Cyril Cook was born in Easton, Hampshire, but at the age of five was brought to live on a farm in Mottingham, Kent. Educated at Eltham College, he matriculated in 1939, joined The Rifle Brigade in 1940, and was commissioned and transferred to The Parachute Regiment in 1943. He saw considerable service in the 6th Airborne Division in Europe and the Far East where for a period he commanded, at the age of 22, a company of some 220 men of the Malay Regiment.

His working life was spent mainly as the proprietor of an engineering business which he founded, until he retired to start the really serious business of writing the six volumes of The Chandlers.

By the same author

THE CHANDLERS

VOLUME ONE – THE YOUNG CHANDLERS
Published in 2005 (Vanguard Press)
ISBN 1 84386 199 2

VOLUME TWO – THE CHANDLERS AT WAR
Published in 2006 (Vanguard Press)
ISBN 978 1 84386 292 5

VOLUME THREE – THE CHANDLERS FIGHT BACK
Published in 2006 (Vanguard Press)
ISBN 978 1 84386 293 2

VOLUME FOUR – THE CHANDLERS GRIEVE
Published in 2006 (Vanguard Press)
ISBN 978 1 84386 294 9

THE CHANDLERS

VOLUME 5

The Chandlers Attack

Cyril Cook

THE CHANDLERS

Volume 5

The Chandlers Attack

Vanguard Press

VANGUARD PAPERBACK

© Copyright 2007
Cyril Cook

The right of Cyril Cook to be identified as author of
this work has been asserted by him in accordance with the
Copyright, Designs and Patents Act 1988.

All Rights Reserved

No reproduction, copy or transmission of this publication
may be made without written permission.
No paragraph of this publication may be reproduced,
copied or transmitted save with the written permission of the
publisher, or in accordance with the provisions
of the Copyright Act 1956 (as amended).

Any person who commits any unauthorised act in relation to
this publication may be liable to criminal
prosecution and civil claims for damages.

A CIP catalogue record for this title is
available from the British Library.

ISBN 978-1-84386-295-6

*Vanguard Press is an imprint of
Pegasus Elliot MacKenzie Publishers Ltd.*
www.pegasuspublishers.com

First Published in 2007

**Vanguard Press
Sheraton House Castle Park
Cambridge England**

Printed & Bound in Great Britain

I dedicate this volume to my wife

EILEEN

who, shortly before we were married, suffered the trauma of being bombed out of her family home, and had only a three-day honeymoon following our wedding day before I was whisked away to the battle in the Ardennes. A year later she was to bear our daughter on her own while I was in the Far East, in danger yet again.

Courage comes in many forms.

MAIN CHARACTERS FROM PREVIOUS BOOKS

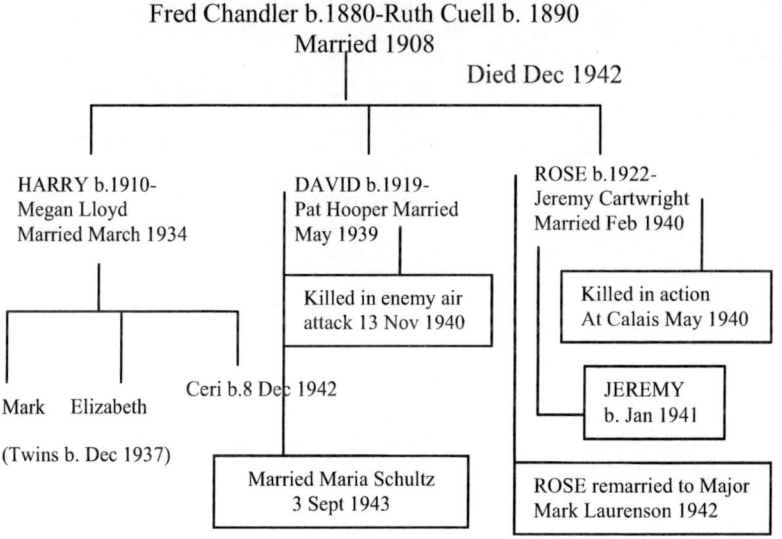

OTHER FAMILIES

JACK HOOPER   Now Sir Jack, Pat's father.
                     Married MOIRA EVANS, Megan's Aunt.
                     Moira is a Top Civil Servant involved in the
                     Atom Bomb project. Son JOHN born August
                     1937.

TREFOR LLOYD   and Elizabeth. Megan's parents.

BUFFY CARTWRIGHT   and Rita. Baby Jeremy's grandparents.

KARL REISNER   Refugee from Nazi Germany now naturalised
                     British citizen. Father of ANNI married to
                     ERNIE BOLTON, David's boyhood friend
                     and now Works Director at Fred and Jack's
                     engineering company Sandbury Engineering.

DR KONRAD VON HASSELLBEK and Elizabeth. Parents of David's great pre-war friend, Dieter, now fighting in a panzer division in Russia. All fervent anti-nazis. Also daughter, Inge, ardent Nazi married to Himmler's nephew. Dieter married cousin Rosa April 1940. Rosa subsequently confined to Ravensbruk concentration camp for six years, now released to work at Bruksheim Klinik as a doctor but still a prisoner.

CECELY COATES with children Oliver, now 18, and Greta now 16 caught in England when Japs invaded Malaya. Husband Nigel and Nigel's brother Judge Charles Coates in Jap internment camp if still alive.

CHARLIE CREW Son of Brigadier Lord Ramsford, David's previous C.O., and grandson of the Earl of Otbourne. Charlie is a great friend of the Chandler family. Engaged to Wren Emma Langham.

HENRY SCHULTZ and wife Susan. David's parents-in-law whose son, Cedric, had been killed at the battle for Calais in 1940.

GLORIA TREHARNE Lost her daughter and son-in-law in the Blitz. Now lives with Cecely Coates at "The Bungalow", along with Cecely's two children and her own two grandchildren, Eric 9 and Patricia 11. The Earl is very fond of Mrs Treharne.

Chapter One

New Year's Day 1944 dawned dull, overcast, dry, but bitterly cold. It was to be a momentous year for all the Chandlers.

"Snow on the way, I reckon," Fred Chandler observed to Rose, as he brought the milk in to the kitchen from the front porch. And snow it did. A quarter of an hour after Fred's prediction a veritable blizzard descended upon them, swiftly covering the surrounding countryside, bringing gasps of delight from young Jeremy standing on the settle beneath the sitting room window: gasps of delight being repeated by young John Hooper at the Hollies: Mark and Elizabeth at Megan's cottage and young Eric at The Bungalow. It was the first real snow in Kent that winter, although they had seen several thin layers during December which had quickly thawed and disappeared, much to the children's disgust. Now they would all be able to get together and build a whacking great snowman, since each would be accompanying his or her parent back to Chandlers Lodge to say goodbye to all the visitors who had been present at the New Year's Eve party.

It had been arranged that all the previous evening's guests would return at 11am for coffee and to say goodbye to each other before they went their several ways: mainly by train since of those who possessed cars, few had sufficient petrol to be able to use them over any distance – and by the looks of things, those with cars would be more than pleased they had only short distances to cover in this weather.

It remains to be said that one or two of the party arrived still a little hung-over. With alcoholic contributions from several of those attending, augmented by Fred's inexhaustible supply of Whitbread's Light Ale from the cupboard under the stairs, no one went to bed thirsty. A cup of coffee, from a bottle of course – ground coffee was a thing of the past – soon proved to be a restorative, probably a psychological if not a physical consequence.

The Earl and his son Lord Ramsford, were the first to leave, along with Charlie, his new fiancée and her parents. Gradually the others drifted away until those who would be staying for a few days somewhere or other in Sandbury remained. David and Maria, along with Rose's husband Mark, would be going back off leave on the morrow, Tuesday 2nd, David to his parachute battalion at Bulford on the edge of Salisbury Plain, Mark to Catterick where he and Charlie were stationed in a battalion of the City Rifles. The three men were now preparing for the invasion of the Continent, whilst Rose and Maria would be preparing for additions to the

Chandler family at the end of July or thereabouts. Their respective husbands were infinitely more solicitous regarding their respective wives' condition than they were fearful of their own prospects!

Emma would have to return to Deal where she served in the Royal Marine Depot as a Leading Wren. She would miss having the immediate presence of Maria who had now left the service to become a civilian and mother. On the other hand she would be aglow with her having been proposed to by Charlie, with a wedding to look forward to in the summer, and the prestige of joining one of the country's most aristocratic families. However, this latter factor played no part in her decision to marry Charlie, should he ask her; she had made up her mind about him long before she discovered he was the grandson of an Earl. Nevertheless, she was an intelligent girl not given to flights of fancy, and knew, with considerable apprehension, that Charlie, having already fought his way across the Western Desert in Montgomery's Eighth Army, was now preparing to take part in the greatest invasion ever to take place – wherever it was to be. He was still a subaltern, a lieutenant, and lieutenants in the infantry are extremely expendable!

She was not the only one to be apprehensive about Charlie. Lord Ramsford was the Earl's only son and, being now divorced, was not likely to produce another heir, which meant the succession to the titles rested with Charlie. All their eggs, therefore, were in one basket. As the Earl had remarked to David a long time ago, that was not the best of situations, particularly so in wartime! The Earl had a younger brother but as he was as queer as a four pound note there would be no 'first reserves' on that side of the family.

At midday Fred announced, "I must get down to the factory, but with all that snow I shall have to walk – riding a bike is out of the question." Even the managing director at this stage of the war rode a bike for short journeys, petrol being rationed, and far too scarce to use when pedal power would suffice. As he shuffled through the snow on to the hard standing at the front of the works, he saw a ministry Humber parked in the visitors' bay. "What the hell do they want on New Year's Day?" he asked himself. "We plebs may have to work on what should be a bank holiday, but surely civil servants would be having at least a week off to get over their New Year festivities."

As he passed his secretary's office, she appeared at the door.
"I've just phoned Chandlers Lodge, Mr Chandler, they told me you

had left. The two ministry men arrived about ten minutes ago. I had some tea made for them and put them in your office."

"Thank you Miss Russell, and a Happy New Year to you."

Fred walked into his office, hand outstretched to greet his two visitors.

"Since when did civil servants work on New Year's Day?" he asked with a smile, "Or do they pay you double time or something?"

The two men smiled. The leader answering, "I'm Bill Harvey, this is Harry Charlton. We are here on a somewhat unusual mission."

"In which case, to save my being incarcerated in the Tower and then drawn and quartered, I have to ask you for your authority to be here, along with your personal identification particulars, in accordance with section something or other, subsection ditto, of the Official Secrets Act." They smiled at his jocular request, producing the necessary credentials about which Fred had jested, but which, they noted, he now scrutinised very carefully.

"Right gentlemen, before we start, I would like to get my works director, Ernie Bolton, to join us." Looking through the glass partition into Miss Russell's office he saw Ernie was already there. He waved for him to come in. Duly introduced, Ernie joined them at the conference table while Harry Charlton unrolled two large drawings. At first glance they were obviously outlines of tanks, which prompted Fred to immediately exclaim, "Are you sure you are in the right place – we have nothing here heavy enough to build tracked vehicles?"

The two ministry men looked at each other and grinned.

"You think they are tanks? That is very good news, because that is what we want Mr Hitler's reconnaissance people to think. These are made of wood, fitted with lengths of drain pipe to look like guns, and strategically placed to look as though the coming assault on Europe is coming from somewhere where it isn't, if you follow me. Now, you have a great reputation in the hierarchy of the ministry for producing quality wooden products. You make the tail assemblies of the Mosquito bomber, as well as the complete Hamilcar glider. These mock-ups will not need to be of that quality, I emphasise that, but they have still got to be sufficiently durable to stay out in the open, even though we shall cover some of them with sheeting for an extra bit of confusion, for at least six months."

Fred and Ernie looked at the drawings, little more than sketches really, looked at each other and laughed their heads off.

"What did you do in the war Grandad?" Fred joked.

"I built wooden tanks," was Ernie's reply.

When the general levity subsided, Fred asked, "Right. How many and when do you want them?"

"Two hundred by the beginning of March, service vehicles will come and collect them in pairs as made. To be sheeted over for transport purposes and kept out of sight until loaded. This exercise, along with others of a similar nature, is designed to totally deceive the Germans as to where we are going to strike."

Thus it was a very hectic two months commenced, first in procuring the material for which they received ministry priority certificates, and secondly the actual fabrication. They had to make four a day to hit the required target – but they did it – just!! None of their tanks actually ever fired a shot in anger, but their position on the Downs on either side of Dover kept a sizeable proportion of the Wehrmacht dug in overlooking the Pas de Calais to repel 'the invasion', whilst the real tanks thundered ashore later in Normandy, far to the south. It was probably the best hoax of the war, added to by the fact the planners had ensured a real live tank had motored up and down the serried ranks of the bogus ones to ensure authenticity in aerial photographs – even the Germans would be suspicious of rows of tanks without their attendant tracks, particularly on the light chalk soil of the Downs.

After the ministry men had departed Fred called Ray Osborne in to brief him on what was happening. Ray was in charge of the Hamilcar project, housed in a new large bay which had been erected for the purpose. It had to be a large building, the Hamilcar glider was bigger than the four-engined Halifax bomber which towed it.

"Ray, Ernie and I want you to build some tanks for us. It is a bit of a tight schedule, two hundred in the next two months!"

"You are, of course, joking."

"Cross my heart. Your bay is the only one with sufficient space, headroom and an overhead crane to do the job. I should add they are made of wood."

Ray's face was a picture.

"Wooden tanks? I know we build parts of a wooden airplane, along with a wooden glider, but who the hell dreamed up a wooden tank?"

Fred pushed the drawings toward him, Ernie standing by grinning like a Cheshire cat! Now, that's a funny thing; I've seen dozens of cats in Cheshire, I have never seen one grin.

A lot of people credit the Cheshire cat story to Lewis Carroll, that master story-teller, a writer who has never been surpassed for screamingly funny, totally original, way-out script, such as:-

He thought he saw a Banker's Clerk

Descending from the bus:
He looked again, and found it was
A Hippopotamus:
"If this should stay to dine," he said,
"There won't be much for us."

Lewis Carroll's story of Alice meeting the Cheshire cat is a classic of fantasy. The cat appears and disappears. He writes: 'This time it vanished quite slowly, beginning with the end of the tail, and ending with the grin, which remained some time after the rest of it had gone'.

Cheshire, as we all know, is famous for its cheese. Long before Lewis Carroll's birth in 1832, cheeses had been made in the shape of a cat, a cat with a big smile. When they were made in blocks or in the round, the trademark imprinted in it was the smiling cat. Probably, Lewis Carroll got the idea of the cat disappearing, from seeing a cheese being gradually consumed from the tail end until such time as only the smile was left. Who knows?

But to continue.

Ray made a concentrated study of the plans.
"I see what they are up to," he exclaimed. "By putting these things somewhere strategically different to the genuine force, Jerry will have to spread his defences to counter them. Our military planners seem to have learnt a thing or two since the balls-up at Dieppe."
"Well, for one thing, they sent the chief balls-upper out to Burma for a start, didn't they?" Fred was referring to Lord Mountbatten of course who had made such a hash of the Canadian assault on Dieppe back in August 1942. Since the Chandler family lost three very good friends killed in that fiasco, caused directly, in Fred's opinion, by the abortionate planning attributed to Lord Mountbatten, he was not exactly a fan of Admiral Lord Louis.
Ray continued to study the drawings.
"I think we could get perfectly good results with unskilled labour, provided we had a couple of joiners to supervise them; but that's where we shall probably come unstuck, skilled woodworkers are like gold dust."
The three men stood silent for a moment or two.
"I wonder if the RAF people on the airfield could loan us a couple of men for the two months. With the thousand odd blokes there they must have people with that sort of experience, even if they are not doing that particular work at the moment," Ray considered.

"Suss it out. Ernie, get the price out, will you? They want it in the morning to put on the contract, although knowing how fast they work we shall have delivered everything before we even get the order."

Ray and Ernie stood up to leave but turned back as Fred asked, "By the way Ray, how's the love life coming on?" Ernie's Cheshire cat grin re-asserted itself.

"Well, all I can tell you is that it is going according to plan."

"Your plan or her plan?"

"Well, I'm not absolutely sure June has a plan. I have a plan," accent on the 'I' "but I ran into a problem. As you know she works at Chiesman's Department Store in Maidstone. I arranged to meet her there in order to be introduced to the manager of the beds and bedding department. Apparently Mr Chiesman – the original Mr Chiesman that is – always insisted that beds and bedding were to be sold by men, as he thought it unseemly they should be sold by ladies." His two listeners chortled at this – as Ray himself had done when it was first explained to him. "Anyway, I then realised I had a problem. I was a single man; therefore presumably I would, or should, be looking for a single bed. I decided to take the bull by the horns, but fortunately the manager wallah was called away to take an important telephone call from the store director, as a result June asked me if I would excuse her as she had to get back to the Counting House, of which she is the manageress. I breathed a sigh of relief, the bedding man returned, and that's how I bought a double bed and bedding."

"I take it you haven't tried it out yet?" Fred asked slyly. "After all, if it isn't suitable; that is, isn't springy enough, or is too springy for the purposes you intend using it, you may want to take it back."

"I'm afraid my position as an officer and a gentleman – well, a one handed ex-officer, and possibly a gentleman, precludes me from answering that question."

"That's his story and he's sticking to it," Fred concluded to the still grinning Ernie. They went their several ways.

Ray went back to his office and straight away got on to the station adjutant at the RAF HQ on Sandbury aerodrome. Explaining the problem, the adjutant apologised he would not be able to help as every single person they had was flat out on working on aircraft for the day and night offensive shortly to hit France and Belgium prior to the invasion.

"In addition to our usual Spits, we've got two extra squadrons of the Typhoons you have undoubtedly seen zooming around these last two weeks to look after. God knows how we are going to do it, but do it we must."

"You will all have to work eight hours a day instead of the standard

RAF four hours I suppose."

"Cheeky bugger. It looks as though it might be twenty-four the way things are shaping up. By the way, you are the ex-sapper who lost a hand aren't you? – we met at the shindig in the Guards' mess a couple of months back, you may remember."

"Yes, that's right. That's why I contacted you. You, I thought, were such a damned decent fellow who would do all he could to help a damsel in distress. Although I don't exactly fit into the damsel category I thought now there's a chap one can really count on in an emergency."

"Bullshit."

"Oh well, I tried. Now, if you come into town, come into the factory and see our beautiful Hamilcar."

"I'll take you up on that, although I can assure you I would never be taken up in one – frighten the bloody life out of me it would."

Ray sat back, smiling to himself, then had a bright idea. As it turned out it was an extremely bright idea. He had led a bomb disposal team of Royal Engineers based in Chatham until he had an argument with a fuse he was removing from a one thousand pounder, which exploded after he had withdrawn it from the bomb, and blew his hand off. Now, the UXB team, as they were known, comprised a number of men who dug down around a bomb which had failed to explode, a sergeant who directed them, and an officer who finally removed the fuses and rendered the bomb safe for removal and blowing up. When the diggers got down to a certain depth – and a bomb could go down twenty feet in soft earth – they had to shore up the shaft with baulks of timber.

It occurred to our wide awake ex-sapper, (all Royal Engineers are called sappers), that as fewer bombs were being dropped in recent months, the direct result should be fewer UXB's. By extension therefore, shorers-up of UXB shafts would be underemployed. He put a call in to his old friend, the adjutant, at Chatham barracks, explaining the situation, who to his astonishment asked immediately, "How many do you want?"

"How many have you got?"

"Well, we could easily let you have half a dozen, they are standing around doing sod all most of the time at present, except when an old bomb gets turned up in debris somewhere and we have to deal with it."

"Marvellous, we will put them up and give them beer money."

"I didn't hear that last bit."

"Oh right. We'll put them up and donate a suitable amount to the Royal Engineers Fund for the families of those killed in UXB operations. Plus we will give the lads some beer money."

"I didn't hear that last bit."

Ray laughed.

When the lorry with the men arrived the next morning it deposited no fewer than eight workers led by none other than Ray's old sergeant, the man who had carried him out of the muddy hole into which he had fallen when he lost his hand.

"Sergeant Dixon, what a surprise. How are you? And how's that NAAFI girl you were sweet on at Chatham? By jove, you're looking well."

"To answer your questions, sir, I am well, touch wood." There was no wood in the immediate vicinity, he touched his head instead. "And the NAAFI girl is now Mrs Dixon and we are expecting another little Dixon shortly."

"Good for you, good for you. I am pleased to see you. And welcome to you too gentlemen," he added, "turning to the eight squaddies standing waiting.

"The adjutant told me I was to stay in charge of this lot, sir, so I shall have to get billets for them. Captain Bloom told me to remind you that if an emergency arose he would have to whip them away, otherwise you can have them as long as you like."

"Well, we know the local billeting officer very well. We could get them in pairs in civilian billets, or perhaps in the Welsh Guards' camp down the road."

"I think they would prefer civvy billets sir."

"Too bloody right," came a response from a lance corporal. "Who wants to be mucking in with bleeding guardsmen?"

It was pretty obvious the direction in which the thoughts of the eight men, and the sergeant for that matter, were drifting. Civvy billets might mean a daughter in the house, or even daughters. Come and go as you please. Soft beds. Keep your nose clean, cushy number for a couple of months.

"Right then," boomed Sergeant Dixon. "You are here to work. You are working for Captain Osborne who I will have you know has two – repeat two – Military Crosses, so if you think you can bullshit him I can tell you, you are very much mistaken. Not only that you're here to carry out a very important job for the war effort. So no skiving. If I see anyone skiving he goes straight back to Chatham. UNDERSTOOD?"

"Understood sergeant," was the unanimous reply, the lance corporal then adding, "But what is to be done sir?"

"You've got to build two hundred tanks."

"Tanks?" The eight men, plus the sergeant, looked incredulously at Ray.

"Do you mean the sort of army tanks that go clattering around making a lot of noise, sir, or water tanks, or what?"

"Wooden tanks." The mystified looks on the working party's faces was a picture to behold.

Ray continued. "These are wooden, dummy tanks, which will be placed in conspicuous places to bamboozle Jerry's photo-reconnaissance people into believing we have armoured divisions in places where we haven't. Now, it sounds laughable, but it is no laughing matter. It is absolutely essential you tell nobody what you are doing. If it is established that any one of you, perhaps when you have had a drink or two, lets on what is happening, it will be a definite court martial offence. Do you clearly understand?" There was a general nodding of comprehension.

"Right then, let's get to work."

And that was how two hundred wooden tanks were cut, fabricated, assembled, painted with camouflage paint and delivered in pairs, the last pair being loaded four days inside the final delivery period. The men all received two pounds a week beer money, the sergeant three pounds, and Sandbury Engineering donated fifty pounds to the RE Benevolent Fund. Two of the lads found girlfriends in the town, two more were billeted on a lady in her mid thirties whose husband was at sea, and who bestowed her favours on one, one night, and the other, the next, a most amicable arrangement all round, since with the spacing of the nocturnal exercise no appreciable diminution of the work ethic was discovered in either of the two at the factory.

David and Mark travelled together on Tuesday 2nd as far as Victoria whence David made his way to Waterloo, Mark to Kings Cross. London was crammed with British and American forces on the move; mostly it would appear going back off leave. David was met at Andover by a driver from the transport section. He had met Sandy Patterson on the train. Sandy was a Canadian lieutenant who had been posted to David's company some three months before, and had been spending the Christmas leave at Blackheath, in South London, at his girlfriend, Amanda's house.

"We've got to wait for someone coming in from Oxford sir. He should have been here before you but his train is running half an hour late."

"Who is it, do you know?"

"It's a new captain for HQ company I believe sir, I don't know his name."

Twenty minutes later the Oxford train arrived. They saw a tall, immaculately overcoated figure in a red beret with captain's pips on his epaulettes directing a porter to offload a prodigious volume of kit on to the platform. The driver hastened forward, saluted, and asked if the captain was for 'R' Battalion at Bulford.

"I am," he replied, as he spotted David and Sandy, both of whom were wearing raincoats, which carry no badges of rank.

"Are those two going to 'R' Battalion as well?" he asked the driver.

"They are sir."

"You two," he called to them "come and give a hand with this kit, don't just stand there."

Sandy looked at David, David winked at Sandy. "Come on, let's have some fun."

They approached the imperious captain.

"Having problems?" David innocently asked.

"I need to get this kit on to the truck."

David turned to Sandy. "It seems an inordinate amount of kit for a captain – do you think he's genuine Sandy?"

"Look's a bit suspicious to me David."

"Captain," David continued, "we have been warned about a bogus captain wandering around the Salisbury area scrounging board and lodging from different messes until he feels he is about to be found out then he pushes off. You fit his description. I think we ought to see your identification papers."

"Now look here. I am Captain the Honourable Montague Joice-Livett, my father is a cousin of the King, so get on and help with this kit."

"Not without seeing your papers, unless you want to walk to Bulford; that's about fifteen miles."

The captain's face was turning a delicate shade of puce. "Oh, very well." He fished inside his impeccably tailored overcoat, eventually pulling out his officer's identity papers. David examined it thoroughly, passed it to Sandy asking, "Do you think it's genuine?"

"I don't know. It says 2nd lieutenant on here, it doesn't say captain."

The captain exploded. "When it was issued I WAS only a 2nd lieutenant. You don't get new identity papers every time you get promoted, as you will find out if you ever get promoted."

"Now, now, that's very unkind. But you must admit it is a bit suspicious," David replied. He paused for a moment. "I know," he said to Sandy, "identity discs! If he was genuine he would have identity discs." Turning to the captain, "Show us your identity discs."

Now the identity discs are worn on a piece of cord around the neck at all times. At no time should you be without them – except possibly during certain nocturnal exercises when they might get in the way. In that case one would hope you would be known to the other party anyway.

"Dammit – No, I'm damned if I will."

"You are damned if you don't – it's a long walk to Bulford – and you would have to leave your kit behind."

In a fury, the son of the cousin of the King undid his greatcoat again, undid his tunic, undid his shirt, groped inside a thick woollen vest and eventually displayed the two small medallions bearing his name and number.

"How do you spell your name?" queried Sandy.

"J O I C E" the reply began.

"It says J O Y C E here," replied Sandy.

"You sure you're a fella?" asked David, innocent as a babe.

"They bloody well spelt it incorrectly, you stupid asses," bellowed the captain.

"OK, leg-pull over," David announced. "I will give you a bit of advice, son of the cousin of the King, advice which my father gave me when I was quite a young lad. NEVER judge a sausage by its skin. Just because we were standing around in our raincoats waiting for you to arrive, and bloody cold we were too I might add, you assumed we were junior to you. Before you start throwing your weight around establish who it is you are ordering about. I am Major Chandler."

"I see, in that case I apologise."

"I apologise – SIR."

"I apologise sir."

"Right, welcome to the battalion," said David holding out his hand, duly taken by the Hon. J-L "and this is Sandy Patterson of the Canadian Parachute Regiment, presently with us."

They climbed into the truck, a rather chastened Captain Montague Joice-Livett sitting in the back with Sandy whereas he had firmly expected to sit beside the driver. His humility however was short lived. Within three weeks, as a result of his arrogance and high spending in the mess, in addition to his habit of speaking to NCOs and other ranks as if they were his serfs, he came a cropper. The second in command of the battalion was one, Major Hamish Gillespie. A Scot with twenty years service all over the globe, and one who was amiability personified – unless you upset him. The trouble with Joice-Livett was that the arrogance of him and his ilk was in no way matched by his, or their, ability. After two or three occasions he had slipped up and been able to place the blame for the episodes on to his subalterns; they being of the school who did not tell tales to their superiors, kept quiet about it. It is the captain's job in a company to organise, when on exercises or rifle shooting on the range, the ammunition and midday rations for the men in his company. As a result of J-L's negligence, HQ Company arrived at the range without either ammunition to fire, or anything to eat at midday.

Hamish had travelled with them, immediately calling J-L to account when the dearth of food and ammunition was discovered.

"I told the bloody platoon commanders to get it organised," he blustered to Hamish. A young lieutenant was standing nearby.

"Were you told to organise the ammo?" asked Hamish.

"Good Lord, no sir. I wouldn't know where to start."

"What about the other two platoon commanders?"

"Same with them sir, one's Signals, one's Mortars. We have nothing to do with rifle ammunition."

Hamish marched back to where he had left J-L.

"You've just told me a pack of lies."

"Are you calling me a liar, you Scottish nobody? You'll find I have friends in very high places if you have."

Hamish took a step forward and was about to punch J-L very hard indeed when the platoon commander he had spoken to, who had followed him back to find out what was going on, held his arm, saying, "This blabbermouth is not worth it sir."

Hamish paused. "Did you hear his reply to me?"

"Yes, sir."

"Write it down so that it is verbatim, then get one of the other platoon commanders. Captain Livett," (studiously avoiding the double-barrel!) "You are under arrest for insubordination. These two officers will escort you back to your quarters where you will wait until the commanding officer calls for you. Do you understand?"

"Yes."

"Yes WHAT?"

"Yes, sir."

"Take him back to Bulford."

To compound his misbehaviour, when the colonel sent the assistant adjutant, late in the afternoon, to tell him to come to the COs office, he had gone into Salisbury. The next morning he appeared before the CO.

"I'm giving you a choice, Joice-Livett. You can take my award without my calling witnesses regarding your behaviour, or you can be recommended to the brigadier for court martial. What is it to be?" Livett knew he was trapped.

"I'll take your award," and then as an afterthought, "sir."

"Right. I'll tell you straight. We do not want you within a hundred miles of this battalion. You are ranked at present as a temporary captain, you will revert to lieutenant immediately, and you will be posted to Divisional HQ where doubtless they will be able to find something for someone like you, totally without any ability whatsoever as far as I can see. Leave straight away, pay your mess bill before you go, the adjutant will arrange transport for you to Andover and a rail ticket to Div HQ. How the hell you got through Octu I can't begin to guess."

A fuming Lieutenant Joice-Livett gave a thoroughly sloppy salute, turned and left.

"Now we have to get another captain from somewhere," Colonel Hislop declared to Hamish.

"Bloody good riddance to that one sir, I shudder to think of him on active service."

"Which will not be long now I reckon."

Chapter Two

Megan Chandler, Harry's wife, finished her shift at Sandbury Hospital at 10 pm on Friday 5th January. It had been a busy day since she took over as sister on the men's surgical ward at two o'clock that afternoon. It was a very cold night. Some of the snow which had fallen earlier in the week still remained, as a result she had decided to walk to and from work, fearing the roads would have iced up when she came home, and that as a result she might come a cropper from her normal motive power, namely her bicycle. It was not a long walk, no more than fifteen minutes, mainly through the High Street, although of course there were no street lamps to guide her. Everyone carried a torch, as much to be seen as to see, she was more than aware from the casualties they received at the hospital that the blackout caused almost as many deaths as the air raids – particularly in the narrow country roads.

She trudged along the High Street, passing groups of soldiers who had just been turned out from the pubs, in the process receiving many good natured, if not particularly articulate, offers to 'see her home', which she jokingly declined. Turning off the High Street into the tree lined, and always very dark side road leading down to her cottage by the river, she had the feeling she was being followed. She was not unduly perturbed, other people lived down here beside Megan Chandler, she told herself. She crossed the road, earlier than she would normally have done. We all get into a routine as to where we carry out certain required manoeuvres on our approaches to home, shop or factory. The footsteps followed her. She quickened her step, the footsteps followed suit. She swung round pointing her torch toward the person following her, who, seeing her turning, rushed at her out of the darkness knocking the torch out of her hand. As she screamed for help he dragged her on to the bank at the side of the footpath and ripped her top coat open. She fought like a demon, leaving deep scratch marks down his face, using her elbows and knees in an endeavour to keep him off, and trying to poke his eyes with her knuckles. Her screams were heard in the nearby cottages by a neighbour and his sixteen-year-old son, who put their boots on to go out to establish from which direction they came.

In the meantime her attacker had completely overpowered her, pushed her on to the bank, covered her mouth with one hand and having lifted her skirt up was endeavouring to rip down her underwear. As his hand moved on her mouth, so she sank her teeth into it, holding on with all the strength her jaws could muster. He swore a string of filthy oaths, hit her a tremendous blow on the side of the head to make her let go, at the same time kneeing her violently. She let out another piercing scream which provided the bearings the neighbour and his son needed! They rushed toward the scream, the younger man in the lead with his father shining his torch ahead, lighting up the obscene tableau being played out on the bank. The youngster hurled himself at the attacker, getting an extremely vicious back hander across the mouth for his pains, but nevertheless knocking the rogue over. His father was a very burly forty-five year old who ran his own coal business, was used daily to carrying anything up to two or more tons of coal in hundredweight sacks up peoples garden paths into their coal sheds, but on this occasion instead of utilising his undoubtedly powerful hands and arms on the assailant, decided it would be more economic to use his steel toe-capped boot, part and parcel of his tools of the trade. He therefore applied a non too gentle size ten to the ribs of the would-be rapist which had him screaming with pain and fighting hard to get his breath. Despite this he struggled to his feet to receive a punch in the solar plexus which would have done credit to the great Joe Louis himself. He crumpled, motionless on to the pavement.

"Run home George, dial 999 for the police and ambulance, and then phone Mr Chandler at Chandlers Lodge. It's Mrs Megan."

He picked Megan up slowly and gently, took his coat off and laid it on the bank, lowered her back on to it, and wrapped it around her as best he could.

"The ambulance will soon be here Mrs Megan."

To the tradesmen in Sandbury she was always described as Mrs Megan to distinguish her from her mother-in-law, Mrs Ruth Chandler, now sadly no longer with them all.

"Thank you Mr Robbins, thank you so much," she started to cry.

"There, there, now Mrs Megan, it's all over now." He was a kindly man but found it difficult to put his feelings into words at the best of times. His wife had said to him some years back, 'You never say you love me'. He had looked at her in complete and utter astonishment saying, 'What the devil are you talking about, any fool can see from a mile off I love you'. She had treasured that moment although it could not be said to be the ultimate in romanticism.

The attacker stirred. Mr Robbins whipped his neckerchief off and swiftly bound his ankles.

"You move an inch now my son, and I'll kick your bloody head in, so don't tempt me you dirty little slug."

The police Wolseley and the hospital ambulance, coming from

opposite ends of the town – well, Sandbury was only an oversized village really, it didn't even boast a Woolworth's – turned into the lane and pulled up beside the small group, now joined by young George.

"Mr Chandler's coming right over, so is Sir Jack Hooper who was at the Lodge at the time."

"Righto son, well done."

As they were helping Megan into the ambulance Fred and Jack arrived. Jack shone his torch on to the assailant.

"Sergeant, this man fits the description of the bastard who attacked Nanny Cavendish when she caught him looting our house after it was bombed back in October."

"Is it now?" He turned to the prostrate villain. "It looks as though you are going to go away for a very long holiday my son. Now let's get you up."

The sergeant and Mr Robbins pulled him up. He stank of methylated spirit to the extent they both had to turn their heads away. Handcuffs were swiftly applied and the man bundled into the car.

"If I had my way I'd have a cage out in the yard for people like you." Turning to Jack he added, "You would never believe the filth we have to clean up in the cell, sir, when one of these blackguards has been housed for a night, as well as having to delouse it afterwards."

The ambulance moved away, followed by Fred and Jack in Fred's Rover.

"Well done you two. The detective will want a statement from you first thing in the morning. You did a bloody good job here tonight." The sergeant shook hands with them both, his action repeated by both Fred and Jack.

The duty houseman had been alerted and was waiting for Megan's arrival. She was swiftly moved into a side ward, where shortly afterwards Matron Duffy arrived, that is, Matron Duffy as was, now Matron Johnson, as is. A Royal Marines major, Ken Johnson, who had been billeted on the Chandlers in 1942 had fallen in love with the widowed Matron Duffy, and despite misgivings on the part of Ken's family regarding the fact she was a cradle catholic, which unease the beautiful matron had swiftly overcome when she met them, they had married at the end of 1942. The houseman examined the patient under the eagle eye of the matron. Where she had been struck so violently on the side of the head a massive blue-black bruise had appeared, the attendant swelling almost completely closing her right eye. Where the would-be rapist had driven his knee into her side a second large bruise had appeared.

"We'll X-ray the ribs immediately, she's in such pain she may have sustained a fracture." The houseman looked at matron for tacit approval. Matron went out to Fred and Jack, waiting in a little ante-room, where the night-sister had organised a cup of cocoa for each of them.

"There's no point in your waiting any longer. She is badly bruised and has possibly got some damage to her ribs, but otherwise she is alright. I will see she gets a good night's sleep and you can come in tomorrow morning, early, for a few minutes."

They thanked the matron, leaving Megan in the care of people who knew her so well she was almost family to them, from the cleaning staff to the matron herself. There was nothing that would be left undone regarding the care and well-being of Sister Megan Chandler.

Early the next morning a detective arrived at The Hollies to ask Nanny Cavendish if she would kindly come to Sandbury Police Station, in an endeavour to identify Megan's assailant as being the person who had struck her with a poker when she had disturbed him looting the bomb damaged house the previous October. Harold, Sir Jack's chauffeur, an ex-RAF warrant officer employed by the aircraft manufacturers, Shorts of Rochester, to drive Jack, who was the chairman of that company, asked if he could go with Nanny. Jack immediately agreed saying he would contact Miss Watts, his secretary, to re-arrange any appointments he may have. He would not be later than an hour.

Harold and Nanny had been walking out since her brush with the looter, he subsequently having visited her several times when she was in hospital. He was in his early forties, she middle thirties, both had considered love had passed them by, but now it looked as though they were a match.

"Go in the Jaguar," Jack suggested. "Then the detective won't have to bring you back. I'm sure he's got far more important things to do than drive you around," – this all said with a grin, since he appreciated the two would like to be on their own together, even if it was only for a short while. "I was young myself once," he told himself, though to be fair neither Harold nor Nanny could be called, exactly, young. I suppose it could be argued that when you are over the sixty mark, everybody forty or below looks young.

They drove to Sandbury Police Station. The station sergeant had stayed on from his night duty stretch to arrange an identity parade, although it must be said that he had found it difficult to find five other people to even remotely bear comparison with the stinking prisoner.

Nanny had no difficulty and certainly no qualms in identifying him.

"He's the one," she said "Number three. He is even wearing the same clothes as when he attacked me."

"Thank you Miss. Please sign this and you can get away." Harold put his arm around her waist and took her out to the car. Although she had been so positive during the identification parade, the memory of the incident was flooding back into her memory. After all, if you have been brought up in a civilised, gentle household, take a post with civilised employers, even if you sometimes have to handle truculent children, you are hardly prepared for the trauma of being confronted by an evil looking, unkempt, filthy dirty assailant, armed with a poker, furthermore, intending to use it. It is the stuff of nightmares. Harold seated her in the passenger seat, then leaned over and kissed her on the cheek. She grasped his hand and kissed it.

"Thank you, dear Harold." She smiled at him.

Over the weekend they visited Megan in her side ward. The X-rays had established that no bones were broken, but she was very badly bruised, her poor face looked as though it had had an argument with a Maidstone and District bus. On Saturday she asked Fred if he would get Mr Robbins and young George to come and see her, she wanted to thank them both.

The residents of Sandbury were accustomed to seeing Mr Robbins in clothes which would have stood up of their own accord, with hands, and in the summer, arms, as black as the rest of him, a face to match, and a sort of leather sou'wester which covered his head and shoulders, likewise as black as night but highly polished by the continual abrasion of sacks of coal or coke which rubbed against it. When he, his wife, and young George therefore presented themselves to Side Ward A on Sunday afternoon Megan did not immediately recognise the gentleman leading the little procession. He was dressed in a neat pinstriped suit, white shirt with an immaculately starched collar, which held a Royal Artillery zigzag tie; over his arm he carried a coat which a tailor would have recognised immediately as top quality West of England Saxony cloth (and would have added – he didn't get that in wartime nor did he buy it in Burton's). All in all he exuded the impression of a well-to-do middle class member of the Sandbury populace. Only one thing gave him away. No amount of scrubbing could entirely remove the coal dust ingrained in those strong hands. He held his hand out to shake that of the patient. Megan took it, pulled it towards her and kissed it.

"Thank you Mr Robbins, thank you, thank you," she said, dissolving into tears at the remembrance of that evil night, "and you too George," she held her other hand out for an embarrassed sixteen year old to be accepted and be the recipient of a second kiss. Mrs Robbins looked on, smiling.

On Monday 8th January everybody chipped in to help. Nanny had kept Ceri, Megan's youngest, over the weekend and said she would carry on doing so. Mark and Elizabeth, Megan's twins, now six, stayed at Chandlers Lodge from which place Cecely Coates, on her way to Country Style in the High Street, where she worked, collected them and young John Hooper, also six, to take them to school, situated only a couple of hundred yards from the shop. Anni, who lived just off the High Street, had elected to collect them all from school and return them to Chandlers Lodge and The Hollies. It all worked very smoothly.

Rose had to stay at the Lodge as she was expecting a new 'daily' to arrive at nine o'clock. Her usual lady, Mrs Stokes, who had been with the Chandlers since before the war started, had had to have a minor operation, which followed by a week's convalescence would put her out of action for a fortnight. Treasure that she was, she had arranged for a neighbour of hers to come and 'take her place' for the two weeks.

"She'll never take your place Mrs Stokes," Rose had replied, "they broke the mould when they made you." And so they did, Mrs Stokes was an absolute gem.

"Oh get away with you! She's a thoroughly reliable woman and honest as the day is long. You might find her a bit slow but she'll plod on and keep the place reasonable until I get back."

On her first morning Mrs Kinson was ten minutes late, giving Rose the immediate impression that the reliability of Mrs Stokes was to be supplanted by the uncertain time keeping of her successor. When the good lady did arrive, flushed of face and full of apologies, she seemed reluctant to tell Rose the reason for her belated arrival.

"It won't happen again Mrs Laurenson, I promise. You see, I've told him."

"Don't worry about it Mrs Kinson, a few minutes doesn't matter at all. But, what do you mean 'you've told him'?"

"Well, you're a married woman Mrs Laurenson, so you know what they're like."

Rose's curiosity went into top gear.

"What they're like, Mrs Kinson?"

"Yes, you know, wanting their married life. Harry worked all the weekend on a job so he had today off. I took him a cup of tea in bed and he grabbed me. I told him I had to be here at nine o'clock, but he said 'I'm aching Ethel, I'm aching'. He always says that when he wants his married life, and you can't really refuse them when they say that, can you? I mean, they might go somewhere else, mightn't they? So I said, well you had better make it quick then, I don't want to be late on my first day. But he wasn't quick enough was he?" Rose was almost in hysterics within herself, desperately trying not to show it on the outside. The final sentence of this chronicle of human passion was as matter of fact as if she had been talking about the baker leaving a loaf of bread. "Anyway, he went off to sleep again as I was getting ready to come here, so he'll be alright till I get home."

Having put Mrs Kinson to work, Rose could not contain herself any longer, but got on the telephone to Anni to relate, word for word, the happenings earlier on. After a mutual bout of hilarity, Anni asked through her sobs of laughter, "How old is Mrs Kinson?"
"I don't know exactly, late fifties I should think."
"Well, all I can say is that if Ernie ever has to have a blood transfusion I'll make sure he gets it from Mr Kinson – that you can rely on."

As a result of this incident, Anni told Ernie about the cry 'I'm aching Ethel'. Ernie told Fred and Ray, Fred told Jack and Reg Church, as a result it became a form of greeting between them, producing an abundance of merriment all round.

Megan did not lack visitors, not only from family and friends, but also from the hospital staff. Late on Monday afternoon, the detective handling the incident came to take her statement at the end of which he said, "I have to ask you this Mrs Chandler, did you at any time do or say anything to encourage this man?"
Megan looked at him open-mouthed.
"I beg your pardon!" It was the first forceful utterance she had made since being admitted to the hospital.
"Did you at any time do or say anything to encourage this man?"
"You have seen the man?"
"Yes, of course."
"Do you honestly think I would have any truck with anyone like that?"
"I have to ask the question Mrs Chandler. Please answer it."
"No I did not, and I resent even being asked such an offensive thing."

"I'm sorry, but I have a job to do."

When the detective had left, Megan lay back, drained, on to her pillows to be joined by matron.

"Any problems?"

"He asked whether I encouraged that evil swine."

"Well, I suppose that's on their list of 'must-do's'. They get a lot of cases, I imagine, with all the troops around these days, of girls having had a drink or two leading a man on and then not playing ball. In your case you had never met the man before, you are a highly respectable married woman with children, and above all a nursing sister going to her home late at night after serving the community day after day, year after year. I think they will throw not only the book at him, but the bookcase as well, both because of you and Nanny Cavendish."

"Nanny Cavendish?"

"Yes, he's the same man that assaulted Nanny last October. She identified him at the police station this morning. He will be lucky to get away with anything less than life."

He did, in fact, get ten years penal servitude on each count, to run consecutively, with the judge's comment, "You are an evil man to have caused such pain and distress on two eminently respectable ladies. It is only that you have pleased guilty to all charges you have not received two life sentences. Take him down."

Megan left hospital on the Friday. It had been decided she should go to Chandlers Lodge for a couple of weeks at least, until she would be fit for duty. Over the weekend Cecely and sixteen-years-old Greta came to visit her. Greta seemed a little down in the dumps, Megan putting it down to the fact she had to go back to Benenden the following week, where she boarded all the week and came home for weekends. It was a bright cold day. She sat looking out of the window whilst Megan and Cecely were chatting, then turned and said, "Where are the children?"

"Probably up in the playroom."

"Do you think they would like a walk up to the woods?"

"I'm sure they would love it."

"I'll go and ask and then get them dressed to go out."

"That is kind of you Greta, it really is."

When Greta had disappeared to collect the twins and two-year-old Ceri, Megan said, "Greta seems a bit subdued, is she alright?"

"I think the course of true love is not running so smoothly at the moment," smiled Cecely.

"Oh crikey! Well we have all been there haven't we at that age. Who are we talking about?"

"Well, at David and Maria's wedding she met one of Emma Langham's cousins, Peter. The wires hummed daily after that, the post office made increased profits, then at the end of November gradually the letters dropped off and instead of a daily telephone call at the weekends, by the time her end of term holiday came, it became apparent loves' young dream was at an end."

"She will soon find someone else."

"I know that and you know that, but the world at this present moment as far as our Greta is concerned, is almost, if not completely, at an end. Anyway she is going to the church hall dance tonight. Perhaps that will brighten her up."

Brighten her up it did. Girls were in short supply at these hops, as they were known locally. A succession of RAF bods, guardsmen and unusually, a sailor on leave, left her no time to mope. After a number of requests to 'walk her home' after the dance were deftly parried by her reply that her uncle was picking her up – fictitious of course – she began to feel that there were, as her mother had remarked, other fish in the sea. "Not that I have any intention of grabbing the bait again – men are not worth getting worked up about – not that I intend going into a nunnery – I shall be very choosy in the future – if I bother at all!" Her day dream, or to be exact, her evening dream on this occasion, was interrupted by a thickset, good-looking young man, eighteen or so she guessed. Girls at a dance instinctively endeavour to judge the new dancing partner's age, secondly cast a quick glance at their third finger, left hand, to see if they are married or not. They don't mind being chatted up, but have to be constantly wary about being conned by would-be Casanovas with an eye on the main chance. Well, let's say most of them that is. A chap has to get lucky every now and then.

To return to her new, prospective Fred Astaire. He was well spoken, dressed in a neat blazer and flannels, but, she noticed, kept his hands behind his back until the couple took to the floor. He was clean, neat, with chestnutty coloured wavy hair – first impression, very nice being Greta's assessment. As he took her hand the lights lowered for a smoochy foxtrot, which he performed very adequately. The foxtrot over, he thanked her, returning her to where she had been standing, saying, "I'll return you to your friends."

"I was on my own."

So much for resolutions.

They chatted away. She mentioned she had not seen him at the dance before, did he live locally? He said he lived in Hampshire but was staying this weekend with his aunt and uncle, Doctor Power, did she know him? Yes, he was the family doctor. All the time he kept his hands out of sight, it was becoming quite noticeable.

"I don't know your name."

I'm John Power, and you are Greta Coates."

"How on earth do you know that?"

"I saw you with some children this morning when I was with uncle in his car. I asked him who you were and he told me."

"You are not in the forces yet?"

"I'm a Bevin boy."

"A what? What on earth is a Bevin boy?"

"Instead of being called up for the army we have been called up to dig coal." He then showed her his hands. Although they were spotlessly clean, they showed the dark blue rims around the nails, the odd faint blue scar showing recent contact with a jagged piece of the black diamonds he had been called upon to help bring to the surface to enable the war to be prospered.

"Would you have preferred to have been in the army or wherever?"

"Yes, but there is no appeal. One in ten of conscription age is drawn on a ballot system. If you are in that ten percent you go down the mines. Look, don't let's talk about me, how about showing all these people how to do a proper quickstep?"

And they did. He had obviously had dancing lessons; for Greta it was part of the standard curriculum at Benendon. The waltz followed. They stayed together for the rest of the evening.

When the final 'Who's taking you home tonight?' waltz was being played, John asked the inevitable question – "Can I walk you home, I know you live at The Bungalow, uncle told me, it will not take me out of my way?"

"John Power. That is the biggest whopper you've uttered in ages. I know where Doctor Power lives remember – it's the other end of the town."

"Well, let's say the walk will do me good."

"I'll get my coat."

That was the beginning of Greta's second romance. On the way home John told her he had finished his training up at the Cresswell Colliery Miners' Training Centre in Derbyshire which had taken a month. He had now been posted to Betteshanger Colliery near Sandwich in Kent, uncle John suggesting he spend his weekends with them at Sandbury.

"So you will be here next weekend?"

"Yes, will you be going to the dance again?"

"I could be persuaded."

"Consider yourself persuaded."

They parted at the gate of The Bungalow with a chaste handshake, Greta opening the door and going into the sitting room was, to her mother and Mrs Treharne, an entirely different person from the one who had left them at seven o'clock to go to the dance because there was nothing else to do. She was bright-eyed and bushy-tailed, as Cecely later described her to Megan.

Mrs T – "Have a nice time dear?" definitely a loaded question.

Greta – "Very nice, thank you auntie." Mrs T was 'auntie' to Greta and Oliver ever since they first came to live at The Bungalow.

Cecely – "Meet anyone you know?"

Greta – "Well, no, not exactly, that is I met someone who is the nephew of someone we all know."

The two ladies looked at each other – a knowing look which spoke volumes.

Mrs T – "May we ask who this uncle we all know might be?"

Greta – "Doctor Power. He walked me home."

Cecely – "Who? Doctor Power?"

Greta – "No of course not. His nephew."

And then the story came out. John Power was a Bevin boy. What's a Bevin boy? and so on, until the two ladies harboured no doubts whatsoever that Peter Langham was now history.

Both Greta Coates and John Power the younger (his uncle too was John Power) went to bed smiling. For all I know Uncle John might have gone to bed smiling as well, but his nocturnal undertakings do not form part of this narrative.

Chapter Three

On the 5th of January 1944 Harry lay on his charpoy listening to the incessant drumming of the monsoon on the atap roof of his hut. Force 136 would not do much in this weather, he reflected. He was a trifle concerned that he had not heard from Sunrise that he had reached his HQ up in the Cameron Highlands, way to the north of Kuala Lumpur, in Malaya. The colonel had visited Harry's camp before Christmas with half a dozen Chinese guards and his two aboriginal guides – great friends of Harry who he had christened Bam and Boo – but had left over two weeks ago. He should be back by now, Harry calculated. On the other hand the monsoon could make torrents out of little streams, which made travel not only hazardous but also the cause of many unplanned detours.

He moved his arm up to put his hand under his head on the pillows, disturbing the companion stretched out beside him, Chantek by name, who made a little throaty growl and pushed her outsize paws into his side. Chantek was a beautiful leopard cub, found by Harry, alongside her dead mother some three months ago and reared on 'exasperated milk', as Harry had always designated it. She was now the camp mascot, growing more each day and never more than two feet away from Harry if she had her way. Pushing her paws into his side, she leaned her head forward and licked his shoulder, her rough, sandpaper tongue bringing her pleasure which transmitted itself to the opening and closing of her claws into his ribs.

"Hi, cut that out." She gave a little whimper and snuggled up to him.

Sunrise had fallen in love with this beautiful bundle of fur, her startlingly blue eyes, and her large ungainly feet. She, in turn, had taken to him, but was singularly apprehensive of Bam and Boo. She eyed their eight feet long blow pipes with considerable unease, instinctively knowing they meant danger.

The monsoon was debilitating in many ways. Little activity could take place in the form of training, maintenance of the camp, working in the camp garden producing their staple tapioca and other basic foods, or carrying out the incessant war against the jungle to prevent its enveloping their huts, which with some creepers capable of growing a foot a day was a constant struggle. At least they could keep dry now. The interior roofs of all the living quarters were now lined with parachute material salvaged from the bi-monthly air drops they were receiving, which more or less effectively overcame the previous problem of waking up in the night to find you were having a shower bath from a leak in the atap roof caused by the monsoon gale lifting the covering. The main problem however was psychological. The constant rain, the half-light, the noise of the drumming on the roofs, the incessant thunder and lightning, brought on a creeping paralysis of the brain, so that unless the officers made a conscious effort to keep active there was a great temptation to lie back on one's bed. However, between two and four o'clock each afternoon that was the order of the day. As Harry always designated it – 'kip time' – and the period of the day which Chantek loved best, when she could cuddle up to – who? Did that pretty head have a brain that had given a name to the other animal to whom she cuddled up? Did she think it was her mother? Unlikely. Harry always smelt, sometimes worse than at other times, but his smell was nothing like another leopard. And when he told her off for digging her claws in she did nothing to resent it. It was like being clipped around the ear by their mother as happens to all cubs when they do something wrong. There was no doubt about it, it was a complex relationship, showing that cats have very intricate sensitivities in that they can love and care for one person, be aloof towards some others, and positively antagonistic, for no apparent reason, towards others. There must somewhere exist some sort of wavelength which establishes into which category the relationship falls. At one end of the scale you have the most famous man-eating cat – a leopard – who in India killed 125 people over a period of several years before it was finally shot. At the other end you have the famous Elsa the lioness, who after being set free, returned to her human 'mother', to show off her cubs, while her mate looked on cautiously from a distance. One day there will be a university giving Ph D's for the understanding of cats, large and small, you mark my words.

But back to Harry. It was now four o'clock. He heard Reuben Ault, one of his fellow officers, clump along in wooden sandals – nobody walked barefoot in Camp Three, or anywhere else up in the high jungle if they had any sense. Harry knew what was coming next. Reuben was going to get into the shower – a cleverly engineered piece of equipment fed from the adjacent mountain stream, now in spate – during which time he would sing his favourite song. Despite having a voice like 'The City of Canterbury' fog-horn, which ship was known throughout the merchant navy as having the most sonorous, deep bellied, ear shattering, warning device yet produced, he fancied himself as a bit of an opera singer. The unfortunate thing was, he knew no opera. He did however know the great Italian song 'Santa Lucia'. Unfortunately again those were the only words he knew of it. His rendition therefore went like this:-

Santa Lucia, Santa Lucia,
Santa Lucia, Santa Lucia,
Santa Lucia ... and so on.

It was when he started the second verse, the combined howls from Harry, Tommy Isaacs, and Matthew the camp doctor, would tell him to put a sock in it, or worse, at which he would emerge smiling from the shower (one would not stay long in it anyway, it was too damned cold), saying, "I knew you would enjoy that."

By these, and other means, they kept each other amused. However, Harry's amusement was short-lived. There was an urgent hammering on the door of his room, causing him to jump – God; my nerves must be getting bad! – and Chantek to give her throaty growl and thump her tail angrily on the mattress. Knowing that at this time of day Harry would have the leopard in his room, it was a rule that walking straight in was forbidden in case the fast growing little blighter decided to leave the security of the room and its adjacent wire enclosure to have a look at the world outside – an adventure which could easily lead to its demise, it had a lot of enemies out there.

"Hang on." He picked Chantek up and held her close to him. "OK – come in." It was Choon Guan, leader of the communist Chinese, who nevertheless was under the command of Harry and the other two officers. Choon Guan hurriedly closed the door behind him, standing some little distance from Harry and the leopard. He didn't like the leopard very much. The feeling was more than mutual.

"One of the men has deserted sir."

"Which one?"

"Lee Choon Hong."

"When did he go and do you know why he went?"

"He has not been seen since breakfast and nobody knows if he had a reason."

"Well, the point is what do we do now? I am certainly not going to send out a search party, it would be like looking for a needle in a haystack, particularly in this weather. Where does he come from?"

"Butterworth sir, right up in the north."

"Right. Get the radio operator to contact HQ in the Cameron Highlands tonight and give them the man's address. They may well have someone in Butterworth, they certainly have in Georgetown on Penang Island just opposite Butterworth. What they can do about it I'm sure I don't know."

"Don't worry about that sir; we know what to do if we find him."

"Well, I'll question you no further on that score. The problem is what if he is caught by the Japs between here and Butterworth?" Harry reflected on this for a moment. "Presuming of course he is intending to go to Butterworth. He may just have been overcome by being shut in, in this bloody rain soaked place, and heading for the nearest kampong to get drunk and forget it all. Anyway, put the men on a state of alert for a few days, double the sentries and so on. That will do two things, one it will make sure no one creeps up on us should he have been found and persuaded to give our position away. Secondly, it will encourage the others not to be so stupid as to follow his example."

Privately Harry hardly blamed the poor chap, although of course he was more than well aware of the slight possibility the deserter could jeopardise them all. As for deserting, Harry had more than once thought that if he had been subjected to the Marxist indoctrination forced upon him, as it was rammed down the throats of his communist troops, he would have deserted long ago. The commissar who ranked almost as powerful as Choon Guan, spent at least an hour every evening indoctrinating the men, his rantings and ravings being clearly heard on occasion in the officer's quarters and sick bay. On at least three occasions Harry had ordered Choon Guan to tell the demagogue to keep his voice down, they couldn't hear themselves speak. Admittedly that was somewhat of an exaggeration, but it set Harry and the others to wondering how any average person could put up with assaults of that nature on their brains night after night. As Reuben succinctly put it, "If that's communism they can stuff it up their arses." Reuben had a singular ability to break things down to basics. Harry concluded that Lee Choon Hong had just had enough of the brain washing and had no means of escaping it except by taking his chances on getting away from the camp. Let's hope it's not contagious, he reflected, although it would hardly surprise me if it was.

Three days later the monsoon took a break. The sun came through strongly turning the whole camp into a Turkish bath. The parade ground was at the most thirty yards wide, yet the steam from the saturated ground was so dense it could not be seen across. By mid-afternoon visibility had improved somewhat, prompting Harry to say to Matthew, "If it's like this again tomorrow, by lunchtime it should be OK to go to the lake and bag a couple of ducks." This he intended to achieve with his blowpipe – he was going to have to get pretty close to succeed in that!

"Can I come with you sir?"

"Yes of course. We can take a couple of your chaps as well; they don't often get the opportunity to stretch their legs."

The reason for going to the lake, about an hour away, was to get the wherewithal to introduce Chantek to proper feeding. Her diet of 'exasperated milk', followed by small feeds of 'bully', had over the past three months built her into a sturdy little animal, but now was the time to wean her on to a diet which was nearer to that to which she would have been introduced by her mother, had she not been orphaned. In the jungle a leopard will normally hunt small deer, birds, monkeys, tree rats and wild pigs. However, they are good fishermen. Lying on a river bank, when they spot a fish, it will stun it with a flick of its paw, and then dive in and fetch it. The problem with Chantek was that, due to its upbringing, it would never be taught to hunt by its mother. It would starve long before it learnt to hunt of its own accord. It was therefore down to Harry and his willing helpers, to keep it fed.

Over the past two or three weeks Harry and Matthew had designed and made a little harness to fit on a not entirely receptive animal, so that she could be taken out for exercise. They had first made a collar, but this proved unsuccessful in that she developed a knack of lying on her back, putting her two front paws on it, and neatly removing it. They decided that short of strangling the little blighter, it was going to have to be a body harness. Strangely enough she did not seem to object to this too much. After a short while of trying to tear it off with her back legs, she settled down to wearing it without too much commotion. Made from the plaited cords from the 'drop' parachutes – it was quite astonishing the different things which were being fabricated, encased, suspended, reinforced, strengthened or braced by the various parts of the parachute, even the straps found a use by the cobbler to repair every day footwear – the harness was light, being nylon, did not shrink when it got wet, was comfortable to wear, and extremely strong. On her first walk up and down the parade ground, Harry kept her on a short lead at first, gradually lengthening it until she could run little distances, the whole exercise being watched by thirty or forty communist Chinese who laughed and clapped. As Reuben noted afterwards, "I never thought I would see the day when that po-faced lot would all laugh and clap together. There's hope for them yet."

There was no such thing of course. They would virtually all perish in their endeavours to bring communism to Malaya after the war with Japan ended.

The next day, Sunday, dawned bright. During the monsoon season it was possible to have a few bright hours giving the impression of a bright day ahead, when the big black clouds, illuminated by vivid and continuous lightning would appear, and send those who had no cause to be out in the deluge to scurry for shelter. It was still bright by midday, so Harry decided to make his trip to the lake, along with Matthew and two of his Christian colleagues. Although they were non-combatants Harry insisted they carried a weapon, on the premise that even if they were most unlikely to meet nasty little Japs, they could very well be confronted by other denizens of the jungle with which, in an emergency, they might have to deal. He had of course given them strict orders this action should be taken only in a dire emergency.

They made slow progress at first. This absolutely novel experience for Chantek required that, as soon as they hit the game trail, which was the initial route to the lake, she frequently had to stop and sniff out all sorts of scents. After making very slow progress for some twenty minutes Harry said, "Come on, young lady, we will never get there," and picked her up. She sat up on his chest with her front paws over his shoulder looking back at Matthew following immediately behind, not completely sure whether she preferred the adventure of endeavouring to analyse all those different smells, or the closeness and the smell of her protector. She decided upon the latter, laid her head down on to her paws, and dozed off.

When they reached the lake, Harry put her down, and keeping her on a short lead, gave her to Matthew to hold, while he slowly and quietly made his way forward. Through his binoculars he studied the edges. The lake was, if the maps they had were accurate, about two miles long and from a half to one mile wide, at its widest point. As he swung his glasses round he saw, some two to three hundred yards to their left, a small colony, or to be more correct, I believe, to be called a raft, of ducks.

They moved slowly around the lake towards the ducks swimming and diving near the shore line. Suddenly Matthew grabbed Harry's arm, pointing to a mat of vegetation floating on the surface of the water, slowly moving toward the small flotilla.

"What's up?" whispered Harry.

"Crocodile," Matthew whispered back, "underneath the vegetation. Freshwater crocodile. Lives on fish, and any small animal that comes down to drink."

"How big is it?"

"Males grow up to twelve to fifteen feet, females a bit less. They hide under the vegetation and then strike."

As they spoke the vegetation moved closer to the unsuspecting birds. Suddenly there was a commotion in the water and the crocodile could be clearly seen hurling itself at its prey. With its long slender snout wide open it got two of the birds which had collided with each other in the panic, snapped its jaws shut and disappeared beneath the surface. In the meantime the other birds took flight directly towards Harry and his party. Harry quickly loaded a dart into his blow pipe and aimed at the leading bird. As it was flying straight at him, it presented almost a stationary target; at about twenty paces he fired the dart, the duck faltered in its flight, dived to hit the ground only a yard or so in front of one of Matthew's men, who promptly despatched it with a well aimed blow with the flat of his machete. Harry retrieved his dart after which the second man stuffed the bird into a gunny sack brought for the purpose. Harry turned to Matthew.

"How is it I didn't know there were crocodiles in Malaya?" Matthew looked at him smiling broadly.

"Sir, you can hardly blame me for an incomplete education." The other two grinned. Matthew continued. "These freshwater ones with the long thin snouts are not very common. They don't guard their nests, so when they lay their eggs in a mound they build out of leaves or peat, they just leave them. As a result if other predators, wild boar, snakes and so on find them they get eaten. They could lay up to fifty or so eggs, if one or two survive to make their way to the water, they are lucky. With the big crocs down at the coast, in the estuaries or mangrove swamps, they protect their young and as they hatch they carry them to the water, even then the newly hatched have to take their chances against predators, sea snakes and so on, or other crocs."

"Are you telling me the river I swam across, at Muar, has crocs in it?"

"They would be the saltwater ones, the same species as the Australian ones. They are the biggest in the world, anything up to twenty feet long. To answer your question, definitely yes. I have seen them from the ferry there. If you swam that river you were very, very lucky to make it, what with the crocs, the sea snakes and the filth from the mangroves which drain into it." Harry felt his stomach doing a decided rumba at the recollection.

"What do they live on?"

"Anything that moves really, from mud-crabs to buffalo. The buffaloes come down to drink and are grabbed by the leg and pulled in the water to drown, the croc doesn't attempt to kill the animal as it stands."

"How do you know all this?"

"I made a study of it at high school. We all had to give a lecture there for 'The Lecture Prize' – a book, plus, and I repeat plus, a sizeable sum of money, which as you can imagine, was the main incentive. I chose crocodiles."

Harry mopped his brow. "I shall start having nightmares again after all that. I knew about the snakes and I had the wind up for months afterwards, but CROCODILES, I didn't know about blooming crocodiles. Imagine one of those blighters grabbing you and pulling you under to drown in that filth. God Almighty!!

"It was God Almighty who watched over you, He knew you were a good man."

Harry turned to Matthew, put his arm around his shoulder and said, "I'm not as good as you think, but this I promise, I will try to be what you think I am."

The ducks having flown to goodness knows where, and the sky darkening to the north-west, Harry decided that one duck would have to suffice for the purpose of the further training of the little monster rubbing against his legs. They returned to the camp without incident, other than after about twenty minutes on the lead, Chantek ran back to Harry, looked up at him, and said 'Will you carry me?' not in those words, of course, although the little whimper which accompanied the pleading look may well have been panther language for the entreaty. He picked her up; she resumed her comfortable position on his shoulder, looked back at Matthew, made an indeterminate sort of noise to him, put her head down and promptly went to sleep, despite the continual jogging.

When they reached the camp the talk of course was all about the crocodile. Reuben was a mine of information – and kidology – about crocodiles, having been in Northern Queensland for a year before the war.

"You know they can run at twenty miles an hour don't you? So it's no good running away from them, you have to find a tree. They can't climb trees of course, but if it's only a small tree they get hold of it and shake it until you fall off."

"Pull the other one!"

"If it's a bigger tree they make a sort of whistling noise and two or three others appear and they all have a go together."

"Rubbish!"

"The funny thing is when you then fall out, they all start fighting each other as to which one is going to eat you. That's how you escape up another tree."

"Then what happens?"

"Abos come along and the crocs disappear, they don't like the taste of Abos."

The next morning, Chantek was in her big pen, having spent most of the night in with Harry. The thunder had rumbled around nearly all night frightening her to bits, as a result Harry had got up at around midnight and opened the flap. When he got up at 6.30 he put her back through the flap, washed and shaved, had his porridge, which came in the air drop and was a welcome variation to the usual tapioca, then called for Matthew to bring the duck. They tossed it into the enclosure; Chantek pounced on it but clearly had no idea as to what she was supposed to do with it.

"She's not hungry – she had a good meal last night sir," Matthew suggested to Harry, as she looked singularly disinterestedly at the large bundle of feathers confronting her.

"Do you think we should have defeathered it?" Harry asked.

"I wouldn't think so. After all they don't catch them in the wild without their feathers on do they?"

As they spoke she did a half circle from where she was standing, suddenly changing direction with a flying leap landing with her front paws on her prey. Having carried out that incredibly sudden operation, she was still at a loss as to what else she was supposed to do.

"Normally her mother would be teaching her, showing her how to secure it and which parts to tackle first, in animals the soft underbelly, in birds the head and legs."

"You are quite a blooming encyclopaedia in your own quiet way, aren't you Matthew?"

"I suspect there are many things you are far more informed about than I am."

"All I can say is that I'm learning far more from you than you are from me at the moment. But then, I always was a bit thick."

Matthew laughed. "That I do not believe for one moment."

"Well, I must get cracking. We will leave her to it. Don't give her any more to eat. You know the old saying, 'necessity is the mother of invention?' When she gets hungry perhaps she will find a way of getting at it, although if she doesn't touch it by tomorrow, we shall have to bury it, or it will go off."

She played with it, dragged it around, and threw it about, but she made no attempt to eat it. She went to bed hungry leaving the carcase in the pen. In the morning they found a bundle of feathers and bones. Ants had found it and there was nothing edible left.

"So we make the effort of an hour's trip to the lake, run the risk of being eaten by crocodiles, an hour's trip back, all to give a few thousand ants a feast. I am not very happy with you."

Chantek looked at him. Understood every word he had uttered, and rubbed herself against his leg. It was her way of saying, 'Never mind – eh?'

That night they heard on the BBC news, relayed from Ceylon, that Spitfires were in action in Burma, and that thirteen Jap planes had been shot down. Harry jumped off his chair.

"You know what that means don't you? They have enough Spitfires back home to deal with the Germans, so now they can send some to our theatre. That will happen with everything all the time now. They will drive the Japs out of Burma soon, then invade Malaya. It is only a question of time."

He called for Choon Guan. Passing the news on to him he asked him to tell his men. He failed to notice a certain lack of excitement compared to his own, but then Choon Guan was looking beyond the defeat of the Japs, to the defeat of the British. This might include, for all he knew, the deaths of Captain Chandler, Lieutenant Ault and the policeman, Lieutenant Isaacs. Despite his oriental inscrutability, combined with his communist principles, that latter fact disturbed him a little – but only a little, on the day he would have no second thoughts.

Chapter Four

From the end of September 1943 through to the New Year, Rosa von Hassellbek saw and spoke to her mother and Fritz, her new stepfather on a more or less daily basis. Her work in the Klinik kept her very busy. The numbers of female slave workers on the farms surrounding Brunksheim had increased, which directly led to an increase in the numbers of pregnancies with which she had to deal. The fathers, in the main, were other slave workers along with British and French prisoners of war, plus the occasional German farmer, who if it were found out would immediately find himself in a concentration camp. The mothers never saw their infants. Provided the babies were fit and healthy they were immediately given to German families. If they were sickly they were quietly disposed of. In the midst, therefore, of Rosa's gladness of having her mother and dear Fritz close by, she had the continual sadness of seeing mothers separated from their babies, and a few, a very few it must be said, of some newborn just left to die.

Operation Monika had been put into effect. Fritz had written to Rosa's husband, Dieter, serving in a panzer division on the Russian front, telling him that an old flame of his was anxious to hear from him. Dieter, of course, could not write directly to Rosa as she was technically a concentration camp inmate, having been given a six year sentence for possessing anti-war leaflets. Similarly, Rosa could not write to Dieter, even though she was at work in the Klinik, and not in Ravensbruk camp. Having a wife in a concentration camp could well cause him to be under suspicion in the present atmosphere of distrust. So, it was contrived that Dieter would write to 'Monika' at Fritz's address, since 'Monika', being married to a somewhat profligate husband serving in Norway, was living with her husband's parents, she would, therefore, be ill-advised to have love letters from someone on the Russian front, arriving at her husband's home. Any censor therefore reading love letters to and from Dieter, would take no notice – it was happening all the time.

The letters between them provided a lifeline to each of them. Although Dieter's new Tiger tanks had the beating of anything the Russians could throw at them, they were swamped by the seemingly endless reserves of manpower, guns and tanks the communists seemed able to produce. As a result each day they had to retreat. The morale, even in the elite units such as Dieter's was constantly being challenged, and in the allied units, Rumanians, Bulgarians, Hungarians, and so on, was at breaking point. With the recapture of Kiev in November the Russians gained a winter base, the snow came down by the ton, causing the war, apart from a few local skirmishes, to be set aside until the new year at least, probably February. It would continue of course in the South, in the Crimea, but even there not with the ferocity which had obtained all along the fifteen hundred mile front during the last nine months.

Dieter was sheltering in a prefabricated hut against one of his Tigers, the latter sheeted over and provided with an oil heater to prevent it freezing up, when the colonel's runner came to him.

"Herr Major, the colonel wishes to see you."

Dieter hurriedly put the writing pad away upon which he was penning a love letter to Monika, put on his sheepskin parka his parents had sent him last Christmas, and his snow boots, and made his way to the CO's billet.

"Dieter, when was the last leave you had?"

"October last year sir."

"Right. I can send a major, a captain and two lieutenants for ten days leave. That is of course calculated from the time you arrive and return to the railhead in Germany. God knows how long it will take you to get there, and back from there."

Dieter's heart surged. But then he asked, "What about you sir, you haven't had a leave for ages."

"Well there my dear Dieter, I have some news for you. When you come back and I assume you WILL decide to come back," this latter assumption accompanied by the sort of grin rarely seen on the extremely regimental face of his colonel, "I shall take a leave allotment, during which time you will be appointed as acting lieutenant colonel in charge of the regiment. So go and pack and be ready to move off to our railhead at 0800 hours tomorrow, which is the 15th December. You should therefore have Christmas at home."

Dieter thanked the CO profusely, saluted punctiliously, and almost ran back to his quarters. An hour or so later a clerk from the regimental HQ brought him his travel documents, along with a note authorising him to draw Reichsmarks at the paymasters' office at the Russian railhead.

The journey to the German railhead at Frankfurt am Oder was a nightmare. It took three days. Twice they were stuck in snow drifts, twice in the early stages they were attacked by partisans. It was a very stiff, tired, unshaven panzer grenadier major who eventually alighted to get some German money and change trains for Berlin. In Berlin he received a tremendous shock to see the extent of the British night bombing and marvelled at the way in which the railways had been repaired, not knowing that most of the work had been carried out by slave labour. In Berlin, instead of using his travel warrant to Ulm, his parents' home, he bought a ticket to Hannover, from which city he would find his way to Bruksheim. At Bruksheim he would contact Fritz to plan how he could see his beloved Rosa.

"At that point," he told himself, "I shall, I suppose, decide whether I will go back or not." There was of course, no doubt in his mind. He was a soldier, a professional soldier, and there was nothing, not even his beloved wife, which could interfere with his primary duty to the regiment – even if it was in an army commanded by a no-nothing Austrian ex-corporal.

It was the morning of the 20th December therefore that the telephone rang in the apartment of Mr and Mrs Fritz Strobel in Bruksheim.

"Strobel speaking."

"Major Strobel, this is Dieter von Hassellbek. I am in Hannover. I have ten days' leave. Can I come and see you?"

"Dieter, how great to hear your voice. Yes, get the slow train for Kassel. It's the fifth stop. When will you be leaving?"

"On the next train."

"That will be at 11.20. It is an hourly service, bombing permitting. I will meet you at the station."

"How will I know you?"

"If there are more than three or four people in the arrival hall at that time I will be most surprised. I will be the tall, good-looking one."

Dieter laughed. He was obviously going to like his new step-father-in-law.

Fritz went quickly into the kitchen where Gita was preparing some vegetables with which to make soup. Referring to the telephone call, she asked,

"Anyone interesting dear?"

"I will give you three guesses."

She could sense the excitement in his voice.

"Elizabeth from Ulm?"

"No."

"I can't think of anyone else – not Rosa?"

"No."

"Oh, do tell me please."

"Dieter!!"

Gita's hands flew to her face.

"Where is he?"

"In...," he studied his watch. "In one hour and forty minutes he will be here."

Gita flew into his arms, crying unashamedly, until she was struck by the realisation that there would be an enormous hurdle to overcome in arranging contact between Dieter and Rosa. She lifted her tear-stained face.

"How are we going to do it?"

"Do what darling."

"Get Dieter and Rosa together; on their own, they must both need each other so much." She thought for a moment, "and we must contact Ulm straight away and get Elizabeth and Konrad to come and stay so as to see him."

"Well, look, you book the call to Elizabeth and I will walk to the station."

"The station is only a fifteen minutes walk," she remarked mischievously, realising that under that casual exterior he was as excited at meeting Dieter as she herself was. She calculated further, "if he arrives on time at say just before midday, it will be 12.15 when you both arrive here. We shall not be able to tell Rosa as he usually doesn't come into the park until between twelve thirty and one o'clock. Add to that, it is bitterly cold today, she may not even venture out."

"We shall have to plan as we go, there is no other way. If she does appear do you think it would be better if you went straight down and told her, as I did when I brought you here? She should then have a little time in which to prepare herself."

"Yes, I will do that, but it still does not solve the main problem does it?" Fritz was well aware of what the main problem was, and had nothing whatsoever in his fertile brain to solve it at present.

As he made his way to the station he turned thoughts over and over in his mind as to how they could get Rosa away to be with her husband, but produced nothing but a feeling of pessimism at the impossibility of it all. Whatever was to be done to achieve an immediate successful outcome had to be very firmly balanced against jeopardising Rosa's present situation. The absolute first priority was the prevention of her being re-incarcerated in Ravensbruk concentration camp. Even love and passion had to take second place to that.

The train was more or less on time. The two men instantly recognised each other, shaking hands warmly. First exchanges of conversation on occasions such as this are invariably approaching the trivial.

"Did you have a good journey?"

"The first three days were the worst."

They laughed together.

"Thank God I never had that sort of problem. I used to think anywhere more than two hours from Hannover was a bad posting!" There was a short silence.

"Have you seen Rosa today?"

"No, she might well be out in the park by the time we get back." They climbed into a horse drawn cab. Dieter started to ask if he would be able to see her. Fritz put his finger to his lips and nodded towards the driver. Dieter had forgotten what it was like back in Germany. The Gestapo was only a comparatively small organisation. They relied on hundreds of thousands of informers, chief among whom were family members informing against their own kin, waiters and barmen, and near the top of the list, cab drivers. It was astounding what was said (and done for that matter) in the back of a cab, as if the cabbie did not exist. They confined their conversation therefore to the weather and sundry similarly uncomplicated subjects, until they arrived at Fritz's apartment.

Dieter looked at himself in the large mirror in the hallway.

"God, what do I look like?" His eyes were red-rimmed with lack of sleep, he had four days growth of beard, his hair had not been cut for a month, as he slipped his parka off he displayed a creased and crumpled uniform leading him to continue.

"God, if I went on parade looking like this I would be kicked out of the regiment."

"I don't think so, not with those on display," Fritz pointed to his campaign ribbons and his Knight's Cross.

"Let's go to the window and see if Rosa is there." They went to the window from which they could clearly see Gita sitting on the bench. There was not a soul in sight other than her. A lady with a dog then appeared, spoke to Gita, and then sat on the bench beside her, the dog making a fuss of its new friend.

"The lady with the dog speaks to Rosa when she happens to bump into her," Fritz told him.

As they spoke Rosa appeared from the Klinik. Fritz handed Dieter a pair of field glasses which he focussed on the trim, white clad form encased in a heavy black cloak, walking towards the two ladies on the bench. He was overwhelmed with emotion. He saw the lady with the dog speak to Rosa, indicating for her to sit down. Rosa studiously avoided looking up to the window, having given a smiling "Good morning," to the 'other lady' on the seat. The dog, which Rosa had previously been told, was also named Dieter.

"Hello, my lovely Dieter, how are you?"

Two things happened then in quick succession. Gita nearly jumped out of her skin at the mention of Dieter, the dog transferred its tail-wagging affections to his friend Rosa; resting his head on her lap and looking up at her with his big brown soulful eyes. She stroked his head.

"What do you do here at Christmas?" asked the lady to Rosa.

"It will be like every other day," Rosa replied.

"But won't you get some time to be with your family?" Rosa's eyes filled with tears.

"I'm afraid not," she managed to answer.

"Look, my husband is the Burgemeister. He is head of the council which runs the Klinik. I will ask him if he can get a Stellvetreter to be on call so that you have a break." (A Stellvetreter was a kind of locum).

At this, Rosa burst into tears.

"But your husband has already done so much for me, he saved my life, and the lives of many others with me."

Gita, acting instinctively, got up from her end of the bench and came round to comfort Rosa, forgetting for the instant she was supposed to be only a casual acquaintance. Remembering quickly she pulled a handkerchief from her pocket and handed it to Rosa.

"There, my dear, borrow this."

"What is your name, my dear?"

"Rosa von Hassellbek."

"How did my husband save your life?"

Rosa slowly unbuckled the leather strap she wore to cover the concentration camp number stencilled on her wrist.

"I was in a party of one hundred and twenty women marched to the brickyard on the outskirts of the town. We came from Ravensbruk. Most of us died on the way or were executed by the guards. Your husband will tell you the rest. He is a wonderful man."

The short, jerky, account had both of her listeners weeping, until the Burgemeister's wife said in a low voice, "My husband has told me nothing of this." She continued, "Now look my dear, my name is Frau Auerbach, my husband is Doktor Auerbach, not a medical doctor you understand. I will see if he can arrange something."

Gita was in a quandary. Should she risk everything and tell Frau Auerbach that Rosa's husband had arrived from Russia that morning? She looked up at the apartment window where she could clearly see the two figures, one holding field glasses.

"Frau Auerbach, can I speak to you in complete confidence?"

"Yes, of course my dear, absolutely."

"I am Gita Strobel, Rosa's mother."

"I rather suspected that, you are like two peas in a pod."

"Rosa does not know this, but her husband arrived here in Bruksheim this morning on leave from Russia where he is a tank commander. He is, at this moment, standing at our apartment window up there with my husband."

At this Rosa swung round, looked up at the window and saw her darling Dieter for the first time for over a year. As she raised her hand to wave, she felt her head swimming around, her legs unable to support her. She put her arms out; the two ladies supported her and lowered her to the bench. She quickly recovered.

"I'm so sorry; it was the shock of seeing Dieter. I had many times thought I would never see him again."

Frau Auerbach, seated on the bench beside her, put her arm around her. "I lost my son, Dieter, in Russia last year, my heart aches whenever I think of him." She thought for a moment, interrupted by Rosa saying, "I must get back, although how I shall be able to wait until tomorrow to see my husband I just don't know." Still uppermost in her mind was that she must do nothing, absolutely nothing, to imperil her position at the Klinik – a return to Ravensbruk would be a death sentence.

"I shall go and see my husband straight away and see what can be done. Our problem is Frau Doktor Schlenker, I don't know how much of a party person she is – but then my husband will probably know."

"She is always very kind to me, although fully professional."

She took Gita's address and telephone number.

"We shall contact you later today," she said, and with that hurried away, not in her usual direction across the park, but back out towards the town centre, and the town hall. Gita gave Rosa a quick hug. Rosa looked up at the window and waved, they both then walked away. When Gita arrived at the flat, out of breath as the confounded lift was out of order again, she therefore having to climb the stairs to the sixth floor, she was met at the open door by the two anxious men.

"What happened?"

"That lady is the wife of the Burgemeister, the man who looked after Rosa and the women when they reached the brickyard."

"What happened at the brickyard?" Dieter asked.

Gita described the march one hundred and twenty women had endured across Germany from Ravensbruk concentration camp north of Berlin. Most of them died on the way from starvation, or if unable to keep up, by being shot by the sadistic guards accompanying them. Only some thirty survived, totally unable to work at the brickyard to which they had been allocated. The Burgemeister had arranged medical care, subsequently placing them on farms locally to work. Finding that Rosa was a doctor she was placed at the town Klinik, on her honour not to leave the premises. It was during her lunch time sorties to the park bench nearby she met Fritz – he in turn visited Gita in Munich to tell her her daughter, of whom she had heard nothing for months, was safe. Fritz and Gita formed an attachment, were married, Fritz bringing his new wife back to Bruksheim where she could be near her daughter, and see her almost daily.

Dieter had slumped on to a chair.

"Are you saying that German soldiers were used to march women distances like that without proper food or shelter? And then shoot them if they lagged behind?"

"That is exactly what they did. They were SS Totenkopf I understand, camp guards."

In this year of 1944, stretching into 1945, hundreds of thousands of men, women and children experienced the awful ordeal Rosa and her fellow prisoners had endured as the Russians moved towards the camps from the East, and the British and Americans from the west. Very few survived. But that was in the future – the very near future in fact.

"To think my men are giving their lives for scum like that. Something must be done."

That was a moment of decision for Dieter. He would talk to his colonel when he got back as to what they could do to get this evil Nazi system destroyed, a proper peace made with Britain and France, and then concentrate on driving the hated Bolsheviks back where they belonged. He was well aware of the treatment of certain elements of the Russian populace by German troops, but even in his, as he would consider it, fair mind, the killing of commissars, party members and partisans, male and female, was a legitimate part of the war on world communism. This ambivalent attitude to right and wrong was not the sole belief of the German middle classes, many people in Britain would much rather be fighting the Russians than the Germans – as long as the Germans were not Nazis!!

"So what is happening now?"

Gita went on to tell them that Frau Auerbach had gone to talk to her husband to see what can be done. "She took our telephone number, she seemed a very very nice lady, she lost her son Dieter in Russia some while ago."

They each fell silent, pondering separately what the meeting at the park would bring. Rosa would be allowed to visit Dieter? She would be forbidden from so doing? She would be sent away? Worst of all, now that her connections outside the Klinik had been discovered she would be returned to Ravensbruk? Everything depended on the combined decision of Doktor Auerbach and Frau Doktor Schlenker, the final outcome probably contingent on the Frau Doktor's judgement.

"Is my husband engaged Fraulein?" Frau Auerbach had swept through the double doors, past the notice which clearly announced, "No Smoking, No Dogs," taking no notice of the notice, if you follow me. The young receptionist answered, "No Frau Auerbach, the Herr Burgemeister was just going to leave for his lunch."

"He will have to wait for that," and with that she hurried up the stairs to her husband's office leaving the young receptionist with the clear indication that at least one person in the small town of Bruksheim was able to boss the Burgemeister about, a fact of which she had not, up until now, even contemplated, let alone been aware.

"Hello, my dear, what brings you here? I was just about to walk home. Hello, Dieter, have you been a good boy?"

Dieter slobbered his reassurance to his master's husband (he knew who was the boss if nobody else did), that he had indeed been a good boy, flopped out on the carpet, and instantly went to sleep, keeping one ear open for the next command.

"I want to talk to you about the Frau Doktor in the Klinik – Doktor von Hassellbek."

"How do you know her name, or for that matter anything about her."

His wife explained how she had met her some months ago in the park, ending with the details of the meeting that morning.

"Now, her husband, who is a war hero with the Knight's Cross, has come on leave from Russia. She has not seen him for over a year. Is there not a way they can spend time together. It would be desperately cruel if they could not – it might be the last time she ever saw him, you know what happened to our Dieter."

The mention of Dieter made the dog look up, but instantly realising they were not referring to him, he went back to his one ear-open sleep.

The Burgemeister was somewhat taken aback by this appeal from one he would be unable to refuse, firstly because he loved her very much and secondly because he tacitly admitted, but only to himself, she was what is euphemistically known as the dominant partner.

"I will go and see Frau Doktor Schlenker."

"I would like to come with you," adding so as not to appear she was laying down the law, "if you don't mind of course."

"No, no, by all means do."

They walked to the Klinik, Dieter thinking to himself he was getting a decent run today for a change. (We shall get confused if we are not careful, that was Dieter the dog of course).

Frau Doktor Schlenker received them with open arms. "What a nice surprise, how kind of you to call ....." etc etc. The Burgemeister came straight to the point.

"We would like to talk to you about Frau Doktor von Hassellbek," but before he could get further, Frau Doktor Schlenker interrupted.

"Oh, please don't tell me you are taking her away, I just would not be able to manage without her. She is so conscientious and efficient I would find it difficult to replace her and impossible to cope on my own, especially now with the increasing numbers of guest workers in the district, half of whom seem to be getting themselves pregnant by the British and French prisoners of war working on the farms."

The Burgemeister let her go on. His experience of innumerable council meetings at the Rathaus was, that if you let the person taking the floor talk for long enough he either exhausted his argument, or himself, or both, thereafter being at a distinct disadvantage having nothing further to add to his diatribe, request, or whatever.

Having finalised her pleading, the Burgemeister assured her he had not come to take her extremely valuable assistant from her. He too had a vested interest in keeping Frau Doktor von Hassellbek at the Klinik – she was a first class doctor, "And as far as the Town of Bruksheim is concerned we get her services for nothing," he added. He then took the plunge.

"Her husband, who is second in command of a panzer grenadier regiment in Russia, has discovered she is here. He has come on leave. I would add he has recently been awarded the Knight's Cross to add to his other Iron Cross, and campaign medals. I think it is only humane that we allow them to be together for this short time, particularly since it is Christmas, a time of goodwill to all men."

The Doktor remained silent.

"I will arrange for you to have a Stellvetreter during the period of her absence. The way things are it may well be the last time she will ever see him."

The Doktor's eyes brimmed with tears. "That would be terrible. My nephew, Johann, has been posted missing, believed killed in action; I was very fond of him, how terrible it would be to lose a husband."

"Or a son," added Frau Auerbach, her eyes misting over as she again felt the anguish of the loss of her own precious Dieter.

They were all immersed in their own thoughts for a few moments, the silence broken by Frau Doktor Schlenker declaring, "She can go. How long is the leave?" Told it was for eight days after today she added, "But to cover myself, after all the authorities know she is here, she is on sick leave in your care and she will have to report here each day so that I know she has not absconded. Is that agreed?"

"Agreed."

"In which case I shall call her in." She went out into the main building, returning with Rosa.

"Frau Doktor, the Burgemeister has told me of your husband being here on leave from our gallant forces in Russia. I am allowing you eight days' sick leave under the supervision of the Burgemeister, with two conditions you must not contravene under any circumstances. Firstly you are not to frequent the town nor travel out of the town. Secondly you are to report to me at midday each day so that I know you have not absconded, you are still a camp inmate. Is that understood?"

"Clearly, Frau Doktor."

"And finally, my dear," she said, holding Rosa with her hands on Rosa's arms, her tone changing from the authoritative to being almost motherly, "my blessings on you both. You can go now to your husband."

Rosa's eyes streamed with tears as she hugged the somewhat reluctant Doktor, the somewhat embarrassed Burgemeister and the somewhat highly gratified Burgemeister's wife, so pleased with herself at having completed a successful outcome to this romantic saga.

Dieter knew that there was something special afoot and barked loudly, something he rarely did.

Chapter Five

January and February slipped by. Gradually the battalion became welded into a superbly efficient force, ready to go anywhere and do anything. It did not however lose entirely its sense of fun. Towards the end of February, on the day after David's twenty-fifth birthday in fact, the battalion was called on parade for a battalion photograph. This entailed the participants being formed in an arc with a special camera mounted at the centre of the arc traversing from left to right. The men were placed on the ground at the front, then seated on chairs, people then standing behind them, a further row seated in the forward edges of tables, and finally a row of men standing on the tables behind them. By having these serried ranks it was possible to get six hundred officers and men in one long picture so commonly seen in schools, college and military photographs. On this occasion three jokers on the far left of the camera, as soon as it had moved away, ran round the back of the battalion without being seen positioning themselves on the right hand side, thereby appearing twice, with big smiles, in the same photograph. When the proofs arrived, and this escapade was discovered, RSM Forster possessing the eagle eye which spotted it, asked the colonel who was studying the picture would he want the men concerned charged.

"What the devil with?"

"Oh, I will think of something sir, have no fear."

"I think we will leave it as it is Mr Forster, it just shows we have men with lively minds. In time it will be a point of interest to people looking as it as to whether they can see the three sets of twins in the picture."

And so it proved to be that over the years, when the photograph was eventually displayed in the Regimental Museum in Aldershot, three completely unknown paratroopers became celebrities. Sadly only one of them survived to enjoy the joke.

Every two weeks the men got their usual weekend pass, David spending them alternately with Maria at Chingford and at Sandbury. In the middle of January they decided to go to the pictures in Chingford on the Saturday evening. As the main feature got under way they heard the sickening sound of the air raid siren, an event which had become much less common of late. As the warning began an announcement was flashed onto the screen:-

An air raid warning is being sounded.

Will those who wish to leave please do so.

The performance will continue.

David looked at Maria in the dim light now being provided to enable people to see their way out.

"Would you like to go?"

"I don't think so darling, it is probably only a hit-and-run bomber. We have had several of those in the past month."

Hardly anyone left. The lights dimmed again and the showing of the film continued. Five minutes later they heard the distinctively disconcerting noise of heavy anti-aircraft fire a little way away, followed shortly afterwards by the furious firing of a mobile Bofors gun seemingly at the front door of the cinema.

"This I do not like very much," he said to Maria, putting his arm around her and holding her close. As he spoke they all heard the screaming of bombs descending – one, two, three, four – it seemed to last a lifetime. The first explosion was some way away, nevertheless could be felt in the cinema. The second one, much nearer, caused the building to shudder, the third one screamed with such intensity that David automatically hugged Maria to him, firm in the belief that their hour had come. It exploded some thirty yards from the back of the screen. The rear wall cracked and trembled, but fortunately did not collapse; the roof became detached at that point which caused showers of plaster and dust to cover the occupants. Worst of all the lights failed. The strange thing was that despite the terror of it all very few people had hysterics. There were a few who screamed as the bomb hit the ground, but in the main the cinema-goers crouched down between the rows of seats, until they heard the fourth bomb explode in the distance.

A high proportion of the people there had torches; most people venturing out in the blackout carried a flashlight of one sort or another. Instantly therefore the dust laden interior was lit by a myriad of hand held beams which gave a degree of reassurance to the audience that the worst was over. Within a minute of the bomb landing, the manager of the cinema, activating a well-rehearsed procedure, ran on to the stage with a large lamp, which, if it did little to illuminate the auditorium, at least shone on him. He had a megaphone in his other hand through which he bellowed

"Ladies and gentlemen. Please stay where you are for the moment. PLEASE."

Some people were already jostling to get out – not that you could blame them, there was something terribly claustrophobic about even that huge cavern filled as it was with thick dust making breathing difficult.

"PLEASE ladies and gentlemen, stay where you are for one minute. The staff are opening all emergency exit doors. PLEASE move now, SLOWLY, towards them."

David and Maria were almost in the centre of the circle. David shone his torch up on to the ceiling and could see some very substantial cracks, which, and it could have been his imagination, seemed to be getting wider all the time.

The place emptied in a little over five minutes, a tribute to the training of the manager and staff in doing what they did to stop people, rushing to get out, thereby probably knocking other people over, or causing panic. There were two thousand people in that cinema, only a handful suffered minor injuries, whereas, where the bomb actually landed, adjacent to a small nearby pub, seven were killed and thirty-one taken to hospital.

David and Maria made their way home where they were greeted in horror by Henry and Susan Schultz, Maria's parents. The plaster and ceiling dust had impregnated all their clothes, their hair was white and their red-rimmed eyes looked out from faces which looked like zombies. As David said to his father-in-law:

"I'm not coming on leave again – it's far too dangerous being a civilian!"

That weekend was the last they had together for six weeks, for various reasons. They talked regularly on the telephone, David acutely anxious that, in view of her 'condition' she should not be doing too much, should not lift heavy articles, should not go out when the footpaths were icy, should ensure she had plenty of sleep, etc, etc, until his exasperated wife told him to stop waffling, she was just going off to play badminton in the church hall.

"You are what?"

"I'm going to play badminton – only for an hour or so."

"Are you sure you should?"

"Of course. They asked me to go into the ladies' tug of war team, but I did jib at that."

"Are you kidding me on?"

"Now, why would I do that?"

"Who are 'they'?"

"I've joined this new women's organisation Lady Reading has formed. We pack parcels for the troops, and dozens of other things, as well as have a certain amount of social life."

He still was unsure as to whether he was being led up the garden path, but ended with, "Well don't overdo it my love will you?" – a pretty lame surrender he considered afterwards.

On the Friday of the taking of the photograph he started off on a forty-eight hour pass, arranging to meet Maria at Victoria, to then spend the weekend at Sandbury. Everyone came to see them at Chandlers Lodge, Sir Jack and Moira being among the first to arrive. Inevitably the talk swung to discussing the war situation.

"Did you hear the announcement about Tito's army?" Jack asked, knowing that David had been with Partisans a year ago in early 1943. "Now apparently his 'Army of National Liberation', as it is known, numbers three hundred thousand, and is equipped with arms, tanks, even planes which the British have sent him."

David felt an inner glow of pleasure and satisfaction at hearing of the success of this great venture which he and Paddy had been active in putting into operation. "I wonder how Todor Mavric, the lovely Livia, Pero Bozovic, and all the others are getting on," he wondered – if, of course, they are still alive.

Jack continued, "And your old playground took a bashing last week Maria, did you know? Apparently our coastal artillery sank a large German supply ship just off Calais, which as an ex-artillery man myself I can assure you must have required some very accurate gun-laying, after all it must have been ranging at somewhere near twenty miles. Anyhow, Jerry plastered Dover, Deal, Folkestone and Ramsgate with shellfire for four solid hours. The powers that be have not told us yet of the casualty figures – they will probably do that in six months' time if I know them."

As they were talking Anni arrived with her father, Karl, and little David. She walked into the middle of the room, held out her hands, in each of which there was something they had not seen for many a year – an ORANGE. Immediately there was a chorus of, "Where did you get those?"

"Mr Burcham in the market place got a consignment today; they are apparently from Spain, the first since the war started. I had to queue and he rationed them to three per person."

"You know," Jack reflected, "those oranges mean at least two things. One, we can afford our shipping to be taken up with a few luxuries, two, the Spanish obviously think we are going to win the war, otherwise they would not want to initiate trade with us."

"You talk of winning the war, I wish someone would tell the miners there's a war on," Fred complained. "I saw in The Telegraph this morning that in the second six months of last year there were over four hundred separate strikes in the mines, and we lost I think they said, some half a million tons of coal as a result. It's a good job their Uncle Joe Stalin is not in charge of them, he would shoot the lot."

"I don't really know what they have to strike about," Jack continued, "they have just been given another rise. Underground workers now get three pounds two shillings a week basic. I understand the unions want six pounds a week for coalface people – they'll never get it."

Talk continued about the continual bombing of Berlin, despite our heavy losses of aircraft. A report from a Swedish eyewitness arriving in Malmo, Sweden, stated that Berlin was 'dying and paralysed, all public transport had broken down'. The general view was 'so what – who started it?'

On 15th February the heaviest attack in the history of warfare thus far was launched on Berlin. Two and a half thousand tons of bombs were dropped by over a thousand aircraft. The city was now fifty per cent in ruins and seventy four thousand people had perished. The Bishop of Chichester protested bitterly against the saturation bombing which had already left Hamburg in total ruins. It had been announced a new bomb weighing twelve thousand pounds, about five tons, was being used by the Lancasters.

The Germans retaliated on the 18th February with a considerable night raid on London and Kent, followed by lesser incursions on the 22nd, 23rd and 24th, combined with shelling of Hell Fire Corner, as the south east of the county of Kent was known. They might be going down, but they certainly were not out.

Among the dozen or so bombers shot down during these raids, one crashed on to the police station at Dymchurch, killing a number of people. However, the main concern at the moment was the shocking news of the road deaths in the past year. Nearly six thousand people were killed, a quarter of them children. More than half of the total took place during the black out. When the fact that there were so few cars on the roads due to the petrol rationing, the figure became even more appalling.

"Well, enough about the war, how are all our romances going?" Fred asked. "What about you Karl?"

"Now that would be telling – is that what you say? I can tell you that Mrs Gordon and I are very good friends. I am taking her and the two children to London next Saturday afternoon to a cinema and supper afterwards. Does that answer your question?"

"You will be putting the children on the train home by themselves then after supper?"

"I did not think of that, perhaps I should suggest it to Rosemary?"

"And what about you Ray?"

Ray Osbourne, who had been chatting to Anni, asked "What about me?"

"You and the delectable June Morris, who I understand you are bringing to the Rotary do next Thursday?"

"Now as an officer and a gentleman, or at least an ex-officer ...

Ernie interrupted, "And ex-gentleman, according to the stories I've heard about the shindigs that take place in that new flat you have moved into."

"I shall ignore those remarks. As an ex-officer and gentleman, I am unable to substantiate the prurient thoughts going through your mind."

Ernie turned to Jack. "What's prurient?"

Jack replied, "Lord knows, probably to do with being in the Royal Engineers I expect – they are a funny lot."

The weekend was soon over. David and Maria left Chandlers Lodge at five o'clock, he then seeing her on to the Underground at Waterloo. There was the usual milling crowd at the terminus, soldiers, sailors and a few airmen in various stages of sobriety. The Bulford garrison train was in, so he made his way to the first class section, selected a corner seat and sat back, keeping his fingers crossed there would be no raid – at least until after the train had left. As he sat there, in what was, thus far, an empty compartment, he wondered as he so often did, what Harry was up to. Harry had not trained as an infantry soldier. In the Royal Army Service Corps it was his job to ensure all the supplies the infantry and artillery needed were speedily and efficiently brought from the various ordnance depots in whichever country they were operating, so that the front line soldiers remained fed and watered, supplied with ammunition and a thousand and one other items an infantryman and an artillery man needs to combat the enemy. Now he had not only found himself carrying the fight to the enemy, a ghastly obnoxious enemy at that, but he had a necessity to learn how to do it on the job. His admiration for his brother was unbounded, not only because he had taught himself to be a fighting man, evidenced by the Military Cross he had been awarded, but also because of the continual, monotonous, soul destroying endurance of living in a rain soaked jungle, which, in David's eyes was valour of a different kind altogether. Yet Megan had told him his infrequent letters, which she thanked God for, were invariably cheerful and interesting.

His thoughts were interrupted by the door from the corridor being brutally pushed back and the voice of Sandy Patterson bellowing, "Look who we found being accosted by two ATS girls on the forecourt David."

"Who's the 'we'?"

"Miles Rafferty and me – Miles has been at Blackheath with me over the weekend."

"Do you mean to tell me you risked taking him to meet Amanda One?" David asked, "And anyway who have you found?" They pulled a body forward.

"Tis meself sir, so it is."

"Paddy! Come in and sit down."

"Well it is First Class sir, is it not?"

"Oh, balls to that, come on in. I want to hear all the news."

The three took their seats. "Right, who is going to start? First of all, how is Amanda One, Sandy?"

"She's gorgeous."

"The sergeant-major and I could have told you that."

A degree of explanation is required at this point. Amanda One was an ATS lance corporal who was allocated to driving David and Paddy when they first went to Ringway to do their parachute training before jumping into the Balkans to join the Partisans. They all three became great friends. Amanda met Sandy Patterson, a Canadian, when he went to Ringway to do his jumps. She was called Amanda One because, by coincidence the driver allocated to David and Paddy when they returned to Cairo from the Balkans, in a hair-raising submarine journey across the Mediterranean, was also Amanda, thus becoming Amanda Two. So now you know all that we can continue.

David proceeded with the cross-examination.

"Now Sandy, what on earth persuaded you to take Miles here to meet your girlfriend?"

"Fiancée."

"What do you mean, fiancée?"

"I asked her to marry me, she said yes, so it's all systems go in the summer sometime. That part we haven't worked out yet. I have a seven day leave coming up in early April; we shall work out the details then."

"Well, this calls for a celebration, the only problem being we have nothing to celebrate with."

"Now there gentlemen, I may be able to help." Paddy got up from his seat, took his haversack down from the luggage rack and took out a bottle of Jameson's Irish whiskey. "Now, I know the major can manage this without his eyes watering, but whether lieutenants can is another matter."

"We'll try hard sergeant major, of that you can be sure," Sandy replied.

"My grandfather distils this in Ireland," Miles Rafferty interjected, "as a kid I used to have it for breakfast."

"And if that isn't typical Irish bullshit I don't know what is," countered Sandy.

The door from the corridor slid open.

"I thought I heard friendly voices."

At hearing this they all stood up. It was their colonel, Lieutenant Colonel Hislop.

"And look who I found wandering on the station concourse."

Behind him they could distinguish in the pale light the RSM and a lady. David gave a cry of welcome.

"Marianne, come in, how lovely to see you."

David and the RSM's wife were old friends, as indeed were RSM Forster and Marianne with David's family.

"Come on in, there's room for us all, we were just about to celebrate Sandy's engagement to his delightful Amanda with a bottle of whiskey provided by Paddy here. Now, the problem is we have no glasses and we can hardly expect a lady, or a colonel for that matter, to drink out of a bottle."

Marianne held her hand out to Paddy to take the bottle, the top of which he had removed as the newcomers arrived. Raising it to Sandy, she said, "Congratulations to you both," took a hearty swig and handed the bottle back to Paddy. They watched with keen interest to see whether she would choke on the swallow she had taken, whether her eyes would stream or even that her knees might buckle. Nothing like that happened. She smiled at them all. "That's part of the training of being an RSM's wife." The all applauded loudly.

"Right Paddy, I'm next." It was the colonel, with Paddy saying to himself. "Am I dead and gone to heaven with the colonel calling me by my Christian name?"

And so the bottle made the rounds, the niceties of crystal glasses being totally ignored. All of them, with the exception of the delightful Marianne, would soon be only too pleased to be back in the comfort of that railway carriage, glasses or no glasses.

As they got under way David looked across at the colonel seated opposite him.

"Sir, as I know you have a delightful home on your huge family estate in Marlborough, would it be in order to ask what you were doing on a forty-eight in London."

"I was visiting an elderly aunt." There was a universal nodding of heads at this reply, as if to say "We've heard that one before."

"And your elderly aunt, sir, did you find her well?"

"Frightfully, thank you."

"Sir, can you remember the name of your elderly aunt?" The others were all grinning away like mad; it was something completely out of the ordinary to be party to the leg-pulling of their colonel.

"If I tried hard enough I think I probably could. I was visiting my elderly aunt – that's my story and I'm sticking to it."

"Well, we shan't say a word to anyone, shall we?" He looked at the others, who each nodded in agreement.

"Oh, one last thing sir, what colour lipstick does your aunt use?" – looking calculatingly at the colonel's cheek. The colonel grinned at the watchful party.

"Oh, you don't catch me on that one you blighter. I was visiting an elderly aunt, I was visiting an elderly aunt," he repeated.

David sat back, then addressed the others. "Do you know Goebbels said that if you say anything, and I mean, anything, enough times, everybody will believe it?" They all, including the colonel laughed at this observation, and the conversation passed to other topics for the remainder of the journey.

March came in bitterly cold, but training carried on at a furious pace. They had been delivered with the new PIAT anti-tank weapon, similar to a bazooka, carried by a two-man team. It was deadly effective – provided you got close enough to the tank, and to be fair that is exactly the position in which any soldier with any sense would least like to be. Nevertheless, paratroops suffer from being very lightly armed, this weapon therefore was welcomed with open arms, at least you had something with which to attack armoured vehicles. They carried out two night operations. One in company strength on Salisbury Plain, the second in battalion strength on a battle area in Norfolk. They learnt a lot from these exercises, knowledge which would stand them in good stead in the months to come, the chief part being that by dropping in darkness on a landscape criss-crossed with hedges and ditches was the fore-runner of a colossal balls-up unless every single man knew exactly what he was supposed to do when he landed. Always supposing he was dropped in the right place of course!!

On the night of the Norfolk drop that was precisely what happened. The pathfinders were to drop half an hour before the main landing and set up directional beams to guide the incoming battalion, a force of some thirty aircraft. The aircraft were flown by American crews, a factor not exactly pleasing to R Battalion, the stories of Yankee pilots dropping paras and unhooking gliders into the sea in the Sicily invasion still more than current in airborne circles. The pathfinders suffered two problems. Firstly half of them, some ten men, were dropped miles wide, the second half from another aircraft, were dropped on the target – more or less – but in the landing half of their equipment was so damaged it was rendered useless. The upshot of it all was that half the aircraft following got no signal and had to give the green light when they calculated by dead reckoning they were over the drop zone. To add to the problem there was a certain amount of low cloud that night, visibility being further reduced by a ground mist. All these factors meant that the battalion was spread all over the place, some even landing outside the battle area from which the population and stock had been relocated elsewhere, to end up in the back gardens of understandably frightened country folk not terribly pleased at being disturbed in the middle of the night.

David's company was scheduled to rendezvous at a copse near a group of farm buildings. When sufficient numbers had arrived at the RV they were to attack the farm, dig in around it and await further orders. David's stick, which included his batmen, Angus, Paddy and the wireless operators all landed reasonably close to the RV reasonably close being half a mile away. Miles Rafferty and several of his men he had collected on the way – some heading in the opposite direction – had already got to the copse just before David arrived. It was 2.30am. Gradually men trickled in.

"No sign of Mr Patterson or Mr James sergeant major?"

"No sir, not as yet, their platoon sergeants are in, but we're only thirty-two strong." It was then 3.15am.

"Well, we'll give it another half hour then we shall have to move."

At 3.45 on the dot Sandy Patterson arrived bringing four men with him, two of whom were from another company. With others having struggled in, they now had forty-four men – only a third of the company.

"Right, we'll split into two platoons." Sandy you take the left hand set of buildings, Miles you take the right. When you've cleared them, Sandy you dig in on the other side, Miles you dig in on this side so that we have all-round protection."

"Where will you be sir?"

"The CSM and I will be in the front room of the farmhouse, waiting for Angus to brew up."

Elsewhere, other company commanders were carrying out similar mock attacks, all the objectives having been taken by daylight in preparation for the inevitable counter attack. The exercise, however, from the CO's point of view, had it been somewhere in France would have been a very dicey affair. Less than half of the battalion had been dropped in the right place. Despite the lessons learned from this and similar drops by other battalions, the old adage of 'what can go wrong will go wrong', was proved to be true. Furthermore it didn't end with the practise drops, it happened all over again in Normandy 'on the night', doubtless we shall hear more of that in chapters to come.

When all the men had eventually drifted in it was close on midday.

"All in, now sergeant major?"

"We're still one short sir; three men were injured and put in the blood wagon."

"Who is the missing one?"

"Elliott 73 from Mr James's platoon sir."

"Well perhaps he was dropped so wide he had made his way to a village cop shop." The men had been told that in the event of their being totally unable to reach the battle zone in time, to report to the nearest police station, from which they would be collected.

"I've been on to the RSM sir. He sent the runner back with a message no Private Elliott has been reported booking in."

The lorries arrived to take the men back on their long journey to Bulford. Still no Elliott 73.

"We'll move off sergeant major. Elliott will have to find his own way back."

Sadly, Elliott 73, (there were three Elliott's in the company, hence the added number to distinguish one from the other,) could not make his own way back. When he had exited from the Dakota he had spun in the slipstream. As a result his rigging lines from the parachute canopy had wound into a spiral preventing the canopy itself from opening. It was a classic malfunction known in the trade as a Roman candle. Private Elliott hurtled to the ground and died instantly.

The next day, the exercise being over, a detachment of Bren carriers, small open-topped tracked vehicles, were employed in scouring the battle area collecting the parachutes discarded by the five hundred odd men when they landed. Those that landed outside the battle area provided the opportunity to some of the farmers of 'winning' some first class rick covers; at least fifty were never found.

What WAS found by one of the carriers was the crumpled body of Private Elliott. The shocked young men employed on this task had never seen a dead man before, let alone a body so badly deformed as this. They removed the parachute, gently lifted the dead paratrooper up on to the pile of parachutes they had already collected and drove back to their base. The lance corporal in charge, before they left, using the initiative which had made him a lance corporal at the early age of nineteen, carefully folded the parachute up so that it could be examined by the court of enquiry which he calculated would most certainly be held, and at which he would be called as a witness.

It was not until ten o'clock on the morning of Friday 31st March that a runner came to David's company HQ with a request he should go to the commanding officer. With the usual thought, "What the hell have they found out about me now?" he picked up his beret and webbing belt, quickly put them on and walked over to the colonel's office. When he arrived he was bade enter, to find the adjutant and the RSM already there.

"Good morning sir."

"Good morning David. David we have news of Elliott 73. I'm sorry to have to tell you he candled on the drop. The parachute recovery party found his body."

David was shocked. Although all paratroopers knew it could happen to any one of them, when it did happen it was felt very deeply throughout the battalion.

"Tommy," (the adjutant), "has contacted the family, fortunately they are on the telephone, and asked them whether they would like us to provide a military funeral. They had, I hasten to add, already been notified by the military hospital at Colchester to which he had been taken from Thetford, of the accident. The family have told us they would in fact be grateful if we lay him to rest with full military honours, he was so proud of his regiment and his red beret. Now Mr Forster will assist you in selecting a bearer party, and guide Mr O'Riordan in getting the drill right. We have not as yet, naturally, been given a date, but it will probably be in a week or ten days from now, Tommy will keep you posted on that. Finally, I think it would be befitting if you and Mr James attended on my behalf. Any questions?"

"Yes sir, do we know where the funeral will be held?"

"His home is somewhere near Peterborough I believe," he looked enquiringly at Tommy.

"That's right sir."

"Well, we'll leave it in your hands then David. Mr Forster will give you all the help he can from the procedural point of view. I think it might be a good idea to take half a dozen NCO's and men in addition to the bearer and firing parties to show the family he was a valued member of our battalion.

"Right sir, I'll get on to it straight away."

With that he saluted, as did the RSM who followed him out on to the veranda.

David and the RSM walked back to B Company spider, to find all the men on NAAFI break, the CSM and the platoon officers all collected in the company office. David gave them the sad news adding, "When your chaps come back from their NAAFI break will you get them out on to the parade ground for Mr O'Riordan to arrange them in a three sided formation so that I can talk to them." They nodded assent.

Paddy assembled the parade, calling it to attention as David appeared with the RSM, followed by the platoon officer.

"Stand at ease please sergeant major."

"Stand at EASE, stand easy," Paddy commanded.

"I have to tell you of the death of our comrade Private Elliott. His parachute malfunctioned on our exercise in Norfolk. I shall be writing to his parents expressing the sorrow of all of us at the loss of such a staunch member of our company, and express the condolences of each and every one of you." There was utter silence, each one probably thinking 'it could have been me'.

After a short pause he continued. "Will you dismiss four and five platoons sergeant major?"

This done, leaving No.6 platoon, David continued, "This platoon will provide a bearer party of six, a firing party of six, along with two NCO's and four men to attend the funeral. Mr O'Riordan will sort that out now with guidance from Mr Forster. That is all." He turned and left, to the combined salutes of the two warrant officers.

In the meantime, the body of Private Elliott of the Parachute Regiment, previously with the Cameronians, Scottish Rifles, lay on the slab at Colchester Military Hospital, rigor mortis having left him. A sad medical officer, with the aid of a sergeant from the RAMC, carried out the task of having to reposition his head, arms and legs so cruelly misaligned from his fall.

"At least his face missed the worst of it," the sergeant commented.

"Yes, the funeral people will probably cover those bruises up somehow I expect."

It is surprising what has to be done to bodies involved in accidents of any sort, so as to not give their loved ones greater grief than they are already suffering when they view them for the last time.

Chapter Six

In Malaya, January passed in a mixture of utter boredom, Turkish bath monsoon conditions, a cut in rations, depression from having a deserter from the camp, the combination of all these factors not helped by a virtual invasion by kraits, a four feet long very nasty piece of reptilian homework. The living huts were built off the ground, which whilst making them cooler to live in, also gave a certain amount of shelter from the confounded rain for all sorts of unwelcome visitors. The problem is, that different snakes prey on different sources of food. The rat eating snake therefore sought out the rodents under the huts, while the krait, which eats other snakes, sought out the rat eaters. Few snakes are aggressive, certainly kraits are not, but kraits are extremely venomous, moving mainly at night, the consequences therefore of treading on one in the dark, whilst not bad enough to kill a fit, healthy, person are bad enough to make the 'victim' very ill indeed.

When the monsoon eventually eased, Harry decided they would have a snake drive. The procedure was that half a dozen men would be provided with long bamboo poles with a cross-piece on the forward end made from prickly bamboo. Another gang would be positioned on the other side of the hut supplied with heavy wooden, long handled clubs (long handled for obvious reasons), and dressed in boots and double puttees up above knee level in case they were attacked. A snake can only raise itself a third of its length to strike, always assuming it gets the time to do so. Despite these precautions, for some strange reason, there was a marked reluctance to volunteer for the killing ground! The bulk of the Chinese were city dwellers who rarely encountered snakes in their home life, still having therefore the sort of fear their kampong bred brothers had learnt to overcome as children.

Snakes are extremely vulnerable. Their main sensory chord runs right down the top of their body. One heavy blow, if not to kill them, is sufficient to paralyse them, probably this being the reason for their instinctive need to avoid trouble. Harry gave his instructions.

"Now, lay your cross pieces on the ground as close to the next man as possible and push slowly under the hut taking your time from me. The people at the back, let the rat eaters go, but kill the kraits and anything else venomous that comes out."

Reuben was in charge of the killing ground. He had spent time up in

Queensland and the Northern Territory – he knew a bit about snakes!

"Right, with me begin," Harry very slowly pushed his pole under the hut. The huts were about eighteen feet front to back, the poles being a little short of that measurement. From the first hut four kraits attempted to make their escape but were speedily dealt with. There were no rat eaters – presumably they had vacated the premises in favour of the kraits.

The second hut produced a similar result. When they started on the third hut, they had jointly more or less reached the centre, when Harry's pole met with a solid object of some sort. Harry gave it an extra shove which resulted in the pole moving forward another foot or so. Another harder shove and it moved more, to be accompanied by a shout from Reuben "Hold it, come and look at this."

Startled by the shout – one hardly ever spoke above a normal speaking tone in the camp, even lower in the jungle – Harry, followed by the others, ran round to the back of the hut to see the killing team grouped together with Reuben watching the most gigantic snake any of them had ever seen very slowly emerging from under the hut. They had all seen pictures of these monsters, but even though they had been in the jungle now for over two years they had never ever seen one, just as they had never seen a tiger of which there were supposed to be hundreds. But then, the jungle is a big place, and it didn't mean a tiger had not seen them.

"A reticulated python," Harry gasped, "by God, isn't it beautiful?"

The reticulated python shares with the South American aquatic and tree snake, the anaconda, as being the world's biggest snake.

"I wonder how long it is?" Harry asked of no one in particular.

"If we wait long enough we shall possibly find out," Reuben replied, whilst the snake, moving, oh so slowly, headed its way towards the cover of the jungle. About four or five feet from its head there was a distinct bulge, the remains presumably of its previous meal still being digested when rudely interrupted by Harry's prickly bamboo pusher. Its body was beautifully marked and as thick as a man's thigh. They grew up to over thirty feet long and could weigh over two hundred and fifty pounds, although they would not reach this size until they were some twenty-five years old, then living on up to 70 years.

The assembly watched in total fascination as this magnificent reptile slowly made its way from beneath the hut, their normal fear of, and revulsion by, a snake, being entirely lost in their wonderment at being so close to such a unique creature in the wild, an experience of such great rarity.

"How long do you think it is Reuben?" Harry asked.

"I would say it's all of twenty feet," was the reply. Matthew added the comment,

"Look, it is almost straight, its head is by that tapioca plant and its tail has just cleared the hut. We can measure that when it is gone."

They did, and found it to be almost as Reuben had guestimated. It was almost twenty feet. Allowing for the fact the side to side feature of its movement would add a bit more to that distance; it was as near twenty three feet as made no difference, in Harry's view.

"I wish we had had a camera," Harry exclaimed.

"We have the next best thing," Matthew replied, indicating the artist of the camp, in peacetime an illustrator for the 'Straits Times' in Singapore, who was feverishly roughing out a sketch from which he would later make a full sized drawing of the event. He had already made a number of drawings of Chantek in her various stages of growing from a tiny cub to her boisterous present size, some including Harry, some with Matthew. These somewhat bourgeois offerings were frowned upon by Choon Guan, and distinctly discouraged by the commissar, the man who gave them their nightly ration of communist indoctrination. Harry, given the drawings, treasured them carefully, and having knowledge of the opposition previously mentioned, suggested to the artist on one occasion, he made portraits of Choon Guan and the commissar without their knowing and then give them to the two vilifiers.

"After all, most people like to have their photos taken, unless they have something they want to hide, or are wanted by the police or something."

To which our artist friend replied, "in which case that could apply to both of them."

Harry raised his eyebrows but said no more. Most of the fifty odd men under his command had been recruited by the Malayan communist party, and had been taken at face value by their European superiors, no questions asked. Nevertheless, the artist followed Harry's suggestion, and, surprise, surprise, each accepted the offering with a singularly rare smile, causing the later comment to Harry, about the commissar, "I thought he might have cracked his face."

The artist was undoubtedly not a one hundred per cent, fully fledged, totally paid up communist, "I wonder how many more there are in his category," being Harry's thoughts on the subject.

They watched this magnificent reptile make its slow way into the undergrowth. It was one of the few creatures of the jungle which had no predators, other than man.

"Right, back to Hut Four," Harry called, and the de-snaking continued. They had good results from this hut, including a particularly nasty viper, Hut Five drew a blank, but at the main dormitory they had a field day. Whether they disturbed a snakepit, or whatever it is called, or not, suddenly dozens of small and half grown banded kraits appeared, the men having to run between them to finish them off. Even so a few got away as the dormitory was a few yards nearer the undergrowth than the other huts. One of the men had a fully grown krait try to take a lump out of his leg, but he was saved by his thick puttees. The snake however had got his fangs caught up in the material, as a result there was the ludicrous sight of a badly frightened Chinese shaking his leg about, trying to dislodge the nasty thing until Reuben walked across and thumped it, thereby sending it to the great snakery in the sky.

They were all euphoric at the success of their day's work, until two thoughts sunk in to their collective minds. One – how long had they been living on top of that mass of menace without knowing? Two – would another lot, during the night, take the places of those expelled? It was noticeable that few left the barrack room to use the latrine buckets at night for some while after the drive, unless it was absolutely necessary, and then always accompanied by much ground-stamping to hopefully frighten away any unwanted company.

The following weekend they received a coded message from Sunrise asking, "Please resume observation at Ilkley Moor." Ilkley Moor was the code name for an airfield being extended by POW and slave labour at Kuala Lipis, some thirty miles north east of Camp Three. They had carried out observations there before the monsoon, and established the fact that the airfield was being concreted, obviously with the intention to cater for heavy transport or bomber aircraft, whereas it had previously been a fighter 'drome, originally belonging to the RAF before the Japanese invasion. Harry decided to lead the week long patrol himself, which meant leaving Chantek behind in the care of Matthew. She sensed what was going on and was not a little put out by the prospect of losing her guardian.

They left on Tuesday morning, the usual pattern – two scouts forward changed every hour – then Harry and the party of nine men with Tommy Isaacs coming up at the rear. They carried food for nine days, a blanket and mosquito net each – from previous experience they knew that the Kuala Lipis area bred a particularly vicious mosquito – their normal weapons and a parang. There was one medical orderly with a good supply of first aid equipment, if they were to need a stretcher for any reason they would have to make one. On the other hand they each understood from

Harry downwards, if they ran into trouble and one was badly wounded, he would have to be despatched by one of the officers. A wounded man could not be left to the ministrations of the Kemptai, who would eventually kill him anyway. This grim duty had fallen to Harry when they had attacked Kuala Bintang a year ago; the horror of it had been a nightmare to him for weeks afterwards.

They reached their bivvy area before noon on Thursday morning, Harry taking three men forward some two miles to the vantage point they had used during their earlier reconnaissance. He had started to study what further development had been made during the monsoon period, when the monsoon itself decided it had not finished with them, rain falling in torrents. They had no option but to sit it out, although visibility as far as the airfield was concerned was nil. They had rain capes, but in a deluge of that nature nothing is proof against getting thoroughly wet, if not from the head down, certainly from the legs up. At four o'clock, with no prospect of a break in the storm Harry decided to move back to the bivvy area. Here they found the rest of the patrol had managed to build some rudimentary shelter and were knocking up bamboo beds to at least get off the saturated ground for the next couple of nights.

Soon after dawn the next morning Harry's party again moved off, Tommy and his party to relieve them at midday. The rain had stopped but the constant dripping from the trees of their previous soaking made life very uncomfortable for an hour or so until the sun strengthened to give a little very welcome warmth to the patrol's chilled bodies.

Harry studied the airfield through his binoculars. The runway had now been extended, he estimated, to at least a mile, possibly more. The final third still had only hard core laid, rocks dug out from the airfield perimeter by the POW's and broken up to provide a firm base for the concrete. Little concreting had been done during the monsoon, but now some fifty odd bodies were mixing, barrowing and laying the concrete in squares on the final section. As they watched, a 12 seater Fokker aircraft circled the airfield, landing on the completed part of the runway, taxiing up almost as far as the working party. An attendant jumped down from the door in the fuselage, pulling after him a small step ladder, after which there was a pause in the proceedings until Harry saw the very short, rather portly figure of an officer, so short in fact his sword dragged the ground. The officer turned to face in Harry's direction. In the bright sunlight Harry could clearly see his gold tunic patches, signifying he was a general of some sort, but he could not distinguish how many gilt stars he had on the patches to finally determine his exact rank. Nevertheless, he thought, if he is only a major general – the lowest form of Japanese general officer life – this must be a very important project being undertaken here for a general to come and inspect the work in progress.

As the general approached the POW's the NCO in charge obviously gave the order to bow, since all stopped work, turned towards the general and complied with the order until they were told to carry on. Harry's hackles rose at this sight, the fact that fifty odd British soldiers were having to bow to one short-arsed, four-eyed git of a Jap General, raised a fury within him which he would have difficulty logically to explain. Nevertheless, the incident was logged, the further movements of General Short-arse further noted, the whole to be sent back to Cameron Highlands upon their return to Camp Three.

They spent two more days observing the operations on the airfield – in particular estimating the sizes of some corrugated iron sheds being erected. Were they for warehousing? Aircraft repairs shops? Rough sketches were made to give to Sunrise on his next visit.

They spent a further two days which included a patrol around the north side of the airfield until they reached the metre gauge railway which ran up the centre of Malaya to Kota Bharu in the north where the Japanese had first landed in their invasion of Malaya two and a bit years ago. This was significant. The railway was obviously being kept in good repair. Although of considerably smaller gauge than the main railway line running from Singapore to Thailand through Kuala Lumpur it could still carry troops and equipment from north to south, or vice versa, should the Allies invade. Harry decided therefore that further study of this railway line, of which they had known very little, would be required. For now, with rations running out, they had to be on their way back to Camp Three, in his case to the excited welcome by a bundle of spotted fur – a bundle? no longer a bundle, more a hunk!

They broke camp, leaving everything as pristine as they possibly could. They passed the spot where they had found Chantek, newly born from her dead mother. It was overgrown now, concealing probably the remainder of her bones after the carnivores and ants had feasted on her carcase.

The welcome he received from Chantek exceeded even Harry's imaginings.

"She's been dancing on air for the past hour or more," Matthew told him, "how on earth could she know?"

"It's my natural magnetism sending out air waves that she picks up I expect," Harry replied nonchalantly.

"Either that or your smell. You had better get under that shower or no one will come near you."

It is funny about body odour. When you have no means of removing it day after day other than a quick sluice in a cold stream, after which you put the same sweat laden clothes back on, you tend not to notice it, either on yourself, or in your immediate comrades. As soon as you get back into what passes for civilisation, that is, the camp, your first welcome includes the refrain 'What a pong', or words to that effect. The funny bit, already mentioned, is that you still have no idea what they are talking about. It is surprising how quickly one can get used to a pong.

Chantek didn't mind that he smelt like a pole cat, not that she would have known what a pole cat was, anymore than nine out of ten people do who have used that phrase. It is, of course, another name for a skunk, and most people know about the habits of the skunk!

But back to Chantek. She growled until she choked, she coughed her welcome until she choked again. She nuzzled into his sweat stained tunic, she rasped his neck with her tongue; she dug her claws into him until he told her to stop. The smell worried her not one little bit. Now that, I suggest, is true love!

One great piece of news the patrol received upon their return was that an airdrop was scheduled for the night of the 20th of February – two days' time. It was not just the food, ammunition replacement, clothing replacement and so on they had requested, but in the case of Harry and Reuben – their MAIL.

"I wonder if they will include another supply of French letters?" asked Tommy Isaacs. These had caused great hilarity when discovered in previous drops. The opportunities for using these items, totally not indented for, were somewhat limited in Camp Three. They had however, been found useful as teats for Chantek's hollow bamboo feeding bottle, for wrapping matches in to carry on patrols, as sugar containers (provided they were not overloaded so that they split) and numerous other applications where something or other was required to stay dry in an atmosphere where nothing was ever dry for days on end.

They broke camp at noon on the 20th to get to the drop zone, putting men out in groups of three all around the perimeter, each group provided with a torch made from a length of bamboo, into the end of which was plugged a piece of soft wood which had been soaked for days in latex from self-seeded rubber trees near the camp. A reserve torch was always carried by each trio in case the aircraft was late, an eventuality which so far had not presented itself. Harry and his comrades had constantly admired the punctuality of their sky-borne friends; they were always within half an hour of their ETA which, considering the vast distances they had to cover was bordering on the miraculous.

But not tonight.

Scheduled for midnight, at one o'clock the aircraft still had not appeared. Had it got lost? Had it been shot down? Had it been prevented from taking off by weather conditions? Or mechanical failure?

Each torch would last about two hours, but keeping them alight all that time provided a further hazard. Supposing a stray Jap aircraft bringing some VIP or other from Siam down to say Singapore passed overhead and spotted this oval of torches? At the least he would log it, and its position. If it were an operational aircraft it might even come down low, assume there was something funny going on and drop a few calling cards. Of course, in that event, the torches would immediately be extinguished but by Sod's Law, that would be the moment the Liberator would arrive with all their goodies, goodies which would then be taken back to Ceylon again. Harry began to get a trifle anxious.

The torches gradually went out, to be replaced by the reserve. Half an hour later they heard the deep throbbing sound of the four-engined aircraft slowly approaching at about a thousand feet. Harry gave a sigh of relief as he flashed the recognition signal upwards. Immediately a cascade of bundles emerged, supported by white canopies to assist in finding them in the dark. They had to work furiously to get everything unpacked and loaded on to the special back harnesses they had brought with them, each designed for a certain piece or bundle of equipment. An hour or a little more later they were ready to move off back to the base camp some three hours' march away.

Reuben and the ten men, along with the medics, who had been left as camp guard, were up and about when the drop party struggled in soon after dawn. They swiftly off loaded the back packs, laying them out on the company HQ veranda where Reuben would check them in, list them, and compare his list with the inventory provided in the main load, always clearly marked. By this means he could establish they had recovered all the loads, that last thing they would want was to be a load short – still hanging up in the trees somewhere – particularly if it carried the mail, even more so if it carried the rum ration they were now sent! The patrol went off to bed until ten o'clock, whilst Reuben did his quartermaster's job, as he described it. An hour or so later he had established that all had been collected, it now had to be distributed, cookhouse, armoury, medical room, officers quarters, company stores and so on. Receiving and sorting 'the drop' was the highlight of their existence.

When Harry was shaken awake at ten o'clock, this action having interrupted a dream about which we shall say no more, he found a pile of letters, two from people he had never heard of! With great strength of mind he sorted all of Megan's letters, which obviously outnumbered all the others put together, and put them on one side so that later he could have the exquisite pleasure of sorting them into date order, reading them, re-reading them, and reading them again without interruption from any Tom, Dick or Reuben who might barge in on him. Actually he had nothing to fear from Reuben, who, as usual, had received a wad of mail in differently coloured, differently scented envelopes, obviously from different popsies he had been, shall we say, friendly with? in the past. He too had retreated to his room to relive past liaisons.

Megan had said nothing about her being attacked or the subsequent court case. Her letters were lively, informative, loving and naturally carrying the anguish she felt at being without him, and the underlying fear for him in the life he was living. She enclosed fresh photos of the children, news of Carmarthen, and the news she wasn't supposed to let on that Harry would soon be a double uncle, both David and Rose expecting a newcomer to the family.

"I bet dad will be saying, 'another two Christmas and birthday presents to find'," he laughed to himself. He had letters from Ernie and Annie, telling him about Karl's 'romance' with Rosemary Gordon, a lovely letter from Cecely with details of Greta and Gordon, her two children Harry had met at the Coates house in Muar before the Japanese invasion. With several letters from Rose, David, Fred and Jack and others it was an exhilarating, yet at the same time, a draining three hours it took to read them all. However, there was no doubt that the receipt of this mail was, in the long run, the main factor in his being able to stick out the long term debilitation of living in this prison, this dank, unfriendly, unhealthy, and at times, downright dangerous underworld in which he was incarcerated for he knew not how many more months, or years come to that.

Another help in the maintenance of his morale was the receipt of a large bundle of the Times of India. In addition to the excellent news of the war in Russia and Italy, the massive bombing day and night of Germany and French industry – shows they'll soon be landing he forecast to the others – there was also the news of the successes in Burma. Another item that provided interest was a report that four Malay Indians had been landed by a Japanese submarine in Southern India to carry out espionage. They had no knowledge of the local language, were quickly captured, and executed by the Indian Government. The latest paper headlined that the heaviest attack in the history of warfare, that on Berlin on February 15th, when over one thousand British aircraft dropped two thousand five hundred tons of bombs, had paralysed the city.

"Tokyo will be next," suggested Harry.

There were two surprises in the mail. Two letters each to Matthew and to Tommy Isaacs. Harry had mentioned in one of his letters that 'Matthew' and 'Tommy', their families not knowing where they were for safety's sake, received no mail. As a result Megan had suggested to Rose that they get whoever would like to write a few lines to each of them to do so. This idea was seized upon with enthusiasm, as a result some twenty people, including Canon Rosser, John Tarrant and Doctor Carew all wrote half an airmail sheet each, the use of which provided one problem in that Doctor Carew's thick Waterman pen almost obliterated the contribution from someone on the other side of the paper. Airmail paper was not designed to be written on both sides, especially with an ultra posh pen! Needless to say, the two recipients were indescribably delighted, not only by the receipt of the letters, the kind thoughts and comments from another world, but also by Harry having given them a lifeline, if not into, at least from another world.

The monsoon had left them – well not quite. The following night a tremendous storm blew up. Chantek heard it long before the other camp inhabitants were aware of it, and furiously hurled herself against the trap door into Harry's room. Harry got up, flashed his torchlight around the floor to make sure there were no nasties around, and let her in. With a swift bound she leapt on to his bed and cowered back against the wall. He shone the flashlight on her – these torches were a godsend, dropped to them, with spare batteries, two drops back – could see she was very frightened and immediately guessed there was a storm in the distance that human ears would not yet hear.

"Alright, in you come," he said. He pulled the mosquito net down, got back under his blanket and soon they were both asleep. They were awakened an hour or so later by the wind literally screeching into the trees. Harry was not particularly worried about high winds; they had experienced them many times without their causing damage to the camp, cocooned as it was in the shelter of the mass of the forest. However, the fringes of the camp contained some gigantic trees which looked indestructible, but in the wind, which had developed cyclonic force, one of their number gave up the ghost. It fell in slow motion. The top of it seemed to cling to its neighbours for help, ripping away branches as thick as a man's body which in turn, in falling, tore other limbs lower down. The shrieking of the tree's agony rubbing against its surroundings as it fell, the screams of the roots being unearthed and snapping under the strain of this mammoth crashing to earth, awakened every man in the camp. Finally came the thunderous noise of the canopy hitting the ground, the cracking of the branches smashing like pistol shots, the subsequent noise of those same branches trying to reposition themselves in the order to which they had been accustomed, before they had suffered this martyrdom.

And all of this in the space of perhaps a little over thirty seconds, during which even the communists were praying it would not fall on them – not that they would admit to it of course.

In this latter respect they were all in luck. It had fallen on to the parade ground, the main part of the trunk having come to rest between the officers' quarters and the medical room. Another ten feet either way and either Harry and Chantek would have been underneath it, or three of the Chinese who were occupying the hospital beds that night would have been the beneficiaries.

By now, everybody had got their boots on and were milling around outside, until Harry called out, "Right, everybody back in his net, there is nothing to do here until tomorrow."

At dawn the next morning Harry, the other officers and Choon Guan surveyed the problem, the tornado having passed on.

"It will take a month of Sundays to cut that blasted thing up, even if we had the tools," Harry complained. They had three or four handsaws in the camp, but nothing that could even attempt to remove the larger branches to say nothing of the enormous trunk. He continued,
"Well, we'll cut all the vegetation and smaller branches off, then we shall just have to live with it."

"Sir," Choon Guan asked, "suppose I take one of the men with me and go into Raub, I could buy a couple of cross-cut saws there. It's a mining town, there is bound to be a hardware merchant and no one would suspect us."

Raub was about twenty miles from the camp across country. Choon Guan added. "We could bivvy up the first night, get into the town early, and be back here the following day." He added, "We shall never cut any of that with handsaws."

Harry thought long and hard. The only other alternative was to indent for saws to be sent in the next drop, and that was two months away. Again, cross-cut saws, probably over six feet long, would not be easy items to package for a drop, especially from a Liberator.

"All right Choon Guan. But take three men in addition to the man you will take into town with you. They can wait in the bivvy area and look after your arms and equipment – you can't carry them into town with you."

"Right sir, shall we make a start tomorrow?"

"Yes. Do that. I will give you some sovereigns; you will have to get them changed."

"That's no problem sir; there will be a Chinese jewellers there. They will be only too pleased to help."

"And if they are not?"

"I, sir, am very persuasive."

"Well, watch your backs."

"Sir?"

"Yes, what is it?"

"Could we carry one of your darts in case?"

Harry's darts, designed to be fired from his blow pipe, the secret of which he had been given by his orang-asli friends Bam and Boo, when dipped into the resin obtained from the ipoh tree, were silent killing missiles. The poison was carried in a separate container, the dart dipped into it, bringing immediate paralysis and death to the animal, or Jap, which got in its way. Choon Guan knew what the lot of he and his comrade would be if they fell into the hands of the Kempetai. It was an unlikely possibility, but one never knew.

"Very well. I will give you each a small tube of poison, but for God's sake be very careful with it. One drop of that on a cut or something and it will be curtains for you, whether you are caught or not."

"I will take great care sir."

"You had better, I can't do without you."

Choon Guan, a miserable sod at the best of times, actually smiled.

Chapter Seven

Dieter von Hassellbek, his mother in law Gita, and Fritz Strobel, stood together at the window of the flat overlooking the park. They had seen the Burgemeister and Frau Auerbach walk into the Klinik some twenty minutes ago – it seemed like hours. The first sight they had of their return was an unleashed Dieter bounding out from the bushes surrounding the exit, cocking a leg against a lamp-post, running back toward the exit to be put back on the lead again by Frau Auerbach. They each could scarcely breathe in waiting to see who was to follow. Next, the Burgemeister appeared, stopped and turned, obviously talking to the Frau Doktor, then turned again followed, as the onlookers excitedly discerned, by the black cloaked figure of Rosa. Dieter trained his binoculars on the face of his darling, who was looking up at the window.

"She's smiling, she's smiling. It must be alright," he cried, thrilled at the thought that in a few minutes he would be holding her close.

"We must go down to meet her, and thank the Burgemeister and particularly Frau Auerbach for all she has done." Fritz pulled his coat on.

"But we do not know what exactly has been arranged," Gita replied. "We must not get too hopeful."

Dieter caught a glimpse of himself in the hallway mirror as they moved toward the front door.

"God, what a mess I am," he exclaimed.

It was the understatement of the age. Four days' growth of beard, bloodshot eyes, hair like a violinist's, uniform bearing clear evidence of having been slept in since God knows when, along with the ever present smell of tank diesel, if not as pervasive as that of a submariner, still discernible as compared to an ordinary foot soldier.

"She will neither notice, nor care," laughed Gita, "and neither will the Auerbachs."

The lift was working – the second miracle that day! Through the lattice work door they could see, as they approached the ground floor, the stout figure of the Burgemeister leading the way through the front door of the apartment block, with Rosa following, Frau Auerbach and dog Dieter following up at the rear. Fritz slammed the folding door from the lift to one side, allowing Dieter to literally run down the hallway, to be met by Rosa, who had sped past her saviours to throw herself into the arms of her darling husband, who, on many occasions she had thought never to see again. The beaming faces of the onlookers, mingled it must be said by tears of emotion from Gita and Frau Auerbach, said it all – a job well done!

"Will you please come up to the apartment for coffee or a drink?" Fritz asked their benefactors.

"No thank you, we shall leave you to enjoy your reunion." The Burgemeister turned to Dieter. "Frau Doktor will tell you of the terms of her release. In the meantime my wife and I wish you all happiness in your time here together. We would also like to thank you for your heroism against the Bolsheviks," he pointed to Dieter's Knight's Cross, "we know that award is given only for great bravery."

"Thank you sir. You can be sure we shall comply with all your requirements and will not let you and Frau Doktor Schlenker down." They shook hands warmly.

They waved the Burgemeister, his wife and their dog goodbye, then crammed into the tiny lift which again excelled its reputation by working without a single shudder, swiftly taking them to their floor. Well, perhaps swiftly is rather exaggerating its somewhat ponderous ascent, nevertheless they arrived without incident. It was the first time that Rosa had been to Fritz's apartment. It was spacious, high ceilinged, with large windows overlooking the park in which 'Rosa's seat', as it was termed by the Strobels, could be clearly seen. Dieter and Rosa sat side by side on the sofa revelling in their unexpected closeness.

"Now, I shall get a light lunch, and then Fritz and I will go to the market and see what we can buy for a welcome home dinner tonight. After lunch I expect you will want to have a bath and change of clothes Dieter dear, and then a rest after your long journey. As no doubt you will find it extremely difficult to sleep in a nice soft bed after the frozen ground of Mother Russia, I would suggest Rosa joins you to promote security in your being. After all, she is a doctor, and tender loving care is the prime remedy for all illnesses, as taught to all in her profession."

Dieter's old sense of humour flooded back, the sense of humour he had shared all those months with David, Rose and all the Chandlers before this ghastly war separated them.

"I could be forced to forgo lunch." The others laughed. He added, "And the bath, whilst it is highly desirable, could easily be moved down the queue. I shall probably block the drains anyway."

He ate his lunch, but felt the cold, the discomfort, the constant travelling, creeping up on him, so that he could hardly stay awake. The lunch over Rosa announced she and Fritz were off to the town centre, "I will call you in time for dinner at seven o'clock."

When they were alone Dieter took Rosa in his arms and kissed her long and passionately.

"My poor darling, what have they done to you?" he asked.

"I will tell you all about it, but not today, eh? darling, darling Dieter."

"No, not today. I shall bath and shave; you can scrub my back and then warm the bed up. I have just had a thought. When I was with David before the war we were talking about the Duke of Wellington, and how the Duke and the Prussian Marshall fought together at the battle of Waterloo. He went on to say that the Duchess of Wellington wrote in her diary 'The Duke today came home from the wars and pleasured me twice with his boots on! For some reason that has always stuck in my mind, the way some things do. Now the point is, do I take my boots off or not? At least I have no spurs on them as the Duke must have done."

"You are not a duke."

"No, agreed, but I am home from the wars."

"Go and have your bath. I will lay your clean clothes out for you. Have you any pyjamas?"

"Pyjamas? What the devil do I want pyjamas for?"

Rosa ran and turned the taps on for him, hysterically happy.

Dieter shaved, stole a small quantity of cologne from Fritz – "He won't mind I'm sure, it's all in a good cause" – his bath water utterly proved his necessity for its use, he towelled vigorously, looked at his body in the full length mirror for the first time in nearly a year, thought he had lost some weight – not to be surprised at – and joined his beloved.

At seven o'clock they were shaken awake. It was no easy task. The exhaustion caused by days of travel in Dieters' case, the exhaustion caused by the constant work load in the case of Rosa, not to mention the post coital exhaustion to be expected from two lovers after being apart for a whole year, then suddenly reunited, meant that Gita was presented with an herculean undertaking in bringing them back to earth. When they were finally conscious, well, not fully conscious you understand, both still possessed of a kind of listlessness precipitated by the aforementioned causes, she told them,

"Dinner in twenty minutes. Your mother and father will be here in a few minutes Dieter; they got the express up from Ulm. We telephoned them before we went to the market, Fritz has gone to meet them, they were so excited the way things have turned out." She turned away and left them to get dressed.

Dieter turned to his beloved, "We have a very rude saying in the army when we have to get up in the morning."

"What is that?" she asked, relishing the thought of this intimate vulgarity.

"It is – hands off cocks on socks."

"But I don't wear socks."

"Well, you had better unhand me – I do!"

She laughed, held him tight, bit his shoulder lightly, then jumped out of bed. He sat up, looking at her lithe nakedness.

"You are so beautiful." She pirouetted on the polished floor before the dressing table. "Come and kiss me."

"Definitely not, your parents will be here at any moment."

He sat up, smiling, and watched her dress. Oh my God he said within himself, this is what life should be, not killing and being killed, and being cold, being hungry, being afraid, being so lonely in the company of a million others. He brushed the thoughts aside.

"Your wrist-strap," he asked, "have you hurt yourself or what?"

By now she had put all her clothes on and was about to seat herself in front of the dressing table to brush her hair. She stopped, got up and walked over to him, removing the wrist strap as she went. She held out her arm, he took it, saw the number tattooed on it, his face blanching with fury.

"They did this to you? I know about tattooing, many of my men have had it done. It can be very painful."

She smiled at him. "Dieter darling, it was nothing. When this evil war is over I shall wear it uncovered and be proud to do so."

He hesitated a moment. "And you don't wear your wedding ring?" It was more a question than a statement of fact.

"They took all our gold and jewellery from us and threw it in a bucket."

"Who did that?" his fury arising again.

"The SS guards at Ravensbruk."

He was incandescent with anger.

"We have got to stop these bastards," he exclaimed through his teeth.

She took his hand and kissed it. "We can always buy another," she murmured, "now get dressed to meet your parents." He got up, threw his clothes on in a fury he had not experienced ever before. We are losing brave honest men every day out there to try and protect our Fatherland, only to have this filth stealing our wives most precious possessions back here. What he had no means of knowing was that within half a mile of where he stood fuming, there was a jeweller's shop selling those very items ransacked by the SS. At the beginning of 1944 the quartermaster of the SS was so inundated with loot taken from Jews going into the extermination camps of Sobibor, Chelmno, Auschwitz and others, that the pawn shops and jewellers throughout Germany could take no more. The SS were now melting down all the gold and silver and selling it for foreign exchange in Switzerland and Sweden. The Swiss and the Swedes had no qualms in operating this trade, despite the fact they had a pretty good idea of the origin of the goods involved – but, business is business – we must not let a silly thing like morality get in the way of trafficking in precious metals, no matter where they originated.

A knock came on the door.
"Dieter, they've arrived."
Dieter ran out, still buttoning up his shirtsleeves and threw his arms around his mother. He hugged her, held her at arms length, and said, "What was it David said about you? About being lovely?"
"He said the countryside, we were in the Black Forest at the time, was beautiful, just like me. Fancy your remembering that. I wonder if poor David is still alive, and Pat, after all that bombing."
There were hugs all round, Konrad and Elizabeth both in tears as they embraced Rosa for the first time since she was incarcerated in Ravensbruk.

The dinner was somewhat basic. Despite the fact the Nazis were looting food by the ton from Norway, Denmark and France, little of it was to be found in the shops for the consumption of ordinary civilians. In the country, of course, things were not as bad as they were in the towns. It is generally believed that country people are a bit slow in the head, the truth of the matter being they are not as daft as they look. There was therefore a very small number of hungry bellies or empty pots as compared to the cities. Bruksheim was an 'in between' case, in that it was somewhat larger than a village, but not big enough to be called a town. Therefore the surrounding farmsteads still brought their surpluses into the town centre twice a week, although it was unusual for meat to be on sale, and rarely any poultry. Konrad had brought half a dozen chickens with him – dead of course – given him by an old pupil of his who had inherited a poultry farm some thirty kilometres from Ulm in the little village of Ehingen, tucked away on the north bank of the Danube. These had finished their laying days, so had to say goodbye to the free range paradise they had thus far enjoyed, in order to contribute further to the health and welfare of the families von Hasselbek and Strobel. Who would be a chicken? Anyway, Gita had put them in the ice box situated on the veranda, which itself was freezing cold anyway, so they could be used as required.

Of wine there was no shortage, schnapps was plentiful. All in all they spent the next few days up to Christmas Day well fed and well wined. For obvious reasons they had decided that no one would give presents. Fritz had bought a Christmas tree, and decorations to go with it. On Christmas Day they had a sing-song of carols, with a goose for dinner which Gita had managed to buy in the town market – "Highly illegal," she had said, "but who cares?"

"You can be sure the Austrian Corporal and his lot will not go without," Dieter pronounced.

His father considered what he would say for a moment. "Dieter, my son, you must not say things like that. I know here it matters not, we are all of the same opinion, but outside you would be overheard, informed upon, arrested, and at the least imprisoned despite the fact you are a war hero. You have to be very careful."

Dieter pondered over what his father had said. "And is that what my men are fighting and dying for?"

"You are fighting and dying to keep the Bolshevik hordes out of your country. If they got here it would be worse than the Nazis!"

"The only way we can stop them is to make peace with England and America, and he will never do that."

Elizabeth, having listened to this exchange, broke in.

"Now, no more politics, it is Christmas."

...but for a few moments reality had penetrated their season of goodwill and peace.

They had two more days, and in Dieter and Rosa's case, much more importantly, two more nights together before Dieter had to leave. He said his goodbyes to Rosa and his mother, Konrad and Fritz going with him in the barouche to see him off at the station. Then began the long, seemingly endless, drag back to his unit. Mile upon mile of empty, snow-covered steppes, here and there a small forest, every few miles the shattered ruins of a village, a walled cemetery every now and then containing the bodies of German soldiers killed in action at that point. At least they had a grave. Ninety per cent of them were buried where they fell, and in the retreat were often not buried at all. If they were, it would have been in a shell hole and covered up. There were few niceties in the Russian War, especially in death.

At last, stiff, tired, and thoroughly sick at heart Dieter arrived at his unit HQ. Reporting to his colonel he was bombarded with questions about 'did he see his wife? What was the Major Strobel like? Come on, tell me all about it'. He related the events to his commander, ending with the incidents of the tattooing and the theft of the wedding ring. The fury that had consumed him in Bruksheim at what he considered this foulest of foul deeds, was resurrected in front of his CO, to be followed by the question, "How can we get rid of these parasites our men are fighting and dying for?"

The colonel sat back in his chair.

"Dieter, what I am going to say to you is something that could get both of us shot. Do you want to hear it?"

Dieter looked at him intently, paused a few moments before replying, then said,

"Yes, sir, I think I do."

"Then I will tell you on your word of honour you will not repeat anything I say."

"You have my word sir."

"There is a plan to assassinate the Austrian Corporal during this year. As soon as this happens the army will disarm the SS and we shall negotiate a peace with England and America. This plan is being actuated at the very highest level, but people of our rank will be required to augment it at local level. Are you with us?"

Without a second's hesitation Dieter replied "Yes, sir."

"Then we shall say no more. I will tell you what is to be done and when it is to be done. Nothing more will be said about it between us until the assassination. No officer knows of any participant other than his original contact, in your case me of course, and each of we main contactors carry a cyanide pill in case things go wrong so that we do not jeopardise any other officer."

He stood up, held out his hand, which Dieter took firmly, and said, "Here's to a new Germany."

Dieter went back to his bunk, his head swimming with thoughts as varied as a kaleidoscope. Memories of his leave; fury at the Totenkopf, the prospect of the western front divisions currently manning the Atlantic wall being free to come to the east to help push the Ivans back to where they belonged; above all the release of the concentration camp victims, of which he knew, really, so little, and absolutely nothing of the extermination camps.

By the end of January and into February they were on the move again – back towards the Polish frontier. In March the armies managed to stabilise the front in the north and in Dieter's sector in the centre, but in the south they were still in full retreat. "Whatever is going to happen has got to happen soon," Dieter said to himself as spring approached. They were not only on the defensive – being constantly on the defensive is a morale shattering position to be in at the best of times – but the replacements they were receiving to take the place of their casualties were getting both younger and older. Boys of seventeen, men of forty-five or more, drawn from Home Defence units with no combat experience in respect of the former, and at the most trench warfare experience from 1914-18 in respect of the latter.

In Dieter's mind the death of Hitler and his gang had to happen soon!

Chapter Eight

The funeral of Elliott 73 had been arranged for Friday 7th April. It had come to the ears of 'R' Battalion second in command, Major Hamish Gillespie that Private Elliott had arrived in The Parachute Regiment from the Cameronians, a famous Scottish regiment, the home for nearly twenty years of the major himself. He buttonholed the RSM after their meeting with the CO.

"Mr Forster."

"Sir."

"Elliott was a Cameronian. I wonder if we can provide the sort of funeral normally provided for a member of that illustrious regiment!"

The RSM grinned – to himself of course, not to the major – that shower? Illustrious?

"What would that entail sir?"

"Well, first of all, all church parades of any description are held with armed sentries at the church door. Secondly, at the interment, sentries are posted north, south, east and west of the grave at a reasonable distance, facing outwards."

"Is there a special reason for this, sir?"

"It dates back to the Jacobite days. The Cameronians were a protestant regiment so they mounted sentries in order that their church services should not be interrupted by Catholics. Most regiments have some little way of being different."

"Well, sir, in the City Rifles we are of course different to all others by common consent."

"Common just about describes it."

They both laughed. The major was right. Every regiment had its little quirks and fancies, something to make it different from the others. It assisted in making a soldier proud of the individuality of his unit, whether it was wearing a replica of the front cap badge on the back of the head-dress, like the Gloucesters, or NCOs stripes on only one arm like the City Rifles, or a peaked cap so covering the eyes, like the Guards, that they could hardly see, it was all part of family pride.

"Right, sir, I'll have a word with Mr O'Riordan and we will work out a drill." He saluted punctiliously and made his way to "B" Company's spider.

Paddy had organised the battalion pioneer platoon to fabricate a piece of multi-plywood in the shape of the base of a coffin. This they had fixed to a nine inch diameter log about six feet long. The log was normally used in PT exercises, where one group of men threw it to another group and for other uses in negotiating the assault courses – the bane of every infantryman. Using this they had simulated the removal of the coffin from the hearse, the carrying of it, and putting it down. The bearer party would comprise six men of equal height, a sergeant in command, and an orderly to do the odd jobs, carrying the bearer parties berets, arranging the trestle to support the coffin in the church and so on.

Then there would be the firing party who would fire over the grave, commanded by a corporal or another sergeant.

These were all being rehearsed as RSM Forster approached them.
"Mr O'Riordan."
Paddy turned.
"Good morning sir." He did not salute of course. The RSM might, next to the CO and adjutant, be among the archangels of military life, but he still did not merit a salute, despite the fact that chinless wonders of second lieutenants, just out of diapers, did require that acknowledgement.
"We've got to conform to a suggestion by the second in command that we conduct the funeral as carried out by the Cameronians."
"The Cameronians sir? Are they a sort of colonial regiment?"
"Don't let our Hamish hear you say that or you'll be back in the cookhouse washing dishes before you know where you are."
"Well, what do they do different to us sir?"
"The procedure is the same, but we have to mount two sentries at the church door, and four at the cardinal points around the grave."
"What's that for?"
"So that you Catholics don't charge in and bust up the Protestant service."
"Holy Mary, sir, you're kidding?"
"No. That apparently is how it all started, and Elliott was a Cameronian. All it means is that we have two of the smartest men, a lance corporal and a private soldier, to be positioned at the door, and when we get there for you to place the grave watch party, facing outwards of course. They will be the last to march off, after the bearer party and the firing party, when the committal is over."
"Right, sir, I'll work out a simple drill for them."

On the day of the funeral the men paraded for the company commander's – David's – inspection. Six men, a sergeant and the orderly in the bearer party, six men and a sergeant in the firing party, and six men as sentries. With David, Jimmy James, Elliott's platoon commander, and

Paddy there would be a presence of twenty-four of the paratrooper's peers on his last parade, plus a bugler from Battalion HQ.

Command had sent a coach in which to transport the men the one hundred and fifty miles or so to the little village outside Peterborough where he was to be laid to rest. David, Jimmy and Paddy would travel in the CO's Humber staff car.

Arriving at the church in good time, Paddy's first job was to establish where his lookout sentries would be positioned. There were no problems, no wall in the way or any other stumbling block. It was a fine day, graveyards are notoriously slippery if it is, or has been, raining hard.

The hearse arrived, the bearer party took posts facing the back of the vehicle; the orderly collected their headdresses, in this case six red berets. A minor detail – each beret had the name of its owner in white paint inside so that the orderly could return the correct beret to its owner. Such minor details ensure the proper carrying out of any parade.

The sergeant, in a muted voice, (there would be no parade ground commands at this parade), gave the first command.

"Inward turn," the three men on either side turned to face each other, as the coffin, covered by the Union Flag, on the top of which was placed a red beret, was gradually moved out in to the strong hands of the bearer party.

"Lift." They lifted it shoulder high.

"Right and left, turn."

"Step." At this command the left hand file stepped off with the left foot, the right hand with the right foot. This is, in fact, the only time a soldier steps off with the right foot, thus ensuring their burden is carried smoothly.

In slow time the procession made its way down the aisle, the family leaving it to be seated in the pews, the coffin carried forward to be positioned on trestles positioned by the orderly.

"Halt."

"Inward turn."

"Lower." The coffin was lowered on to the trestles.

"Left and right, turn."

"Slow march." The bearer party moved to the rear of the church.

David, Jimmy and Paddy had, in the meantime, been conducted to their seats with the family. As one does, David remembered other occasions in which he had been a sad participant in this service. His first wife, Pat, killed in a German air attack. His mother, dying in the prime of her life and there was his dear friend and brother-in-law, Jeremy, who he buried at the battle of Calais with the accompaniment of only a hasty prayer from the padre to see him on his way.

The parson took his text from St John – 'He was a burning and a shining light' – a text he said was so apt. He had known John Elliott since he was a boy at Sunday school. He knew him as a choirboy and then as a young man, proud of his uniform, and then, so proud of his red beret. His valediction was sincerely expressed and could only, in David's estimation, bring comfort to the mother, father and two siblings who now had to face the world without him.

The service over, the bearer party took up their positions again, lifted the coffin, turned and slow marched to the open grave. As the bearer party emerged from the porch, the NCO in charge of the sentries gave the order.
"Sentries, take posts," at which the four men marched to their previously appointed positions, halted and faced outwards. The bearer party lowered their burden on to the struts positioned across the grave, and took up the tapes with which they would be required to lower Private Elliott to his final resting place. The committal then took place, after which; "Bearer party, right and left turn. Quick March."
The bearer party marched off to a nearby path, where they were ordered to, "Replace Headdress." There is a drill even for that operation.

Meanwhile, the firing party, waiting nearby was ordered.
"Bugler and firing party, take posts."
They slow marched to the graveside, three men on either side, the bugler at the head.
"Inward turn. Present. Fire." The shots rang out over the grave, startling an enormous flock of rooks, gathered in the tall elms nearby.
"Order arms."
Without further command the bugler took a pace forward. It is every bugler's nightmare that, not having had the opportunity to have a few practice blows, he will 'drop a clanger' on the first note. On such an occasion as this that would be a disaster, the thought of which increases the horror. The first call however rang out loud and clear.

| Firstly. | Regimental call. | Each regiment has its distinctive command. |

Secondly.	No more parades today.	Given at the end of each working day.
Thirdly.	The Last Post.	
Fourthly.	Silence for one minute.	
Fifthly.	Long Reveille.	

The N.CO in charge of the firing party waited for a few seconds.

"Firing party. Right and left turn."

"Bugler and firing party, to your duties, quick march."

The party marched off to join the bearer party, the whole then marching off to the vehicle park.

David, Jimmy and Paddy stepped forward, saluted the grave together, and then turned to join the family group.

Only when the mourners had left the graveside were the sentries commanded to fall in, they then being marched off to join their comrades. Everything had been carried out in a solemn, martial manner, as befits the laying to rest of one's comrade, be he a private soldier or a general. During the conversation outside the porch Mr and Mrs Elliott approached David and shook hands with him and with Jimmy and Paddy, thanking them so very, very, much for coming all this way.

"He was our comrade, Mrs Elliott; he was part of our family as well."

Those words remained in the minds of John Elliott's parents all their days, as indeed they did in the minds of others who had overheard them.

The sad thing was that nearly half of those providing the various parties so impeccably, would themselves be placed in the soft earth of Normandy in only a few weeks' time.

Jimmy James would be among their number.

By the time the party departed for Bulford it was nearly 4.30, the staff car leading the way. Between Northampton and Oxford David spotted a largish pub: it being nearly 6.30, he told the driver to pull over on to the forecourt. He got out, walked back to the coach which had pulled in behind them and said to the sergeant in the cab, "We'll stop here for a drink and a pee."

"None of my men drink, sir."

David grinned. "Then they can go through the motions!"

They all piled in to the public bar, David leading.

"Blimey, we're invaded," the landlord exclaimed to his half a dozen regulars in for a pint before going home. David went to the counter, took out a crisp, large, white, five pound note, a note which always looked as though it was worth having, saying,

"Give them what they want – when that runs out let me know."

"Yes, sir, what will you gentlemen have?"

"It's a rule in the army landlord, as you probably already know, that officers, and if it comes to that warrant officers as well, always eat last. So see to them, and then I'll have a pint of Whitbreads Light Ale. Paddy?"

"I'll have a Guinness sir."

"A pint of Guinness – Jimmy?"

"I'll have a scotch if there's any going."

"We'll find one for you sir – somewhere," replied the landlord, with a grin. "By the way, I take it you've been attending a funeral?" They all, of course, were wearing the standard wide black armbands.

David replied, "Sadly yes. One of our comrades was killed in a jump, his parachute malfunctioned."

The landlord, and his wife who, hearing the hullabaloo, had joined him behind the bar, looked very sad, the landlord saying softly, "Poor bugger."

With the assistance of the barmaid called in from the saloon bar, the men were swiftly served. Standing a little to one side David and his two companions were approached by a middle aged, well set up gentleman, wearing, David noted, a well cut Harris Tweed jacket and cap of the same material, heavy cavalry twill trousers, and an expensive, if somewhat worn, pair of brogues. The Fifty Shilling Tailors didn't supply that lot was David's immediate thought.

"Excuse me major, may I ask your sergeant major how he came to be awarded the Military Cross. I have never seen a WO2 with that decoration before."

"May we assume you are an ex-army man sir?"

"Yes, thirty years altogether, mostly with the Royal Warwicks, although I ended up with a brigade in the last lot."

"Go ahead sergeant major," David urged.

"Well, sir, it was like this. They wanted to send the major here to Yugoslavia to suss out whether it was worth our while helping Tito. They knew that the chances were he would get lost – he gets lost the minute he is outside the barrack gate here at home –"

By now all the squaddies were listening in.

"So they said I ought to go with him to look after him, you might say. He did all sorts of brave things while I hung back a bit you understand, so they gave him an MC. And then my union, we've got a sergeant majors union in the army now sir, as you probably know, it's called COSMU, my union said they would bring us all out on strike if I didn't get one as well. The powers up there," he pointed upwards, "like you yourself was, sir, thought, if they do that who will we have to bash the defaulters, so they gave me one, so they did."

The ex-brigadier looked at Paddy in astonishment, and then at David, who, along with all the other listeners, was grinning all over his face. Paddy continued, "Sir, I have to tell you, I have waited twenty years to pull the leg of a brigadier, now I've done it."

The Brigadier started to laugh. He laughed loud and long.

"By jove – wait till I tell my family about this – it'll go in the archives. Well, now, tell me how you were awarded an MC."

"Well, sir, Kings' Regs allows for it, which most people don't seem to know," David butted in. "Sergeant Major O'Riordan, sir, is a bit of a shrinking violet."

"By God, I've never seen a violet that size, shrinking or not."

"Well, sir, we got into some trouble with an SS Mountain Division where they almost encircled some ten thousand partisans in a valley. Like a sack, really. The sergeant major led attack after attack on the mouth of the sack to keep it open so that the partisans could get out and up into the mountains. As a result a large proportion of them got away to fight another day."

"And you?" pointing to David's MC.

"For the same action sir."

"And what happened to the partisans who were unlucky enough not to get away?"

"They were all butchered sir, and their bodies left behind for nearby villagers to bury."

The men were listening open mouthed at these disclosures, the story never having been told before.

"Now I know what those are," pointing to David's other gallantry medals, the Distinguished Conduct Medal, and the two French gallantry medals.

"The DCM you got in the ranks?"

"Yes, sir, I was a corporal with the City Rifles at Calais."

"By jove, you've seen some action in your young life, have you not?"

"Just a little sir. Nothing, I imagine, to compare with a spell in the trenches in France in the Great War."

"Well, I've no doubt you haven't finished yet by a long chalk." He raised his voice for all to hear.

"I wish you chaps well in what we all know you are going to have to do soon. I must go home now or the memsahib will put me on fatigues. Good luck to you all." With that he shook hands with Paddy and the two officers, and made his way out of the bar.

David waited for a couple of minutes.

"Right, drink up, or the cook sergeant will be on at me for keeping him waiting around." They were all now looking forward to their supper with some relish, having not had a hot meal since breakfast. Very soon now a hot meal would become a considerable luxury, certainly not something to take for granted.

David shook hands with mine host.

"There's twelve shillings odd in the kitty sir," he was told.

"Put it in the Spitfire box," was David's reply.

Every bar in every pub throughout the land, had a Spitfire box. Organised on a county basis monies were collected: when sufficient to pay for a plane, the plane was named after the county raising the money, and handed over to the RAF In this manner everyone contributing felt he, and she, were doing their bit towards the war effort.

When David arrived back at the mess, having with Jimmy and Paddy seen the men 'fed and watered', as Paddy put it, he found letters from Maria, Anni, Rose, and last but by no means least, from Charlie Crew. Having eaten the supper kept back for Jimmy and himself by the officers' mess cook, he wandered off to the quiet of the billiard room – being Friday night it was empty – to read his letters. Maria's was what his brother Harry would call 'mainly luvvy duvvy'. She was now five months pregnant, protesting she was getting more and more unlovely and waddling like a duck. He smiled to himself at the thought he had told her at their last weekend together, two weeks ago, she was 'blooming like a rose', and the waddle was in fact 'the proud walk of pregnancy, envied by all'.

Anni's letter was full of news of her two children, three-years-old David and Ruth, now nearly a year old, along with a report on the 'love life' of her dear father. She ended her letter with the thought, 'I wonder if Dieter is still alive, and his cousin Rosa. They were such nice people'. David had met Anni first, before the war, when swimming starkers with Dieter's friends, in the ice-cold lake near Dieter's home.

The chirpy letter from Rose, again giving all the news of young Jeremy and her husband Mark. Rose too was expecting at the same time as Maria, and was keeping very well.

Finally he turned to Charlie's letter. Grandfather, the Earl of Otbourne was well and kicking, conducting, he understood, lively telephone conversations and correspondence with Mrs Treharne. Father, Lord Ramsford, seemed more and more absent from London than before, 'organising the Frog resistance for when it all happens I suppose', being his considered opinion. 'Oh, and Emma and I are getting married on the 8th of July, all things being equal, and you are detailed as best man, my old sport'.

Never was there a truer aphorism than Robbie Burns – 'The best laid schemes, etc etc'. On the 8th July neither Charlie nor David would be in a position to attend a wedding.

Feeling now very tired after a long day, he had a quick nightcap in the bar and wandered off to his room. "I wonder how much longer I shall have a comfortable bed to rest my weary bones in," he said to himself. Thinking of the discomfort of the nights spent in the trenches at Calais and living in every conceivable rat infested, flea infested, farm building for the best part of six months in Yugoslavia, he wallowed in the luxury of clean sheets, blankets and pillow cases he at present enjoyed. He thought of his father in the trenches in the Great War. Five days in the mud and filth of the front lines, five days in the reserve trenches just behind the front line, then five days back in some flea-bitten accommodation for rest. A relentless cycle in which the best you could enjoy to keep yourself clean was an overall wash from a bucket when you finally got to the rest area, after which you scraped the lice out of your tunic and trousers, only within a day to have the eggs, buried in the cloth, hatch out to carry on the purgatory. With leave once a year if you were lucky, how did they stand it? The longer he served in this war so his estimation of his father, and others like him, intensified.

He slept soundly until Angus woke him with his tea and shaving water.

"What time is it?"

"Seven thirty sir."

"Seven thirty on a Saturday – what's going on?"

"CO's parade. Ten o'clock sir. I have heard a bigwig's coming to see us. We were only told yesterday while you were away."

"Well, it serves me right. I didn't read Part One Orders last night as I should have done."

"I'll get the sergeant major to put you on a fizzer sir, shall I?"

David grinned. "I hope he's read them."

"Oh the RSM will see to that sir, you may be sure."

If there was someone of importance visiting the battalion, no matter how little notice had been given, the RSM would have his boot behind all the senior NCOs and warrant officers to make sure the swank factor of his fiefdom was not impaired in any way. Not only that, the colonel and the other officers kept out of his way so that he could do it. Every man knows his place in the army, and on an occasion such as this the RSM was next to God.

When David reached the breakfast room, his first question to his neighbour was, "Who's coming today?"

"Well, don't you know?"

"If I knew do you think I would be asking a bone-headed nit like you?"

His friend Major Claude Warren, officer commanding A Company, grinned amiably.

"Windy Gale in person."

General Gale was the commander of the 6th Airborne Division, of which David's brigade was a part. David had seen photographs of him. He was everything a picture book representation of a paratrooper should be. Big – very big, a face as rugged as any Hollywood tough guy, giving the automatic impression of not having been born, but of having been quarried. Things must be getting close, David reflected, he's obviously not coming to inspect the officers' mess bar, he's going to do a 'King Harry' job on us; stiffen the sinews and so on, lend the eye a terrible aspect, greyhounds in the slips straining at the start. He couldn't remember any more, in fact he astonished himself that he had remembered those bits of what is probably the most famous speech attributed to any Englishman. Then he remembered the starting lines about, 'Once more into the breach, dear friends, once more: or close the wall up with our English dead'. Well, we don't want too much of that, he considered.

And it happened as he had anticipated. The general mounted a rostrum, told the parade to break ranks, having inspected them, then told them of the great enterprise they would soon be undertaking and as the 6th Airborne would be first in, to give the Jerry hell and let them know the measure of the hundreds of thousands of soldiers who would follow them.

"Our red berets frightened the hell out of them in North Africa and Sicily, now it's your turn to scare the shit out of them in Europe – wherever that landing may be. Good luck to you all."

The RSM took over.

"Parade, attention. Remove headdress. Three cheers for the general. Hip hip" – a roar of hoorays.

David wondered to himself again, bearing in mind the stories he had heard from his father and Jack Hooper of the anger of, and distrust between, the men in the trenches and their generals twenty miles away, whether a general, other than perhaps Monty, had received such a spontaneous and enthusiastic reception as Windy Gale did wherever he went in the division. The fact that he would be jumping with them, not following up days afterwards made him, as Angus said later that evening – and Angus was not one given to hyperbole – 'one of us'.

Chapter Nine

It was Monday 28th March when Maria and Rose, complete with barely discernible bumps under their hip length jigger coats, emerged from 'Country Style' in Sandbury Market Square. They had visited Cecely to see what she had in the shape of maternity wear, or as they had joked, in the shapelessness of maternity wear. Both were now nearly four months 'in the club', as David had so elegantly described it. David's first wife, Pat, killed in an air attack over three years ago, was the original owner of Country Style, its proprietary rights having passed on to David, the business being run by Mrs Draper, with Cecely's help.

As they got to the War Memorial they were tooted from a black Austin car. Being respectable married ladies, albeit very attractive pieces of crackling as would be the description of them by a passing motorist, they took no notice, until a blast from the same vehicle made them look across to see a smiling Emma Langham waving to them. As they waved back she got out of the car, ran across, dodging the traffic which comprised a farmer's Dutch cart, a bicycle and one hundred yards away a Maidstone and District bus. It was a busy morning. She was greeted with, "What are you doing here?" There followed kisses all round, interrupted by the voice of a strikingly good looking naval officer asking, "Do I get included in this oscillatory frenzy?"
"Oh, this is Lieutenant Commander Renfrew, my friends Maria and Rose. Maria was a chief Wren at Deal; Rose is her sister-in-law. Their husbands are both army majors."
"How do you do. But the point is, you haven't answered my question. Do I get a welcoming kiss or don't I?"
A smiling Maria looked at a smiling Rose and said, "Have you ever been kissed by a sailor?"
"I work on the premise that I say nothing which may incriminate me."
With that they each kissed the gallant seafarer – an occurrence observed with interest by Fred Chandler from the window of his accountant's office overlooking the market place.
"Do you know, I never have any luck when it comes to the fairer sex. I get introduced to the most delightful girls, only to find, in this case, the person introducing me is engaged to an Earl or something, the girls in question are both married to soldiers, of all things, leaving me high and dry you might say."
Rose quickly replied, "Now, that we know is absolute tosh. Sailors

have a girl in every port, that is a well known fact."

"It may well be, but the trouble is they share out their favours ship by ship, as it were, so they do get a trifle second-hand."

Emma butted in. "Were you going home? We could drop you off if so – I'm sure the commander would be delighted to do that."

"No, we're going to have lunch at The Angel, would you care to join us commander?"

"We would be delighted," came the reply.

They moved the short distance to The Angel, greeted by John Tarrant, the landlord, who speedily organised two extra chairs at their pre-booked table. Having got themselves settled, Rose, who was seated with her back to the door, received a hand on her shoulder. Turning, she said, "Dad, what are you doing here – oh it's Rotary lunch day isn't it?"

"More to the point young lady, what are you doing snogging with a sailor in broad daylight in the middle of the metropolis of Sandbury?" The commander in the meantime had stood up to be introduced.

"Dad this is Lieutenant Commander Renfrew, my father Fred Chandler."

Shaking hands the commander said, "Now wait a minute, you're the gentleman who has the boundless supply of Whitbread's Light Ale under the stairs of your family mansion I believe."

"How the devil did you know that?"

"Your fame has spread via one, Charlie Crew, to Leading Wren Langham, thence to me."

"Well, all I can say is that if you fancy sampling some of it at any time, just knock on the door of Chandlers Lodge. Now I must rush or that blasted sergeant-at-arms will fine me again for being late. Enjoy your lunch – 'bye now."

Having ordered – it must be said that menus at that stage of the war were somewhat basic in their content, the maximum charge each being five shillings, all four meals costing only one pound – Rose started the conversation off.

"If it is not an official secret, which branch are you part of commander?"

"Let's cut out all this commander lark, my name is Baird, an old family name."

"And that's a Christian name?"

"It is, it certainly is."

"But you're not Scottish?"

"Through and through, although I have to say I was born in Kenya to

Scottish parents and went to school here at Cantelbury College. In fact the reason we are here in Sandbury is that I was going to have a quick look at the old school, out at Mountfield."

"My brother David went to Cantelbury and we are great friends of Doctor and Mrs Carew."

"What year was he?"

"He started in 1930. He is twenty-five now."

"Was he in the 'A' form?"

"Yes."

"That's why I don't remember him by name; I was in the 'B' form. I had come from a prep school in Kenya and was pretty dim. Otherwise we must be the same age. I could possibly remember him by sight."

Maria dived in to her capacious handbag, bringing out their 'close-up' wedding photo.

"I remember him. He got gored by a bull or something, did he not? He was in all the papers, I remember."

"Well, it wasn't quite as dramatic as that, but yes, he was badly hurt saving a cowman from being gored."

"Isn't it a small world? Well, give him my regards when you next write to him Maria, and ask him why he didn't join a civilised organisation, namely the Royal Navy, rather than the very plainly named 'Army'. I know we are pretty fussy as to whom we allow to join us, but I'm sure that being an Old Cantelburian he would have got in."

"I will do that," replied Maria. "I think his reply will certainly be, how would we describe it in the navy? Salty?"

They enjoyed a lively, if not cordon bleu, lunch, until Rose said, "By the way Baird, you still did not tell us what you do."

"I am a submariner."

There was a distinct pause in the conversation. Rose continued, "As David's Irish company sergeant major would say 'that's an awful dangerous thing to be, so it is'."

"How would he know?"

"He and David were brought back from Yugoslavia to Alexandria in a submarine and got depth charged on the way. They said it was distinctly unpleasant."

"What do they do?"

"They're paratroopers."

"Well, I tell you this; you wouldn't get me up in an aeroplane, let alone jump out of one. Do you know the name of the sub they were in?"

Maria answered "It was Thunderer, a 'T' class boat."

Baird's face changed from a smile to a distinct degree of sadness.

"That was Rusty Gates; he was a friend of mine. Thunderer was lost about six months ago with all hands off the Italian coast somewhere. Look, I'm sorry, I shouldn't have spoilt the party bringing that up, please forgive me."

"It can't be helped," Maria resolved, "it's the age in which we live, we've all suffered."

There was a renewal of kisses all round as Baird and Emma said their goodbyes, after which Rose and Maria made their way back to Chandlers Lodge.

That evening Jack Hooper and Moira came over to see Fred, Rose and Maria.

"What's the news on your front Jack," Fred asked, having provided him with a pint of Whitbread's, with the remainder from a quart flagon positioned conveniently adjacent to his right arm.

"Well, now we're in this new coastal ban area which goes right up to Northfleet and for ten miles inland, we are meeting one or two problems with the powers that be in getting passes issued for our workforce who live beyond the pale as it were."

"Where does it start and finish?"

"It starts way up at the Wash, and goes right the way down to Cornwall. No one can enter it, other than residents, unless for exceptional reasons. In an organisation of our size we have dozens of people every day wanting to come to the factory for one reason or another. Union officials, sub contractors from all over the country and so on. They are all positively vetted in and out at the check points and on the trains. It's a massive business."

"Well if it stops enemy agents seeing what's going on it's well worth it."

"They caught a chap called Oswald Job I hear, I don't know his nationality, but he was executed at Pentonville last week for espionage."

"The Telegraph reported last month's raid casualties today." Fred lifted the paper – all eight pages of it. "They are the highest monthly returns since the big raids in '41. 961 were killed, 350 men, 425 women and 186 children. All those children killed, it doesn't bear thinking about. And all the time we are hitting them. The slaughter in Frankfurt, Stuttgart, and so on, must be horrendous. The slaughter in our lot in 1914 was horrendous enough but at least they were soldiers not civilians."

"All I can say, as I have said many times before – who started it?" Jack's question was left unanswered. "Another six inch column in The Times yesterday described how the tuck shop at Harrow School had been destroyed by incendiary bombs. I ask you, churches, hospitals, railway stations, all sorts being blown to bits and The Times devotes a six inch column to describing the demise of a blasted tuck shop."

The conversation brightened on to other subjects after that. How Jack's chauffeur, Harold, was progressing with his courtship of their Nanny Cavendish.
"Going strong I believe."
How Mrs Treharne's friendship with Charlie's grandfather, the Earl, was continuing.
"I understand from Cecely they talk over the telephone most days."
How Ray Osborne was faring with his new-found lady friend June Morris.
"He comes to work each day with a face like the cat who has just eaten the cream. I reckon they might well get spliced in the not too distant future."
How Karl's romance with Mrs Gordon was prospering.
"Slowly but surely, so Anni tells us. She and Ernie are very happy about it."
How young Greta, sixteen this month, was getting on with her new beau, John Power.
"He comes from Betteshanger most weekends to stay with his Uncle John, but apparently spends a good deal of his time with Greta."
"Wouldn't it be nice to be sixteen again?" queried Moira.
"And know what you know now?" asked Jack.
"Oh no, I don't think so, you'd run a mile from every young man you met."
"Now that reply doesn't quite add up. Did you run a mile from every young man you met?"
"No, but neither did I know what a licentious, predatory, profligate lot you all were at that age, otherwise I would have done."
"And since then?"
The others were all listening and smiling at this domestic cross-examination. Moira thought for a moment.
"Now, I must confess, I am beginning to see there are two sides to every question. But I still say you are a predatory, lustful lot. If I had my way all men would be fitted with chastity belts, taken off only when required by the female. Come the revolution that will be my first ordinance."
There was general laughter at this suggestion followed by Jack, still teasing, asking, "How would you design a chastity belt for men for goodness sake?"
"We three girls will get together on the drawing board tomorrow,

you see if we don't."

There was general laughter at this. What they were not aware of was that one of the couples they had been discussing, had run into a temporary set-back. Chauffeur Harold James knew, deep inside him, that he loved Eleanor Cavendish very much. He had a good job, a sergeant's pension, and being a steady sort of chap, a healthy bank balance. Those three components normally would go a long way towards providing the pluses on the balance sheet of a proposal of marriage. However, there were two main factors which he considered could outweigh the pluses. Firstly he was illegitimate, a state of affairs in the year of grace 1944 unfairly causing as much of a stigma to the unfortunate child as it did to the errant parents. In Harold's case, he never knew his parents. He was dumped on Doctor Barnardo's as a one-year-old tot and brought up by them, therefore was very conscious that he was a bastard, and that even if he so succeeded that he became an air marshall or something, he would still be a bastard.

The second factor was that although he had been surrounded during his twenty odd years of service in the RAF, before being invalided out, by unbridled barrack room licence, being stationed in places where brothels were the main places of entertainment, and because of his attractive looks having received all manner of covert or direct invitations from wives and daughters in the married quarters, he was still a virgin! As he told himself, "People would laugh their bloody heads off if they knew." He was faced with the dilemma that if he told Eleanor everything, she might very well ditch him: on the other hand, if he didn't, she would have to know all eventually, then would censure him for keeping it from her.

What he had no means of knowing was that Eleanor too had a far more difficult hurdle to overcome. She loved Harold; he was everything she had looked for in a man. Courteous, kind, witty without being brash, and utterly reliable. If he asked her to marry him, she thought that he had been close to so doing on occasion recently, and she said that she would, there would come a time when they would be naked together, except perhaps for their wedding rings, and he would clearly see the stretch marks on her abdomen brought about by her child bearing when she was a young woman.

Eleanor Cavendish had attended an extremely reputable school for nannies when she was eighteen, a school from which the gentry and aristocracy invariably recruited the staff intended to look after their progeny. She had come from a small Wiltshire country village, where her father was the incumbent. He took little heed of her since her mother died when she was only six years of age; being so wrapped up in his misery he had time and inclination only for his pastoral duties, leaving the care of his daughter to an ageing housekeeper. When Eleanor found herself at the nanny training institution among an assortment of other young women of a similar social standing, she came to realise how little she knew of the world. Nevertheless, she threw herself into the tuition she was given, as a result passing out top of the twenty young ladies taking part in the instruction.

At the end of the course she was interviewed by the principal of the college and given her diploma, a most handsome document produced on parchment as befitted a nanny from this illustrious establishment. She was also permitted to wear the distinctive clothes, almost a uniform, that nannies from this renowned sisterhood so exclusively enjoyed.

"I have had a request from Lady Harriet Harris for a nanny to look after her four-year-old son and one-year-old daughter," Miss Anstruther-Robyne informed her. "She would have preferred a Jewish girl, but we do not have Jewish girls here of course."

Eleanor wondered why 'of course', she knew little of the outside world yet.

"I have therefore recommended you, as being our leading graduate. She and Sir Julius will be here this afternoon to interview you."

The interview was conducted in a most polite and friendly fashion, most of the questioning being carried out by Lady Harriet, the most significant question from Sir Julius being: "I take it you are not walking out?"

"Walking out?" It was an expression she had not met up until now, but her natural intelligence immediately guided her.

"Oh, no sir, no, most definitely not."

"Good. Can't have that. Definitely not."

Thus began five happy years living an in-between life at the palatial home of Sir Julius and Lady Harris in Golders Green. An in-between life because she was superior to the remainder of the staff, except the butler with whom she was roughly equal, but, inferior of course to her employer, his family and guests. Her father died two years after she had first taken up her appointment. She was given leave to attend his funeral, after which the family solicitor had informed her that, although her father lived in some comfort, like most parish priests he in theory owned the freehold of both his rectory and, strangely enough, the church and churchyard, at his death this all reverted to the Diocese again. His furniture and fittings could be sold, but in the event they were far from new and brought only some two hundred pounds. In his bank account he had the sum of three hundred and four pounds five shillings and threepence, which was a reasonable amount considering his stipend was only three hundred pounds a year, plus the usual Easter offering from which most clergy benefited.

So Eleanor Cavendish was left with an aunt living at Tankerton in Kent, and the not inconsiderable sum of around five hundred pounds in the bank. You could, in 1926, buy quite a reasonable house for that sort of money, or live reasonably comfortably in rented accommodation, without having to work for at least a couple of years.

Each year Sir Julius and Lady Harriet moved to Antibes for the month of September where Sir Julius's parents owned a villa. For this whole month Eleanor was excused wearing the 'Nanny Clothes', as she called them. In addition she was given each Saturday and Sunday off, along with a little extra spending money above her normal salary, during which time the children were looked after by their doting grandparents. In 1929, at the age of 23, Eleanor was enjoying her annual stay at Antibes, the freedom she had, the thrill of exploring the Cote d'Azur on her days off using the very inexpensive buses which plied along the coast, the sun, the sea, the beautiful food and the very friendly people. On the Saturday of the second weekend off, she took the bus to Cannes. She walked through from the bus station to the Croissette, turned west until she found herself outside the Carlton Hotel where she sat on her favourite bench beneath the palm trees, looking out over the parasols and mattresses on the sands, to the children and grown-ups frolicking in the beautiful, crystal clear sea.

"And to think I get paid for this," she chuckled to herself. She was still smiling at the thought, when she turned her head towards an extremely well dressed gentleman in his thirties sitting at the other end of the seat. He, turning his head toward her at that moment registered the smile, thought it was for him, and smiled back.

And that's how it all started!!

He addressed her rapidly in French, Eleanor quickly telling him she was English, her knowledge of French being very limited. He at once apologised and immediately spoke to her in very clear grammatical English. Doffing his hat he said, "Allow me to introduce myself mademoiselle, I am Count Pietro Bassanetti." He handed her a small, gold edged visiting card, which indicated his address as being in Via

Civitavecchia, Milan.

"You are here on holiday mademoiselle?"

Eleanor hesitated for a moment. She was reluctant to tell a fib; on the other hand she was equally as reluctant to tell a count she worked for a living. In the end she decided that honesty was the best policy.

"I am a nanny looking after Lady Harriet Harris's two children. Saturday and Sunday are my days off."

If she had known what was flashing through the count's mind at that announcement she would either have fainted or run the length of the Croissette, for Count Pietro Bassanetti was no more a count than she herself was. He was of a breed of con men who flourish on the Cote d'Azur during the season, feasting mainly on middle-aged American ladies, pleasuring them as required, and earning good money in the process. It was now the end of the season, he had a more than satisfactory balance in the bank to carry him through the winter, it looked as though fortune had further smiled upon him by providing him with an attractive, virginal young English girl with which to finish off a profitable four months. He so rarely enjoyed the delights of accommodating a virgin these days; after all, he was on the wrong side of thirty-five. In a good year he had been able to sail off from Genoa to Singapore, Saigon, or even Hong Kong to gratify his predilection for such females, where they could be bought for a few dollars at the age of twelve or thereabouts, after which he would return to the South of France in the summer to carry on his normal occupation. This year he had not made quite enough for such a trip, so this chance meeting looks like manna from heaven, he told himself.

"Mademoiselle, I was just leaving to have lunch, you would not care to join me I suppose. I usually go to a small but very select bistro behind the Croissette – the food is extraordinarily good."

Eleanor hesitated, but not wanting to seem stand-offish as she believed English people were regarded by continentals, answered it was most kind of him, and accepted.

It would be pointless to go over his game plan, since it would be much more obvious to an outside observer than it would have been to poor, innocent, Eleanor, a parson's daughter who thus far had lived the life comparable to that of a convent girl. It progressed from the occasional touch of hands on that first day, to a meeting on the Sunday at which an arm was slipped around a compliant waist and a passionate kiss goodbye until the next weekend – and so on and so on, until the last Saturday and Sunday together he persuaded her, after plying her with some rather second rate champagne, that they were truly in love, and that that was what true lovers did together. He would be coming to London on business in a month or so and would get in touch again – how could he wait so long?? etc etc.

The first week in October the family returned to Golders Green, and Eleanor resumed wearing her nanny clothes, living in a haze of euphoria, tempered after a week or two by not hearing from her lover, but excusing that with the further thought he was probably very busy. On the one hand she suddenly realised he had never told her what his business was. On the other hand again, perhaps being a count he had private means and had no need of a business. I should have asked, she decided. A month or so later she started having sickness in the mornings, and looking peaky. On one of her rare visits to the nursery Lady Harris asked, "Nanny, dear, are you alright? You look a little off-colour."

"Oh, I imagine it is just something I ate – but I can't think what?" was Eleanor's reply, fully believed by her Ladyship who would not have dreamt the indisposition could be for any other reason.

"Nanny, Sir Julius and I have to go to South Africa at the end of next week. We shall be away for eight weeks altogether including the voyages. Will you be alright? We shall be back for Christmas."

"Yes, of course Lady Harris. The children will miss you."

"Oh I think they probably would prefer to be with you anyway," she replied with a smile. "Anyhow, if you have any problems with the children, just call Doctor Forbes, he is only five minutes away."

"Yes, Lady Harris."

Two days after Sir Julius and his wife left, their young daughter, now nearly six, had been coughing badly in the night. Eleanor in the room next door had got up and given her some Galloway's, in the morning took her temperature to find it was at 100 degrees, upon examining her throat found it to be very sore, so she immediately called Doctor Forbes. A quarter of an hour later the doctor arrived.

"I thought I would nip in before my morning surgery," he announced in his bluff, friendly way. He examined his small patient, told Eleanor to keep her in bed for a couple of days and to collect some medicine from his dispensary at any time after midday. It was quite common for doctors to mix their own remedies in those days. As he spoke to Eleanor she suddenly had to turn and run, he being clearly able to hear her retching in the nearby nursery lavatory. When she returned, watery-eyed, pale faced, and in obvious discomfort he asked, "And what is the problem with you young lady?" She led him into her room, telling her young charge she would be back in a minute or two, where she described her symptoms.

114

The doctor looked at her benignly.

"You were at Antibes last month. Did you meet anybody – any man?"

"Well, yes." She took the gilt-edged card from her bedside drawer and handed it to the doctor.

"And did you make love with this... Count Bassanetti?"

"We fell in love, yes. He is coming to London soon."

"You say you fell in love. Did he make love to you... physically?"

"Well, yes, he said that was what all people really in love did."

Oh my God, the doctor was saying to himself, how is it that a woman in her twenties can be so naive? But then, thousands were.

"When did you last have a monthly period?"

"Just before we went to Antibes, at the end of August."

"Look my dear. It is pretty certain you are with child. I want you to come to the surgery some time this week so that Nurse Kirkpatrick and I can carry out some tests. Lady Harriet will be back on the 20th of December I believe. So as not to affect their Christmas arrangements I should delay telling her of your condition until after the festivities, but you should be prepared to leave your employ in the new year, as soon as her ladyship can replace you. In the meantime may I keep this card?" Eleanor nodded, too upset and frightened to say anything.

Eleanor walked around in a dream for the next four days until she visited Doctor Forbes's surgery and had it confirmed she was pregnant. The doctor asked where would she go. "I have an aunt at Tankerton I could ask," she replied.

"Write her a letter. Tell her truthfully what has happened. Now, I sent a telegram to my wife's nephew who is in the British Consulate in Milan. He has replied there is no such person as a Count Bassanetti in their equivalent of 'Who's Who', and that the address on the card is that of a newspaper office, in which he is completely unknown. I am afraid you have been cruelly deceived my dear."

Eleanor's letter to her aunt received the reply that of course she must come and stay and have the baby there. Once it was delivered they would make further plans.

The further plans were simple. Aunt Esther would bring the child up as her own until she was of an age to be told, her real mother was the 'cousin' who visited them from time to time. Doctor Forbes told Lady Harriet the story, as a result Eleanor stayed on until February 1930, being most surprised and touched by the kindness of both her and Sir Julius, who gave her a cheque for six months' salary when she left, "This will help you out my dear." She gave birth to a beautiful daughter which she named Sophia Esther, and a few months later got another post as a nanny without difficulty, having received a thoroughly generous reference from Lady Harriet.

So. The path of true love never runs smooth, or so we are told, certainly Harold and Eleanor's path was more than a little rocky, or at least could be. It really does depend on what sort of person each of them is, does it not?

Chapter Ten

Choon Guan's sortie to Raub was successful in two ways. Firstly he ran into a relative of his he had not seen since they were boys together back in Singapore. As a third cousin, he was still, by Chinese standards, close family. One disappointment as far as Choon Guan was concerned was that the cousin, John Tham, was a Christian, but as Choon Guan had learned in the past two years from Captain Chandler, you can't have everything. As a result of meeting cousin John early after his entering the town he had no need to search for the premises from which he, firstly had to change his sovereigns into occupation dollars, and secondly find a suitable hardware store, run by Chinese who would not ask questions. Having purchased two heavy cross-cut saws, two smaller bowsaws, a vice and a set of sharpening tools, and having left them at the store to be collected later he and cousin John had a meal together in an eating house owned by the family on the eastern side of the town.

"I am reluctant to ask what you are doing and where you are from, cousin, but I naturally am very curious."

"If you don't know anything you can't tell anything. That is one of our watchwords."

"Last June there was an attack on the gold mine here, many Japanese were killed and a great deal of damage done. I wonder who carried that out? They must be very well organised. The Japanese went through the town with a fine toothcomb. Some thirty odd Chinese were taken away, only three have returned. Six they beheaded and put their heads on poles at the entrance to the mine. One of those was from our family, cousin Wei Tung."

"Is the mine working again?"

Yes. It took them nearly six months to replace everything you destroyed."

"Why do you assume I destroyed it?"

"I didn't mean you personally. I meant your organisation. I know you have belonged to the Malayan Communists since before the war – all the family knows it. I am not a communist as you know, but I would like to join you to help drive these foreign monkeys out."

"And when they have been driven out, what about the other foreign devils?"

"You mean the British?"

"Of course."

"I shall have to think about that when the time comes. In the meantime I would like to join you in what you are doing."

"It is a long time since we last met. What do you do for a living?"

"I trained as a dentist. I have a small practice here. I could be very useful to you and your comrades."

"Not married?" John paused.

"No. I was to marry Mary Chan from our church, but the Japs killed her father and two brothers after the raid, so her mother took her back to Singapore. We are going to wait for each other until the war is over."

They finished their meal. As they emerged from the little eating house they were confronted by two, obviously off duty, Japanese soldiers. Immediately John pulled on Choon Guan's sleeve, and bowed to the two conquerors, Choon Guan rapidly following suit. The two Japs took not the slightest notice, but passed by, chattering away, leaving the cousins seething with rage.

"They come from the old mine," John surmised, "judging by the direction they are taking."

"What's in the old mine?"

"I don't know for sure, but by the heavy lorries which go in there, we suspect it must be ammunition – probably shells or even bombs – they are extending the old RAF airfield just south of here on this side of the Bilut river."

Choon Guan kept silent about the other airfield being extended some thirty odd miles north where they had been keeping a watch at Kuala Lipis.

"Can we get near it?"

"Yes, there are dwellings fairly close. I have a friend there we could call on."

"Reliable?"

"Yes, as good as gold."

They strolled the half mile to where the houses and shacks began to peter out, John turning into an enclosed garden housing two pigs and a number of chickens. He knocked at the back door, opened by one of the ugliest men Choon Guan had ever seen in all his life.

"John, hello," then suspiciously, "who's this?"

"Simon, this is my cousin Choon Guan. We wondered if you would mind our looking from your front upstairs window?"

Without a word Simon led the way up the narrow, somewhat rickety stairs, to a small room with a double bed in it, a chest of drawers, and little else except for a large crucifix on the wall above the headboard. Choon Guan had a moment of inner, non-communist hilarity, wondering whether Simon turned Jesus' face to the wall while he was on the job. They went to the small window and looked through the net curtains towards the mine entrance. Choon Guan immediately assessed the situation. Unlike the open cast mine they had attacked, this mine originally had been dug into the hillside, had given up all the gold it had contained, leaving a big entrance cave with probably many tunnels from it, which had followed the seams. When they petered out it was abandoned. Now it would be a perfect bombproof storage centre.

Choon Guan turned to Simon, and saw that he had been joined by his wife. To his utter astonishment she was as beautiful as her husband was ugly. She stood next to Simon, her arm tightly around his waist, and politely said, "Good afternoon" as she saw Choon Guan look at her. He was lost for words. He had lived now for years without the benefit of talking to women, and although he had passed a good number in Raub, and even talked to one in the hardware shop and another in the eating house, it had to be said his conversational powers when it came to the female sex were decidedly limited. Furthermore, this particular female was undoubtedly one of the most beautiful he had ever met.

John introduced them. "This is Simon's wife, Ann Ng – my cousin Choon Guan."
"Welcome to our house Choon Guan. Would you care for some tea?"
"Thank you very much," he managed to splutter. She disappeared below. Quickly he recovered himself.
"Have you ever been in the mine?" he asked Simon.
"Many times when we were young, we often used to play in there."
"Is it guarded?"
"Oh yes, there are two Japanese officers, half a dozen Koreans, and a dozen or so Indian guards. The Indians do the guard work; the others carry out the unloading work I imagine."
"Do they live there?"
"The Indians do, so do the Koreans, the Japs live in the town."
"Thank you Simon. Tell me, do you have any relatives you could visit for two or three weeks if I asked you, and of course compensated you?"
"If it is to do harm to these monkeys, yes. Both my wife and I have many relations in Kuala Lumpur."
"Good. John will come and see you again in two to three weeks." They adjourned downstairs to drink tea, Choon Guan again marvelling at this exquisite lady being wedded to such a diabolically ugly man, his lewd thoughts bringing the conclusion that Simon Ng must have hidden charms of a very considerable grandeur to compensate for his lack of handsomeness.

Whilst drinking their tea, in the pouring of which Choon Guan noted that Ann's fingers, hand and wrist were as beautifully and delicately formed as the rest of her, he got John and Simon to sketch out the interior of the cave as they remembered it, complete with measurements, positions of tunnel workings and so on. They then returned to the upstairs window and drew as accurately as they could the perimeter fencing, sentry positions, exterior sheds and vehicle ports. He wanted, if possible, Captain Chandler to be able to decide or not on an operation without having to return for further reconnaissance. When it was time to leave Simon went out to 'feed the chickens', to make sure no prying eyes witnessed the departure of the visitors.

From Simon's house they went on to John's practice. He lived in the two small rooms above the surgery, from which he collected his mosquito net and such clothing as he would need. This, along with his instruments and a couple of medical books he stuffed into an old rice sack, which he could sling over his shoulder with the object of its being less conspicuous than a suitcase or haversack. They collected their goods from the hardware store, steadily made their way to the edge of town where, once they found they were unobserved they made their way into the beluka to meet up with the three man standing patrol Choon Guan had left to take care of his equipment and weapon.

It was already getting dark when they hit the secondary jungle. Choon Guan decided to 'bivvy up' – a phrase they had learnt from Harry – but not to brew up in case their fire was spotted or smelt. They feasted on a sachet of rice each, finishing off with delicious papaws John had stuffed into his pockets from the earthenware fruit dish in his living room, which went a long way to reducing their need for a hot drink.

After an eventful climb up to their camp on Mount Baju, having been challenged by a sentry so well concealed they were within a yard of him and still could not see him, they arrived on the parade ground to be welcomed by their comrades.

For John it was an eye-opener. Like most Chinese, he had lived near the jungle – after all, in Malaya one is not far from it at any time – but the thought of venturing into it would be the last thing he, and people like him, would ever consider. Now, not only had he slept out in it, he had followed game trails, in the middle of it all finding himself in the equivalent of a small village, totally concealed beneath the forest canopy, a fallen member of which being spreadeagled before him.

A slim, weather-beaten white man, accompanied by a very large man and a much smaller dark skinned Eurasian, came from the huts to welcome them back.

"Who have we here?" Harry asked.

"Sir, this is my cousin John Tham, he wants to join us. I can vouch for him. He is a dentist, and has brought his instruments with him." Turning to John he added, "This is Captain Chandler, our commanding officer, he has killed many Japanese," this latter phrase obviously being the highest accolade he could bestow on any man.

Harry studied the newcomer, he held out his hand, receiving the strong grip of the professional tooth extractor, belying the apparent delicacy of his hand and arm.

"Welcome to Number Three Holiday Camp. I will hand you over to the Medical Section Officer, Matthew Lee, who will check your credentials, though if they don't add up for any reason we have to keep you in that cage over there." He pointed to Chantek's home, "You will soon get used to the leopard."

"The leopard?"

"Yes, it will be your job, as you are the newest recruit, to take the leopard for a walk each day so that she can catch her prey."

The listeners tried hard not to grin. John turned to Choon Guan. "You didn't tell me about a leopard." Choon Guan carried on with the leg-pull.

"You don't have to worry, she has only mauled two of her walkers so far, and they both survived – well, only just."

Harry looked at Tommy Isaacs, they each raised their eyebrows. Choon Guan making a joke??? There is hope for him yet was in both their minds. Reuben however was more outspoken. "You'll end up in the salt mines Choon Guan if you're not careful." With that John recognised the leg pull and started to grin, until he saw Matthew bringing Chantek towards the little group, held by a long lead affixed to her body harness. She bounded toward Harry, John speedily distancing himself from Harry's side, when six feet away she did a flying leap, which of course Harry was expecting, and landed on his chest with her front legs on his shoulders. For a moment John thought she was going to seize on Harry's neck, instead, she rubbed her face against his ears and rasped his shoulder with her rough tongue. John was mesmerised.

"Could I stroke her sir?"

"Hold your hand out to her first so that she can smell you, then move it slowly. You'll frighten her if you move quickly."

"Me frighten her? She's frightened the life out of me already." Then hastily adding, "Sir."

They all made a fuss of their mascot until Choon Guan broke in.

"Sir, we've found another target you may like to consider."

"Right, let's go into the office." He put Chantek down, the beautiful animal trotting along on the lead for a few paces, then, like a nine year old boy, suddenly changing direction and pace, running back for the length of the lead, then bouncing back to keep up with Harry again. Harry spotted Matthew.

"Matthew! This is John Tham, cousin to Choon Guan. He tells me he is a dentist. Will you have a chat with him and I will talk to you later."

"Yes, sir." Matthew shook hands with a fellow Christian. "Welcome to Camp Three."

Harry, with Choon Guan and the two officers went into the small company office.

"Right. Tell us about this target you've found."

Choon Guan spread his sketches on the table. They discussed them thoroughly, at the end of which Harry summarised. "It is a very good target. There are, as I see it, two major problems. One, it's on the far side of the gold mine we hit before, which means to get to it we shall have to make a wide sweep around it and come in from the east. Now, that's no problem going there, but coming back the place will be swarming with Nips and we could easily land in trouble. The second problem is, that unlike the gold mine, which was surrounded only by a wire mesh fence and was therefore easy to get into, this has a very short wall in front of the mine with a heavy double entrance door, all, according to these sketches some eight or nine feet high, with the guards posted inside the perimeter actually at the mouth of the mine."

They each digested this appreciation of the situation, as the manual on tactics so succinctly puts it.

Tommy Isaacs broke their ruminations.

"If this mine is built into the hillside, would it be possible to get in from off the hill rather then make a frontal assault over the wall?"

A further silence. Tommy continued.

"Then perhaps you could bump off the sentries with your blowpipe, get into the cave, set the charges, and we could get an hour or two start on the way back before the balloon goes up."

"Choon Guan, how did you manage to make these sketches without being noticed?"

Choon Guan told him of Simon's house, that it could be used, and that he had offered to pay for Simon to take his wife to Kuala Lumpur for a spell while they used it, in order to divert any suspicion from him, or the possibility of his being involved in any reprisals by the foreign monkeys.

He failed to mention Simon's beautiful wife, the thought of whom made his mouth water, but she came back into his mind, and thoughts, and dreams for a long while afterwards.

"Can you see this cave, or whatever you call it, from the observation point we used on the gold mine job?" Harry asked.

"You cannot see the entrance; you can see the hill behind it."

"Well, Sunrise is coming in two weeks. We will put it to him, perhaps he would like to go and have a shufti at it. In the meantime, enlarge these sketches so that we can present them to him. Now. How about this blasted tree. You have two cross-cut saws?" Reuben nodded.

"And a saw sharpener as well. One of the men was apprenticed to a saw-doctor in Port Swettenham; we'll need him to keep them sharp. That tree is as hard as iron."

"Right. Get out a rota will you Reuben. Two pairs, one hour, saw like mad. As one pair finishes its hour, a new pair takes over. Everybody to do a stint, hospital staff, cookhouse and officers as well. We must get all the branches cut off and sawn up before Sunrise gets here. We can't do anything about the trunk, that will have to stay there."

So operation 'Clear-up' was put into effect. At first, one hour's sawing didn't seem much of a problem – until you had to do it! Harry had carried out a good deal of tree felling and logging up in his early days on the farm. "The secret is, let the saw do the work," he bellowed at the first operators, who raced away like blue posteriored flies at first, until they learnt to move the heavy saws backwards and forwards steadily, letting the weight of the metal and the sharpness of the teeth do the work.

Sunrise arrived on Sunday 12th March, accompanied as always by Harry's old friends Bam and Boo who he welcomed with big hugs as always. John, the newcomer, found this quite unbelievable. An English officer hugging two smelly aborigines like long lost brothers would be the last thing on earth he would expect to see in the Empire upon which the sun never sets. But then he was learning a lot of things in this new environment, some of which, like snakes, centipedes and the continual all enveloping atmosphere of the jungle crowding in on him from all sides and overhead giving a feeling of claustrophobia it would take some weeks to overcome, as it had all the others.

With Sunrise and his party was a fresh face, introduced as Major Lister, a pre-war Malay Regiment officer who had hidden up when the peninsula was overrun and then found the Force HQ up in the Cameron Highlands.

"Harry, this is David Lister. He will be taking over from me in a month or so. My eye problem is gradually worsening so it has been decided to take me out to have them seen to."

"How do you do sir."

"David!"

"David it is. But when you are a colonel presumably you will be Sunrise?" Harry asked, smiling.

"I don't know if it is when, or if!" replied the major. Harry's first impression of him was that he was a typical pre-war looking army officer. Lean, an air of authority, and considering the fact he had been traversing the jungle for the past week, still looking reasonably tidy. His second thought was, let's hope he is not as bloody thick as most of his brood. We shall see.

The next day Sunrise told him that he and Reuben could give him letters for home – "Though God knows how long it will be before they get there."

This news brought a great surge of happiness to them both, the inevitable comment to Reuben being, "You seem to have a lot of female cousins, Reuben, I do hope the contents of these letters will not provide too much of a shock to the censors?"

"All strictly benign, sir, as you would expect from an officer and a gentleman."

"I notice you had your fingers crossed when you said that! Now, Harry, what's this little caper you mentioned?"

Harry explained how Choon Guan had discovered a cave, in fact an old worked-out mine, close to the gold mine they had attacked last year.

"It is considered to be either full of ammunition, or possibly bombs, since the airfield to the south is being extended and a runway made to accept heavy aircraft. The POW's there are being made to work fourteen hours a day I understand from our Chinese sources."

"God, I do wish we could do something for them," the colonel said sadly, "but we can't. I've heard that thousands have died up north on a railway in Siam which has been pushed through to Burma. Someone is going to have to pay for this inhumanity one day."

But of course, few did.

David Lister chimed in. "sir, how about my going to have a look at it with Harry and the two orang asli. It might be a good parting present for you."

Sunrise looked at Harry. "What do you think?"

"Good idea sir. Perhaps we should take Choon Guan and the new lad, John Tham, who knows the district well. We could do it in two days, three at the most. When are you thinking of returning?"

"In about a week. If you start off on Wednesday you will be back by Friday. I can then move off on Monday the 20th which will give us plenty of time to discuss a plan."

At first light on Wednesday the little party set off, much to the disgust of Chantek, who knew straight away something was in the wind. Harry gave her a big cuddle and set her down in her enclosure. She looked at him with big, doleful eyes, which clearly asked, "Why are you leaving me?" then slunk away to the far corner turning her back on him.

Choon Guan led the small crocodile out of the camp, up the stream, until they came to the game trail which would be the first part of their route to the beluka hide-out overlooking Raub, where they would bivvy-up. At one point they had to cross a deep ravine. Luckily a fallen tree, which they had found on a previous expedition, straddled the ravine, was used by the local game, and could with care be negotiated, thus saving the effort of having to descend into, and climb out of, quite a deep, heavily wooded gully. As they emerged from the close cover in front of the tree trunk Choon Guan suddenly stopped, Harry bumped into him as he was on his heels, John and the two natives a little further back automatically coming to a halt, Bam and Boo sniffing the air.

"What's up?" Harry whispered, then looking over Choon Guan's shoulder he found himself confronted, at a distance of only some ten paces, by a magnificent tiger standing on the far side of the trunk, ready to cross over. In the meantime Choon Guan had sunk on to one knee and was slowly unslinging his tommy gun.

"Don't fire unless he attacks," Harry whispered. Firstly, there was no way he would want to destroy this beautiful animal. Secondly, a burst from a tommy gun would be heard for miles. Harry and the tiger stood looking at each other for, it seemed, an age, yet it was probably only a little over a minute. It swished its tail and gave a low growl. Choon Guan slowly raised his gun. Whether some inborn instinct in the tiger led him to fear danger in that thing pointing at him, we have no means of telling. He bared his teeth, snarled at them, jumped off the tree trunk and disappeared into the undergrowth in the gully. Harry was consumed with two totally different sensations. Firstly the euphoria at having experienced a face to face meeting with, without doubt, the most beautiful and probably the most dangerous animal on earth, and secondly the automatic fear the meeting had engendered in him evidenced by a distinct rumbling in his stomach, and a most positive weakening of his knees. To cover his fright he whispered, "Two years or more in this jungle and that's the first time I've seen a tiger."

"Let's hope it is the last sir," replied Choon Guan," it frightened the life out of me."

They pushed on to their vantage point which they reached mid-afternoon, giving them two hours to find the best place to observe the cave, and then prepare their beds and evening meal – cold of course, they could not risk lighting a fire. After scouting along the crest line for half a mile they found themselves looking over the hillside into which the mine had been tunnelled. It was not very high, running in a long rump like an oversized 'barrow', Harry described to himself, like those on Salisbury Plain. The wall enclosing the front of the mine was continued along each side of the barrow, and then joined over the top, by a close mesh steel fence with coils of barbed wire inside and out, and a further coil fixed to the top of the fence itself.

"A few minutes with wire cutters will soon get through that lot," was Harry's second thought. The two objects which interested him most however were two brick chimney-like structures appearing from the mound, and at about thirty yards from them two galvanised steel ducts emerging for about four feet. At least, they had at one time been galvanised, but now were decidedly rusty in parts. They kept watch until it was time to hasten back to the bivvy area.

The next morning they were about at dawn to try and establish what movement took place at the dump – they assumed it was either an ammunition or bomb dump in the workings. They established the guard changed at 6am. Sentries stayed on duty for three hours at a time. There were no prowler guards around the perimeter fence. Three large, covered, lorries arrived during the day and drove away empty with covers removed. They could not establish what the lorries had been carrying as they were unloaded out of sight of the observers. At around noon Harry grabbed Choon Guan's arm.

"Look!" He pointed to one of the brick chimneys. It extended some six feet from the mound itself. From it was emerging a thin column of smoke.

"They are either cooking something or it's a blacksmith's fire perhaps," he ventured.

"Well, whatever it is, sir, something dropped down there would do no harm."

Harry watched the smoke rising and drifting away in the damp, windless air.

"Supposing you and I get through that fence tonight with a plumb line to find out if all four ducts are unblocked. We can calculate roughly how much cord we would need to reach the bottom, and if we test the one that's smoking now we can check it against the others. If they work out roughly the same there's a good chance none of them are blocked up."

"How do we get through the wire, sir?"

"Good question."

John had been listening to this conversation.

"Sir, I could go into town and get some wire cutters."

"I am a bit worried about that. You are not as used to covering your tracks, as we are, you might not even be able to find your way back if you are held up and it gets dark."

"I'll go with him sir," Choon Guan suggested.

Harry gave the suggestion considerable thought. As he stood there he was the absolute image of his father. Fred Chandler was known never to make instant decisions, except in emergency. Every pro and con had to be digested to arrive at a sound conclusion – you could almost hear his brain whirring at times! Now Harry was not only, as always, looking like his father, he was intuitively acting like him.

"OK," and then he thought – 'I haven't said OK in years! I used to be always saying it!'

"OK, take a couple of sovereigns and get the strongest cutters you can – and be back before dark or I shall worry." Again he thought 'I sound like an old mother hen'.

The two Chinese, the communist and the Christian, set off into Raub. It would take about an hour to get there, say an hour in the town, to get the sovereigns changed and buy the cutters, and a little more than an hour to climb back up to the bivvy area. They should be back well before dark was the general conclusion. However, as a certain Mr Murphy is reputed to have said, "What can go wrong, will go wrong." In this case the Chinese owning the hardware store had shut up shop for the afternoon to go to a family funeral in Fraser's Hill, about twelve miles away.

"So what do we do now?" asked John.

"Is there no other shop?"

"No, this is the only one which sells heavy equipment like this. There would be one in Fraser's Hill I expect."

"But you don't know for sure?"

"No, sorry."

"We have only one option. We walk away, swearing." Choon Guan looked at John. "Well, alright, I'll do the swearing." John grinned. A respectable rapport was growing between these two opposites.

"I have been known to blaspheme a little on occasion – in a good cause of course."

"Well, this is the best of causes. So we walk away, swearing, get to the end of this row, make our way round the back, break in, take our cutters and leave the money."

"How will you know what to pay?"

The point John was making was that there would be no price marked on the cutters – presuming the shop possessed any, another obstacle which had to be considered – for the simple reason the shop owner would ask a prospective purchaser the highest price he could think of within reason, the purchaser, unless he was an idiot, would turn to walk away then offer the lowest price he could legitimately arrive at, then after a few minutes they would arrive at a price somewhere in the middle, and the article would be wrapped up and paid for. The Chinese had to get their pleasures one way or another!

The two young men sauntered back past the few small shops until they came to what was little more than an alleyway. A quick look around to see they were unobserved and they moved into the little lane. The buildings each had low outhouses, and small yards in which one or two had chickens scratching around, all contained by a substantial fence, since they backed on to open ground not far from bamboo thickets and secondary jungle. The area was deserted; it was after all the hottest part of the day when anyone with any sense would be having a snooze. They slipped along the back fence until they came to the rear of the hardware store. Now would be the part that could go wrong – getting over the fence. It was a little over six feet high. They heaved themselves up, rolled over the top keeping as low a profile as possible, and dropped into the yard, quickly then moving close to the building. To their astonishment, confronting them was an open kitchen window! Not fully open, but open just a little so that a cursory glance by a family member leaving the establishment could easily have missed it. The family of course lived at the rear of, and over, the shop.

They got in through the window and made their way forward. The door to the shop was locked, but Choon Guan made short work of that by the simple means of inserting a spade, standing in the corner of the kitchen, into the door frame and levering the door open. It was dark in the shuttered shop, but enough light filtered through the misfit in the shutter doors to allow them, once their eyes became accustomed to the gloom, to search for their wire-cutters. This shop, like all hardware shops, is a miniature Aladdin's cave. Drawer after drawer. Box after box. Shelf after shelf. There were even items hanging from the ceiling, dozens of them.

"How the hell does he know what he's got and what he hasn't got?" asked Choon Guan of the world in general.

"I bet he knows his stock down to the last nut and bolt," grinned John.

At last they found the cutters – no price on them of course. They left the equivalent of the two sovereigns with just 'Thank you' on a piece of notepaper, and made their way out into the yard, carefully closing the kitchen window before locking the back door from the outside and pushing the key under the door, back into the kitchen. Deliberately not hurrying, they made their way across the open ground at the back into the beluka, once there they speeded up to get back to the bivvy area before dark.

What they didn't know was they could have got the cutters for the equivalent of one of the sovereigns had the shopkeeper been there. But then, His Britannic Majesty had plenty of sovereigns to be used in a good cause, did he not? From an alternative point of view they could have nicked them for nothing. There is no doubt the Chinese shop keeper would have sleepless nights worrying about who was so honest as to burgle a property and then leave the money, superior in value, to the goods which had been taken. It was against all reason.

Having rejoined the little party, Harry and David Lister had a talk together, whilst the others joined some lengths of parachute cord together, cord they always carried to hold up overhead shelters in their bivvy area. Harry had calculated that from the top of the chimneys to ground level inside, provided it did not slope too drastically, would be about fifty feet. They had, between them, some sixty feet. The next decision to make was, what to use as a weight on the end of their make-shift plumb line. They found a pebble, about the size of a large potato. Bam, immediately guessing what they were trying to construct, told them to wait a few minutes. David Lister, who spoke their dialect having served in the Cameron Highlands area for a number of years, translated for them. The two disappeared for a few minutes into the beluka coming back with some lengths of thin, but obviously very strong vine, which they wove into a mesh net bag. In the bag they stuffed some moss, put the pebble in, drew the neck up tight, then wove the end of the parachute cord into the mesh. Having done this, Bam stood up, gripped the cord about eight or nine feet from the stone and commenced whirling it around his head. At first it made a low, buzzing sound, which as he speeded up changed to a high pitched whirr. He and his companion smiled at each other as he did this.

"As children they would have made toys like this to play with," David Lister told the interested watchers, "they wouldn't have Meccano or Hornby like you rich people. The main thing is, you know now the bob is not going to fall off your plumb line."

As soon as it was dark, Harry, Choon Guan and David moved off on a circuitous route around the gold mine presently being worked, and which they had so successfully attacked the previous year, to eventually reach, after some hour and a half of careful movement, the barbed wire perimeter of their proposed target. Their main problem, Harry had considered, would be to keep as low a profile as possible once they got on to the top of the ridge. From all directions they would then be silhouetted on the skyline. They therefore would have to crawl the last twenty yards or so, until they reached the two ducts and the two chimneys. To the uninitiated that would not provide a problem, but this was not a nice, grassy, English type slope, this hillside was covered in all sorts of stinging, spiky vegetation, containing all sorts of stinging, biting creatures, including possibly the odd snake or scorpion, which all combined to object to being knelt upon or disturbed in any way. Nevertheless, there was no alternative, down on to their hands and knees they eventually had to go, having got through the wire with little difficulty.

After many muttered curses, and many more unmuttered ones, they reached the flat skyline and crouched by the first chimney. Slowly Harry lowered the plumb line until it went slack with six feet still left to go.
"Fifty-four feet," he whispered, David jotting it, by feel, on to his notebook.

They repeated the exercise on the other three outlets, only one, one of the galvanised ducts, required the full length of the cord. Satisfied with their reconnaissance they retreated to the opening in the wire which they had marked with a small piece of white cloth, joined the hole they had made up again, so that it would take very close inspection to discover it, and made their way back to the bivvy area. It was now well after midnight. They slept until dawn, then moved off back to camp.

That evening they commenced discussing the plan for the raid. It was simple. They now had plastic explosive and timers which had been included in the last two drops. They would simply scale the barrow, as they had already successfully demonstrated to be a comparatively simple task, lower four lots of explosive fitted with two-hour timers, and then hop it back to the bivvy area to watch the firework display.

They discussed the size of the explosive charges.

"They must not be too bulky," Sunrise advised. "Your plumbs were quite small; the chimneys themselves may be irregular, although the ducts will probably be the same diameter all the way down."

"Don't over-egg the pudding. I would think a maximum of ten pounds per charge would do enormous damage in a confined space like that. However, if the place does contain bombs I doubt if exterior explosive charges will set them off, but you never know, you could be lucky."

And so they talked on.

"The final question is – when?" Sunrise asked. They all looked to Harry, it would be his decision. He again went into his thought sequence.

"It has got to be a fairly dark night; moonlight would be too risky with our being silhouetted on that skyline. We have some swampy ground to cover behind the working mine, which was OK on the reconnaissance as we had had little rain, so we would not be able to go after a heavy rainstorm. I suggest we go on the weekend 25th/26th, provided the weather is reasonable. That will give us ample time to practice and prepare."

"That's settled then, good luck to all of you," and with a final thought Sunrise added "I wish I were coming with you."

The conversation then drifted into other subjects.

"What is that I hear about your finding a fifty foot python under one of your huts?" Sunrise asked.

"That story has obviously grown with the telling," laughed Harry. "We calculated it to be a little over twenty feet."

David chimed in. "We had a lot of them in one out of the way district I had before the war, until some Chinese moved in to hunt them for their skins."

"Why are they called reticulated – what does it mean?" asked Reuben.

"Well, a reticle is a sort of network bag, as I understand it, and since the python has intercrossing lines all over its body, giving it considerable camouflage properties, its been dubbed reticulated. As you probably all know they prey on deer, monkey, wild pigs, even human beings, by first seizing them with their backward curved teeth. I have actually counted their teeth – on a dead one I hasten to add – they total about a hundred. Having grabbed their prey they then wrap their body around the animal and crush the life out of it, swallow it whole, then snooze for two or three days to digest it."

Comment from Harry... "Bloody hell."

David continued. "I am told that a female lays about a hundred eggs, and then wraps her body around them to keep them at a regular temperature for nearly three months, during which time she eats virtually nothing. When the young pythons emerge they are then on their own, two or three feet long, and at the mercy of hawks, wild pigs, or other snake eating snakes, like the Krait. Very few of them survive I believe, but those that do can live as long as a man. There is no doubt they are most magnificent creatures."

"All I can say is, I shall have nightmares about the blasted things for the rest of my days," Harry commented, the remark bringing laughter from the others, in at least two cases, an extremely sympathetic laughter at that.

"One last thing I forgot to tell you," David continued, "they are also very good tree climbers; you have probably walked beneath one many times without knowing it!!"

"You're kidding?" from Reuben.

"God's honour," from David.

"Bloody hell," from Harry.

Chapter Eleven

The first week in April was unseasonable to say the least. The wind had changed round to the north. On three nights running they had suffered a hard frost causing Fred to remark that he would have to put his winter combinations back on again if he had to continue to cycle to work in these temperatures. As he remarked to Ernie on arrival, "I thought we had lost this brass monkey weather." The cold however was overshadowed by the news in the Telegraph that day. Winston Churchill had sombrely given to Parliament the previous day, the numbers of Britons killed by enemy action in the war, up to September 1943.

The armed forces	230,000
Seamen	6,000
Civilians	49,703
Total	**305,730**

To add to the sorrow engendered in the minds of the people reading these figures, was the thought that the worst was still to come. The invasion was obviously near. Hitler was boasting he had a secret weapon with which to hit Britain. Would this be gas? or would it be something more deadly? or a super bomb of some sort? Whatever happened it was obvious that many, many, more people had to die before this evil man was defeated. Contrasted with a couple of years back there was no one in the country now who did not believe he would be defeated. Further evidence of the impending assault on the continent was recognised by a further extension on April 8th of prohibition of access to coastal areas to cover the South Wales coast and Bristol Channel. No person was permitted to carry binoculars or telescopes in the coastal areas anywhere. The telephone service to Ireland and Northern Ireland was withdrawn. There were to be no further airmail services to Gibraltar, Spain and Switzerland among other countries. The despatch of daily and suburban newspapers overseas was banned, except to forces serving abroad. Everything that could be done to perfect security was being done; it was a masterpiece of organisation.

Following these restrictions, diplomatic missions were clamped down upon. All diplomatic telegrams overseas now had to be in plain English. All diplomatic bags would be searched and items censored. Finally no departures of staff would be permitted from embassies and legations. In applying these draconian measures the Government apologised and stated the restrictions would be removed as soon as possible. This was total war.

An item which would indicate a reaction to another and greatly increasing problem, was that, whereas all divorces had to be heard, until now, in London, as a result of so many married couples being torn apart by the war, to say nothing of the effect of the influx of allied troops from overseas, divorces could now be heard at all assize towns as well as London.

"A sad sign of the times," was Fred's comment. Divorce before the war was usually the province of the well-to-do and film stars, now it was becoming commonplace. Even Fred could not have envisaged how commonplace it would be in a few years' time. Even less could he have envisaged a time when half the population would not even bother to get married in the first place!! That circumstance at least should reduce the number of divorces.

Air raid casualties for March 1944 had been announced. 279 had been killed, comprising 125 men, 116 women, and saddest of all 38 children. Another 633 were wounded and in hospital.

"I wonder if Goebbels tells the German people how many of their countrymen are being killed?" Fred enquired of no one in particular as the family sat in the kitchen that evening. By family, I mean the Chandlers, the Hoopers, Ernie and Anni, they all considered they were one family.

Jack broke the ensuing silence.

"I don't think there's much chance of that. On the other hand I think a lot of people here in Britain have a conscience of what Bomber Harris is doing in carpet bombing their towns. There is a feeling in some quarters that, just as the Blitz on London only raised a greater determination among the people to fight on, the same may happen with the people of Hamburg, Essen, Frankfurt, and so on. One wonders what degree of lying in waste would induce capitulation. Bomber Harris seems to think he can reach that, and that the end justifies the means."

What, of course, Jack did not know, was that Hitler was intending to win the war by doing exactly that with his V1's and V2's, shortly to rain on London and the people of Kent, and the other south eastern counties.

Their somewhat sombre conversation was interrupted by a knock at the front door.

"Who the devil's that at eight o'clock on a Saturday evening?" asked Fred – again of nobody in particular. Rose in the meantime had hastened to find out.

"Ray, how lovely to see you, and June – do come in." She led them into the kitchen where the others were scattered around the huge table. When Ruth and Fred were house-hunting before the war, Ruth had always stipulated 'I must have a big kitchen', and it was not until they inspected Chandlers Lodge that she found one to meet her requirements. And now, sadly, Ruth was no longer with them.

As June Morris followed Rose in, the men stood in welcome. She had met Fred before, now being introduced to the others for the first time.

"This is a pleasant surprise," Fred joked, "did they throw you out of the pictures, or the pub, or wherever?"

"I, that is, we, have an announcement to make, and as all of you have been so good to me for the last two years, we felt you should be the first to know except for June's mother and family of course."

"Is he trying to tell us something, do you think?" wondered Jack aloud.

"I have to tell you, dear friends, that June and I are to be married." There was a hubbub of cheers, claps, how lovely's, when's, and all the other exclamations which inevitably follow an announcement of this nature.

"We have known each other now for over six months, which is not a long time, but we both know that we are a couple. In fact I think we both knew it the first evening we met."

"Love at first sight eh?" boomed Jack.

"Do you know, I think it was," Ray replied. "Anyway, we are setting the date for sometime in September, details of which I shall be sending out in Part One Orders in due course."

"What the devil are Part One Orders?" Ernie queried.

"You'll find out when they arrive, my dear Works Director."

As is the norm on an occasion of this nature the girls all clustered together. 'What will you wear?' 'Is your mother pleased for you?' 'Have you decided where you will honeymoon?' and all the usual excited questions asked of a prospective bride. The men behaved more prosaically, merely topping up their glasses and expressing the opinion 'You are a damned lucky fella', and so on.

At roughly the same time Ray was making his announcement, Harold was making the decision that would either make or break his future. It was nearly eight o'clock, just getting dusk – double summer time being in operation. He and Eleanor were strolling towards The Angel for a quiet drink, it being Nanny's evening off, when they came to the church. Inside the lich-gate there were benches on either side. Harold took his courage in both hands saying:

"Can we sit here a few minutes dear Eleanor, there is something I must tell you."

She looked at him, her thoughts a melange of 'is he going to propose to me?' 'has he decided he does not want to see me anymore?' She sat beside him.

"Eleanor, my dearest, I want to ask you to marry me, but I have to tell you of a stumbling block first, since you may not want to consider my proposal once you know."

If her thoughts had gone into top gear before they were now supercharged. 'Is he already married?' 'No, he's too honest, he would have told me'. 'Has he been married before?'

He broke into her anxieties.

"You see," and with a big breath, "I'm illegitimate. I was brought up in Doctor Barnado's; I never knew who my parents were."

"And that is the stumbling block?"

"Yes, my love."

Thinking of her own, as she considered it, dreadful situation, his admission seemed so trivial. She sat, without saying anything, clutching his arm, her head in a total whirl. I have now GOT to tell him, she told herself. If I leave it now, and he proposes and I accept, leaving him to find out when we are married, he will consider it deceitful at the least, and hateful at the other extreme. And I would not blame him if he did.

"Harold dear. What you have told me is of no importance, really it isn't. In no way can a person be responsible for his or her parents. It is what you yourself are that counts, and I admire you beyond all others. But there is still a stumbling block, as you put it, a much larger – a very much larger one than the one you have described." She paused for a few moments, almost afraid to go on. Harold put his arm around her.

"What is it my love, there is nothing you cannot tell me."

She softly told him the story of the bogus count, how kind Sir Julius and Lady Harriet had been to her, and that the teenaged Sophia he had met when he took her to Tankerton to her aunt's house after the attack at The Hollies, was in fact, her daughter. He let her talk on, and when she had finished, held her very close. At last he said.

"So, if you accept my proposal, we shall already have a daughter to start our family off?"

"You still want me?"

"Yes, darling Eleanor, will you marry me?"

She cried and cried, repeating "Yes, oh yes," over and over. When she at last settled herself she said what any woman would have said under the circumstances, "My God, what a mess I must look."

Harold wisely said nothing. In fact, when you come to think of it there is little that can be said when confronted by the obvious, would you agree?

When they broke the news to Sir Jack and Lady Moira the next day, Jack asked, knowing Eleanor had no male family, "Could I have the honour of giving you away?"

"Oh, Sir Jack, would you really?"

"It would be a privilege."

Eleanor had another little weep.

"Why is everyone so kind to me?"

"Because, my dear, you yourself are kindness personified, as we have discovered time and again whilst you have been with us. Kindness begets kindness." Jack was not given to philosophical utterances; this therefore held a genuine conviction of his feelings on the matter. He swung into typical Jack mode.

"This calls for a drink. It's Sunday lunchtime so we are entitled to open up something special." He disappeared to a cupboard door beyond the stairway; a door which they knew opened down into the cellar, and returned with a bottle of champagne.

"I'm keeping a few of these for when the war ends," he revealed, "but this being such a special occasion we are fully entitled to raid the stock."

Moira hastily found glasses as Jack expertly eased the cork out of the bottle.

"To Eleanor and Harold."

They drank their champagne, the conversation then turning to the future.

"Where will you live?" Moira asked, following the question with a tentative "shall we be losing you?" adding, "soon?"

Harold answered the questions.

"We shall have to look for a flat somewhere in Sandbury, Eleanor wants to stay in her job until...," he was then lost for words, although his drift was very clear.

"Now look, this is a suggestion, turn it down if you like. Those two bedrooms beyond the nursery can easily be turned into a double bedroom and sitting room. Why not stay here until you want to set up on your own? There is a separate stairway down to the side door, you can live your own lives, this house, heaven knows, would be home to half a dozen families if we were in Soviet Russia, it's so big. Then you can save to buy a place when you've a mind to."

Moira looked a little undecided about this. Nanny was used to living with the family, Harold was not. It might be a bit overpowering for him. On the other hand, look at the Earl down at Ramsford. He had half a dozen people living, if not cheek by jowl, at least under the same roof as he did.

Eleanor looked at Harold. He nodded.

"We would like that very much," she replied.

And so it was settled. The banns were put up at the end of April, the wedding to be on Saturday 24th June.

The evidence of the coming invasion of France became more and more apparent to the people of Sandbury, and in many places elsewhere for that matter. Daily, the Typhoons were taking off from Sandbury Aerodrome, sometimes twice in a day, to hit railways, bridges, river locks, coastal batteries, airfields and factories in Northern France. All through April and into May the assault continued. The population, from eight-year-old boys through to old-age pensioners, got into the habit of counting them out as they circled into formation over the town after take off, counting them back afterward to make sure all were safe. It was a fabulous airplane, fitted with cannon or rockets. It could fly faster than a Spitfire and became famous as a tank destroyer, one day in August despatching 135 enemy tanks. Now it was being used as a low-level bomber carrying a pair of 1000 lb bombs, the heaviest load of any single-engined plane. We shall hear more of the Typhoon!

The second piece of evidence was, at the beginning of May, the disappearance overnight, almost, of the Welsh Guards from the camp out on the Maidstone Road. One day they were there, the next day they had gone, leaving a small force to garrison the camp and accept new recruits from the training battalion as they arrived. There was no farewell party; no band to play them off as there had been when they arrived. They went to war without a single cheer to send them on their way.

Before this, on the night of 23rd April, the South Eastern counties were awakened soon after midnight by the shrieking howl of the air raid siren. Rose slipped a dressing gown on and hurried into her father's room. He was awake, but in no hurry to rouse himself.

"Do you think we should go to the shelter?"

Fred considered the proposition for a moment or two.

"Let's see if there is any gunfire anywhere in the distance. It could well be a general alert about a couple of planes. They could be going anywhere."

This was true. Apart from the big raid on London on the 24th March, there had been only isolated hit-and-run raids since then. The problem to be faced was therefore in which direction were they running on this occasion, and more importantly, who were they going to hit?

Rose turned to go back to make sure Jeremy had not awakened when a thunderous cannonade sounded from the anti-aircraft batteries around the airfield, reinforced recently by the arrival of a battery of 3.7 inch guns designed to augment the Bofors which normally defended it.

"I think we had better retire in good order," Fred quickly decided. In fact I will delete that statement and replace it with, "Let's get the hell out of here," or words to that effect. He hurriedly slipped into a pair of boots, kept since the big air raids at the head of the bed, grabbed a coat, although it was April it was still quite chilly at night, and would be damned cold in that blasted shelter, ran out on to the landing to take Jeremy, now three years old, from Rose's arms, wrapped in the eiderdown from his bed.

They hurried to the shelter, keeping their torches down as they went. Getting into an Anderson shelter required a certain amount of agility, since the floor of the shelter itself was three feet below the level of the ground outside, and the opening, for obvious reasons which gave access to the shelter, was small, only a little less than three feet square. You had therefore to sit on the ground, put your legs inside and push yourself forward to land on the shelter floor, the rest of you slithering in behind without, hopefully, banging your head on the corrugated iron at the top of the opening.

Alternatively, of course, one could sit down, turn on one's stomach and slide in that way. Whichever way was chosen, a degree of bodily elasticity was required to negotiate the entry to and exit from an Anderson shelter. Elderly people found it quite difficult, but soon learnt the art when they could hear shrapnel falling or bombs coming down as they stood out in the open garden.

Once in the shelter Fred pulled the heavy curtain across the entry, and switched on the low wattage light and small electric fire. After the shelter had been delivered and installed he had got a jobbing builder in to concrete the floor – he had heard of people climbing into their shelter into six inches of water after heavy rain. In addition, he had paid his work's electrician to run a supply from the house so that they could see to read, and keep warm. It was widely suspected that getting into a freezing cold Anderson at eleven o'clock on a November evening caused more deaths than the bombers.

As he switched the light on they could hear the throb-throb-throb of the Heinkel bombers, followed by the screaming of several bombs being aimed at the airfield. Parachute flares had been dropped by the first flight which clearly lit up the hangers and the aircraft out on the dispersal points. The second flight, braving the ack-ack fire, came steadily in to drop three sticks of bombs across the target. Coming in from the east, as they did, the final two or three bombs in each stick missed the airfield landing in the outskirts of the town causing considerable damage and casualties. One of the bombs landed twenty yards from Fred's office in the front car park at Sandbury Engineering. It had failed to explode, as did two others elsewhere.

After some twenty minutes or so, the all-clear sounded. Fred climbed out of the shelter, taking Jeremy from Rose and then helping her out. As he turned to the house he heard the persistent ringing of the telephone.

"Run and answer it, Dad, I shall be alright," Rose assured him.

'My blooming running days are long gone', Fred said to himself, nevertheless breaking into his version of a bit of a gallop. He grabbed the receiver.

"Chandlers Lodge."

"There's an unexploded bomb just outside your office sir." It was the foreman in charge of the fire-watchers. Being a Sunday night, or to be more correct at this time it was Monday morning, there was no night shift at work. "I've informed the police and the ARP people."

"Where are you phoning from?"

"From Miss Russell's office Mr Chandler."

"Does it occur to you the bloody thing might go off?"

"I didn't think of that."

"Well get your party out straight away. Go to the main gatehouse and I'll be there in ten minutes."

"Righto Mr Chandler."

Rose, still holding a three-year-old now gone back to sleep again, asked, "What's happened?"

"Unexploded bomb outside my office. I am going down. I don't suppose for one moment we shall be able to let anyone in to work. Give Ray a ring, and Ernie, ask them to meet me down there, will you dear?"

Rose went off to put Jeremy back to bed, while Fred got dressed. Things happen in threes. Fred got his bicycle from under the lean-to at the side of the house, pedalled off toward the factory, was half way there when his front tyre came into contact with a chunk of shrapnel as sharp as a razor. Not only did it deflate the tyre but also caused a pronounced wobble to the steering, resulting in his hitting the kerb and depositing him on the grass verge.

His comments considerably increased the immediate ambient temperature.

Picking himself up he pushed the bicycle on towards the factory, only to hear the siren going again, the same throb-throb of bombers and the opening up of the ack-ack guns once more from the airfield. He was nowhere near houses, under the doorway of one of which he might have been able to shelter from the shrapnel, now clinking down on the roadway only yards away. He had no steel helmet on, not that the would have been much good if a sizeable piece of 3.7 shell had fallen from ten thousand feet and hit it, but it would have been some defence against the smaller pieces. As he considered what the devil he could do, the planes had overflown, probably heading for Biggin Hill he guessed, and the anti-aircraft fire from the aerodrome ceased.

Hurrying along now, he reached the gatehouse to find Ernie there along with a civil defence unit standing by.
"I telephoned the UXB people," Ernie said, "they're coming from Chatham, should be here within the hour. They have given us priority as we are on war work, although I understand there are similar incidents in the locality, mainly in rural areas."

Ray arrived shortly afterwards.
"Have you had a look at it?" he asked Fred.
"No, and I don't bloody well intend to either," Fred replied. "I am where I am today by not sticking my neck out or poking my nose into other people's business."
Ray laughed. "And that's how you got the Military Medal?"
"Everyone's entitled to one mistake."

Ray walked across the hardstanding to where the bomb had fallen. He had dealt with many of these incidents as a bomb disposal officer in the Royal Engineers, and had one hand missing to prove it! He could not tell how deeply it was embedded, but since it had crashed its way through the four inch screed of hardcore and concrete and had not exploded, it could be either a dud or fitted with a time-delay fuse. The Luftwaffe was making increasing use of this type of bomb, which it had been discovered often caused more chaos just being there than the explosion itself. He walked back to Fred and Ernie.

"I reckon you are going to have to wait seventy-two hours for that one," he prophesised. As he spoke a PU and three-tonner arrived. A young lieutenant climbed out of the PU.

"I understand you have received one of Fatso's calling cards," he said breezily to the assembled trio.

"Over there, under the window," Fred replied, shaking hands with the ebullient young subaltern, and in the half-light raising his eyebrows to Ray.

"By the size of the hole it looks like a thousand pounder," Ray told him.

"And am I to assume that you are an expert on these matters sir?"

"Well, let's put it this way, I have encountered one or two in my short and not uneventful life thus far."

Fred butted in.

"Captain Osborne was in your lot."

"You are Captain Osborne? The adjutant told me about you. You still hold top score at Chatham you know." He thrust his hand out to shake hands, and was just a little disconcerted to have it taken in Ray's left hand.

"Well, I will go and have a shufti. Care to come with me captain?"

They walked across the hundred yards of hardstanding to the hole. The lieutenant studied the hole and the site, his sergeant who had followed them stood by.

"We are going to have to break up this concrete with a pneumatic drill," he said to Ray. Ray nodded agreement.

"And you know that problem. If the bomb has a number 50 fuse on it the drilling could set it off."

The number 50 fuse referred to was an anti-handling device which activated the bomb if it was moved only a millimetre or two, designed of course to dissuade people like the young lieutenant, and Ray before him, from trying to take it out of the hole. The number 50 itself only became activated once the bomb became impacted. It had already caused a lot of trouble.

"In any event," continued the young lieutenant, "we can't do anything for seventy-two hours."

They walked back to the gatehouse.

"It looks as though we've got three days' holiday," Ray informed Fred.

"I can't afford to stop the factory for three days," Fred protested.

The lieutenant proceeded to point out the obvious.

"It would have been longer than three days if it had landed twenty yards to the north and exploded, instead of being a UXB. Even now if it does go within the seventy-two hours it will certainly do a lot of damage to the front buildings. As it is, if you can get one of your chaps to telephone my boss," he handed a card which Ernie accepted, "at say eight o'clock each evening, if it is still dormant on Wednesday evening, we will come in and start tunnelling at midnight."

"Tunnelling? Why tunnelling?" asked Fred.

"We'll dig in that flower bed just at the end of your office, go under the hardstanding and then down. We can't risk breaking up more of the concrete."

"You say eight o'clock in the evening. Won't your boss be boozing it up in the mess?" Ernie asked.

"Of course, that's why I've given you the mess number." They all laughed at this rejoinder, although in the situation in which they found themselves there was really little to laugh about.

"Well, three days' holiday, plus however long it takes to get it out! Crikey, it will break us. Incidentally how long will it take to get it out – any idea?" asked Fred.

"With a bit of luck, late afternoon on Wednesday," replied the lieutenant. "By the way I'm Archie MacClintock should you need to get hold of me."

The factory workers arriving at eight o'clock were all sent home, the staff at nine, and told to report on Thursday. The first question asked by virtually every one of the hourly paid workers was 'what happens about our pay?'

Technically the hourly workers were not entitled to pay. A quick telephone conversation between Fred, Jack and then Reg Church the accountant, came to the decision they would pay the basic rate, Reg expressing the view that they would be able to recoup at least part of the outlay from the War Risks insurance. There were still moans from people on piecework, those who would expect overtime work and so on, but then it is a worker's privilege to moan just as it is a soldier's.

Chapter Twelve

On Friday 28th April David set off for Sandbury on what was to be his last forty-eight hour pass before the Normandy invasion. He had no way of knowing this for sure of course, but all sorts of tasks they were being called upon to carry out pointed to their imminent contact with the Wehrmacht. All equipment, clothing, boots and weapons had been checked and checked again to ensure they were perfect. Benjamin Franklin had said, two hundred years before:

> 'A little neglect may breed mischief:
> For want of a nail a shoe was lost:
> For want of a shoe a horse was lost:
> For want of a horse the battle was lost!

Lieutenant Colonel Hislop of 'R' Battalion, the Parachute Regiment, had no intention whatsoever of an un-zeroed rifle causing the battalion to lose a battle, everything was to be inspected all up the chain of command, nothing was to be left to chance. And nothing was.

David travelled to London with Sandy Patterson, who was to stay with Amanda at Blackheath, and Jimmy James, another of his platoon commanders. They parted at Waterloo, David making his way to Victoria. As he waited for his train to come in to the platform his mind went back to when, as a young indentured apprentice engineer, with hardly a penny in his pocket, he had stood on this platform after his day's work in Victoria Street.

He thought of the journeys he had made with Pat before they were married, when she had come up to town and they had supper in the Corner House in Coventry Street. How they would walk the length of the train to get into an unoccupied apartment so as to indulge in some serious snogging on the way home. How they had been caught out one night by the ticket collector, who David calculated had seen it, and more, many times before and who didn't turn a hair. He smiled to himself and then thought 'we must go and see Pat and Mum over the weekend'. Pat and his mother lay side by side in Sandbury churchyard.

Arriving home he was welcomed by Maria, who had travelled down earlier in the day from Chingford, and the rest of the family. They too were well aware of the fact that soon he would be snatched away from them all again, but each put on a brave face despite what they might be feeling inside.

"Has the bomb been removed?" was his first question to his father, and as it was only 6pm. followed it with, "who clocked you off?"

"The answer to your first question is yes, they dug it out without incident. It had no funny fuses on it so they steamed the explosive out and were away by Thursday lunchtime. The lads left behind to fill the hole didn't rush themselves, they have just gone. All I hope is bloody Jerry stays on his side of the Channel tomorrow night as we are having a few people in. Mark and Charlie will be here in about an hour, and Emma will be here in the morning. The Earl is coming up and staying at his club tonight and with John Tarrant tomorrow night, although it will probably be well in to Sunday morning before he gets to bed. I think he wants to have some time with Charlie before the great day."

"The great day?" queried David.

"You know what I'm talking about. Everybody knows. I reckon even bloody Hitler knows; though he doesn't know where," then as an afterthought, "at least I hope he doesn't."

Fred moved away. Maria, who had been standing beside David held his arm tight against her at the thought of what she knew was to come. He looked down at her.

"Darling, can we slip out and see Pat and Mum?" David never said he was 'going to the churchyard', it was always 'go and see'.

"Yes of course. I'll get my coat."

They walked arm in arm to the church. They would have no opportunity to buy flowers, although secretly Maria was scolding herself she had not thought to buy some before the shop closed.

The churchyard was calm and peaceful. The sun shone fitfully through the elms which bordered it to the south and west. They reached the neatly tended graves where Ruth, Pat and Lady Halton lay together, the latter a great friend of the family who was killed with Pat when their canteen vehicle was destroyed by a Messerschmitt on Sandbury aerodrome. Standing there side by side, Maria, holding David's arm tightly, wondered what was passing through her husband's mind. Being a second wife is invariably, at least in the early stages, a position needing a great deal of discretion and sensitivity.

"I think we had better get back," David whispered.

They turned and retraced their steps to the lich gate, the same spot at which Harold and Eleanor had 'plighted their troth', as they might have described it. Once clear of the church, David asked, "What's all this I hear about our young Greta going steady?"

"Oh, I hardly think it could be described as going steady. After all she's only sixteen."

"How old is the young man?"

"John Power? – he's eighteen. He is a Bevin boy, based at Betteshanger colliery near Deal."

"Does he like it?"

"I think he dislikes it intensely, but has accepted it as being his part in the war effort."

"I would like to have a chat with him."

"He and Greta will be going to the hop tomorrow night. Why not ask them to call in on the way home? It finishes at 10.30."

"Why not ask them to the party?"

"When you were sixteen would you like to have been surrounded all the evening by a load of old fogies like us?"

David halted, turned towards Maria, and for all Sandbury to see, that is to say one stray dog and two crows perched on a nearby wall, kissed her extremely firmly nearly taking her breath away.

"Do I feel like an old fogey?" he asked

"I haven't felt you recently so I reserve my reply," she replied. They both walked on, smiling as they went. The solemnity of the churchyard had been left behind.

When they reached Chandlers Lodge, Mark and Charlie had arrived. After much banter and hugging the three got together for a few minutes on their own.

"Well, are you all ready?" asked David.

"As ready as we shall ever be I reckon," replied his brother-in-law, "except for Charlie's lot of course, I have dreadful problems with them."

"Now look here, dear old company commander, my shower, despite constant interference in training schedules sprung on us from higher authority, namely yourself, are the best in the battalion." He added, "As we shall undoubtedly show you in due course."

Mark and Charlie, in a battalion of the City Rifles. were in an armoured division. In the desert they rode in small vehicles behind tanks. When the tanks were held up they were called upon to attack the enemy strong point so that the tanks could move forward again. They were to find that operating in the close confines of fields and hedges in Europe was to be a vastly different kettle of fish to the wide open spaces of the desert.

Rose, spotting their heads together, came across declaring:

"Now then you lot, no shop today, or was someone telling a joke?"

Mark took her hand and held it to his lips.

"Now you know, my little treasure, that we three would not indulge in such a low, basic, other-ranks, form of humour as that, don't you?"

"I was merely asking so that I wasn't left out, that's all. We haven't heard a good one here for at least a week, at least until last night."

Mark continued to hold her hand.

"And what was the last one you heard?" he asked. "Come on, spill the beans, as our transatlantic cousins, I believe, express it."

"It was from Emma."

Charlie interrupted. "Emma? My Emma?"

"Yes, you're Emma, when she phoned last night to say she will definitely be here tomorrow. Now, apparently a teacher in a class of ten year olds told the children they were going to learn about 'averages'. 'Can anyone tell me what I mean by the word average?' she asked. No one spoke until one little lad, put his hand up and said 'it's an animal miss'. 'How do you mean, it's an animal' she queried. 'Well miss', came the reply, 'I heard my mum talking to Mrs Brown over the garden fence the other day and I distinctly heard her say she got a ride on an average three times a week'."

A roar of laughter greeted the end of the story, with Charlie finally remarking,

"Two of the most beautiful, innocent looking young ladies in the world, and they tell rude jokes to each other. What on earth is the jolly old world coming to?"

They all went to dinner at The Angel that evening, where they were joined by Jack and Moira. The talk was about Fred's bomb, as it came to be known, the disappearance of the Welsh Guards, the Typhoons operating daily from Sandbury airfield, the new tented camp beyond Mountfield, the presence of a small group of American Army Air Corps officers visiting the airfield, and so on. A subject not raised, instinctively it would seem, was what the three young soldiers had in store for them, although they all suspected this would be the last week-end they would all sit down to a meal together for a long while to come.

They were in the middle of the main course – since the first course was inevitably a fairly basic soup and the sweet some roly-poly or something similar – the main course was aptly named. But then, as Charlie had remarked when the menu had been discussed, "What do you expect for five bob?"

Anyway, in the middle of the main course, David, facing the door, was surprised to see Charlie's grandfather, the Earl, enter, followed by Charlie's father, in civilian clothes. The Earl, seeing he had been spotted, put his finger to his lips, walked through the crowded restaurant to where Charlie was sitting with his back towards the door, clamped his hand on Charlie's shoulder and stated, "I hope you are behaving yourself young man."

Charlie turned, knocking his chair over in the kerfuffle, quickly retrieved by a nearby waiter.

"Grandfather, pater, what a lovely surprise. We didn't expect you until tomorrow. In fact pater, we didn't expect you at all."

"I can always go away again if that's the case," his father answered, "but I wanted to have a further chat with the delectable Emma to let her know what she's letting herself in for."

The Earl put up a hand. "Now, we have eaten, so we will let you get on and see you in the residents' lounge after your meal. I've arranged coffee, and we have a little something to go with it I believe."

They finished their meal and moved into the resident's lounge. The little 'something to go with it', was a bottle of finest French cognac produced by Lord Ramsford, which effected the comment from Fred that 'this wasn't bought from the Sandbury off-licence'. They would have been surprised to know that Lord Ramsford had, only seven days ago, been drinking an identical beverage in Normandy.

"I arranged the glasses with Mr Tarrant," Hugh Ramsford confided to Fred in response to his quip. "He said that he would have to sample the goods to see if they were of a suitable quality to be put into his glassware. I gave him a generous measure to which he replied 'I think you shall have to have the crystal ones out of the locked cupboard', and here they are." The wine waiter, an elderly, long serving member of The Angel staff arrived with a tray of beautiful crystal goblets, a smaller tray with three methylated spirit lamps surmounted by cradles being carried by a young woman assistant.

"Thank you William," Lord Ramsford said as the trays arrived, Fred immediately musing his lordship had done his homework, otherwise how would he have known the chap's name!

Whilst the young lady assistant proceeded to pour the coffees, William placed three of the glasses in the cradles, rotated them half way after a few seconds, then taking them by the base, placed them one by one in front of the three ladies. In the meantime his assistant having finished pouring the coffee, placed three more goblets on the lamps. In a short while all had been provided with their warmed glasses and the delicate amber liquid added, giving a bouquet as delightful as the delicate taste of the liquor itself. It was the high spot of the evening, not only for the guests but also for William and his assistant who left the room one pound, and ten shillings, respectively, in reward for their ministrations.

Leaving the Earl and his son at The Angel, the others walked home back to The Hollies or Chandlers Lodge. Everybody mucked in on Saturday morning to get ready for the party except Fred of course who would be at the factory all day. Buffy Cartwright and Rita would be arriving at about eleven o'clock to stay for a couple of days with Jack and Moira. Anni and Ernie with Karl and his friend Rosemary Gordon would be there, as would Cecely and Gloria Treharne from The Bungalow. It was hoped that General Sir Frederick Earnshaw and his wife would join them; they were old friends of the Chandlers. Finally Greta had said she and 'her friend' John would call in after the dance finished. Altogether it was to be the biggest party at Chandlers Lodge since dear Ruth died.

The party went with a swing, aided and abetted by a continuous flow of Whitbread's Light Ale from Fred Chandler's renowned cupboard under the stairs, augmented by a couple of bottles of Scotch and sherry brought by Buffy, another bottle of Scotch from Jack, along with offerings from other guests in the form of Green Goddess Cocktail and so on. At 10.30pm Greta arrived with a very shy young John Power. Cecely, who – surprise, surprise – happened to be talking earnestly with Hugh Ramsford, went across and collected them, bringing them back to introduce John to Hugh and the Earl – who – surprise, surprise – was in deep conversation with Gloria Treharne.

After the initial small talk, the Earl said, "John, my boy, I am told you are one of Mr Bevin's boys. Now tell me, what were your first impressions when you went down the mine for the first time?"

A small group of people nearby, hearing the question, broke off their conversations to wait for the reply.

"Well sir, to be honest, I was scared out of my wits. When you get into the cage to go down to the pit bottom you only have about five feet of head room, so you have to stand with your head all on one side if, like me, you are nearly six feet. The cage starts off slowly and then speeds up in the dark to, I am told, 35 feet per second. You feel your stomach come up into your mouth. Halfway down there is a thunderous noise as you meet the other cage coming up. The pit bottom is 3000 feet down and then you first get out you are in a big cavern, well lit, but from here the colliers and other workers have to walk as much as a mile to the coalface. The dust, the extremes of heat and cold depending on where you are in the mine, are indescribable."

Maria asked, "Do you still have the ponies down there to pull the trucks?"

"No ma'am. They all went before the war. It was said it was not humane to keep animals under those conditions." He paused for a moment or two. "Apparently it is humane to keep men locked in there for eight hours every day."

The Earl took his arm. "We all admire greatly what you are having to do, you may be sure," he said, to the accompanying expressions of 'Hear, hear', from the immediate listeners. The Earl continued, "Now give us a rough idea of your day."

"Well, sir, I am totally unskilled of course, so I am called a dataller, in other words paid the minimum basic wage. Those at the face are all on piecework. I get fourteen shillings and threepence three farthings a shift which when my stoppages are taken leaves me with around three pounds five shillings a week for a five shift week. I get up at 4.30 for the day shift, have breakfast and collect my snap from my landlady, that's a couple of sandwiches and an apple if I'm lucky, to eat mid-shift."

He looked around at the increasing number of listeners, including David, the General and Lady Earnshaw, with whom he had been in conversation.

"Look, sir, I'm terribly afraid of boring you all." John was totally unused to being the centre of attraction as he now was.

"No, not at all, my boy, this is the most interesting conversation I have had in a long time."

"Well, I take my snap tin, it's always a tin. If you take sandwiches in a paper bag or whatever and leave them down somewhere the mice soon find them and you've no snap left."

"Are there any rats down there?"

"No, I believe when the ponies lived down there, the place was infested with them, big brown ones. They used to come in with the fodder. Now the animals have gone the rats have been eliminated. But the mice are everywhere. They are quite blind, what they find to live on, goodness knows. Anyway when I get to the pit I go into the clean locker room and leave all my clothes, then on to the dirty room and put on what they call 'pit black'. Then I draw my lamp and I am ready for the cage, only at Betteshanger we call it 'the chair' – I don't know why. The chair goes down at six o'clock."

"So all that preparation is done in your own time?" queried the Earl.

"That's right sir. When we get to the pit bottom the people doing a regular job, colliers, and so on, go off, the rest of us are what is known as 'on the market', we can be detailed by the pit deputy to fill in wherever we are needed. I have a semi-permanent job at the moment as mate to an electrician which means I travel all over the underground workings with him fixing electrical breakdowns, moving motors and so on. I probably walk about five miles a day, sometimes standing up, sometimes bent double, sometimes on my hands and knees. It's an interesting but thoroughly dirty life."

"You'll have to write a book when you are demobbed," the general suggested.

"I'll be his typist," Greta suggested seizing John's arm, thereafter continuing to hold it close.

"But you can't type," John countered.

"I shall soon learn, you see if I don't."

"Well, when you two have concluded your warm-hearted polemics, perhaps we can hear how you get out after your day's work," the Earl jested.

"Well, we have twenty minutes mid-shift to eat our snap, then at a quarter to two we assemble at the pit bottom to go up, so that we finish the eight hour shift on time at two o'clock. We then hand in our lamps and go to the dirty locker room, into the showers, where I have to tell you we need to scrub each other's backs, no way can you get the muck off on your own. Then it is on to the clean locker room and away."

"So you have to shower and change in your own time?" the Earl asked.

"Yes, sir, of course in the old days, not so long ago I might add, the men went home dirty and bathed in the wash house or in front of the fire. Pit head baths are a godsend, no doubt about that."

"Well, I'm sure there is so much more you could tell us, but we had better let you off there. The last thing we want to do is to spoil your party." At this final statement from the Earl there was a spontaneous burst of applause from the listeners, received with considerable embarrassment by the young Bevin boy, who up to that moment had considered he was a nonentity – not being a service man, yet here he was addressing an earl, a lord, a general, a knight and a host of important people, all of whom were taking in every word he uttered. It raised his morale considerably, particularly in respect of the regard he was held in the eyes of a certain young lady to whom he was becoming very attached. It had been a cause of considerable dismay that he was 'only' a Bevin boy, not a soldier. This assembly had indicated there was a certain cachet to working underground, an occupation as difficult and perhaps far more dangerous than many service jobs.

The party was a great success, the pleasure dampened to a certain degree of those being left behind knowing that the three warriors would soon be in the thick of it. Emma was staying the weekend with Megan so Charlie walked them both home. Hugh Ramsford and his father walked Cecely and Gloria to The Bungalow, John and Greta trailing a short distance behind. Perhaps I should amend that. It started as a short distance behind, but seemed to get more distant until they were able to indulge in some serious canoodling without being spotted. When it was necessary to catch up, that is, some one hundred yards from The Bungalow, they moved into a higher gear in order to close the gap. Needless to say the people in front were far too involved in each other to have even noticed whether the youngsters were with them or not. Funny thing, love.

On Monday morning, it was May Day but there would be no celebrations in the town centre this year. Miss Russell had arrived at eight o'clock to find the telephone ringing furiously. 'Someone's in a blooming hurry', she said to herself.
"Sandbury Engineering, Mr Chandler's office." Until the switchboard girl came in the line was put through to Fred's office.
A pleasantly modulated American lady's voice asked, "May I ask to whom I am speaking?"
"I am Miss Russell, Mr Chandler's secretary."
"Oh, Miss Russell. I am Major Coulter. I wonder if colonel Rathmore and myself can come and see Mr Chandler this morning?"
"At what time Major Coulter?"
"Well, we shall be coming down from London. Say ten o'clock?" put as a question Miss Russell noted, not as a demand, and was impressed by the courtesy implied.
"Yes, that would be alright. Can I give you directions?"
"Well, I have plotted the route to Sandbury. Perhaps you can give me final guidance."
"When you reach the clock tower take the turning opposite, down to a 'T' junction. Turn left and you will see the factory on the left about a quarter of a mile along that road. Oh, and major, there are certain parts of the factory which cannot be visited without authorisation, so we have to be particularly careful in examining visitors' identity documents."
"I quite understand; I shall ensure that the colonel, who has a habit of leaving his wallet behind, is well prepared. I would add that the habit referred to is generally as an excuse not to have to buy a round of drinks when called upon so to do." A pleasant laugh accompanied the final quip.
"We shall look forward to your visit major," Miss Russell replied, looking up to see Fred coming through the doorway with eyebrows raised

enquiringly.

"So which major is visiting us and when, and moreover, why?" asked Fred.

"Well Mr Chandler, it is a lady major, an American, along with a colonel, and they will be here at ten o'clock."

"A lady major eh? Not many of those around I shouldn't think. What do they want?"

"I didn't think to ask. She asked for you by name so someone we know has put them on to us."

"Did she sound like best teacups?" asked Fred mischievously. It was a stock joke in the office that Miss Russell immediately sized visitors up on arrival as being in the best teacup, the ordinary teacup, or plain mug division, and instructed the young lady in the canteen accordingly.

"Well, we had better find out if they would prefer coffee, I don't think Yanks drink tea." Fred continued, "I'll ask them when we get them settled. Better tell Ernie and Ray, will you please?"

A few minutes before ten o'clock a large Chevrolet staff car pulled into the car park. A very large, considerably overweight officer alighted, followed by a tallish, slimly built lady of around the forty mark, Fred judged, watching them through his office blind. She had obviously been driving. I would have thought they would have had a driver he mused.

Miss Russell showed them into Fred's office, the colonel pushing past Major Coulter with hand outstretched, Fred registering the thought that courtesy was not top of the colonel's attributes.

"Mr Chandler. I expected to find a much bigger plant than this." Fred's second thought was that tact seemed not to be high on his agenda either.

He made no attempt to introduce the major, Fred's third thought being he was being confronted by a pig-ignorant sod who should be sent back to military school, or wherever it was they bred him.

Fred came round his desk, shook hands with the major saying, "Welcome to Sandbury Major Coulter, please sit down." He pulled a chair from the boardroom table and placed it for her in front of his desk. He left the colonel to get his own.

"How can we help you major?" he asked pointedly ignoring the overweight colonel. However, the colonel was not to be ignored.

"We've come to find out if your facilities are good enough to make some matériel for us."

Fred knew damned well what matériel was but had decided he had already had enough of this bombastic colonel.

"Oh, and what is matériel?" he asked as innocent as a babe. "We are very simple country folk down here and as such are unaware of these posh words."

The major suppressed a giggle. The colonel floundered.

"Well matériel is, well I suppose you would describe it as, well I suppose it is anything to do with arms, and all that kind of stuff."

"But we don't make arms or all that kind of stuff, so how can I, and my little plant, help you?"

The major had to turn her head and heroically prevent herself from bursting with laughter at the subtle mickey-taking, the latter naturally being completely lost on the colonel.

"Well, I will leave the major to sort it out with you while I have a look round."

'No, please – where WAS he dragged up?' thought Fred, the thought being duplicated almost word for word in the mind of, by now, a somewhat embarrassed major.

"Certainly colonel, but first we have to go through certain procedures, as a good deal of our little plant is covered by the Official Secrets Act."

"But surely that doesn't apply to us?"

"It would apply to Winston Churchill or General Eisenhower himself if either of them came here."

"So what do you want?"

"I need to see your personal identity documents. I then need to see the authorisation from the Ministry of Defence, the Ministry of War Production, or the Chief Inspector of Armaments, the Inspector of Naval Ordnance or the Air Ministry so that I can determine which part or parts of our little plant you can visit. I have no doubt you were informed of these requirements?"

The colonel was lost for words, and for the first time addressed himself to the major.

"Did you know all about this?"

"Oh, yes, sir, I included it in the memo to you of 29th April." She stopped briefly. "I have of course got all these authorisations for both of us."

"Well, why the devil didn't you say so?" He was somewhat put out at being wrong-footed.

Fred interrupted, "I'll organise it," he said, lifting the telephone. "Ernie, can you take a gentleman round the plant for me?" He turned to the major. "Can I see the documents please?" and to the colonel "May I see your identity papers colonel. I have to ensure you are the person referred to on the authorisations."

The formalities concluded and Ernie having collected the colonel, who pointedly did not shake hands with his guide, Fred leaned back in his chair, looked at the major, and they both burst into peals of laughter.

"Where did you find him?" Fred asked.

"His father and his brother are both senators," she replied. "He has some sort of fancy liaison job at SHAEF headquarters which carries the rank of lieutenant colonel, but he has never seen any real soldiering in his life. He will report the results of my visit when we get back, and probably be awarded another medal for the hard day's work he has put in. We have a number of political hangers-on like him at HQ. In the west of the United States they would say he was 'all hat and no cattle'. We just have to put up with them."

"Well, I'd rather you than me, that's for sure. Now, down to business. What can I do for you? Firstly would you like tea or coffee? I have to tell you the tea is good, the coffee is like strained horse manure, straight out of a bottle."

"In that case, tea please." Fred signalled Miss Russell through the window, mouthing tea please."

The major took some folded drawings from her briefcase and handed them to Fred, who got up from his chair and walked across to the boardroom table to lay them out.

"Wait a minute" he exclaimed, "these are copies of our drawings."

"That's right, with modifications in respect of the attachment units. You see, we have a super fighter plane which you call the Mustang. We want to extend its range so that our Fortresses can keep fighter cover right across Germany. At present the fighters have to leave them sometimes a couple of hundred miles from their targets, as a result we are losing too many of our bombers, and more importantly too many of our crews. Having been advised of the quality of your workmanship and the reliability of your delivery schedules we would be interested in placing a monthly rolling order with you."

The item they were discussing was an auxiliary fuel tank which Sandbury Engineering were currently manufacturing for the RAF. Attached to the underside of the airplane, it was jettisoned when used, thereby giving a far greater range to smaller aircraft.

"Tell me major, how did you get into this technical work?"

"My father was an engineer, so I was brought up with the smell of cutting fluids in my nostrils. I took Engineering Sciences at University, the only female in the student group, and passed out top, to the chagrin of some of my critics I might add. I then went to work for an oil company in Texas, eventually becoming Vice-President-Procurement. That's how I got my commission and the job I am doing now."

"I notice you wear a ring. Would it be impertinent to ask if your husband is in England with you?"

"I lost my husband ten years ago. He was trapped in a fire on an oil rig in the Gulf. I've never had the desire to replace him." She looked sadly out of the window as Fred replied,

"I'm sorry, I should not have asked."

"It's OK Mr Chandler, it's OK. Now, can you see any problems with this project?"

"You haven't told me how many, and the required delivery schedule yet major," Fred joked.

"Please call me Margaret; I am still not used to this 'major' tag. To answer your question we need five hundred by the end of this month and then five hundred each week for the next six months, a roll-over order to be decided at the end of the year."

Fred looked at his customer. "That, Margaret, is a whacking great order for such a small plant," they both enjoyed the joke.

"Can you start straight away? The ministry assures me there will be no problem regarding licences for materials."

"Yes, we have a good stock of metal, we shall have to get the release mechanisms organised, they are different to our current ones. Now supposing you and the colonel go up to The Angel and have a somewhat spartan lunch compared to your usual fare while Ernie Bolton and I go into the drawings and confirm the production run. If you then come back here we can ask you to sort out any queries which may have arisen."

"We'll do that." Fred lifted the internal phone.

"Miss Russell, can you get John Tarrant for me?" Miss Russell swiftly complied.

"John, it's Fred. I've two very important American officers coming up to you for lunch. In the first instance try and give them something better than the usual mouldy cheese sandwiches you feed us with, and secondly put it on the Sandbury Engineering tab. Oh, and make the wine something a bit more drinkable than that bathroom tub vintage you give us. OK?"

The major sat there smiling widely.

"He must be a very good friend of yours?"

"Why do you say that?"

"Only very good friends could insult one another as you were doing."

"Ah, but then I was only telling the truth." His grin belied his words.

Ernie returned with the colonel. Ernie's normal genial countenance had been replaced by a mask of controlled animosity. To put it bluntly, the colonel had more than got on his tits, as he described it after to Ray and Fred.

"Did you see everything you wanted to see in our little plant colonel?" Fred asked. Margaret again had to turn away.

"Well, your lad here showed me everything. I should think it will do."

"My lad, or rather my works director as he is normally described, will now go over your drawings whilst you go to lunch. Perhaps you and the major will then return to see if we have any problems?"

"Very well. I hope it won't take too long. I have an appointment this evening."

Ernie could not resist it. "Have you colonel? What's her name?"

Fred grinned. Margaret nearly exploded. Ernie's face was a picture of innocence. Whilst the colonel was trying to think of a suitable reply Fred addressed Margaret.

"You will find The Angel in the town centre major. It's an old coaching inn, drive through the archway and park in the rear yard."

"Thank you Mr Chandler."

They left, Fred and Ernie noting the colonel climbed in the back of the car leaving the major to open her own door and get in.

Ernie commented, "What a boneheaded heap of crap he was. What was she like guvnor?"

Fred paused before replying.

"She, as they say on the films, was something else!!"

Chapter Thirteen

David arrived back at Bulford in the early evening of May 1st. The first thing he did, so that he was not caught on the wrong foot, was to read what was known as 'Part One Orders'. This section of the daily orders issued by the commanding officer gave instructions as to which individual, platoon, or company, was to carry out a specific task on the date specified. Failure to read Part One Orders, or having read them, failing to comply with them, was a major crime. The first thing he read informed him that B Coy CQMS (his quartermaster sergeant) was to draw twelve rubber dinghies from the QM stores on Tuesday 2 May at 1030 hours.

The second thing he read was that B Coy would parade at 0800 hours on Wednesday 3May in full battle order to embus on TCVs (troop carrying vehicles) for a three day exercise, returning on Sunday 7 May. His first thoughts were, one, that's five days not three. His second, if it takes a day to get wherever we are going and a day to get back again we must be going to make quite a journey. His third thought was, what the hell do airborne soldiers want with rubber dinghies? Only prats like commandos and the navy idiots who go and recce enemy beaches need rubber dinghies.

Claude Warren, OCA Coy, came up behind him.
"Want any help with the long words my son?" he asked.
"Do you know anything about this dinghy lark?" asked David.
"No, and since mucking about in such things usually results in one getting one's arse wet I really don't want to know. Why do you ask?"
"I've got to go on some exercise or other, taking with me a dozen dinghies."
"Oh that's easily explained. They haven't enough aircraft for all the battalion; you therefore have got to paddle across to wherever it is we're going. You will of course have to leave two days before us and will be given a full navy escort." And as an afterthought, "I do hope it's not too rough and there are no Unterseeboots around to interfere with your journey."
"Claude Warren, how did you ever become a major?"
"Family influence old boy, family influence. My brother used to sleep with a lady who used to sleep with the Prince of Wales. Not that she got a lot of sleep I understand, but doubtless you comprehend the underlying nuance in the expression. Anyway, if you read on beyond the

boating pond detail, exciting though it is, you will note that my lot, A Coy, have to also board TCVs to go to Battersea to learn about street fighting in the bombed out square mile there."

"You jammy blighter. I suppose you'll be up in the West End every night living it up."

"And why not may I ask? Incidentally, your lot will be going up next week, so I hear, so you had better organise that delightful wife of yours to get herself booked into some nearby hotel so that you do not stray from the straight and narrow. I suppose there are such things as hotels in Battersea. I know there is a park there, perhaps you could pitch a tent in it if you are unlucky with the hotel."

"I should think getting a hotel in London with the millions of Yanks there are floating around will be a bit difficult."

"A friend of my family runs a club – members only I add – not one of your low dive, drinking clubs, with which I understand you are more than familiar. He tells me that the influx of Americans and Canadians on leave has suddenly evaporated, I wonder why that is?"

"If you don't know, nobody does. Anyway, it's a rattling good idea, thanks for the tip. I'll ask the adj when we're going etc. and see the colonel for a sleeping out pass."

"Well, don't bank on it. There may be plans for night ops which would directly cancel your plans for night ops."

David made his way to the telephone to tell Maria the news and to ask her if she would do some reconnaissance regarding hotels. He would let her know the final details, hopefully, on the morrow. He got through fairly quickly to be answered by the deep-throated voice of Henry Schultz.

"David, how nice to talk to you," etc etc as invariably opens most telephone conversations. Having passed the time of day, or evening in this case, he asked if he could have a few words with Maria.

"Yes, of course, she has only just arrived from Sandbury, I will call her." A breathless Maria came to the telephone.

"Am I so precious you can't live without me for more than a few hours?" she asked laughingly.

"Not even for a few minutes," he replied gallantly, and went on to explain the reason for his call, telling her he would telephone again tomorrow, hopefully with firm details, but she was not to be disappointed if it all fell through.

The next morning David received a call to go and see the CO. When he arrived Hamish Gillespie collared him.

"The CO has asked me to deal with you David."

"Well, don't deal with me too harshly, I'm only little," he cheerfully replied. Hamish grinned.

"These boats. Your company has been selected to carry out an assault river crossing should the bridges over which we intend to cross become blown by the enemy. Where, when and how will be detailed to you, and to me for that matter, in due course. In the meantime you are to go down to South Devon to practise, the instruction being provided by RAF wallahs, since they are the normal users of this exciting equipment."

"And that's all?"

"That's all. For now anyway. When you come back on Sunday you have a day on Monday to prepare, then off you go to Battersea to practise street fighting for five days, so I suggest you lay off the scrumpy, or whatever they call that jungle juice in wildest Devonshire."

David went back to his company office and called an 'O' group of his platoon officers and Paddy, his CSM, put them in the picture as far as he could and went to look at the dinghies. Since they were contained in rubberised canvas holdalls there was nothing to see. Ten of them were comparatively small, the size of a small kit bag, two were very much larger. He picked one up. It seemed to weigh a ton. "How the hell do we carry that?" he asked the CQMS.

"Perhaps you might find a pram or a wheelbarrow to put it in," was the somewhat unhelpful reply. Actually it turned out to be not as daft as it sounded.

The next morning Paddy had B Coy on parade at seven a.m. ready for inspection by firstly the platoon commanders and finally David, to ensure each man had his full kit, plenty of spare socks and in particular to ensure they had not packed out their haversacks with cardboard to make them look as though they were full, but would be only a fraction of the normal weight. They would be lucky to get that one past CSM O'Riordan, particularly since he had succeeded in doing it himself long before some of them were out of diapers.

"Where are we going sir?" Paddy asked.

"I've just been told," David replied, "Exeter Barracks. The TCVs will be staying with us as the exercise takes place up the river somewhere. An instructor will meet us there."

"Why go all the bloody way to Devon. Surely we've got enough rivers around here?"

"I understand this location is very similar to our eventual landing site. Where that is I am as much in the dark as you are."

It was roughly one hundred miles to their destination which they reached soon after two o'clock, being held up on two occasions by massive convoys moving north to south. One of these contained American troops, which resulted in a lot of good-natured banter from the red berets, as they had to wait to let them pass. Although the roads were crowded it was nothing to how it would be in two or three weeks time, when every verge, every village green, every lane within a few miles of the coast would be packed with unbelievable numbers of troop carriers, tanks, trucks and all the impedimenta so patiently built up for the great assault on fortress Europe.

Having arrived at the barracks, the platoon officers saw their men were to be housed and fed properly, an unnecessary concern in view of the fact they were being hosted by the Devonshire Regiment, well known for their hospitality. The Devons had a battalion of glider troops in the 'Airborne', so were more than welcoming to the paras.

The next morning they boarded their TCVs again to travel some miles along the river to a spot where it ran parallel to a canal. They were some four hundred yards apart. A road ran over a bridge above the river, then on over the canal, it was all very peaceful and serene. An Intelligence Corps major, along with an RAF warrant officer and several sergeants, all, they noticed, being PT instructors. The major welcomed David.

"Major Chandler? I'll just put you and your officers in the picture; then I will push off and leave you to Mr Douglas here." The one hundred and twenty men were in the meantime being marshalled by their sergeants into platoon order.

The major continued.

"The plan over the other side is that gliders will land silently as close to these bridges as possible and capture them. The paras will reinforce them as quickly as possible. Now it is possible that Jerry will have the bridges ready for demolition and will blow them. If they do we have to get a nucleus of one company over the two water obstacles, to stop an enemy approach up the main road running parallel to the canal. So your men will be provided with these inflatable boats, get across the river then the canal, dig in and provide a defensive position facing south. All clear so far?"

David was a bit puzzled. "Why can't we be dropped on that side in the first place?"

"The short answer is that the terrain on that side is not suitable."

The major continued. "So today and tomorrow Mr Douglas and his men will show your chaps how to use the boats and on Saturday we will stage a mock assault with bags of smoke all over the place, and on Friday night we will repeat it in the dark. I am led to believe this, properly executed, could well be absolutely critical in the successful outcome of the British landings."

He left them in the care of WO Douglas, who in turn despatched three of his sergeants to each of the three platoons.

There were two types of dinghies. The first, a small one to take one, or at a stretch two men, the other a collapsible canvas unit to take nine men. The instruction commenced with showing the men how to inflate the small ones, and to assemble the large ones. Following that how to carry and put them into the water, first from a low bank, secondly from a high bank, they would of course have no idea of the type of water's edge they would meet; in fact the river edge would almost certainly be different to the canal edge.
Then the fun began.

The first two men to actually launch their inflatables waded into water, pushed down on the edge of the dinghy to lever themselves in, the dinghy promptly upending causing the first soakings of the day. The dinghy fortunately had a long length of rope on it being wisely held by the instructor otherwise it would have disappeared down the river. They had instructed budding RAF crews on this lark before.

During the day the whole company came to accept the fact that if they did not get wet getting into the boat, they would certainly get wet getting out of them.

The next day they practised getting across, two men at a time, others on the near bank holding a rope to pull the dinghy back for others to cross, those already on the far bank holding another rope to pull the dinghy over again. It would be quicker than paddling; furthermore they would not get dispersed in the dark, if the two groups were connected by the rope attachments. Finally they practised crossing the river, racing across to the canal, crossing the canal and finally running forward to their defensive positions. The officers and Paddy were far from divorced from all this frenetic activity, getting wet and so on. After all on the night – and they assumed it was to take place at night, an airborne assault in daylight would be a pretty horrendous affair as they were to find nearly a year later when they jumped the Rhine – on the night, they would be called upon to lead it all. It followed therefore they had to be even better trained than their men.

They trained in the collapsibles, with hilarious results to start with, in that the men on one side were infinitely better paddlers than the four men on the other side, which tended to turn the boat downstream and eventually would have described a complete circle had not the rope attachment not been brought into use and prevented them from being washed out into the English Channel.

At four o'clock they called it a day. In varying degrees of discomfort, from being soaking wet up to the knees to being soaking wet all over, they travelled back to Exeter to baths and hot meals, with wet clothes taken away to be dried ready for the morrow. They would not enjoy these facilities when it came to the real thing as they well knew!

On Saturday they arrived to carry out the daylight attack. Since paratroopers would be dropped at all sorts of distances from the crossing point a rendezvous had been arrived at. When enough men had arrived to fill the collapsibles, the senior officer or NCO present would lead the men some two miles to the river, confirm the bridges had been blown and then make the double crossing. A man would be left on the banks of the river and the canal respectively to pull the boats back for further arrivals to cross.

When they debussed at the RV they were surprised to find the CO there.

"Good morning David, 'morning sergeant major."

"Good morning sir, come to watch the fun?" replied David.

"I've come to put a little realism into the caper. Now, you and the sergeant major will be in the same stick I presume?"

"Yes, sir, that's correct."

"Well you see, your aircraft has dropped you and your stick well wide of the target. In addition, the two collapsibles haven't turned up. This means therefore that the platoon commanders have got to organise the crossings without the boats, just using the dinghies. Now Miles Rafferty is 4 platoon is he not? So he is to take the first dozen men chosen at random with say three dinghies and make his way to the crossing point. After twenty minutes Sandy Patterson will take a further thirty men and half a dozen dinghies and twenty minutes after that Jimmy James will take the remainder to arrive, say another dozen, leaving a sergeant to muster those arriving in dribs and drabs to move when he thinks fit. All clear?"

"Yes sir, but that leaves some fifty or sixty men unaccounted for, including myself and the sergeant major."

"Exactly. And that could very well be the case when we do the job.

When we have taken your first batch, we will come back and the second lot can have a bash, only then you, the sergeant major and I can act as platoon commanders. Clear? Can't have the three youngsters wearing themselves out by doing it twice. Especially when tonight they have got to do it again in the dark." He thought for a moment. "Correction. We have got to do it in the dark."

David looked at Paddy. Paddy looked at David.

"What rollicking fun, sir, what rollicking fun," and then he added, "by the way sir, no one has told us how these boats and dinghies are being dropped to us."

"Haven't they? That's most remiss of somebody. A court-martial offence I should think. In fact, I've kept it back deliberately, well, at least that's my story and I'm sticking to it. The collapsibles are to be dropped by the Stirlings in containers marked with phosphorescent yellow paint. The dinghies will be put into kit bags and strapped to the legs of the chosen carriers, which in the main will be each officer, warrant officer, and senior NCO in the company."

David looked at him in astonishment. "But with our parachutes we are already carrying about 90 pounds, how much do they weigh?"

"About 30 pounds."

"Well, they say donkeys go best loaded," David joked, "I hope the RAF are providing lifts to get us on the aircraft."

"Coalmen carry hundredweight sacks of coal about all day long, up and down stairs, up garden paths – piece of cake, is that not so Mr O'Riordan?"

"It's one reason I was never a coalman sir, so it is."

All being debussed, David called them together and told them the plan.

"You are to move from here at rifleman pace. Speed is the essence. You have two miles to the first crossing. We'll have a competition as to which squad gets there the quickest. Right Miles, take your lot, and we will see you, dug in, later on."

Having given instructions regarding the second phase of the operation David, Paddy and the colonel piled into the Humber staff car and drove off to wait on the bridge to watch the crossing. There were one or two mishaps as the three squads arrived in turn and were pulled across the obstacles, finally digging in astride the road as instructed. There were a couple of soakings as men tried to rush getting into the dinghies, two men lost their rope requiring them to plunge waist deep into the water to retrieve it, but all in all it went quite well.

"Right, once more into the breach etc etc," said the colonel, "let's get back and bring our squads down. David, you go first, then Mr O'Riordan, and I'll follow up at the rear."

David knew without a word being said exactly what would happen. The colonel was, come what may, going to get a ducking by one means or another. The men of B Coy, R Battalion, The Parachute Regiment, would not get a chance like this again, probably ever. It would be sacrilegious almost, to spurn such an opportunity as was being presented to them.

And it was done very cleverly.

The colonel was the last man to be pulled across with the exception of a tail-arsed Charlie who would be holding the rope from the rear of the colonel's dinghy so that it would be pulled across in a straight line. In addition t-a-c would be holding the rope of his own dinghy into which he would pile as soon as the colonel was across.

As soon as the CO commenced his journey the man holding the other end of t-a-c's rope passed it under the rope pulling the CO's dinghy, walked down stream a dozen yards, while t-a-c walked up stream a dozen yards. This, as you will immediately have realised, produced a sunken rope over which the CO's dinghy would have to pass. The timing of the next part of the operation had to be spot on, and spot on it was. Just as the CO's dinghy passed over the submerged rope, made submersible by its being thoroughly soaking wet, the men on each end pulled hard on it. As a result it caught under the front end of the colonel's dinghy, neatly transferring him into the river before he realised what was happening to him. Quickly the men holding his ropes manoeuvred his dinghy back along side for him to hold on to until he was pulled gasping to the bank. David ran down to him.

"What happened sir?" he asked in all innocence.

"I know bloody well what happened, just as you do. I give you fair warning. If anyone comes up before me from B Company the least he will get will be six months, even if it's only because he had a button undone on parade."

Surrounded as he was by a sea of smirking faces his threat was not being taken that seriously. The smiles increased as he unfastened his gaiters to let out copious quantities of river water trapped in his trouser legs. Miles Rafferty added insult to injury.

"Did you catch anything sir?"

Blankets had been brought with them in the trucks to put round any involuntary swimmers. B Company had the unusual spectacle of seeing their colonel stripped off to his long johns and wrapping himself against the somewhat chilly spring air. The story went the rounds, the two perpetrators swiftly attaining cult status.

It was no surprise that Paddy's lot won the time trial.
"The bugger had us running all the way, in full kit too," David heard one squaddie telling another as they embussed to go back to Exeter.

The night crossing went very well. There were going to be three variables on the night of the actual drop. Would the company be dropped in the right place? Would the bridges be defended, in which case crossing under their noses would be a bit dicey? When they had dug in would half the German army decide they were not wanted? Well, one day all would be revealed.

They made their way back to Bulford, again witnessing the movement of thousands of lorry-borne troops moving south.
"It's when you see this you can appreciate what the various staff-wallahs do to earn their money and six months' leave a year," the colonel joked to David, riding with him in the Humber, "every man, every vehicle, has an appetite of some sort. They all expect to receive their mail no matter where they are. What it must have been like when everything was horse-drawn I shudder to think. This lot has now to be loaded on to ships, the ships marshalled into the right order for disembarking, contingencies made for bad weather or breakdown. I'm beginning to be glad of the simple task I have at the sharp end."
"You do have one disadvantage sir."
"Oh, what's that?"
"You stand a far greater chance of being bumped off than those poor over-worked staff wallahs."
"I hadn't thought of that."
But his wife, and his pretty twelve-year-old daughter Sandra had. As had Maria, and Rose, and Emma, and a host of other family members whose nearest and dearest were part of that enormous throng poised to assault the Atlantic Wall. Thousands upon thousands of people of all ages lying in their beds at night wondering whether their loved ones were yet facing a foe, barricaded in behind defences they had had four years to bring to perfection.

They arrived back at Bulford soon after 2pm. With the inevitable weapon inspection concluded David and his officers went back to the mess for a somewhat delayed lunch. Later in the afternoon he put a call through to Maria which was answered in a quarter of an hour. After enquiring how the little one was coming along, and being told he was going to be a footballer judging by the activity in which he was indulging...

"How do you know it will be a boy?"

"I made that plain on the order form."

...Maria told David she had been able to get a room in a small hotel just across Battersea Bridge in Edith Grove and had he organised his sleeping out pass yet?

With panic gripping his vitals he suddenly realised he had not. However, he instantly crossed his fingers and replied, "That's all arranged," swiftly changing the subject by telling her about the fun the men had had with the CO.

Leaving the booth he bumped into the adjutant.

"Tommy," he asked "can you fix me a sleeping out permit while we are at Battersea, I've rather jumped the gun in that I've got my dearly beloved to find a hotel nearby, which she tells me that after dint of scouring the directories she has been able to do, only to realise I haven't organised my end of the operation."

Breathless after that peroration he waited for a reply.

"What's it worth?"

"What do you mean, what's it worth?"

"It must be worth at least a tenner to judge by your present state of agitation. I mean I wouldn't like to be in your shoes if the memsahib has to cancel all her arrangements through no fault of her own."

"Tommy, I will thump you in a minute."

"You can't do that. You are a major. I am a captain. It is strictly forbidden for majors to thump captains – read your Army Act, section fourteen. Anyway, if you read the movement order sent you regarding Battersea you will note that due to lack of accommodation officers may board out should they so desire."

"You bugger. I'll buy you a drink tonight all the same, since you have saved me from a fate worse than death."

The next day the company got themselves ready to move out to Battersea. On Tuesday they were taken in TCVs at the unearthly hour of 6am. and by noon were having their first instruction in house to house fighting. A halt was called at 4 o'clock. David, having seen the men were all comfortably billeted under canvas in nearby Battersea Park, walked through to Battersea Bridge Road where he was lucky enough to get a cab for the short journey to Edith Grove and the welcoming arms of his beloved.

As he and his men practised fighting from house to house, room to room, and on rooftops (those that remained), it was driven home to David that people were living in these streets of houses only a short while ago. As he clumped up the narrow stairway in these typically working class dwellings to take up firing positions at the windows, he speculated on the room's previous occupants. Love, lust, procreation, birth, sickness and death all could have existed or taken place here. He had this strange feeling of being an intruder, such as he had experienced when they took up their defensive positions in the small French houses at the battle of Calais four years before. There they had even used the solid furniture as part of the defences. That had really upset him. It had been his first experience of total warfare.

And now, after five years of action in various countries, he was to take part in this great assault to reclaim Europe from the Nazis. Like most soldiers who had come through the war unscathed thus far, he was wondering whether his luck would now run out, whether the 'one' with his name on had been issued to some square-headed bastard tucked away in an emplacement somewhere over there, patiently waiting for him.

He shrugged off the feeling.

The three days, and the three nights, passed quickly. Finding themselves back in Bulford on Friday afternoon they were greeted with the news they were to do a brigade night drop preceded by a four hour flight, on Sunday night, weather permitting. Weather permitted and they found themselves in a long convoy of trucks moving to God knows where to jump, they were told at the last minute, from Stirlings. Stirlings were massive four engined bombers, superseded in the main by Halifaxes and Lancasters, now to be used for the transportation and delivery of paratroopers to the continent. Jumping from a Stirling was simple, in that there was a whacking great hole in the floor of the fuselage at the rear end to which one just walked and plunged through feet first. The slipstream from the massive Bristol Hercules motors meant the parachutes were instantaneously opened, in the process causing a jerk to the neck and body much greater than from the Whitley or the Dakota, from which the men had previously jumped.

There were a few minor accidents on landing after the four hour circular flight bringing the brigade back to Salisbury Plain. That was to be expected. David's company got off scot-free.

From the DZ they had to march back to Bulford, some fifteen miles. It was a piece of cake. They arrived soon after dawn on the Monday, but were then kept working all day on bayonet drill, PT, weapon training, and finally at five o'clock the full battalion was assembled on the main parade ground for an hours drill under RSM Forster. The RSM, at the end of his systematic torture finally assembled the four companies in a square. An orderly ran forward carrying a large square box some three feet high and three feet square, almost rupturing himself in the carrying out of the action, followed by Colonel Hislop, who promptly stood on it, asked the RSM to stand the men at ease, and then began to address them.

"You have just experienced two full days of considerable activity without sleep. It is highly likely that in the near future that will happen to you fairly regularly. You have done well. From this moment the division is to become incommunicado. Tonight you may write letters home but no mention must be made that you are on the move. Platoon officers will censor all mail; any references that should not be there will mean the letter will not be sent. So that you know this applies to officers and warrant officers as well, mail from these illustrious people will be censored by the adjutant. He has, I believe, learnt to read especially to carry out this task."

There was a murmur of merriment around the square.

"No one may leave the camp, police pickets will be at both exits. All telephones have been cut off. Tomorrow you will be issued with ammunition and on Wednesday the battalion will move to a tented camp where you will undergo very detailed instruction regarding our divisional objective, our battalion task, and your own specific missions, until you can carry out your own particular job in your sleep.

We all know in our heart of hearts, that 'R' Battalion of the Parachute Regiment is the 'crème de la crème', as our froggy friends would say. Now we shall prove it to others beyond all doubt. Good luck to you all."

The RSM came forward.

"Remove headdress. Three cheers for the colonel. Hip hip..." and so the parade was dismissed, the men going to their billets telling themselves 'This is it!' It was the 16th May, in exactly three weeks' time they would be finding out what 'This is it' really meant.

Chapter Fourteen

The raid on the old gold mine at Raub took place as planned. Harry and his small party moved out on Friday 24th March and bivvied up on the ridge some miles away in the beluka overlooking the target. Working on the premise that Saturday night would be the best night for the job, the Nips having been paid and all but the immediate guard in the town indulging in their preferred recreation, they got everything prepared.

Four ten pound plastic bombs in thin wall tubes of female bamboo were fitted with two-hour timers and securely fixed to the lowering cords. At 10pm. they moved out, reached the wire and cut their way through, crawled again up to the summit and set the timers. Harry crawled to each point to check they had been correctly prepared, then signalled for them to be lowered. The timers, not being particularly sophisticated, would not, as Harry full appreciated, be actuated at exactly the same time. In fact there could be as long as ten minutes between the first and the last to explode its charge.

When all the devices had been lowered the party made their way back to the wire, marked as always with a piece of white cloth, carefully joining the gap up again as they left so that it would take a very percipient eye to discover it. All was going so well that Harry had a funny feeling that things were going too bloody well. He had a further feeling immediately that he was becoming more of an old woman every day.

They reached the beluka and lay up, watching in the direction of the mound. It started to rain. It started to pour with rain. Visibility fell to next to nothing. They stood up, if they could see nothing, nothing could see them. Harry looked at his watch. "Another ten minutes," he whispered. The ten minutes passed. Nothing happened. Another five. A terrific and seemingly endless display of sheet lightening suddenly lit up the countryside, followed by a rolling rumble of thunder, in the middle of which they heard a muffled explosion from the direction of the mound. Unaccompanied as it was with any display of pyrotechnics they were not absolutely sure it was one of their bombs or whether it was part of the thunderstorm. A minute later they were left in no doubt.

Where they were standing they could not see the entrance to the mine. Choon Guan's original sketches had shown the original cave-like opening to have been boarded in and fitted with large double doors. A high, enclosed perimeter fence was positioned in a semi circle some thirty yards from the double doors, this fitted again with solid double gates. The guard hut was just inside the gates. As they watched they saw a huge flash of flame emerging into the night sky from the front of the building. Burning pieces of timber were thrown a hundred feet into the air, this display being followed by a booming explosion reaching them some seconds later.

"I think we have won the pools my sons," Harry exclaimed to his excited group, and to Choon Guan he said, "and it's all thanks to you." As he spoke there was another explosion. Whether that was another of the bombs going off or whether it was a chain reaction from the previous explosion they had no means of knowing. It really did not matter; whatever they were using the old mine for was now immaterial.

It was still raining hard as dawn approached and they set off back to Camp Three, to be met enthusiastically by Reuben and Tommy and the rest, and ecstatically by Chantek, who again as Matthew told Harry, knew he was coming an hour before he actually arrived.

That night they sent a coded message to Sunrise to acquaint him of the success of the operation. As Harry said to his fellow officers, "It's a pity we can't go back in to see what actually happened. One thing in our favour is that they will not know for sure that it was an outside attack, it could have been a spontaneous explosion in whatever it was they had in there."

But in this point Harry was seriously mistaken.

When the flames had been put out and the smoke had cleared from the cave, the local commander called in the Kempeitai to investigate, as much to cover his own tracks as for any other reason. Much of the cave had, to quote a phrase, caved in, but still hanging from one of the metal ducts, now blackened and distorted from the heat, they found a length of some sort of cord literally welded on to the metal. The Kempeitai warrant officer had been a detective back in his home town of Kanazawa, some two hundred miles from Tokyo over on the west coast, this item he immediately considered to be out of place, and as a result should be further investigated. He carefully removed it from the duct, put it in a paper carrier bag, and the next day took it to headquarters in Kuala Lumpur.

The headquarters had a small forensic department, poorly equipped, but staffed by two or three extremely bright young graduates who had been trained in the Kempeitai school in Keijo (later to be known as Seoul) in Korea. They carefully unravelled the charred cord, from the centre strands being able to establish the fibres were synthetic, probably nylon, and the only force using nylon as far as they were aware, were the Americans, although of course they could have supplied the British or Australians. Whatever the case might be it seemed probable that a raiding party had lowered explosives into the cave via the ducts.

Warrant Officer Tadayuki Sasagawa bowed his thanks to the young scientists and left for his headquarters at Frasers Hill, where he was the second in command of the small military police detachment.

He put his suspicions to his superior officer, a lieutenant, who immediately authorised him to investigate further. He suggested to the warrant officer that if he found it likely there had been a raid, that he take a small party of men, and using the services of two Dyaks brought over from Sarawak, try and trace where the raiding party had come from. These Dyaks, head hunters and renowned trackers in their own country, were to be paid in gold, it was the only currency they acknowledged, the Japanese Military Police Provost Marshall General himself having been required to authorise such a method of payment.

Sasagawa assembled his small force. He fully realised the possibility of finding tracks or clues more than a week after the explosion, was remote. Nevertheless, he had been well trained in positive thinking; some small discovery might well lead to guidance on the numbers involved, the nationalities even. There was no doubt in his mind it was the work of Chinese blackguards, but were they a force holed up in the jungle, or were they saboteurs living perhaps in Raub itself? The piece of nylon cord, a critical piece of evidence to decide this conundrum, led him to believe they were one of the insurrectionist gangs known to be concealed somewhere in the thousands of square miles of mountainous and almost impenetrable forest running from Siam to Singapore. This cord was almost certainly from a parachute. A parachute meant supply by aircraft. Supply by aircraft meant sophisticated communication between supply and delivery.

'Start at the beginning', he told himself, and with his two Dyaks made a thorough survey of the wire defences. The heavy rain had washed away all hopes of finding footprints. The barbed entanglements were made up from all sorts of odd pieces, the place where it had been cut for

Harry's party to gain access therefore exciting no extra interest. He ordered the Japanese NCO, a corporal, to get his men, four Koreans, to cut a hole in the wire so that he and the trackers could go to the top of the mound. The corporal bowed, respectfully suggesting it might be dangerous for the warrant officer to ascend, should he, the corporal, not go up first to ensure the explosion had not weakened the structure. Saragawa brushed him aside.

When the policeman reached the top he found the surface to be crisscrossed with cracks and fissures. The two chimneys had largely fallen in; the two ducts were twisted and blackened. When one of his legs started to disappear into soft earth he decided to take the corporal's advice and retreat to safe territory. Nevertheless he was too old a hand at detective work to expect to solve anything in five minutes. Sometimes it could take five years!

He took his trackers back down through the wire, and painstakingly moved round and round the barrow moving outwards all the time. His two natives, and for that matter his military squad began to show signs of boredom by early afternoon, until one of the Dyaks stopped suddenly, pointing to something metal in the harsh grass at that point. Sasagawa approached. Carefully he pulled away the green stuff to ensure the object was not booby-trapped, although he considered that most unlikely, to discover a British army issue clasp knife, in good condition, therefore newly dropped. He picked it up carefully; there might still be fingerprints on it, which would be of no use whatsoever he told himself. Nevertheless his training had taught him to examine any and every unusual object and hope for a miracle.

One of the Koreans was carrying half a dozen white painted posts about three feet long. Sasagawa took one and pushed it into the soft earth at the point at which they had found the knife. He then took a compass from a pouch on his belt, took a bearing on the mound, followed by a reverse bearing from the post to indicate in which general direction the raiders would have taken in their retreat. It pointed direct to a clearing on the edge of the jungle on the forward edge of the escarpment which overlooked Raub.
"That's where they came from," he told the corporal.

He should have remembered the part of his training which said that you never make definite assumptions of fact from mere conjecture. He could not of course have known it but he was dealing with Harry Chandler who had spent over three years now in the jungle and in that time learnt a thing or two. One of these things was, never go in straight lines. Near the point the warrant officer had found the knife, Harry had made his first dog-leg, going half left from his previous line of retreat to make for a point on the escarpment almost a mile from the opening his tracker had identified.

Sasagawa called it a day, returned to the mine and then drove himself back in his two-seater Kurogane to his base at Frasers Hill, having arranged for the party to meet the next morning to go up to the escarpment. During the half hour drive he pondered as to what he should do next. He had no desire whatsoever to pursue these bastards into the jungle. He was a town man. He would not of course admit it to anyone, but he was petrified at the thought of, even more petrified at the sight of, and even more petrified than that at contact with, the smallest spider. Then he told himself being petrified had no scale or degree, you were either petrified or you were not petrified. This internal line of reasoning however did not mask the fact that he had been told there were spiders in the jungle big enough to snare birds the size of chickens which they would poison and eat. The very thought turned his bowels to vapour. He had in the past fought and conquered miscreants twice his size, but a spider dropping on him engendered total panic. He had been brought up on the Bushido principle that the greatest honour he and his family could achieve would be for him to die for his emperor. Even when in an impossible situation, fighting against horrendous odds, he should, and would, save his last round for himself. He would never surrender. Somehow that samurai code did not extend to combating spiders.

As a boy back in provincial Japan he had never liked spiders, even though they were only the common household or garden type which he could easily swat or tread upon. After his training he had been posted to southern Indo-China. He had a comfortable room in a military complex on the outskirts of Saigon, the room looking out over some bushes and miles and miles of paddy fields. One morning he awoke soon after dawn with a feeling he was being watched. Becoming fully conscious he found himself looking into the eyes of a gigantic spider, fully eight or nine inches across from leg-end to leg-end, crouched on the end of his bolster only a foot or so away. It had a yellowy-brown speckled body, hugely thick legs covered in black hairs and intense, unblinking eyes. He was terror stricken, totally transfixed for many seconds.

At last he recovered his wits sufficient to enable him to let out a piercing scream, lift up his end of the bolster thus tilting the spider back against the mosquito net which enclosed the bed space, pulled the net up and saw the ghastly creature fall to the floor. As it scuttled to the corner of the room his bearer, a young Vietnamese boy came running in to see this mighty Japanese warrior cowering against the wall pointing toward the spider, now stationary in the corner. The lad walked over to it, swiftly bent down and picked it up, walked to the door and put it on the veranda outside. It disappeared down the steps and into the bushes.

"Why didn't you kill it?" screamed the fearless member from the hand of the Rising Sun.

The bearer understood not a word, but smiled and bowed, saying "It was one of God's creatures!"

It was then Warrant Officer Sasagawa became conscious of the fact that since he had been so tucked in beneath his net that a mosquito could not penetrate his sanctuary, the spider must have been in with him, crawling over him, even sucking his blood without his knowing, all night long! This thought so unnerved him he had to run to make the latrine, thereafter each night making a thorough search of the folds of the net and taking a flashlight into bed with him to finally convince himself, when he had tucked the net in, he was alone.

The degree of arachnophobia from which he suffered is not unusual, but he didn't know that. Most people suffer from it to an extent, few to the extreme of the warrant officer. It was something about which he could tell no other soul; he would lose face beyond retrieval.

While the policeman was thinking about the spiders and trying valiantly not to soil his breech clout which he wore under his tropical trousers, Harry was having a meeting with his officers and Choon Guan. He thought it would be a good idea if Reuben and Tommy took a patrol of a dozen Chinese who were not involved in the undertaking at the mine to see the results of the operation from the hiding point. It would give the men some exercise after being cooped up for several weeks, and at the same time hopefully get some accurate detail regarding the results of the operation.

The next morning, soon after dawn, they moved out of Camp Three, having been told not to engage in any action, they were going there purely to observe. They reached the bivvy point, meeting no problems on the way. It was a fine, clear day. Reuben and Tommy intended to observe during what remained of the day while half the squad made up the bivvies.

They would resume the observation the next morning and leave for camp three by 11am in order to get back before darkness fell.

Likewise the next morning, Sasagawa marshalled his little squad, although he had no stomach for the task he was being called upon to carry out. They made for the white stake, he took the compass bearing again and they slowly made their way toward the escarpment searching all the time. Nothing more was found. To give him credit he did consider that the raiders might not have taken a direct route but could have zigzagged. He then discounted that thought; they would not expect to be tracked, they would be anxious to put as much distance between them and the target as they could in the shortest possible time.

Having reached the top of the escarpment, he studied the jungle before him. Solid, forbidding, stretching three thousand feet above him, full of every imaginable stinging, biting, bloodsucking creature ever created. How was it these evil looking Dyaks could make their way through it wearing next to nothing and come to no harm? The truth was, they did not – come to harm that is! They were as capable of being bitten by a snake or a mosquito as anyone else, with more or less identical results. Few lived beyond the age of thirty years in their own environment back in Sarawak, speedily succumbing to diseases endemic in more civilised communities, if you could class a society of which the Kempeitai was part, civilised.

What Sasagawa did not know was that his trackers had, in fact, felt unwell that morning when shaken awake by the guard commander. Although it was a cool morning, cool by Malaysian standards that is, they were both sweating and dry mouthed. Nevertheless when the warrant officer arrived at 6.30 they moved out. A temporary malaise was not uncommon with native people living under the conditions they did, but because of their built-in ability to combat many diseases they frequently could shrug them off. This, however, did not apply to influenza, and it was influenza they had caught from two of the Korean guards with whom they had been on patrol the previous day, and who now lay in the sickbay at the main mine.

Now, having climbed the escarpment, itself an exhausting exercise, Sasagawa directed the trackers to move two hundred yards either side of where they had arrived, where he had driven in another white stake. At the end of the two hundred yards they were to go forward five paces, turn inwards and move back to the start point. When this had been carried out, say three times, should nothing be found, they would move the operation to the left and start again on a new front.

The trackers moved steadily on, each gradually feeling more and more ill, until eventually one of them collapsed. Immediately Sasagawa ran to him, saw that he was sweating profusely and immediately thought of all the most horrible, contagious, body destroying illnesses with which the man could be inflicted. Simple flu did not occur to him. In the meantime the other tracker walked from the section he had been searching, he too looking as though he was on his last legs, promptly collapsing alongside his companion.

Sasagawa was in a quandary. His first thought was to leave the savages there where they were. Then he called to mind the Imperial Japanese Army had spent money on bringing these people to Malaya, they were enrolled in the books. He had therefore to take them back to Raub, where if they died, their deaths could be properly registered and they would be written off the strength. He ordered the Koreans to pick them up to carry them back. They shrunk away. The natives could have typhus or any other tropical disease the Koreans had never seen or heard of for all they knew. Sasagawa stepped forward to the Japanese corporal in charge and slapped him hard around the face and head.

"Tell your men to pick them up."

This physical abuse was systematically instilled into the Japanese. Any officer or NCO was fully entitled to ill-treat subordinate ranks by slapping, punching, kicking, and by warrant officers and officers, beating with the scabbards of their swords. The recipient of this treatment was not to respond in any way, but to accept the brutality. It was no wonder they themselves performed such acts of barbarism on civilian and military prisoners as they did.

The corporal gave the order. Knowing what would happen to them if they demurred; they lifted the semi-conscious evil smelling bodies, leaving the blowpipes and dart satchels on the ground. Reuben Ault, two hours later, spotted these items through his field glasses, then carefully ensuring it was not a lure, collected them to take back to the camp. He had spent time on his travels in Borneo and regions adjacent, and immediately recognised the blowpipes for what they were and from whence they came.

"These are not our orang asli blowpipes," he told Tommy Isaacs and the listening Chinese, "they are from Borneo." He gingerly abstracted one of the darts from a satchel. "They use curare which totally paralyses the victim, man or animal, so that they can be despatched without danger."

His mind went into top gear. What were they doing here? Why would they leave weapons behind which had probably been in their respective families for generations? Most bizarre of all why would they leave their most important valuables, their darts and poisons, lying around?

He had no answers to any of these questions.

They carried out their tasks and made their way back to camp. Harry, coming out to meet them exclaimed, "What the hell have you got there?"

Reuben told him of the find, and when the men had been fed, the officers, along with Choon Guan and Matthew, sat down together to try and sort out the mystery. The solution they arrived at was not far from the reality. The Nips had brought these trackers over to try and find the people they knew to be holed up in the mountainous jungle. They had died from some sort of disease or had become too sick to continue. The Jap troops had taken them back to their base, but had no desire to lay their hands on either the blowpipes, or more importantly, the poison and the darts. If they were Koreans, which as was known by Harry and his men most of the garrison troops were, they were more than happy not to have to slog their way through jungle to find a foe who would probably kill them anyway.

One factor that would not have occurred to them, one to which they would not even have given house room even if they had thought of it, was that since the trackers had died from their influenza, the warrant officer was more than pleased he had good reason not to penetrate an environment where spiders existed which were large enough to devour chickens!

Chapter Fifteen

When Colonel Rathmore and Major Margaret Coulter returned to Sandbury Engineering from lunching at The Angel, the major was most complimentary regarding the fare they had received.

"Mr Tarrant looked after us extremely well Mr Chandler, and the wine was first class. Thank you very much for your hospitality."

The colonel, Fred noticed, did not reiterate her thanks, but did add, "The service was slow, so as we are running late perhaps we can get down to sorting out any problems."

"Certainly colonel. Now perhaps you can give us the benefit of your experience. You see, on this release gear, here, you appear to have the fixing pin on one side fouling the weld on this part of the body. It will therefore be impossible to get either the pin in after the weld, or do the weld after the pin. How would you get round that?"

Margaret, having speedily realised what Fred was up to had moved away to look out of the window across the hardstanding, where the bomb had fallen, across the fields to the wooded downs rising in the distance. It was May Day, the hedges were covered in the white flowers of the blackthorns, it really was a beautiful panorama stretched before her. In the background she could hear the colonel trying to bluster his way out of answering Fred's question.

"Er, yes, I can see that. Well. Surely it can't be too difficult. Either move the pin or move the weld I would have thought. What would you do?"

"Well you see sir, we are not allowed to do or recommend anything. They are your drawings after all."

"Well, if they were your drawings what would you do?"

"I would get someone in from my little plant and get them to work it out." Margaret was thoroughly enjoying her afternoon.

"Well can't you do that?"

"The problem is sir, they are not my drawings. We could be put in The Tower for taking liberties with your drawings."

The colonel was getting more flushed every minute, the bulk of the bottle of claret John Tarrant had found for them and which he had consumed, leaving one small glass for Margaret, assisting his increasingly rubicund appearance.

"Major, can't you help here?"

Margaret let him off the hook.

"Put the pin in from the other side Mr Chandler. I'll get a detail sent to you tomorrow to cover the modification."

"Thank you major, we'll do that."

The colonel swiftly regained his overbearing posture.

"Well, if there is nothing more I must get away."

Fred looked at Margaret.

"I will have the price telexed to you this afternoon by the time you get back, and the quotation and terms of supply in the post tomorrow."

"Thank you Mr Chandler, and thank you again for your hospitality.

Fred found himself replying, as he took her outstretched hand, "I trust we shall have the pleasure of seeing you again."

"You can be sure of that," was the reply.

The colonel shook hands brusquely and led the way out to the car.

"And if I never see you again I shall lose no bloody sleep," Fred said out loud as he watched Lieutenant Colonel Rathmore settle his well upholstered frame into the rear seat of the Chevrolet. As she started away, Margaret looked across at the office window and gave a little wave. Fred waved back.

Ernie gave his usual respectful knock on Fred's door and walked in.

"Any problems, guvnor?"

"No, all's well. I had mister loudmouth over a barrel for a minute or two which gave me a certain amount of pleasure, and the major too I fancy."

"Talking of pleasure, that major would certainly get nine out of ten, in my humble opinion."

"She's too old for you. I reckon ten out of ten would be nearer the mark. Anyway, down to business."

They got down to business, but as soon as the details as to how their existing line could be modified and increased to cater for the additional work load, and Ernie had left to start getting it organised, Fred sat back, thinking about Margaret Coulter.

Since Ruth had died nearly eighteen months ago he had gradually withdrawn from the deep misery into which he was plunged at her passing. He was sixty-four now; far too old he felt to have any romantic attachments. At sixty-four one could see only too clearly the shortcomings and funny little ways in women which in youth passion would ignore. Being a reasonably fair person he also realised one or two minor little fads and affectations of his own. The funny thing is, that at sixty-four you don't feel old. He knew several people in their sixties still playing cricket. He had to admit to himself he knew none whatsoever who were still playing football although Alf Rosen at Rotary was still refereeing at sixty-five. 'It's no use having flights of fancy about an extremely captivating American woman who I shall possibly never see again. She is probably twenty years or more younger than I am, so put her out of your mind', he told himself.

But the trouble was he found it easier said than done.

On Thursday 11th May, ten days after the visit, Miss Russell stopped Fred as he went back to his office, having been watching the loading of the latest completed Hamilcar glider on to its transporters.

"There has been a telephone call from Major Coulter. She asked if you could ring her back Mr Chandler."

"Get her for me, will you please Miss Russell?"

Ten minutes later the call came through.

"Good morning major, to what do I owe this pleasure," he joked.

"Oh, Margaret, please Mr Chandler."

"In which case I am known to all and sundry as Fred."

"Well, Fred, I was so taken by the beauty of the countryside where you are that I thought I would take this weekend off to come and stay at The Angel, and that perhaps you would care to join me for dinner one evening."

"Have you booked The Angel yet?"

"No, I was going to do that and to ask if I could mention your name in the event John Tarrant might be fully booked. Perhaps he would be able to recommend somewhere else."

"In that case why don't you stay at Chandlers Lodge, my home? My daughter and I would be most pleased to have you." And then as an afterthought, "Did you propose to be on your own?"

"Mr Chandler, what are you suggesting?" He heard her chuckling as she continued, "Yes, definitely."

To cover his confusion at the suggestion he joked, "I just wondered if the colonel was to bless us with his presence."

"Oh, he has moved on to better pastures, thank God. Engineering Procurement was a bit mundane for a mind of his calibre."

"Well, I suppose it must have been a bit embarrassing for him to have to take his shoes off every time he needed to count beyond ten."

Again than animated chuckle.

"So, how about staying with us, and I will have a few friends in to meet you on Saturday evening. I shall not be able to see anything of you on Sunday though, as I have a Home Guard exercise all day, but Rose, my daughter, will look after you."

"How old is Rose?"

"She is twenty-two. Her first husband was killed in France in 1940 soon after they were married. She has a little boy three years old and remarried a year or so ago."

"How very, very, terrible to lose a husband at such an early age."

"Yes, but then you too have suffered in that way as well, haven't you? So, how about staying with us?"

"What about the food situation? I understand having visitors is not exactly easy for you Brits."

"Oh, we'll find something, somewhere, have no fear."

"Then I will accept with great pleasure. I will raid our PX store to see what I can contribute, and I shall come by car, we get a recreational petrol allowance each month – not a lot but it will more than cover my journey to Sandbury."

Fred gave her directions to Chandlers Lodge and the home telephone number, then sat back and told himself 'now you've got to tell Rose'. At this thought he had a few misgivings. Would Rose get the wrong idea? Come to that, was he getting the wrong idea? Oh, stop worrying silly sod; it'll all work itself out.

Margaret arrived at lunchtime the next day, Friday, introducing herself to Rose, and reiterating her sincere thanks for their kindness in having her for the weekend. Little Jeremy was standing behind his mother as she welcomed their visitor on the front porch, clutching her skirt and peeking around at this stranger.

"You must be Jeremy. I've heard all about you. Your grandfather tells me you're a little rascal," she said with a smile.

Jeremy thought for a moment or two.

"Are you a Canadian?"

"No. I'm an American."

Jeremy thought a little more.

"Uncle Alec says an American is like a Canadian but not as clever."

"Oh does he? I shall have to have a word with Uncle Alec."

"I am afraid," said Rose "that will not be possible. They have all been spirited away. Alec is a major in the Canadian forces who lived with us when they first came here in Christmas 1939. He and his friend Jim and their colonel, Tim, were great friends of ours, family almost. Jim and Tim were both killed at Dieppe."

They both suddenly realised they were still out under the porch and moved into the large hallway, Rose suggesting they went into the kitchen.

"Now this is what I call a kitchen," Margaret exclaimed. "I am billeted in a small flat in West London. You hardly have room to fill a kettle in that kitchen, and there are three of us to use it."

They chatted on, Rose taking to the newcomer more and more.

When Fred had arrived home the previous day and asked Rose if she would organise a room for a forty year old, or thereabouts, American officer, it was some little while before it transpired it was a 'lady' officer. She readily agreed. Like her mother before her, having guests was always a pleasure – well, nearly always, they had had one or two they wouldn't want to see again – but she reminded her father that Maria was coming for the weekend and Emma was coming up on Saturday for the night.

"I thought we might have a few people in on Saturday to meet Margaret," he had replied. Immediately Rose's antennae started to vibrate. Margaret? Since when did her father call recently encountered people, especially ladies, by their Christian name? Why, he has known Gladys Russell, his secretary for years, and he still calls her Miss Russell. Interesting.

When Margaret had consumed the inevitable cup of tea in the kitchen she told Rose "Oh, I told Fred I would raid our PX to see what I could find to help out with the food situation." Rose's antennae showed another blip. Fred eh?

"Oh, that was kind of you. I shall never forget my mother cutting off Dad's butter ration when the war started and showing it to him. It was roughly enough for two pieces of toast on a Sunday morning, full stop! He said then he would never survive – that was more than four years ago."

"I think you are all marvellous the way you have endured all this, the food, the bombing, the blackout." She paused for a moment.

"Well I am afraid butter wasn't on the availability list, so I shall not be able to bring a smile to his face in that respect. I'll get my overnight bag and the goodies I could lay my hands on." Standing up she added, "By the way, it is most remiss of me. I have not asked you when your baby is due."

"Maria, my sister-in-law, and I are due more or less at the same time, at the end of July. She will be here at any minute for the weekend, and another friend Emma, will be here tomorrow to stay overnight. Father has asked some friends in on Saturday evening for you to meet. They are nice people, I'm sure you will like them."

Margaret disappeared to the car, returning with a canvas grip and a largish box tied with string which, by the way she was carrying it, was of no mean weight. She put the grip down and lifted the box on to the large deal table using both hands. Rose produced scissors and cut the string, carefully rolling it up for re-use. You wasted absolutely nothing in wartime.

The first item from the box was a round tin of cheese. 'Six people's rations for a month' as Rose described it later. Next came powdered egg, a large tin of peaches, two tins of Canadian salmon, a large tin of ham and last but by no means least, a large, sealed, tin of coffee.

"My word, how did you get all this?" asked an overwhelmed Rose.

"That's not all," was the reply, as she dived into her holdall and produced a large slab of chocolate for a wide-eyed Jeremy, and three pairs of nylons for an even wider-eyed Rose. Margaret explained.

"We live out, so we are entitled to draw certain items for use in our quarters, although we take our meals in the main building. The PX is normally for families of serving personnel, but they of course are few nowadays."

"Well, I know what my dad will say – invite the lady every week!" They both laughed.

Actually she was quite near to the truth.

The Saturday evening went with a swing. As usual at nine o'clock everything stopped to hear the news, the main item of which was that Ernie Bevin had issued new Defence Regulations which included five years' penal servitude for inciting strikes or lock-outs. The previous coalminers strikes had affected three million people in the gas, shipbuilding and engineering industries. That could not be allowed to happen again.

During the evening Margaret met Megan, Anni, Jack and Moira, and all the extended Chandler family. Soon after 10.30 Greta and young John Power arrived from the hop, and were introduced. Jack came over to the little group, put his arm around John's shoulders and asked, "Well, how's life in the depths of Kent these days John."

Greta answered first. "John's got a new job now, he's a loader."

"And what may I ask does a loader do?" asked Jack, adding for Margaret's benefit, "Our John here is what is known as a Bevin boy. Instead of being drafted into the forces he has been incarcerated in one of our coal mines, and doing a marvellous job I hasten to add. Without the coal there would be no munitions, without munitions Hitler would walk over us. So what's this new job then John?"

"Well, a loader extracts the coal from behind the collier and loads it on to the conveyor." He went on to explain.

"If you imagine a wall say eight feet high, the bottom half of which is the seam of coal the upper half is rock. The collier works at that seam tunnelling under the rock. He has what is called a stint, say 12 yards long, where another collier joins up with him on either side. As he pickaxes the coal away the loader, with a spade shaped shovel, loads the coal on to the conveyor which takes it to the main gate where it automatically is discharged into tubs."

By now all the gathering were clustered around a somewhat embarrassed John Power.

"I say, this must be terribly boring," he spluttered, "after all, it's only a glorified way of labouring."

"You carry on John old son, you're showing us another world," Jack assured him.

"Well, I also help to collect the props and bars from the main gate to wedge under the rock roof."

"So does the collier have to work in four feet of height to get the coal out?" asked Margaret, who had been fascinated by the story from this very nice looking young man.

"Yes ma'am, we both do as he progresses into the seam. Sometimes the seams are smaller and then the collier has almost to lie down to get at it. The problem where we are at the moment is that it is very wet, so we are working with no clothes on except boots and helmet because of the excessive heat, and constantly walking or kneeling in water." He stopped for a moment, then continued, "Not that you would recognise it as water since it is like a pitch black slurry."

Fred broke in. "So he digs the coal and you shovel it on to the conveyor. How much do you have to extract, or whatever you call it, in a shift?"

"We are on piecework. We have to shift four tons to make money, but we only have about five and a half hours out of the eight hour shift to actually coal. We have a two thousand yard walk to the coalface and back again from pit bottom. Timber to shaft, cut and install. Sometimes the coal is so hard they have to use explosives on it to start it off. That all takes time."

"Well, I think you're a bloody hero, and that's a fact," Fred told him, "now, come and have a drink, I expect you need it after steering this young lady around the dance floor all the evening and then entertaining our curiosity." There was a chorus of 'here, here's' as John, his arm securely held by an extremely proprietary young Greta, was led off to the Whitbread's Light Ale dispensing department, namely the kitchen table, groaning it seemed under the weight of innumerable quart flagons. Actually the weight was not all that considerable, since the majority of them would appear to be empty.

The party over, Fred, Rose, Anni, Maria and Margaret sat around the deal table, drinking cups of real coffee for the first time in a very long time, for which they each thanked their very welcome guest.

"It is my place to thank you all," Margaret replied. "It is so many years since I had a real family evening. I have been to parties of course, usually where a fair proportion of those present are bent as fast as possible on getting, what do you call it, three sheets in the wind. The remainder usually saying how many deals they have done and the amount of money they have made. Tonight, you were all one big family, nobody showing off, it was really great." They all smiled at her, Rose took her hand.

"You must come again," she said.

"What also struck me," she continued, "and I hope I am not reviving past sadnesses, but so many of you since the war have suffered so much. Rose, David, Megan at being without Harry, Anni and Karl, poor Cecely and Greta without Mr Coates, Mrs Treharne's great loss and Sir Jack and Lady Moira. You all act so bravely. It is so unfair." Her eyes misted over. "I'm sorry, I really am."

"Just shows what a jolly nice person you are" Fred assured her. "We shall never forget all those you mentioned, just as we keep Ruth in our thoughts all the time. She was the rock we all clung to. Now, I don't know about you lot, but I've got to be on parade in the morning, so I'm off to bed." He got up, made the rounds of the table kissing each and everyone goodnight, including Margaret, checked the front and back doors and made his way aloft. The others sat for a while, chatting away, Emma telling them of the recent shelling at Deal and of the two big guns there which pounded the French coast and German shipping passing through. Emma's two favourite spots, The Park Tavern, and Deal Library just opposite, were demolished by shellfire earlier in the year. On one day in March, forty-four shells had hit Deal, shells from very heavy guns indeed being fired from twenty-five miles away and more.

On Sunday morning Fred was having his breakfast in the kitchen when Margaret came down accompanied, hand in hand, with young Jeremy, still in his pyjamas.

"I've had a visitor," she announced.

"Good morning Margaret, did you sleep well? He didn't wake you up did he?"

"To answer your questions, yes, I slept very, very well thank you, and no, he didn't wake me up, I'm usually an early riser anyway."

"Well, excuse my being in my shirt sleeves; I didn't expect you to be about yet. Hang on a minute and I will get you some coffee."

"Look, I know you have to get away. I can look after myself, honestly I can."

As she spoke Rose arrived. "So there you are you rascal. Did he wake you Margaret? No, you are dressed, so he couldn't have done."

Fred finished his breakfast, swallowed the remainder of his mug of tea, and announced he must be off. He went into the sitting room to collect his battledress blouse, and was putting it on as he returned to the kitchen.

"Where did I put my cap?" he asked of the world in general.

As he turned Margaret spied the two rows of ribbons above his left breast-pocket.

"Fred, you didn't tell me you had been a solider," she began, "and I know already that the British Army does not throw medals at everybody as we seem to do. I know of one lieutenant colonel in our HQ with three rows who has never experienced the front end of a bullet in all his life. For that matter, not even heard one being fired. Tell me, what are they?"

"He won't tell you, but I will," Rose declared, "starting from here, this is the Officer of the Order of the British Empire, we call it the OBE, next is the Military Medal, which Dad won in the trenches when he led an attack by his company after all the officers had been killed. The next one is for the campaign on the North West Frontier in 1898, the next two being the Queen's and King's medals for the war in South Africa against the Boers. After that is the 1914 star, the rosette on it is known as the Mons decoration, then the British War Medal and Victory Medal 1918. These latter three became known as Pip, Squeak, and Wilfred, after famous comic characters. The oak leaf on the Victory Medal shows he was 'Mentioned in Despatches' for gallantry. Now, have I made any mistakes Dad?"

"No, you are about right I reckon."

Margaret was open-mouthed at all this.

"But if someone passed you in the street they wouldn't know what an extraordinary man you are, would they?"

"And if you two don't stop mucking me about I shall be very un-extraordinary when I am cashiered for being late on parade. See you tonight," and with that he put his cap on, picked up his stick and was gone.

The two ladies stood smiling at each other until Rose said, "What would you like to do today?" adding, "We all usually go to church, but we could go out somewhere."

"No, I'd love to go to church with you. Tell me about the building; it looks very old from the little I've seen of it."

With Maria and Emma joining them, they had a really chatty hen party over breakfast after which they all sat and read the papers until it was time to walk to St Johns for Matins.

As they left the church Canon Rosser stood at the west door shaking hands with his parishioners and in particular the few servicemen left locally who had become regular attenders. As Rose and her little party approached, he picked young Jeremy up and said, "I didn't hear a squeak out of you today, what happened?"

Jeremy looked at him solemnly.

"Mummy told me I had to be good today and not show up Auntie Margaret."

"Who's Auntie Margaret?" Jeremy pointed her out. Rose introduced her as being an American major – she had been wearing civilian clothes all over the weekend. After the usual courtesies Margaret stated, more as a question than as a fact.

"The church is very old, it makes you feel very humble when you think of all the people who have worshipped here over the centuries."

"The chancel end and part of the nave are 12th century, the remainder 16th. However there was a church here, the foundations of which you can see at the east end, in Saxon times, so the people you refer to go back well over a thousand years. Kent of course was probably the first part of England to become Christian. Have you been to Canterbury yet?"

"No, I only arrived in England a few weeks ago and have seen very little yet."

"Then you must come again. There is so much to see, once they let us see it that is." The Canon was, of course, referring to present travel restrictions in force all around the coast.

Fred saw Margaret off on Monday morning. She thanked him profusely for a wonderful weekend with such nice friendly people.

"Perhaps you would care to come and stay again in a week or two?"

"I would love to do that."

Fred left for work wondering what he could possibly concoct in the way of a reason for succeeding in that eventuality.

Chapter Sixteen

On 25th May 1944 David and his men said goodbye to Bulford knowing that for some it would be the last time they would ever see it. They were, nevertheless, in excellent spirits, as was evidenced by the extremely unmilitary display of balloons attached to the TCV's in which they were riding. This display however soon attracted the attention of the padre, who complained to the adjutant, with whom he was travelling, that the balloons were in fact blown-up French letters, this spectacle being in his view, most unseemly. The adjutant grinned, promised to have them removed at the first stop, then promptly forgot all about it.

The journey to the transit camp, although only some seventy odd miles, took five hours, their long crocodile of vehicles having to negotiate numerous points where other similar crocodiles were trying to cross their path, to say nothing of the complete chaos at several roundabouts. The military police endeavoured to keep everything moving but inevitably convoys got broken up, those leading having to wait for the detached units to catch up again. At least the weather was fair, so that when they did eventually arrive, to find themselves in a tented enclosure surrounded by masses of barbed wire entanglements, they were not up to their knees in mud.

An advance party had been sent the day before which speedily conducted the various companies to their sectors and within an hour of arriving every man had a bed and blankets, things they would undoubtedly miss in the not too distant future.

Over the next few days the officers, the NCO's and the men were taken in groups into a large marquee to view a sand table of the divisional objective. Having had the bigger picture explained to them each soldier was given a one to one three hour briefing later in the week on the exact part he and his platoon were to play in the operation. It would be fair to say that never before had the individual fighting man been brought into the picture in such detail as he was on Operation Overlord, which was the code name given to the invasion. After the intensive preparation he would know exactly where he had to go, what he had to do, and if he was dropped wide how to get to his rendezvous to rejoin his comrades. Dropping paratroops is a somewhat inexact science as everyone knew from General Gale downwards.

There was inevitably a good deal of waiting around, although they were visited by General Montgomery and by their own general. On the morning of the 3rd June they all assembled in full fighting trim to go to the airfield near Gloucester for take off. David looked up at the scudding clouds and remarked to Paddy, "If it's like this over there we are in for a rough landing."

"And well spread out too I shouldn't wonder," was Paddy's lugubrious reply.

In the event, because of the weather, D Day was put back for twenty four hours, the men slept on the airfield and on the evening of the 5th, with the wind still stronger than David would have liked, they emplaned, twenty to an aircraft, on the giant Stirling bombers newly converted for paratroop use. At half an hour before midnight their plane started to roll towards the end of the runway. The noise of these thirty odd, four engined monsters lining up to carry 'R' Battalion to battle was incredible. Many men said a little prayer for the first time since they had been in Sunday school, many were smiling excitedly; many were thinking 'what the hell did I volunteer for this lot for!' David looked at Angus, his batman, and in the dim light read the calm indication on his face of a well-trained soldier prepared for whatever may present itself. From him he looked across to Paddy seated opposite, who despite the noise, and the fact that he was seated only six feet from the hole, had leaned his head back and appeared to be having forty winks. David laughed inwardly – 'what a man' he thought.

He felt for the reassuring bump on his chest, beneath his jumping smock, of his mascot. Cedric was a golliwog which his wife had given him before they were married when he first went to Ringway for his parachute training. Since then Cedric had accompanied him on all his training jumps, exercises, and operations. He smiled to himself at the thought of this talisman now to exert its magic power and keep him safe, a keepsake his darling Maria had held close to her during innumerable nights when she was a child, and from which she would never be parted.

His retrospection was halted by the sudden 180 degree turning of the aircraft, an immediate increase in the already deafening noise of the engines and a jolt as the machine moved forward for its seemingly endless take-off. At last it lifted its mighty body off the ground. Next stop France.

David looked across the fuselage. Paddy was still having a doze.

The flight lasted just over an hour before the order came to hook up.

David was to jump number one, Angus number two, Paddy number three. They stood up, hooked their static lines on to the wire secured on the upper side of the fuselage, each man checking the man in front of him to see it was properly secured. They waited for the red light to come on which indicated they had twenty seconds before they were to trust their lives to a few square yards of nylon, but before that was to take place they were welcomed by a most unfriendly barrage of anti aircraft fire intermixed with streams of light machine gun tracer drifting up towards them, clearly visible by those near the hole. At only eight hundred feet altitude the shape of their Stirling could be clearly seen by the coastal batteries over which they were now flying. Fortunately the aim of these gentlemen would appear to be in the main, somewhat below marksman level.

In the middle of this short burst of unwelcome hostility the red light went on. David stood at the hole, Angus and Paddy hard up behind him intent on getting as close to him as possible when they were eventually on terra firma. They were to be followed by company headquarters and a section of Jimmy James's platoon, Jimmy being the last one to jump.

Green light on!

Away they went. Superbly trained they moved swiftly down the fuselage – number ten, number eleven, until just as number sixteen went through the hole an anti-aircraft shell hit the port wing of the Stirling and at the slow speed at which it was travelling, tilted it enough to send Jimmy James and his last three men reeling against the starboard side of the fuselage. Swiftly they sorted themselves out and away they went. However in the three quarters of a minute they had taken to pick themselves up and get into jumping order again the aircraft had cleared the drop zone and they were to land far from the place indicated on the sand table at their briefing in the transit camp.

David and Paddy were each carrying a dinghy strapped to their leg. As soon as they were airborne they pulled the quick release gear and lowered the kitbag in which it was carried until it swung about twenty feet below them on the end of its rope. They then took stock of the place at which they were to land. To David's horror he appeared to be coming down into a lake, a very large lake at that. No amount of juggling with his parachute rigging was going to steer him away from it, but before he could put into operation the drill for landing in water, it rushed up to meet him and he found himself rolling over in about two feet of very smelly liquid which he immediately realised was an area the Germans had flooded. From his concentrated study of the sand table he immediately knew that this would be land near the River Dives, in which case they had been dropped at least six miles from their rendezvous point and the river and canal they were supposed to cross.

Coughing and spluttering he shed his parachute, collected his kitbag and looked around for other signs of life. The water, polluted by centuries of cow droppings in these meadows, poured out of his sleeves and slopped around his knees. He was quite unhappy, until his spirits were given a boost by his seeing the unmistakable frame of Paddy moving towards him accompanied by Angus and three men from Jimmy James's early numbers.

"Where the bloody hell are we sir?" were Paddy's first words.

"I reckon we must be on the western bank of the River Dives," David replied. "We'll hang about here for a few minutes to see if any others turn up, then make our way to where we should be."

"How far do you reckon sir?"

"Five or six miles. If you look in that direction," he pointed westwards, "you can just see trees on the horizon, so this flooding can't last for ever."

They waited for about five minutes during which two more men from the stick found them; then David decided to move off. They had only covered some twenty or thirty yards, David leading, sloshing through the water knee deep, in a couple of parts up to their thighs, when suddenly David found himself slipping down an underwater bank and was up to his waist before Paddy grabbed his shoulder webbing and held on to him.

"Get hold of his pack," he ordered Angus.

Angus swiftly slung his Sten gun over his shoulders and got two hands under his major's pack and between them they pulled David out of what was obviously a dyke. Had he been on his own he would have gone fully in and heavily laden as he was would have drowned. This was in fact the fate of so many men dropped wide, in some cases their bodies never ever having been found.

"Bloody hell Paddy," David said, "that's one I owe you."

"That's one less I owe you, you mean, sir, so it is."

"Right, let's get a dinghy inflated."

Swiftly Paddy took the cover off the one he was carrying, pulled the D-ring and in seconds the inflatable was ready. A post was sticking up out of the water some twenty yards away. "See if you can pull that out," David ordered one of the party. The man splashed his way back, grabbed the top of the post but had no luck in removing it. Another of the party hurried back to him and between them bent the post one way, then the other until with a muffled 'snap' it came away. They took it back to the officer.

"Now, if you hold the dinghy so that I don't tip it up, I'll get in and paddle it across the dyke until I can feel hard ground again with this pole. Then we will ferry you over one by one."

It was strange that while all this was going on there was a deathly quiet all around them. To the west they could hear the odd rifle shot now and then, but nothing resembling a war. The noise, chaos, tracers, shell bursts and general pandemonium that had existed as they flew in seemed to have evaporated. Obviously the thousands of men who had been dropped were now all urgently trying to find their rendezvous points, they were far too occupied with that problem to start shooting at anything, except perhaps when they bumped a German patrol or outpost.

David rolled himself into the dinghy, laid the pole beside him and using his Sten gun handle as a paddle gradually moved himself generally in a westerly direction. After about six yards he plumbed the bottom with the pole – very carefully, the last thing he would want to do would be to capsize this not particularly stable example of aquatic conveyance! He did not reach bottom. He paddled three or four more yards, put the pole over and struck solid ground in less than two feet. Carefully he got out of the little craft, slipped, and ended up sitting up to his armpits in the water. He scrambled up, retrieved his Sten gun, and holding his rope, called quietly, "Right, come on over."

They swiftly, one by one, joined him until the small party of eight moved off again towards the ever welcoming trees ahead. They encountered one more dyke, which they successfully crossed, before they at last splashed out of the water on to dry land. They were all soaking wet, from top to toe, chilled to the bone, but glad to be out of that death trap. "Thank God we had a dinghy," one of the men exclaimed.

"Amen to that," added another.

"Right, let's get moving," David said, consulting his compass. After nearly an hour, steadily climbing, keeping in the cover of hedges as much as possible, and staying off roads, they came to the summit of the ridge they had been mounting. David took out his binoculars and having cleaned the eyepieces as best he could, scanned the country in front to try and get a fix on their position.

"Got it," he breathed.

Paddy nearby whispered, "Got what sir?"

"Ranville Church – separate spire – over there to the left. We should be at our RV in less than half an hour."

But things don't always go according to plan; in fact some soldiers will tell you that if they do go according to plan there's something wrong somewhere. At one point, they skirted a wood and were fired on from close range. They all flattened themselves, until David heard a distinct Brummie voice saying, "Did you get the bastards?" He immediately shouted back.

"Hold your fire you bloody idiots."

The noise of the firing obviously alerted a German patrol some three or four hundred yards away which commenced spraying David's immediate area with continuous bursts from their very lethal machine gun known as the MG42. The men hugged the ground as the bullets cracked over and around them. When the firing stopped, David called out, "Right run for it, make for the hedge."

Running, carrying some sixty to eighty pounds of equipment, is not exactly an expeditious activity. Nevertheless when an MG42 has you roughly in its sights it does give you a certain degree of encouragement, along with the fact that the above average effort produces a bonus to the drying out process.

They found their RV. Major Hamish Gillespie had been left there to marshal all the stragglers, the CO in the meantime having taken the first arrivals to their operational area.

"David, how great to see you. What happened?"

"We've been bathing in the river. It was quite refreshing but a trifle pongy."

"You don't have to tell me – I smelt you coming over the ridge."

"How many in from my company Hamish?"

"Only about thirty percent. Fifty per cent from A Company, about thirty from C. HQ Company seemed to have been dropped miles away. We've no mortars, no machine guns and only one usable wireless set."

"Is Jimmy James in?"

"No sign I'm afraid. Sandy and Miles are down there though. And you are the first company commander."

"What about the bridges?"

"They were taken by the Ox and Bucks without being blown."

"So we can throw these dinghies away?"

"You may. Now get on down over the bridges and the adjutant will book you in."

David, Paddy and Angus and the five from Jimmy James's platoon moved off at rifleman pace down the road. There was sporadic rifle fire in all directions indicating two things. One, there were Germans about in small numbers, two, nothing heavy in the form of tanks or artillery had yet appeared on the scene.

They crossed the river bridge where they met the adjutant.
"The CO is just this side of the canal bridge David. He will tell you what's what."
They broke into a double to cover the four hundred yards to the canal bridge.
"David, good to see you. And you Mister O'Riordan. I'm afraid we've got a bit of a mix-up at the moment. Your company is digging in about a quarter of a mile down the road towards Caen. 'A' company are digging in facing west, and what there is of 'C' Company is occupying the dwellings on the road to Ouistreham. However, the platoons are all mixed up; we will have a sort out later."
"Righto, sir, we'll get cracking."

They doubled off over the canal bridge, passing the bodies of several Germans who had been killed in the brief but superb action by the Oxfordshire and Buckinghamshire Light Infantry – the Ox and Bucks, old comrades of the Rifles David recalled from the Peninsular War days – who had crashed landed in their gliders only yards from their objective, a superb example of airmanship by their pilots of the Glider Pilot Regiment. In the dark they also spotted a small group of German prisoners of war seated in a small depression and being guarded by a regimental policeman.

As the small party reached what there was of 'B' Company they were met by Miles Rafferty.
"I've divided those we've got into two platoons," he rapidly told David. "Sandy is dug in on the edge of that orchard facing south west. The other platoon, or what there is of it, is covering the road with Sergeant Webb in charge."
"Right Miles. You go and take over there. As stragglers come in we will build a reserve platoon here under the sergeant major so as to be able to support either of you when you are attacked. They may come up the road from Caen or they may come over the fields, or both. Have either of

you got Piats?"

Piats were the only weapon parachute troops had with which to engage tanks – and even then their maximum range was around fifty yards.

"Yes, there are two on the road and one in the orchard. But there is a problem."

"What's that?"

"We've got hardly any projectiles to fire from them until the men arrive who are carrying them."

As they spoke mortar bombs came whistling in, landing in the orchard.

"I think we had better get prepared for at least a probing attack," David said. "Miles. Tell your people to hold their fire as much as possible. Keep Jerry guessing as to how many we are, and if they do try to rush us then give them everything we've got. How many Bren's have we got?"

"Four. Two with each group."

"Right. I'll reinforce you as soon as I can."

David looked at his watch. Despite its two soakings it was still working. It was just turned three o'clock. Making a quick calculation he arrived at the conclusion they must have made good time cross-country despite the water hazard.

There was a small two-up, two-down cottage a little ahead of where they were standing.

"We'll make that company headquarters," David indicated to Paddy. They moved on to occupy it, only to find it locked and bolted. David banged on the door. Nothing happened. They went round the back, same procedure. Nothing happened. He was just going to break a window to get in when they heard a movement inside, the bolts unbolted, and the door opened a fraction.

"We are English, we are the Liberation Army," he said in his somewhat basic French. The door was flung open and an elderly man in a long nightshirt grabbed his hand and kissed it repeatedly. It occurred to David afterwards, it could not have tasted particularly agreeable in view of the liquid into which it had been repeatedly plunged only an hour or so ago.

"We must take over your house. We are expecting the Boche to attack at any minute."

"You must do what you have to do. My wife and my two daughters are in the cellar. We will stay there. God Bless You. Vive la France." He turned and disappeared down a steep flight of stairs pulling the trap door down behind him.

David and Paddy, closely followed by Angus made their way upstairs to a window in one of the two bedrooms which looked out on to both of the platoon positions. He told Angus to run back to the CO and tell him where his company headquarters were, and ask him to let them have more Piat projectiles as a matter of urgency. This would not be the only run Angus would make in the next few hours, during which time he was hit no fewer than three times, all wounds dressed by the company medics, since he refused to be evacuated to the field ambulance.

It was still very dark. Faintly they could hear the noise of tanks in the distance.

"They won't use those in the dark," David suggested to Paddy, "they're probably moving them down the road towards us behind an infantry screen. You stay here; I'm going down to have a look at Miles and Sandy's defences." As they spoke four more men arrived, one with two cases of Piat projectiles.

"You come with me," David told him, "you three stay here with the sergeant major."

And so the long long day started.

As David and Angus, with the Piat man, made their way towards 4 platoon more mortar bombs rained in. They dived into the ditch at the side of the road, which fortunately was dry, or nearly so. When the short deluge ceased they continued to Miles's platoon HQ, situated in slit trenches at the top of the bank looking down the Caen road.

"Brought you some more tank busters," David said, and to the carrier of same, "Take four out and give them to Angus." With that he added to Miles, "I'll take them over to Sandy."

He made a quick inspection of Miles's layout then made his way to Sandy. Satisfied with the defensive positions the two platoon commanders had created, he made his way back to company HQ to find another four men had arrived. By dawn they were up to fifty percent strength, but still no Jimmy James nor the company second in command, Captain Rogers. We know now what happened to Jimmy, but Rogers's body, along with numbers seventeen and eighteen in Jimmy's stick were never found. They almost certainly ended up in the River Dives and sank like stones, as did so many on that night.

As dawn broke, all hell was let loose. Two Mark IV panzers appeared some six hundred yards down the straight road from Miles's position and commenced loosing off with both canon and machine gun. They were firing blind, making a lot of noise but doing no appreciable damage other than to one or two houses and outhouses as the men sat out the storm in the bottom of their slit trenches. Over on the right Sandy could see considerable movement behind a hedgerow two hundred yards away, followed by some fifty men breaking through to come towards 5 platoon in the orchard. Sandy's men were well concealed. He softly called, "Hold your fire until I give the word." He allowed the long line to get within fifty yards then gave the order. The two Brens opened up, the riflemen chose their targets and in seconds half the attacking force was wiped out. Some that were not hit threw smoke grenades to cover their retreat, but the resultant screen was not dense enough to be of real help. Few made it back to the hedgerow.

5 platoon paid for their first victory. In a quarter of an hour the orchard was deluged with mortar fire, some bombs exploding in the trees and causing two deaths and two serious injuries to the men sheltering in their slit trenches. Sandy, keeping as low a profile as possible, kept a careful watch of the hedgerow through his field glasses to ensure another attack was not being set up under the cover of the bombardment. When the let-up came, the two wounded men were evacuated to company HQ to be patched up by a battalion medic before being sent off down to the casualty clearing station, when it could be arranged.

The tanks in front of Miles's defences, receiving no reply to their exhibition of force concluded there were no anti-tank guns ahead of them so they started to move forward. Tanks are stomach churning, incredibly menacing objects to have to face. However they themselves when in action are extremely vulnerable in that they are almost blind. A high bank ran down the road on the canal side. When they had approached to some two hundred yards from Miles's position and halted, still not receiving any welcome from the enemy they believed to be ahead of them, Corporal Tug Wilson, in charge of the left hand section decided he would pay them a visit. He had two 'gammon' bombs, which nearly all parachutists carried. With two men from his section he slid down the bank and, doubled up, the posture soldiers of all armies seem to adopt when moving towards the enemy, or the imagined enemy, moved quickly along through low bushes, when they were level with the two tanks, they crawled up the bank.

The first tank had no idea what hit it. Tug lobbed the gammon bomb – two pounds of plastic explosive which detonated on impact – on to the air intake behind the turret. Immediately after the explosion a sheet of flame emerged followed by the exit hatches being thrown open and the attempted rapid evacuation by the crew. Whilst they were being despatched by Tug's two comrades, at that short range aided by the light from the blaze they could hardly miss, Tug quickly moved to the second tank a few yards behind. The driver must have been waiting to move, since the minute he saw the tank in front 'brew up' he moved into gear, locked one track and swung his twenty tons round so as to make a hasty retreat. As Tug threw his second gammon the panzer's side was exposed to him. The bomb hit the upper track, promptly blew it off, as a result, the engine being at full throttle, the whole tank rotated on its good track, the tank commander immediately realising what had happened, giving the order to bale out. Again as they emerged Tug's men dealt with them.

"Come on, let's get out of here."

They slid down into the bushes and ran back towards their platoon post before the surprised German infantry, who had taken cover as soon as the first tank caught fire, started to fire wildly after them. It was at this point their luck ran out. Jock Thompson running just ahead and to the right of the corporal, suddenly gave a cry, staggered on two or three more paces and fell forward face downwards. Tug stopped, turned him over to find half his face missing, the bullet having hit him in the back of the neck and gone right through.

"We'll come back for you son," Tug assured his lifeless comrade, running for his life through a hail of bullets to regain his slit trench.

David had kept his binoculars glued on the two tanks, wondering why it was they had stopped where they had when they could have motored through 'B' Company's defences if they had moved quickly enough. He gave a shout of surprise, which had Paddy running to him, as he saw the first one go up in flames.

"What happened sir?"

"I don't know. I saw this arm come up and throw something. The next second all hell seemed to be let loose."

Paddy surveyed the scene through his field glasses.

"They've done the second one sir, look, so they have. I wonder who it is. By God whoever it is has got some guts."

"I remember seeing you do a similar thing in Yugoslavia, as I recall."

Paddy looked at him.

"I was young and stupid then."

"It was only two years ago."

"Bloody hell, it seems like twenty sir. I reckon whoever has done that deserves a gallantry award."

"Let's keep it on the record; we may have many more examples before we're much older."

As they still kept the tank area under observation, a runner from Sandy's platoon arrived, breathless and sporting a neat bullet hole through the edge of his steel helmet where a sniper had just failed to blow his brains out.

"Mr Patterson says there's a force of about eighty moving around behind you sir, and they've put several snipers up into those trees over to the right of our position. Range about two hundred yards. One of them nearly got me as I left our orchard."

"Right, well done Rawson. Get back to Mr Patterson and take care."

"You can be sure of that sir." David grinned at him.

"Sergeant major!" Paddy came running back into the room. "Will you organise 6 platoon to about face – it looks as though they are trying to get behind us." Paddy clattered back down the stairs to reposition his defences. As he left the doorway a bullet cracked past his ear and splintered a chunk out of the door frame. The enemy snipers were getting serious. He ran the fifty yards to 6 platoon area and got them facing the expected direction of the enemy attack. They were well dug in, by now had three Bren guns, and were more than ready. Having carried this out, he gave thought to where the sniper might be. From Mr Patterson's information, the line of flight of the bullet which missed him and subsequently hit the door post, he judged the only place the sniper, or snipers, could be was in two heavily leaved trees some two hundred yards away. He jumped into the slit trench containing one of the Bren guns.

"Get ready with another magazine lad," he ordered the young number two on the gun. He put 200 on his sights and aimed at the centre of the left hand tree. The number two, observing the strike, called, "Up fifty sir." He raised his sights, and put three bursts into the left hand tree, re-aligned the gun on to the right hand tree and put another three bursts into that one. Nothing happened. 'Perhaps he's higher up', he said to himself, and put the remainder of the magazine, in short bursts, further towards the top.

"You got the bastard sir," yelled the number two, as they watched the body slowly drop from branch to branch until it lay spreadeagled on a fork about ten feet from the ground.

Their animation was short-lived as almost immediately mortar bombs started to rain in on their position, accompanied by a new ordeal to initially frighten the life out of the recipients keeping their heads down in the slit trenches. There was a succession of screaming noises followed immediately by the same sorts of explosions to which they were rapidly becoming accustomed.

Some of the mortar bombs dropped beyond 6 platoon's position landing in the cottage garden, subsequently to hit firstly an outhouse, which had its roof removed to reveal a somewhat basic bucket type lavatory, then to score a direct hit on the cottage chimney. The chimney in turn fell through the roof, then through the ceiling of the room from which David was currently enjoying a birds-eye view of the residents thunderbox, a heavy piece of chimney pipe flying off as it hit the bedroom floor, gashing David's leg quite severely. His immediate thoughts were...

"How did you get your wound major?"

"I was savaged by a rampaging chimney pot?"

Angus ran in from downstairs.

"You all right sir?" David took one of his bandages out of his field-dressing pocket.

"Put this on will you?"

Angus quickly cut the trouser leg and bound the wound. "You'll have to have some stitches in that sir, and a good dollop of antiseptic I reckon." As he spoke another salvo of mortar bombs dropped in, this time killing two men with a direct hit on their slit trench.

The two young officers, and Paddy guarding the rear of the position were all warning their men that the mortar attack was the precursor to an attack by enemy infantry. David's suspicion was that the Germans were trying to get in behind them, thereby surrounding his small force pinning them against the canal so that they had nowhere to retreat.

A final, furious shower of screamers, later to be known as 'Moaning Minnies' deluged the position. There was then a complete silence.

"Watch your front." Paddy's stentorian voice sounded all over the company position. 'B' Company waited for the onslaught. They had not long to wait. The attack had obviously been well co-ordinated, particularly since whoever had planned it had had little time to either establish the strength or the location of the forces he was attempting to wipe out. The paras too were very well trained. Platoon commanders and section NCO's all automatically ordered, "Hold you fire until you get the order." The force on the road from Caen started leapfrogging through the trees and bushes towards Miles platoon. On the western side they had put smoke down behind which to attack across the open ground against Sandy's defences on the edge of the orchard. On the north side, again behind smoke, they were moving rapidly against Paddy.

The attackers lost a lot of men. The paras were well dug in, had sited their Bren guns professionally, and the riflemen were all class one shots. The two groups emerging through the smoke suddenly found that although it had concealed them in their first approach, they were now silhouetted against it. They tried to make themselves as small as possible by adopting the usual doubled up position as they charged, a few getting into Paddy's position where they were speedily despatched, in two cases by the use of the paratroopers fighting knives.

No one got close to Sandy's defences. He had a much better field of fire than the other two platoons. As soon as they burst through the smoke the attackers realised they still had fifty metres of totally open ground to cover, promptly therefore turning back. Few of them made it.

The attackers on Miles's front were more fortunate. As they had a good deal of cover they gradually got close to 4 platoon slit trenches, and from behind a bank began to lob the famous 'potato masher' stick grenades on to the defenders. They came in thick and fast. David, from his elevated position in the bedroom immediately realised the danger. Several men were already casualties.
"Angus, get the sergeant major."
Angus ran out of the cottage towards 6 platoon position calling, "sir, the major wants you."
With the last shots being fired in his sector Paddy told a sergeant to take over and doubled in to company HQ.
"What's up sir?"
"It looks as though they are going to rush Mr Rafferty. Get your men turned about ready to counter-attack them if they do will you. Go in with the bayonet. I will fire a Very flare for you to go."
"Right sir." Paddy ran back to his platoon.
"Sergeant Bright. Stay here with three men and face the way you are. The rest of you, fix bayonets and follow me." They moved on to the shelter of the cottage.

As David had suspected the stick grenades ceased being delivered, a couple of phosphorous bombs were lobbed, from behind which a mass of some thirty Schmeisser and rifle bearing troops charged against Miles defences. From his vantage point David saw his men cutting down the attackers, but still they came on. He saw Miles Rafferty standing fully upright calmly sighting his revolver and shooting three of the attackers until a burst of Schmeisser fire nearly cut him in half, at which point the slit trenches were overrun. He fired the Very pistol. Paddy yelled,
"At 'em."

Firing from the hip they rushed at the enemy, half of whom immediately turned and ran, the other half putting up a fight until they were gradually eliminated. 'B' Company had held their position, but had sustained serious losses.

It was still only a quarter to seven on the morning of the sixth of June.

"Get a strength return as soon as you can sergeant major," David asked. He knew that his original maximum when the last stragglers had arrived was sixty-eight, including himself and Angus. When Paddy returned some ten minutes later having been targeted by snipers on three separate occasions he gave David the figures.

"Mr Rafferty is dead. Corporal Wilson is in charge of 4 platoon. He has only got ten men. Mr Patterson in 5 platoon has two sergeants and eleven men. I've asked him to send Sergeant Holbrook over to take charge of 4 platoon – is that alright sir?"

"Yes, excellent idea. Holbrook is a good solid chap."

"Ex-regular rifleman sir, bound to be."

David grinned.

"My little lot – and didn't they go in at those bastards sir – God, I was proud of them. My little lot comes to three NCOs and nine men. Total for the company thirty-nine, including us. All the wounded are in the rooms downstairs being looked after by the medic and being helped by one of the daughters who has had nursing experience. She's not a bad looking piece of crackling either sir, so she is. How's your leg sir?"

"Hurts like hell. Perhaps the nurse ought to come and look at it." It was Paddy's turn to grin.

Both David and Paddy were giving their watches more than usual attention, a movement interrupted by the sound of heavy tanks moving up the road from Caen. They ran to the window and through their glasses saw three Tigers halted about half a mile away.

"Christ, I hope we haven't got to face them," exclaimed David, "even a Piat head-on wouldn't stop one of those."

"They are not moving sir," Paddy observed. "They seem to be having some sort of 'O' Group."

Having forgotten their watches momentarily they heard the long awaited thunder, scheduled for seven o'clock, of the big guns from the British and American warships which would herald the initial attack on the defences on the 'D' Day beaches. Even at that distance it was frightening.

"Jesus, but I wouldn't like to be on the receiving end of that lot,"

Paddy exclaimed. He took another look at the panzers.

"They are getting back in sir. They're turning round. They're not coming at us at all."

"I reckon they've been ordered to the beaches and are going to by-pass us. After all, they don't know our strength."

"Bloody good job they don't sir."

For the next hour the company, or what there was of it, was continually sniped. There was ample cover at a distance all around their position from which snipers had the advantage of being on higher ground than David's reducing force dug in by the canal. Just after eight o'clock another attack was made on Sandy's front, again beaten off after which the mortars rained in once more.

"What time are the commandos supposed to get here sir?" Angus asked.

"Midday. They will be the first to land along with some French commandos and take Ouistreham, then push on here." He paused for a moment. "I hope our green-bereted friends don't stop for a drink or two on the way."

"What about the gliders sir, the ones with the anti-tank and field guns?"

"They start landing at 2100 hours I believe, along with the rest of the Ox and Bucks, the Devons and the RURs. Another brigade will certainly make all the difference to us. I think there is an anti-tank group with the battalions on the other side of the canal already, but whether they made it or not who can tell. There are none with us that's for certain."

At 7.30 the bombardment had suddenly terminated. The silence which ensued and the vibration of the earth having ceased cast a peculiar sense of isolation in David's small force. Even the birds had discontinued their chorus when the guns had opened up as if they too were in dread of this awful power, only to start up again a few minutes after the ceasefire. The men in the slit trenches had looked at each other in awe, each one trying to imagine what feelings of terror the German defenders must have been experiencing. Mortar bombs were bad enough but being plastered by sixteen inch shells was in a different league altogether.

The attack on Sandy's position at eight had shaken them out of their lethargy. When it had been beaten off and things seemed a little quieter, David decided to get to his three badly depleted platoons and see for himself how they were faring.

He and Angus were sniped several times as they made their way to the three platoon positions. They were very, very thin on the ground. If the Germans were to consolidate their attack instead of the piecemeal probes they had indulged in thus far it would be a walkover. They got back to the cottage, looked in on the wounded on the ground floor, where David thanked the young daughter for her help, in French which had not improved over the years. She smiled, realising what he was trying to say, he came to the conclusion she was definitely eight out of ten.

Back in the room upstairs he said to Angus, "Do you think you could get back to the battalion HQ at the bridge and tell the colonel the poor state we are in? If we are overrun, they would be in trouble."

"Leave it to me sir," replied Angus, and picking up his Sten he clattered off down the wooden stairs. He was winged on the way there, but he got there. The colonel had another twenty men, not all from 'B' Company, not all in fact from 'R' Battalion, but twenty stragglers who had come in since dawn, along with a young lieutenant from the Canadian battalion, who he instructed to fight their way down to Major Chandler and stay with him until after the commandos arrived. This they did. Angus leading them was winged again, as were two of the reinforcements. Apart from that they arrived safe and sound for David to get Paddy to split them up between the three positions.

It was still only ten minutes to nine.

Chapter Seventeen

On Saturday 25th May Rose, Maria and Emma each received a letter from their respective loved ones.

From then on – nothing. No letter, no telephone call – nothing.

On Saturday 25th May Megan received a letter from Harry, along with the drawings of Chantek all of which produced great excitement in the Chandler household.

And then a miracle.

On Saturday 25th May Cecely received a letter in an International Red Cross envelope from Nigel. It was dated September 1943. It comprised a single, very thin sheet of paper, written closely on both sides, saying they were being well treated and that he was well.

The reaction of the recipients of these communications, and subsequent lack of same, was predictable. From now on Rose, Maria and Emma would have that fear for the safety of their loved ones constantly gnawing at them, relieved only from time to time by having to concentrate on some specific task, or engage in conversation with others. The nighttime was the worst time. When they at last lay in bed, wondering what sort of dangers Mark, David or Charlie were facing, or were about to face, sleep, when it did come, came very slowly. Rose had experienced it all before when her beloved Jeremy had been sent to France in 1940. She had known the sickening experience of receiving that buff envelope with the dreaded telegram inside – 'The War Office regrets..'. She tried to console herself that her husband, being a major, would not be in the same danger as her Jeremy had been, he an NCO right in the front line. Common sense, however, told her that in modern warfare even generals were at risk. Her final decision was that she should think positively, her baby would be here in a couple of months, she must, for its sake, keep well and as happy as she possibly could.

But it was not easy.

Maria, being well cosseted by her mother and father, and without the trials Rose had endured, still had those moments when she was alone, and again at night, when she gave involuntary little sobs of distress at the not knowing. This was not new to her. Before they were married, when David had to go away on a mission, she had developed this little mannerism when she thought of him. She was on a bus at Chingford on one occasion when David was away, she knew not where. Thinking of him, and fearing for him, induced this little sob, resulting in a kindly lady on the other side of the aisle asking, "Are you alright dear?"

I suppose we all have our little idiosyncrasies.

Emma was perhaps a little luckier than the others, in that her day was mapped out for her, but she still had the nights to face. Again, once asleep she was not disturbed by would-be footballers or female kickboxers as were her two friends. That doesn't mean that her stomach didn't churn – it did – frequently.

Cecely's letter, having been read, re-read and read again, asked as many questions as it had answered. Nigel was alive in September of last year. Did that mean he was still alive? As the letter was nearly nine months old, what was Nigel's situation now? She took the news that he was being well-treated with a very large grain of salt – he would have to say that wouldn't he? or the swine would tear the letter up.

On the 4th of June the tension was alleviated to a small degree by the announcement that the Allies had captured Rome, another step forward on the path to find victory in Europe.

And then the greatest news of all.

'D' Day. 6th June 1944.

Winston Churchill announced that the biggest combined operation in the history of warfare had started on the coast of Normandy.

Hitler didn't believe him! He thought it was a feint! As a result panzer divisions looking towards the expected invasion in the Pas de Calais were left facing the wooden tanks that Sandbury Engineering and others had built, for two vital days before the Fuhrer would sanction their transfer to Normandy.

In the evening the King broadcast to the nation saying, "Four years ago our nation and empire stood alone against an overwhelming enemy, with our backs to the wall." He went on to describe this great enterprise unleashed today, ending, "We pray the Lord will give strength unto his people."

In the minds of all the Chandlers and their extended families there was a conflict of feelings. First the euphoria of the knowledge that this was to be the final round in the defeat of the barbaric Nazis. With this elation was the sobering thought that David, Mark and Charlie, along with Alec in the Canadian assault, would be in the forefront of the battle against a deeply entrenched formidable enemy. They waited with great anxiety.

As had happened repeatedly during the war, on the occasion of a great event, be it a disaster, a family affair, or a triumph to be celebrated, everyone gravitated to Chandlers Lodge. Conversation naturally comprised large chunks of the 'I wonder' variety. What little news coming from the conflict thus far was examined in great detail. It was obvious we were well established on shore already, it would be impossible, the opinion of all maintained, for us to be driven back into the sea. The enormous weight of our warships heavy guns seeking targets inland, our complete air superiority, all combined to give the feeling, 'Here we are, here we stay until we move forward'.

The next evening they all met again to be told on the nine o'clock news by Alvar Liddell (who as we have noted previously, had such a beautiful voice he could only tell the absolute truth) our advances inland were being maintained.

On the 8th of June came news that the 6th Airborne Division had been the unit to secure the bridges over the Orne river and canal and the eastern flank protecting the beach landings. There was no mention of casualties. They gathered together again that evening around the kitchen table in Chandlers Lodge. Jack stormed in just after nine o'clock, his face red with anger. Fred asked the inevitable.

"What's up Jack?"

"You know the Independent Labour Party had its conference today at Leeds?"

"Yes, it was announced on the wireless this morning."

"I've just heard what they've resolved. In the middle of the war, at a time when all our thoughts and prayers are with those fighting in Normandy and elsewhere they say they 'Condemn the war as an imperialistic struggle camouflaged as a struggle against fascism'." There were gasps of disbelief. He continued, "They demand that steps should be taken to appeal to the German workers to revolt to end the war." There was risible reaction to this proposal, emphasised by Fred remarking,

"Hitler would shoot the bloody lot."

"Finally – and can you believe this during a war? They demand full political and trade union rights for service men and women, increased pay, more leave, abolition of saluting and the total abolition of officers' messes."

The anger felt by them all at the beginning of Jack's report dissolved into laughter at the stupidity of wasting time making such farcical resolutions as the final one.

On the same day another gathering – The Cooperative Conference, a body of considerable influence in the Labour Party – called for the nationalising of the coal mines and the organisation of agriculture on cooperative lines as in Russia. The former did eventually come to pass; the latter would have been as big a disaster as it had proved to be in the Soviet Union.

On Friday morning 9th June, Fred received a telephone call soon after eight o'clock. As Gladys Russell did not arrive until nine o'clock, officially – she was always half an hour early – the call was fed straight through to his office.

"Fred, its Margaret. I wondered if you could come up to town and have dinner with me sometime over the weekend?"

"I'm terribly sorry Margaret. We have some people coming in on Saturday evening and I have a church parade on Sunday morning – a special one to celebrate the invasion. Having said that, what's wrong with your coming down here for the weekend if you are not already committed elsewhere?"

"It seems such an awful cheek to impose myself on you again."

"You, my dear young lady, would be as welcome as the flowers in May at any time. We would all love to see you again."

"Thanks for the young lady bit." They laughed together. "Can I then accept your kind offer? I'll raid the PX before I come. I shall have to come by train this time."

"Can you get the 4.12 from Victoria this afternoon? If so, I will meet you at Sandbury station in the Rover, and drop you back there first thing on Monday morning."

"Yes. I can make that. But are you sure that staying all that time will not put you out? Especially if you have guests on Saturday evening?"

"Good Lord no. It happens all the time!"

"Then I will look forward very much to seeing you this afternoon."

'Not half as much as I shall look forward to seeing you', Fred thought to himself.

Miss Russell appeared in the doorway.

"Can you get me Chandlers Lodge please Miss Russell?"

Duly put through Fred said to Rose, "We have a visitor for the weekend if you can arrange it, love." There was a trace of inveiglement hidden in the request.

"And who might that be?" 'As if I didn't know', Rose added to herself.

"The major who came before – you know, the American one."

"Oh yes, you mean Margaret of course, funny how you have forgotten her name already." The irony was not entirely lost on Fred. "And is she coming on business or on pleasure, and if on pleasure who is it she is particularly pleased to be meeting again?"

"She is coming down to see us all and because she loves the countryside here."

"Have you got that in writing?"

"Go and get your Mrs Stokes to get her bed ready and stop wasting my time." They replaced their respective telephones each smiling broadly.

Margaret was met off the first class section of the train by Fred with a handshake and a kiss on the cheek from an elegantly clad lady who immediately took his arm – the one which was not carrying what looked rather more than a weekend case. This little tableau, witnessed as it was by the wife of Canon Rosser and her friend Mrs Church, wife of Fred's accountant, caused them to look at each other with raised eyebrows, particularly as Fred, usually such an observant sort of fellow, didn't seem to notice they were only thirty yards away. When these two ladies returned from the pictures in Maidstone that evening they played out the little drama to their respective spouses, neither of whom evinced any surprise, the Canon saying, "I noticed when she was here before she seemed very tactile in respect of Fred."

"She's a lot younger than he is."

"You are a lot younger than I am."

"You've always got an answer." He smiled affectionately at her.

"It comes with the job."

Reg Church was intrigued by the embellished account given to him of the event. His wife Catherine, a pure romantic, could visualise only the advent of wedding bells, the relief of Fred's desolation at the death of his beloved Ruth by the kindness and devotion of his new partner, and the fact she was in on the idyll from the very beginning. Reg on the other hand, was scheming in his own tiny mind how they could get considerable mileage out of the situation in the form of pulling Fred's leg at Rotary. He asked, "How old is she?"

"Around the forty mark I should think."

"Bit young for Fred in that case isn't she?"

"Depends what she sees in him."

"What did you see in me?"

"I married you for your money."

"I didn't have any money."

"But I knew that all accountants end up with pots of money."

"Only Scottish ones."

She was unable to quite understand why that should be the case, although of course everyone knows it to be a fact.

On Saturday Fred took the day off, and with some movement restrictions now having been lifted, took Margaret, Rose and young Jeremy to Canterbury, mainly to see the cathedral. They lunched in The County Hotel, where curiously enough there were several American officers.

"What sort of unit do they belong to?" Fred asked.

"They are artillery men," she replied, "I would think probably first reserve for those already in Normandy." Since the three grown-ups were covertly regarding the Americans, Jeremy decided they must be of interest and promptly stared at them. At that, one of them, wearing the two silver bars of a captain, caught his eye, grinned at him, Jeremy waved, he waved back, this being repeated two or three times until the Captain got up and came over to their table.

"Good morning, or rather good afternoon" he said looking at his watch, "one o'clock, must be afternoon. I seem to have made a friend."

Fred in the meantime had stood up, but before he could say anything Jeremy had asked the inevitable question.

"Are you a Canadian?"

"No, I'm an American."

Before Rose could hush him up he followed up, as he had when he first met Margaret, with, "Uncle Alec says an American is like a Canadian but not as clever."

"Does he now, I shall have to have a word with your Uncle Alec."

"You can't, he's in ....." and there he was stumped, "where is he mummy?"

"He's in Normandy dear."

"Yes, that's right, Normandy, with the Canadians."

"Right. I'm Captain Artur Brodowski, everyone calls me Art." Fred, shaking hands, took over the introductions.

"This rascal is my grandson Jeremy, my daughter Rose Laurenson, this is Major Margaret Coulter a compatriot of yours, and I am Fred Chandler."

"Major, which branch are you in?"

"I am in Engineering Procurement."

"You are an engineer? That's unusual ma'am."

Fred chimed in, with some emphasis.

"Major Coulter is a very unusual person."

The captain laughed, the major smiled, the daughter analysed the remark and came to the conclusion that her father, as she had already suspected, if not enamoured of this extremely engaging lady was very close to being so. The suspicion nevertheless was tempered immediately by the thought that he was much older than she was, but then they were both intelligent enough to realise that.

After the usual 'where are you from' and so on, Art told them he and his two friends had visited the cathedral before having lunch.

"We are taking Margaret to see it after lunch," Fred informed him.

"Well, we are going to look around the town, so why don't we all meet back here for tea around four o'clock and have a chinwag as I believe you English call it?" He paused for a moment. "I've made a mistake, haven't I? Since there is a cathedral here, Canterbury is a city – right? not a town. I remember it said so in our do's and don'ts literature we were given when we arrived – you only call places with cathedrals 'city'. Back home a place with three hundred people and one bar often calls itself a city." They all laughed with this engaging young man, who had been joined by his two fellow captains.

Fred looked at his companions. They nodded in agreement.

"Right, four o'clock it is then. On one condition." They regarded him inquisitively. "As it is my county, and my city, I pay the bill."

They laughingly agreed, saying they would all have double portions on the strength of that remark.

The cathedral at Canterbury is almost hidden from the High Street. They left The County Hotel and took the narrow side street which runs to the cathedral. At one moment they were enclosed by the overhanging town buildings then without warning they debouched on to an open space with a full, glorious, awe inspiring view of this magnificent building. The suddenness of the transition made Margaret stop in her tracks and gasp in wonder. She had visited St Paul's and Westminster Abbey, but the approach to them had been gradual, as a result the impact was unhurried. At Canterbury the beauty was immediate, striking, spectacular even. She would never forget that moment.

Inside the vast building Rose indicated she was feeling a little tired, she, along with Maria, being now eight months pregnant. She suggested her father show Margaret around while she sat and waited for them.

"Come on then young man," Fred said to Jeremy, who immediately took his hand giving the other to Margaret. As they walked away, Jeremy chatting away to one, and then looking up at the other, doing a little skip every now and then, swinging on his supporters from time to time, Rose smiled, a smile which gradually faded as she thought of her husband, her two brothers, her dear friends Charlie and Alex, Kenny Barclay, the general even, all in so much danger while she was enjoying a pleasant day in a beautiful city.

Her fears were banished by the sight of young Jeremy loosing his grip on the hands he had been clasping and running towards her excitedly.

"Mummy, I saw the place where wicked men killed Tom – Tom – what was his name granddad?"

"Thomas à Beckett."

"Yes, that's right. Tommy Bucket." They all laughed. He continued, "They stabbed him and stabbed him until he was dead, mummy, wasn't that naughty?"

"It was very wicked dear, very wicked."

"Did they get caught?"

"I don't know dear, I shall have to look in the book about it."

"Which book?"

It is amazing how many questions a very young child can find to ask about the smallest incident, Jeremy having a particularly inquisitive nature.

They visited the 'ducking stool', the Poor Priests' Hospital, then made their way back to The County. Meeting their new friends they had a very pleasant hour together before Fred announced they would have to 'get their skates on' as they had visitors coming this evening. As they enjoyed each other's company, the amusing banter that always arises when young, and not so young, get together, combined with the excellent scones and jam (no butter unfortunately) provided by The County, they could not have imagined, in their wildest dreams, the iniquity being perpetrated at that very moment in a small village in the south of France.

It was a bright, sunny afternoon in the small village of Oradour sur Glane when the peace was shattered by the arrival of a convoy of German troops. The inhabitants were not worried; in fact they came to their doorsteps to watch what was going on. They had rarely seen a German soldier in their little backwater all through the war; they were therefore unafraid of this sudden intrusion. Oradour had never harboured resistance fighters, or been in any way in trouble with the occupying forces – so what was happening?

They had not long to wait. The big drum was sounded which was the signal to assemble in the village centre. One small boy took to his heels and ran to the woods unobserved. He was to be the only child of the 247 schoolchildren left alive by the end of the day.

The SS marshalled the women, some pregnant, some with babes in arms, along with the children and separated them from the men, then marched them to the parish church where they were locked in. After an hour or so the men were marched off in parties to three barns, two garages, a warehouse, and another outbuilding. Here they were machine-gunned to death, except that some did not die. Their end was even more horrific. As they lay wounded the SS spread straw over them and set it alight. In the meantime others were searching the village and killing those who had failed to answer the call to assemble, including the old, the infirm and the sick. They were shot on the spot.

The women in the church, unspeakably afraid for the safety of their menfolk as the noise of shooting increased, at last saw the door open. Two soldiers brought in a large box-shaped object from which fuses protruded. These they lit and retired rapidly, their exit followed by a loud explosion from the box which produced clouds of suffocating smoke. In the ensuing panic the women hurled themselves against the sacristy door which burst open. There was no escape. SS men, outside, machine gunned those in the doorway, other SS had positioned themselves at the windows raking the victims inside with magazine after magazine from their Schmeisser machine guns. Finally, the troops opened the main door and used all of their remaining ammunition to ensure no one stayed alive.

To be doubly sure the soldiers then piled up all the wooden benches and pews and set fire to the church.

Over five hundred women and children perished in the church. A similar number of men died in the orgy of shooting. Miraculously fifteen people including the young Roger Godfrin and one woman, Madame Rouffanche, survived, despite being badly injured.

The beasts then burnt the village to the ground.

WHY DID IT HAPPEN?

All sorts of reasons and conjecture have been put forward, the most probable of which being they attacked the wrong village – even the wrong Oradour, there are other Oradours in France. Certainly Oradour sur Glane had created no reason for this dreadful carnage, if indeed, a reason could be found for such an appalling outrage.

The local authorities decided not to rebuild Oradour sur Glane, a new village was built some little way away. It is said that now no birds sing in the old village, there is a deathly silence, broken only by the sighing of the breeze through the ruined houses and the soft footsteps of those who come to pay homage to the victims of this massacre of the innocents.

No one was impeached for this atrocity.

No one was punished.

But then millions died in this war for no good reason. Few ever paid the price for their deaths.

Chapter Eighteen

The twenty reinforcements Angus had brought back from Colonel Hislop were shared out among the three platoons, David sending the new Canadian lieutenant and ten men to 4 platoon, where Miles Rafferty's body still lay, covered by a small tarpaulin. The remainder he split between Sandy and Paddy. He told Angus to let him see his wounds. Two of them were in his left upper arm and had bled copiously, saturating his battledress and Denison smock. The third was on his right hip.

"I think you had better have a session with the delectable daughter," he told him, "get her to clean you up until we can get you back to the regimental aid post."

"If I get a couple of bandages on I won't need to see the MO," Angus replied. "I don't want my parents to receive one of those 'wounded' telegrams; it would frighten the life out of them."

"Alright, we'll see how it goes."

Twenty minutes later there was further movement down the road from Caen. An armoured car appeared, behind which could be seen a considerable number of men. The action started with the car blasting 4 platoon's position with its heavy machine gun, some of the poorly aimed benefaction finding its way through the window in David's observation post bringing down more of the ceiling and covering him with white powder. Angus came racing up the stairs. Well, perhaps racing is rather exaggerating his progress. His hip was giving him a certain amount of pain and his arm was stiffening up.

"You alright sir? Crikey, talk about Snow White." It was the first time Angus had ever spoken words beyond the proprieties to be observed between major and batman. David grinned.

"We've got company," he replied pointing towards 4 platoon's position.

Angus carefully edged to the window.

"They're moving this way sir, shall I go and warn the new officer?"

"No, he's got his glasses on them. Go up that gully to Mr Patterson and tell him to prepare to wheel his lot round when I fire the Very and take 4 platoon attackers in their flank, then get back to his own position p.d.q. On your way back tell Mr O'Riordan to prepare to do his charge of the light brigade again if I fire a second Very. Got all that?"

"Right sir," and he was away.

It was of necessity a narrow front upon which the Germans were starting their attack on 4 platoon. The eight wheeled armoured car moved forward at walking pace, now firing its two machine guns in short bursts, the supporting troops trying to shelter behind it. The men in 4 platoon knew that all the time the machine guns were firing they would not be receiving the unwelcome attention of the assaulting troops, so they kept well down in their slit trenches. On the other hand the commander in the armoured car could read their thoughts, that is why he had given the order to the two gunners to fire in bursts, with a short delay in between. The defenders experiencing the delay might think the assault was coming in, so would pop up out of their slit trenches only to be the recipients of another burst or two from the enemy. It was cat and mouse at its deadliest.

Their new platoon commander, they were even ignorant of his name, had yelled, "Keep down until I tell you," which meant in effect he was going to keep his head above the parapet to ensure they were not surprised. Another reason for the fact that platoon commanders in action lead very exciting and sometimes very brief lives.

The machine guns on the armoured car ceased firing to be replaced by a deluge of Moaning Minnies as the infantry moved out in front to make the final assault. Throughout the action David had been observing from his bedroom window. One of the mortar bombs burst in a tree right outside the window sending a lethal shower of metal fragments through the opening and peppering the wall outside. Standing back as he was at an angle from what was now more a hole in the wall than a window they whistled past him, shattering a sepia picture of a long dead ancestor of the family safe in the cellar below. As the mortaring ceased the attackers moved forward. They were obviously well trained. They did not bunch. They advanced steadily and purposefully. The lieutenant, who had stayed exposed even during the rain of mortar bombs, called out, "Watch your front. Make every round count. Fire at will" – he could have been on a battle school exercise.

David calculated the time at which Sandy's platoon – or what was left of it – if they wheeled round from their present position, would meet the flanks of the attackers. He decided to fire his first Very. Having done so a dozen or so men left their slit trenches, were formed up quickly in a line and doubled forward to a ridge overlooking the roadway. As the advancing Germans came level with them Sandy gave the order to fire down on to them. A number fell, but the remainder carried on the attack. In the meantime the armoured car commander had identified what was happening, turning his machine guns on to the ridge. Three of Sandy's men were hit, the remainder sliding back down the ridge out of harms way, although unable to regain their original positions as they had to cover ground in the field of fire of the machine guns.

4 platoon in the meantime had opened fire on the advancing troops. David could see that despite those eliminated by Sandy's 5 platoon they greatly outnumbered the defenders. He prepared to fire the second Very for which Paddy and his gallant band were waiting. Just as he was deciding to commit his small reserve force there was a noise, the like of which he had never before experienced. It sounded like a screaming express train, albeit to imagine a sound like that takes some doing. Anyway everything stopped. The express train noise was immediately followed by the mother and father of all explosions some four or fire hundred yards down the Caen road. Before Paddy could say 'bloody hell' a second express train arrived and then a third. At this the armoured car did a three point turn and hurtled off towards Caen, the Germans left defenceless stood in the middle of the road not knowing what to do until one man threw his rifle down and put his hands above his head, quickly to be followed by the remainder. Sandy in the meantime had led his men down on to the road behind the surrendering troops, urging them on towards 4 platoon. There were some thirty in total. They could have done a lot of harm to 'B' Company if the express trains had not arrived.

And the express trains?

They were sixteen inch shells being fired by one of the huge battleships covering the bridgehead. A FOO – forward observation officer – a navy man, had landed with the general and had started coordinating the covering fire in front of the airborne forces' known positions. They were not always as accurate as might have been desired, but they certainly put the wind up Jerry.

It was now eleven o'clock.

As the prisoners came in, David limped downstairs to listen in to their conversation, hoping to glean some intelligence from them, he being a fluent German speaker. They were however strangely silent, in a state of shock almost. He decided to approach them.
"Which of you is the senior?"
They all looked at a feldwebel.
"You have no officer?"
The feldwebel replied, "No sir, he was killed in the previous attack."
David decided it would serve no purpose in his attempting to do an

elementary debriefing. He called out to Paddy.

"Sergeant major. Get an escort of four with a sergeant in charge and get these men back to the CO at the bridge will you?"

"At once sir." Paddy looked around.

"Sergeant Eames. Take four men and get these people back to the bridge. Don't, repeat don't, take all day relieving them of their watches, and get back here on the double – understand?"

"Yes sir," replied the sergeant knowing only too well that the CSM was not joking – if he hung about he would be for it.

"Right, get back to your positions," David ordered. He called the Canadian officer over who had conducted 4 platoon's defence so capably.

"Your name?"

"MacDuff Sir," David shook hands with his replacement platoon commander.

"You did bloody well out there; I was watching you most of the time."

"Thank you sir."

"Right, we will talk more later – that's if you stay with us of course."

4 platoon commander doubled off to his slit trenches, followed by David trying, successfully as it happened, to remember Shakespeare's famous lines,

'Lay on MacDuff
And damned be him that first cries,
Hold, enough!'

This MacDuff, despite their very short acquaintance, he felt, would not know the meaning of the word 'enough'.

For half an hour there was comparative peace, except of course for the odd mortar bomb and to their absolute surprise, a strafing from an ME109 flying very low over the bridges through an absolute tornado of light machine gun fire – fire which in the main missed since the gunners, unused to operating against aircraft, fired at the visitor, instead of well in front of him so that he flew into it. It all added to the livening up of the proceedings.

After that unwelcome incursion they began to be the target of a number of snipers. Two men were hit in Sandy's platoon, one fatally, and another in Paddy's position. Around the bend in the road some one hundred yards away, or perhaps a little more, Paddy saw Sergeant Eames and his four men doubling towards their slit trenches. Now, whether they had doubled all the way, or only when they knew they would be seen by that Irish git of a sergeant major I leave to your imagination. Seeing they would very quickly be in the sight of the snipers from the ridge above, Paddy stood up and yelled at the oncoming group.

"Snipers!! Keep in close to the bank."

They immediately realised the danger, crouched down and kept in the shelter indicated by Paddy. As he spoke Paddy felt as though someone had kicked his steel helmet. At that moment Sergeant Eames arrived telling his men to get into their trenches. He looked at Paddy.

"When did you get that sir?"

"When did I get what?"

The sergeant pointed to the CSM's helmet. Paddy undid the chin strap and took it off. As he did so, a small lock of hair fell on to his chest, landing on one of his ammunition pouches. He looked in astonishment at two holes right at the front, one where the bullet went in and the other, two inches away, where it had come out. A parachutist's helmet is different to the ordinary infantry type, in that it has thicker padding, thus the metal stands well clear of the head. An inch further back the bullet would have blown Paddy's brains out.

"Bloody hell," was his inevitable comment as he coolly replaced the perforated headgear.

Soon after midday a further deluge of Moaning Minnies descended on 'B' Company. They were obviously being fired from behind a small wood, the front of which could be seen from David's observation post, but since the wood itself was on a reverse slope there was no way of pinpointing the actual firing position. Not that having that information would be of any use, they had nothing to attack it with until the guns arrived on the gliders scheduled for later that afternoon. However, bearing in mind the mortar attack usually heralded a ground attack, he gave the order to stand-to. As the mortaring ceased and the men strained eyes and ears to try and anticipate the direction and content of the next onslaught, in the distance they heard the unmistakable sound of bagpipes! Each man knew what this meant; Lord Lovat and his commandos had linked up from the beach landings. If they were through, the infantry division planned to relieve the paras would not be far behind.

Their euphoria was short-lived as they heard the dreadful roaring, clanking sound of a heavy tracked vehicle, a noise guaranteed to unsettle the bowels of any foot solider in its path. David, high up in his window compared to those in the slit trenches, was the first to establish it was a self-propelled gun, a most fearsome piece of machinery if ever there was one. It has one disadvantage however; it is open-topped, unlike a tank. Sandy Patterson must have caught a glimpse of it from his elevated position on the ridge, and ignoring the snipers, got four of his men to load up with grenades, and in less than a minute to run with him full pelt on a repeat of his previous flanking attack. The gunners in the armoured vehicle had already fired two of their 88 millimetre shells, blowing the rest of the roof off David's command post and injuring his other leg with a piece of the shrapnel. As they prepared to fire the third round Sandy and his men hit them with their Mills bombs, holding them with the pins out for a second or so, then lobbing them into the open top. Two of the crew jumped over the side to escape, as did the driver, but a few short bursts from Sandy's Sten gun dealt with them. Two of the crew were still alive, although wounded. They got them out and shouted for 4 platoon to come and collect them.

"Now, what the hell do we do with the gun?" asked Sandy of no one in particular.

"We can't leave it here sir; if we drive it up to company HQ we may be able to find out how it works and blast those snipers with it."

"Williams, that's the first intelligent thing I have ever heard you say," replied Sandy, grinning at him and thumping him on the back, "can you drive it?"

"I've driven a Caterpillar tractor sir, I'll have a bash."

And that's how 'B' Company 'R' Battalion The Parachute Regiment captured their first self propelled gun, although to be fair they had a bit of cleaning up to do to get rid of the gore they had created inside before they could use it, added to which in endeavouring to steer it into the back garden of company HQ Williams 83 completely flattened the residential thunderbox, an establishment which had provided many pleasant hours of reading the local newspaper on a sunny afternoon in Normandy over the years.

David's second wound was more serious than the chimney pot assault, but fortunately no bone was broken. Angus helped him down into the only room in the house now fit to be in, full to overflowing as it was with the wounded. The French girl slit his trouser leg and bound the wound tightly. As she did so, Paddy appeared.

"I'm going to get Sergeant Eames to get back to the colonel and get some ambulances up here sir – that OK?"

"Yes, please do that sergeant major, I'll get this bandaged and go upstairs again. Oh and tell Sergeant Eames to tell the CO we are down to whatever it is – have a roll call will you?"

"I've done that sir, 4 platoon have ten, 5 platoon have twelve and I have fourteen."

"Good God, a company of a hundred and twenty and we are down to around forty including us."

"I expect others have wandered in by now sir. I'll get a full tally of killed and wounded sir, but of course several of them weren't ours in the first place."

Paddy did his calculations. 'B' Company had suffered twelve killed and twenty-seven wounded. It was still only one o'clock on the afternoon of 6th June, but they had held firm and prevented the enemy from attacking the bridgehead from the south. They were tired, desperately tired. They had been awake now for thirty hours, most of that time in a highly stressed situation, and they had no real idea of how much longer they were going to have to hold their position until the Warwicks relieved them. The commandos had forced their way through but had been deployed on the eastern side of the canal to assist the main force in keeping the bridges open, bridges so vital to the protection of Gold and Juno beaches.

They were attacked four more times during the afternoon, but at least the wounded had been evacuated during the lulls – such as they were.

"Why don't they co-ordinate these attacks, not send them in in dribs and drabs?" asked David of Paddy.

"If I knew what co-ordinate meant I'd answer that sir, so I would. But if it means put them all in together I would be glad if you don't talk too loud for them to hear, the bastards have caused enough trouble already."

It was eight o'clock that evening before the Warwicks reached them. It took another hour to hand over before 'B' Company trudged out of their positions, back over Pegasus Bridge as it was now already being called, and back into reserve to eat their first hot meal for nearly two days, and to sleep, many of them falling asleep as they ate.

Having made his report to Colonel Hislop and seen his men as comfortable as possible, David reported to the regimental aid post to have his wounds dressed. The MO took one look at the chimney pot gash and immediately ordered an ambulance to take him back to the field ambulance, army term for hospital. David was very concerned at this.

"Look, Mike," he said to the MO, "can you send a letter off for me?" Mike knew immediately his concern.

"Sure," he answered, "they're collecting them at six tomorrow morning, it should get there first."

David scribbled a note to Maria; Mike gave him an envelope. He wrote.

'Darling. I have had a couple of scratches, one on each leg. As a result you will get a wounded telegram as I have had to have the cuts stitched. I am perfectly OK and rejoining my company in the morning. Love David'.

He turned to Mike, "She's having our baby any minute now, I don't want her getting upset. I'll write properly as soon as I can get a few minutes."

David's letter went off at six in the morning. It was on a returning landing craft by ten o'clock, in Portsmouth at eight o'clock that evening and delivered to Chigwell by first post on Monday 12th June. The telegram arrived four days later!!

The battalion went into three days' rest to refit, during which time a further number of stragglers rejoined, most of whom had been fighting with other units. On the fourth day, as part of a brigade, they were moved to a sector which for the time being at any rate was fairly quiet, mainly because all the bridges had been blown over the River Dives; as a result the enemy could not advance against them, except on foot. However, this lasted only for a few days before a panzer division circled to the south over the first unblown bridge and started to probe north against them.

Whilst things were quiet Paddy pondered to David as to what had happened to Jimmy James. "We've seen no one from the last five in our stick, Captain Rogers and Mr James among them."

Captain Rogers, David's second in command we know dropped into the river and was drowned. Jimmy James landed on the eastern side of the river, missing it by no more than a couple of hundred yards. He quickly shed his parachute and made his way towards some farm buildings. He knew the river must have been the Dives, he was miles from where he should have been, and what was more he was on the wrong side of a river over which all the bridges had been or would be blown.

"I am decidedly unhappy at this situation," he told himself, or words to that effect.

He approached the buildings carefully. He had a funny feeling he was being watched. When he was about ten yards away he heard the 'click' of a cricket, a small tin object with which all ranks had been issued so that when pressed, they could recognise each other in the dark. He gave his 'two click' reply and hurried to the door in the building. Inside he could see the shadowy forms of three men and the sergeant who had clicked him.

"Have you contacted the farmer yet sergeant to see if he knows any resistance people to lead us out of here?"

"No sir, none of us speak French."

"Alright, let's knock him up and see if he can help."

Jimmy's very adequate school French was sufficient to put the picture to the farmer, a sturdy, pugnacious looking man in his late fifties Jimmy judged, who told him there was nobody local who could help but he knew two men in Bures, some five kilometres away who could. He would go and see them at first light; in the meantime he and his men should hide in the loft of the barn and pull the ladder up behind them.

At about three o'clock in the morning, the five men heard considerable truck movement along the road about two hundred yards from the farm, this occurred intermittently until daylight. They breakfasted on their hard rations and water from their water bottles and waited anxiously for the farmer to return. He had told them he should be back by eight o'clock.

It was nearer nine o'clock before he did return. He had good news. Someone would come an hour after dark that night and lead them across country to a farm on the river where one of his comrades would ferry them across. They would have to find their own way then.

"Well, that's better than nothing I suppose," said Jimmy, "but it's going to be a long day I reckon."

It wasn't. Just after three that afternoon a party of some twenty troopers from the SS, led by a captain, drove into the yard, walked into the barn, fired half a dozen shots up through the loft floor, followed by the captain shouting in good English, 'Come down or we will burn you out'. Jimmy had the ladder lowered and climbed down, thinking 'how did they know we were up here?' automatically assuming the farmer had betrayed them until he saw the unfortunate man being held by two of the SS. Obviously his friend in Bures was the informer. 'I hope he rots in hell', Jimmy said to himself.

Clambering down, he turned and saluted the officer in charge and handed him his revolver. There was no return salute. The men were disarmed and relieved of their grenades.

"Which unit are you from?"

"I am Lieutenant James. No 306010."

The captain gave him a vicious swipe across the face. The sergeant and one of the paras stepped forward to protect the officer but were brutally beaten back with rifle butts.

"Which unit are you from?"

"I am obliged only to tell you my name and number. I am Lieutenant James 306010."

He received another backhander which nearly knocked his teeth out.

"You are all parachutists, you are saboteurs."

"We are not saboteurs; we are part of a military force, as you will shortly find out."

He received another backhander, or at least he would have done had he not anticipated it, ducked his head and saw the captain stumble as he lost his balance on missing his target.

"I give you one last chance, what is your unit?"

"I am Lieutenant James 306010."

He turned to a feldwebel telling him to line the men, and the farmer, against an outside wall. This sergeant was an old soldier and protested this was not right. The officer told him that the Fuhrer had issued orders that all commandos and parachutists were to be treated as saboteurs and shot upon capture. The feldwebel reluctantly obeyed the order, lined the men up against the wall, the farmer among them, where his men executed them with magazine after magazine from their sub machine guns, but not before Jimmy looked the officer straight in the eye and said, "You are a disgrace to the name of soldier." In seconds the bodies lay on the cobbles, the farmer's wife and fourteen-year-old son ran out at the shooting crying in anguish.

The captain ordered the youth, "Get them buried." The men mounted their two vehicles and drove away.

This was not the only incident of this nature faced by captured British and American paratroops.

Chapter Ninteen

As David was preparing to drop into Normandy on the 5th of June 1944, so Major Dieter von Hassellbek was preparing to leave Russia, but not a voluntary departure by any means. His Tiger battle group had been moved up to the west of the ancient city of Minsk in an attempt to stop the Russian hordes pushing the Wehrmacht of the Central Army back into Poland only twenty-five miles away. It was a hopeless task. Despite the fact that the Russians could not begin to match them tank for tank the Soviets had the advantage now in three ways. Firstly they had five tanks for every one of the Germans – sometimes it felt like fifty! Secondly the Luftwaffe seemed to have entirely disappeared from the skies, leaving Soviet tank busters free reign to attack anything that moved, and last, but by no means least, some one hundred and fifty thousand Russian partisans had infiltrated behind the German lines causing morale of support troops to collapse utterly.

When news arrived at their regimental HQ on 6th June that deep advances had been made by the Ivans north and south of Minsk, and that as a result Dieter's unit was to withdraw towards Bialystock some one hundred and fifty miles away, morale sank even lower. As it was they were surrounded for three days in a pincer attack, but fought their way out doing a great deal of damage to the Russian T34 tanks in a sixteen hour battle near the small town of Kolosov, just over the old Polish border. But they had lost six of their Tigers, and not a hope in hell's chance of getting them replaced. They then received the calamitous news of the D Day landings. They were now fighting on four fronts, Russia, the Balkans, Italy and France. They could not possibly win this way.

By the end of June they had established firm defences. In the late evening of Friday 30th a runner came to Dieter's tent saying the colonel wished to see him. Dieter hurried back to the command post. Instead of talking to him from behind his portable table, the colonel took his arm and led him outside to the edge of a small coppice of birch. Dieter sensed immediately something was afoot.
"Dieter, I live in hopes our time has come."
Dieter remained silent.
"I have to go back to the Fuhrer's HQ in East Prussia to consult with certain people there. A Fieseler-Storch is coming for me at 1000 hours tomorrow morning. I have signed the necessary papers ordering you to take over the regiment in my absence which also means should I not

return. I shall be away until the end of July. I have cleared my absence and your taking command with the general. I don't think there is anything else for you to know at this stage. You will take the rank of acting lieutenant colonel."

"This is, Herr Oberst, what I think it is, is it not?"

The colonel gave one of his rare smiles.

"I am not responsible for your thoughts, Dieter, though knowing what a clear thinker you are; you are probably somewhere very near the mark. Now, listen carefully. You are to monitor the Reich news bulletins particularly from the middle of July onwards. You will get a very clear picture from those what the situation is."

Dieter thought deeply. "I wish you well sir, may success follow your endeavours."

"Thank you Dieter, and should I not see you again I would like you to know that in over thirty years of service to my country I have never met an officer I hold in higher esteem than you, both as a courageous soldier and a thoroughly honourable man."

"Thank you sir. I would respectfully like to return my tribute to you in exactly those terms."

The colonel and the acting colonel walked back to the command post. Dieter gave his superior officer an impeccable Potsdam salute which was returned in the same manner, turned smartly about and went back to his quarters. They were attacked by partisans that night, who were very swiftly beaten off leaving behind three wounded. At dawn Dieter performed his first duty as commanding officer. The three men were carried in front of him. They wore no uniform. He questioned them in his fluent Russian. They refused to answer. He ordered them to be shot. They could not stand up, they were therefore sat on camp chairs and summarily despatched. You cannot afford to waste time when you are at war.

All through July the battle in the centre raged. Dieter, as second in command of the regiment under colonel Metzner had made it top priority the radio systems in the regiment were kept at the highest peak of efficiency. His maxim had always been 'knowledge is everything'. If you don't know where each tank is, what it is doing, what it is facing, in fact everything about it you cannot make it an effective part of your battle plan. Any tank commander therefore who neglected his radio maintenance, failed to notify faults or failed to request replacement for a dodgy piece of equipment got it very severely in the neck. As a result of the fact they were outnumbered at all times during that terrible month's fighting, their very survival was the result of the close control of the battles by Dieter in his command tank. The Ivans might be able to throw tanks at him but their communications were either second rate or non-existent therefore there was little co-ordination of attack. Dogged retreat may have been the order, nevertheless it was orderly dogged retreat and the Russians suffered badly in the process.

Each evening when the darkness brought relief, not that in July there was all that length of darkness, furthermore it did nothing to stop the infantry and partisan attacks, Dieter listened carefully to his short wave radio tuned in to Radio Berlin. In the early hours of the 21st July a special announcement reported that an attempt had been made on the Fuhrer's life. It had been unsuccessful. Although four of his officers had been killed in the blast, the Fuhrer himself had received only minor injuries and had taken control of the situation. Eight of the plotters were shot immediately. Others had been arrested.

Dieter held his head in his hands. Now he knew there was no hope whatsoever. He almost certainly would die on these featureless steppes or on the plains of Poland, and for what?

His second thought was, of course, of the fate of his commanding officer. Even Dieter, knowing as he did from his own experience of the SS in Russia, and of the scum back in his homeland, could not have imagined what they would do to his beloved Colonel Metzner. In the next two days the plotters – of which the colonel was identified as one, otherwise why would he have deserted his regiment in Russia to come back to East Prussia? – the plotters were rounded up, the senior ones including Colonel Metzner were taken to a basement in the Berlin Army HQ and hanged on loops of piano wire from overhead beams. Hitler ordered a film to be made of the slow strangulation of these traitors, their gyrations and contortions, as they spent the last agonies of their time on this earth. He enjoyed watching it on many occasions in the months that were to be left to him.

It did not end there. The SS spread its enquiries far and wide until up to three thousand officers and officials had been arrested and summarily shot. The fact they did not get to Dieter, although he was investigated, was due to the skill of Colonel Metzner in covering his tracks. Whereas association with one of the plotters would normally automatically assume guilt, in Dieter's place, since he was at the time involved in bloody fighting two hundred and fifty miles away, he was given the benefit of the doubt.

Meanwhile, back at Bruksheim, Fritz and Gita Strobel, Dieter's in-laws, on hearing the radio announcement of the assassination attempt were anxious to learn whether Dieter had had any hand in it. They thought it unlikely since he was at the front, not in some sort of staff position which would give him access to the organisation of a plot to carry out the act they would each welcome.

Rosa, since the kindness shown to her by Frau Doktor Schlenker at Christmas, had developed a different relationship with her superior. This was undoubtedly due to the rose-tinted spectacles having been removed from the Frau Doktor's eyes in respect of the real world of the Nazi system. They were now taking in wounded from the Russian front, up until now they had been accommodating only civilian patients. Rosa had thrown herself into the training of volunteer nurses to carry out basic duties, working very long hours. This particularly commended her to the Frau Doktor, enabling her to create another ward from what had been a gymnasium attached to the Klinik.

On 6th July they had received their first patients from the fighting in Normandy, an overspill from a hospital train sent to Hanover. No matter what propaganda was being spewed out by the Goebbels' fabrication factory in Berlin, it was becoming patently obvious to people like Frau Doktor Schlenker, one-time believers in every word he uttered, that they were now being squeezed from both sides, and from Italy in the south. Goebbels was making great play of the assault by the Reich's great new secret weapon which had started to lay Britain to waste, the V-1 – 'Vergeltung' which means retribution. These had been, according to him and his odious lackey Lord Haw-haw, raining in on London and the south of England since the middle of June, soon to be joined by a missile of even greater terror. The V-1 and the V-2 would win the war for Germany. The majority of the German people believed them, but a substantial minority, knew in their hearts they would soon be a conquered people for the second time in a quarter of a century. The greatest fear of all was that they would be overrun by the Russian barbarians, the 'untermenschen' from the east, that assuredly would be a fate worse than death.

Rosa therefore threw herself into the alleviation of the pain of her patients, saw her mother and step-father at lunchtime most days, was given Saturday evenings off by the Frau Doktor to spend with her family, and prayed nightly for the safety of her darling Dieter, along with supplication for the war to end.
But prayers are not always answered.

Chapter Twenty

On Tuesday 13th June Leading Wren Emma Langham stood by her Humber staff car at the entrance to the Royal Marines garrison headquarters awaiting the arrival of a senior naval officer she was to transport to Chatham. As he emerged a low flying aircraft appeared from the east. They both looked up.

"What on earth's that sir?" she asked.

"God knows," came the reply, "perhaps it's some sort of pilotless drogue the anti-aircraft people use to practise on, that's gone astray."

They had, in fact, just witnessed the first V-1 to be launched against Britain, the fair county of Kent to be the recipient. It would not be the last. Nearly 1500 hit London and the South East in the remainder of June alone, swiftly to be named 'buzz bombs' by the British and 'doodlebugs' by the Americans.

The first doodlebug was not the only manifestation of Hitler's wrath to be inflicted on the county on that day of 13th June. German artillery brought into service massive railway guns, which along with the standard fire power with which Deal, Dover and other channel towns had been plastered over the years, provided heavy shelling for over five hours. The big guns, firing from Cape Gris Nez, reached as far as Maidstone, a distance of nearly sixty miles. Emma and her commodore, having passed through Canterbury, travelled the old Roman road of Watling Street, along which the legionaries had received their first sight of the cold damp land on the edge of the world to which they had been posted. When they were some five miles from Faversham there was an enormous 'whooshing' noise followed by an ear-shattering explosion in an orchard a couple of hundred yards in front of them. There was nothing on the road at that point, but as Emma quickly braked the road ahead became covered in branches from the apple trees along with copious quantities of good Kentish soil. It was completely blocked.

"What the devil do we do now?" her passenger asked. "It really is very important I am not late at Chatham." Emma turned to him and smiled.

"Two hundred yards further on and you would have been too early for everything."

He considered her rejoinder.

"You are right of course, and by jove, considering we have come as close as that to pushing up the daisies you are remarkably plucky." He paused and repeated, "You really are extraordinarily plucky. What is your name?"

"I am Leading Wren Langham sir."

"Leading Wren Langham. I shall remember that."

He had good cause to remember it at a later date.

"Well now, what do we do?"

"There was a gate into the orchard a little way back sir, if I could get that open perhaps I could drive around the shell hole hopefully to find another gate out on to the road. These Humbers will go anywhere."

"Good show, let's try."

Emma reversed the staff car for about a hundred yards, jumped out at the gate, found it opened readily and started her detour. Behind her, two army three-ton lorries, spotting the blocked road ahead, and the staff car with its one star badge on it indicating it contained a brigadier or someone similar intending to circumvent it, decided to follow. However, Kentish fruit trees are not grown to a great height, it makes picking a lot simpler! The Humber just scraped underneath most of the branches, but the three-tonners with their high bodies, and even higher canvas canopies, soon got stuck. Emma, seeing this in her rear view mirror, chuckled out loud, causing her commodore to ask, "What's so amusing Leading Wren Langham?"

"Have a look from your rear window sir."

The commodore did as she suggested, it was not intended to be an order of course, leading wrens do not order commodores about, although under certain circumstances I suppose it would not be beyond the bounds of possibility, but we won't go into that.

The commodore chuckled as he saw the army vehicles stationary with branches of trees penetrating their canopies.

"Someone will be in trouble tonight, and it's all your fault," he chuckled.

Emma's amusement ended when she reached the perimeter fence where it joined the road and found no gate. There was no ditch there; the ground in the orchard was more or less level with the verge of the road, although there was a slight dip on to the road itself.

"Hold on sir," she called out, and increasing her cross country speed aimed her vehicle at a wooden post holding the four strands of barbed wire separating the orchard from the A2.

The Humber was built for far rougher usage than splitting a barbed wire fence, added to which the barbed wire had been placed there some ten years before, so readily gave way to a ton and a half of solid metal.

There was a distinct bump as they hit the dip, the commodore's head making hostile contact with the unyielding roof.

Back on the road they made good time to HMS Pembroke at Chatham – strangely enough a shore station. Apparently the Naval Discipline Act required all naval personnel to be entered on the books of a ship. Therefore Chatham Barracks, hundreds of tons of bricks and concrete, becomes HMS Pembroke! They're a funny lot in the navy.

"Now get yourself some coffee – I shall be about an hour, then we have to go on to Short's at Rochester, where I hope they will give us some lunch." Emma saluted as the commodore made his way into the building.

As she was stationed with the Royal Marines at Deal, Emma of course wore their regimental cap badge on the front of her hat, which drew a number of good-natured comments from passing matelots and again from those in the NAAFI where she ordered her coffee and bun. Now NAAFI tea has the reputation of being similar in composition to the fluid output of a gnat. NAAFI coffee was only marginally better, but it was wet and warm, helped the bun down, and generally assisted in passing the hour (less five minutes – he might be early!). Having held the door open for her illustrious passenger, saying (under her breath) 'My Lord, your carriage awaits', he announced,
"On to the great plane makers then, leading wren."

Emma negotiated the somewhat ample bulk of the Humber expertly through the narrow streets of Rochester turning down on to the riverside to the factory gate. An enormous gateman, probably an ex-copper Emma conjectured, beamed them in after pointing out where they should park. As she parked her vehicle, so a Jaguar pulled in to the adjacent space marked 'Chairman', the chauffeur of which got out and held the rear door open for his passenger, Sir Jack Hooper no less, to alight. Jack took one look at Emma who herself had got out to open the door for her passenger, but before being able to carry out this task she was enveloped in a bear-like hug.
"Emma my love, what are you doing here?"
In the meantime the commodore had got himself out. Sir Jack, keeping one arm firmly around Emma held his other hand out to great his visitor.
"Commodore Jenson I take it?"
"Yes, Sir Jack, how do you do? Oh, and by the way, we normally charge for people who embrace our ratings."

"Does that apply to the male ones as well?"
"We charge double for them."

Harold, the chauffeur, who in the meantime had shaken hands with Emma, saying 'how nice to see you Miss Langham' stood in surprise to hear a very senior naval officer exchanging banter. All the air commodores he had seen or heard in his twenty years in the RAF, admittedly their numbers did not reach double figures, had been a miserable lot of you know what's.

"Well now, come on in. We'll join the senior staff for lunch today in view of the elevated rank of our guest. Do you object to Emma joining us commodore? She's a great friend of ours and we shall not be talking shop over the meal."

"Not at all, not at all."

During the lunch Emma kept herself in the background to a certain extent, although she contributed lively conversation when called upon to so do.

"So have you heard from Charlie?" Her face took on a heavy-hearted look. Jack looked at his navy guest and started to explain.

"Our Emma is getting..."

Before he could continue she put her hand on his exclaiming, "Don't say any more, it could be unlucky."

Jack put his other huge hand over hers, completely enveloping it. "Sorry my dear," and turning to the commodore told him, "Emma's fiancée Charlie Crew is in Normandy."

"Which ship is he on?" asked the commodore.

"He's in the army, in the City Rifles, they are in an armoured division," Emma replied.

The commodore was just going to make a jocular reply about lowering herself by consorting with soldiers when he realised the strain on Emma's face at the thought of her beloved probably in great danger at that very moment.

"Where did you first meet?" he asked, hoping to take her mind off the present.

She explained how her best friend at Deal had been engaged to a fellow officer of Charlie's and that it had been suggested she became a pen pal to Charlie, at that time fighting in the desert.

"And," she ended, "it all grew from there. We had a pretty good idea we were kindred spirits before we even met. Mind you, I had collywobbles when we did first meet after all that letter writing but it all went off very well."

The question and the animated answer served the purpose intended, Emma's usual composed expression having returned. She turned to Jack.

"Sir Jack, when is Harold's wedding? I must send them a card."

"24th June, Sandbury Parish Church, and I am giving the bride away. We are having a small reception at The Angel for family and friends; after all, Nanny is as good as family to us. So please join us if you can."

The commodore was listening with interest to this somewhat domestic interlude.

"You mentioned Sandbury?" It was more a question than a statement of fact.

"Yes, we live there. Harold is my chauffeur and Nanny Cavendish has been with us ever since my son John was born." He hesitated for a moment.

"Do you know the mighty metropolis of Sandbury then commodore?"

"Very well. The first time I ever got three sheets in the wind was in The Angel at Sandbury. I was in the sixth form at Cantelbury at the time, waiting to go to Dartmouth."

"Well I'm blessed. Doctor and Mrs Carew are great friends of ours, as also is colonel Scott-Calder. Do you remember him? He was badly knocked about at Calais, and runs an Octu now."

"I remember them well. Salt of the earth those two. Couldn't say that of one or two of the others, but then you can't like everybody, can you? I was there from 1912 until 1922. My father was a navy man and in those days you might spend three years at a time on the China station or in Malta or wherever. As a result I was packed off to Cantelbury at the age of eight and only saw my father once after that – he went down at Jutland. My mother married again and went to live in New Zealand, so from the age of fourteen I was brought up during my holidays from school by an aunt, bless her, who was very kind, incredibly spinsterish and fortunately fairly well off. It had always been assumed I would go in the navy, so into the navy I went."

"And may we ask if there is a Mrs Jenson?"

"No. 'fraid not. I again have suffered the navy problem of three years here, three years there. I'll have a scout around when this lot is over."

"Good idea. Find a widow with a pub. We will all come and visit you then."

They all laughed. Jack and his visitor went off to discuss their, doubtless, highly secret business, leaving Emma to wander back to her Humber, and to wonder how she would explain the deep grooves in the paintwork made by the somewhat hostile barbed wire. 'I'll think of something' she told herself.

As they drove off down the A2 they saw two more flying bombs, presumably on their way to London. They reached Deal at six o'clock in time to hear the last shell of the day bursting down towards Walmer. Considering they were on what could be described as a 'Home Station' they had experienced a certain amount of active service in one short day. As they pulled up at the officers' quarters, Emma got out to open her passenger's door to find he had already alighted and was stamping one food on the ground.

"Damned foot's gone to sleep" he said, "does that every now and then. Now Leading Wren Langham, I have had quite an eventful day, mainly due to you, and to a lesser extent the shelling. I am going to be here for at least three weeks, that is I am being based here. However I am having to visit a number of establishments along the east and south coasts, so I shall need a permanent driver. I am going to ask your chief officer if I can be afforded your services. Would you be interested in the job?"

"Yes sir, very much so sir." Emma had thought quickly. Travelling to different places would be very interesting. This officer is obviously not one of those she frequently had to deal with – on the make, or at least trying it on.

"Right then. Unless you hear to the contrary here at 8am tomorrow with an overnight bag for two nights. We are going to Portsmouth. Weekend free. Sheerness on Monday, so start working out your routes." As he turned to go Emma saluted correctly, which salute was courteously returned.

When she got to her room she found to her great excitement a letter from Charlie – the first, apart from an 'I am well' card, she had received from France. He was very cheerful except when he devoted a page to saying how desolate he was that their wedding had had to be postponed. Planned for the 8th July, with David as best man, they had always known the war might well interfere with their plans. However most of the remainder of the epistle fell into two categories, the funny things that had happened to him, like falling over in the briny when he was wading ashore, and the tender, amorous passages which was for her the focal point of the correspondence. She went off for her supper with mixed feelings of love, pleasure, and desolation, feelings experienced by millions of couples torn apart by this beastly war, having just heard from their husband, wife, lover or whatever.

Back at Sandbury Jack called in at Chandlers Lodge – he often did that in the evenings when Moira was away.

"I saw a friend of yours today," he told Rose.

"I'll buy it – which one?"

"Have you got more than one then?" He continued, "The delectable Emma. She was driving a commodore who had to come and see me."

"Why would a navy person, I assume it was a navy person, although they do have commodores in the air force I believe, why would a navy person want to come to see you? You don't make ships."

"We make craft which float on the ocean. The navy has a Fleet Air Arm. That could be a reason do you think? I shall do no more than to suggest that as of course you may well be a Nazi spy for all I know." She turned sideways.

"Do I look like a Nazi spy?"

"Ah, but then, these Germans are devilishly cunning – you never know who you are talking to these days. Anyway, Emma sends her love to you all."

"What was this commodore like and how does his rank compare with army rank?"

"He was a jolly nice chap, went to Cantelbury, got sozzled in The Angel once, is unmarried, seemed a rather lonely sort of fellow, and his rank is equivalent to a brigadier in the army. Any more questions?"

"Yes, would you like a Whitbread's?"

"I thought you would never ask."

As they spoke Fred arrived. "Did you hear that peculiar airplane go over this morning?" he asked Jack.

"No, I was at Rochester early this morning, but everybody is talking about it. Did you see it?"

"From a distance, through my binoculars I always keep in the office."

"What, so that you can see clearly who's skiving off early?"

"That, and the young mums bending over their prams when they take the kids out over in the park opposite. Anyway, it was pilotless, seemed to be just a body, short wings and an engine of some sort. Not a radial engine, like a big firework at the back."

"Well, I expect we will be told in due course."

They would be more than just 'told in due course', they would soon be at the receiving end of these evil, indiscriminate weapons Hitler was firmly convinced would win the war for him, those and the V-2 yet to be launched.

They listened to the news as usual that evening which contained an item causing great excitement in the Chandler household. The mellifluous, measured tones of the announcer told the nation, and presumably anyone else who might be tuned in, of a huge, new, up until now, secret, motorless aircraft operating with great success in Normandy. It was known as the Hamilcar. The newsreader stated it carried a tank, whose engine is started while it is still airborne. On landing the pilot operates a system which causes the nose to swing back, the fuselage sinks to the ground and the tank races into action. The glider can land on a cabbage patch and the first one to land silenced an enemy gun post within two minutes of landing.

"I wonder if it was one of ours?" exclaimed an excited Rose.

"Well, now everybody knows all about it, perhaps we won't have to perform the great inquisition lark before anyone can come and see it," was Fred's hopeful comment. Nevertheless, there was great pride throughout the factory, the factory workers' families as well as the extended Chandler family that something they had built, or had been built in their small town was proving to be such an asset to their loved ones in Normandy.

June 1944 was a long month. We were securely ashore but the fighting was hard indeed. Maria telephoned Rose when she got David's letter, they were all most concerned he had been hurt, although he made light of it.

"Bound to, wouldn't he?" being Fred's opinion to Jack and Ernie.

Every night the three girls went to bed with a prayer for the safety of their men. They knew their loved ones were in the very sharp end of the action. As the casualty figures started to be announced in The Times, The Morning Post and The Telegraph, and they realised how many were giving their lives, the night-time torment increased. There was no let up, nor would there be for a very long while.

The buzz bomb raids continued day by day. On 19th June details were announced over the wireless regarding this new weapon. It was to all effects a flying bomb carrying two thousand pounds of explosive. It had a range of one hundred and fifty miles, the launch sites therefore being in Northern France, Belgium and Holland. These sites were now being searched out by photo-reconnaissance aircraft and our agents in those countries and were being bombed heavily.

"Not heavily enough," Fred commented "we are getting more and more every day, and every night as well."

On the 23rd of June it was announced that a Belgian, Pierre Neukermans, working for the German Secret Service had been executed at

Wormwood Scrubs prison. "I would have pulled the lever myself," being Jack's comment.

By the end of the month the RAF had developed a method of 'downing' the buzz bombs. They flew alongside them with the Spitfire or Hurricane wing just under the buzz bomb wing. They then flipped it up, which upset the V-1's gyroscope making it turn over and crash to the ground. The end result of this clever manoeuvre was that the bomb exploded in the green countryside of either Kent or Essex, instead of on the dwellings of greater London. The drawback to this excellent theory was of course that the green countryside of Kent and Essex also contained a goodly proportion of farms, dwellings, villages and towns. In one week Sandbury was the recipient of four of these incidents, which whilst they did not get deposited directly on buildings, nor did they cause any fatal casualties, they blew out virtually every pane of glass in the place, except strangely enough The Angel. The Angel got off scott free, the suggestion being that John Tarrant must be a secret agent of the Nazis.

Along with the serious resumption of the shelling of Dover and the other coastal towns, Kent was taking a real hammering, second only to London. We may have been winning the war but Germany was not finished yet, and was boasting over its air waves that an even greater secret weapon would soon be making its presence felt. And how right they were!

Chapter Twenty-One

During the evening of 6th June, Matthew ran in to Harry's room without knocking – an act he would normally never perform, firstly because of his innate courtesy, secondly there would always be the possibility of Chantek running free. The last thing he would want to do would be to set her loose into a very inhospitable jungle the art of survival in which she had never received instruction from her mother.

Since the raid on the old gold mine at Raub the men on Camp Three had increasingly been going down with sickness. It was expected that in the conditions under which they had to live, and the territory over which they had to operate, the sickness rate would be high. With the very strict hygiene controls and the constant preventative measures instituted by Matthew and rigidly reinforced by the officers and Choon Guan, the sick list was kept at between five and ten per cent. Now however, from somewhere or other one of the men had contracted ringworm, which being highly contagious, quickly spread. In itself not being incapacitating, when it spread to shoulders, back, and so on, which it frequently did, not only was it a most distressing affliction, but the patient could not wear equipment on the tormented parts. The temptation to scratch was overwhelming and when this occurred, being a fungal disease, the skin was removed by the fingernails, thus causing further problems. For nearly a month therefore over half of the company was unfit for operational duties.

More serious than that, Matthew had diagnosed tuberculosis in one of the men, and suspected a second to have contracted the disease. It being highly infectious he called a meeting of the officers and Choon Guan.

"We have immediately to send these men away," he announced.

Choon Guan replied vehemently. "They are two of my best men. And anyway, where can they go, they have no families left?"

"They will have to get urgent medical treatment, otherwise more and more will become infected, even you yourself, or anyone of us would not be immune," Matthew argued.

This was the first time in either of the camps that a situation like this had arisen. They had had deaths from malaria, tick typhus, rubella even, but TB was a different kettle of fish. They looked to Harry.

"We shall have to give them sufficient sovereigns to get medical treatment. What can we afford Tommy?"

"I would suggest fifty each; they would get a substantial amount of local currency for those."

They all looked at Choon Guan.

"I am worried about this. They are not used to having money. I am afraid they would spend it instead of getting treatment."

Harry came in firmly. "If they are stupid enough to do that they must take the consequences. It is either that or we turn them out with nothing. I am worried about the security situation – suppose they get drunk and talk?"

Reuben came up with a suggestion. "Other camps must have this problem by now, probably to a greater extent than we have. Suppose we get Sunrise to organise a central sanatorium type set-up, put them all in together to be looked after, and get whatever drugs needed dropped to them. The men are fit enough to make the journey now, but probably won't be in a few months, by which time they may well have infected others."

Harry did not consider this with any degree of enthusiasm, but in the absence of any other plan of action, decided they should send a message to Sunrise that night pointing out the problem. The 'received and understood' acknowledgement came by return and three days later a coded message came that the problem had already been encountered elsewhere and was giving concern. It had been decided therefore to set up an isolation unit adjacent to Camp Four, supervised by Firefly.

"Who the devil's Firefly?" Harry asked.

"I believe it is the lady at Camp Four, sir," the radio operator replied.

The lady at Camp Four Harry knew well was Marian Rowlands, wife of arch-traitor Rowlands who would be high up on the 'Most Wanted' list after the war. She was also the mother of his brother David's first wife Pat, so cruelly killed by enemy action in 1940. Harry's inbuilt antagonism toward Marian Rowlands was as a result of her leaving her daughter Pat at six years of age to run off to Malaya with Rowlands. The fact that she was endeavouring to expiate the selfishness and wrongdoing of her earlier life by serving her country and her fellow-man at Camp Four, only marginally reduced Harry's hostility towards her, but reduce it, it did.

"How are we to get our two bods there?" Harry asked the operator.

"Your Bam and Boo are bringing a patrol in the next few days to take them. It's not far apparently, only three days."

When one thinks that on a good day one can get from London to Brighton in a little over an hour, that is the equivalent distance of three days in the jungle, and that by using a good proportion of known game tracks. Without those it could be a week or more.

The news that night was eagerly listened to. The 14th Army was advancing on nearly all fronts in Burma showing that the Japanese infantry were far from invincible. This, combined with the news from Normandy, raised the spirits of these men locked in this green hell of constantly advancing vegetation, the keeping of which at bay being itself a perpetual battle.

Bam and Boo, along with three Chinese, arrived on the 24th of June, having taken four days. They rested for two days, then started off at dawn with the two prospective patients, both of whom were more sick than Matthew had been able to judge, making it a very slow journey back to Firefly at Camp Four.

Gradually the ringworm epidemic was more or less eliminated, in the process the shaven heads, and other body parts, covered with large patches of gentian violet, the only material Matthew had with which to treat it, gave a psychedelic relief to the eternal green jungle background. It was however mid-July before Harry was able to take on a full strength operation. Even then, full strength was only barely a fraction above half his available forces, the shortfall being due to normal sickness and the necessity to leave a garrison section behind to defend the camp should he be operating away at any distance.

Harry had been sending four-man patrols regularly to the airfield at Kuala Lipis, an old RAF aerodrome, which since February had been in the process of being extended by British and Australian POW labour. The last patrol four weeks ago, led by Tommy Isaacs, had reported that twin-engined aircraft, transports mainly, but including three Mitsubishi attack bombers were positioned near to the corrugated iron sheds the POW's had erected on the western edge of the airfield. To Tommy's delight, these aircraft were not dispersed, presumably because of firstly the lack of concrete hardstanding, and secondly the supposed impossibility of their being attacked from the ground or bombed from the air. Harry had therefore requested sanction to pay them a visit.

On the night before they left for Kuala Lipis, another piece of news came to them over the airwaves. An assassination attempt had been made on Hitler. The fact that an event on the other side of the world would be of any great interest to people cooped up in a tropical jungle could be quite understood. However, Harry and his comrades more than appreciated the fact that matters of that significance had a direct bearing on their very survival. That the attempt was a failure still showed there was internal opposition to the Fuhrer and his gang, as soon as he would be brought down, it would be the Nips' turn.

They moved out at dawn on Friday 21st July. They were lucky with the weather. As a result they made good time arriving at their bivvy area without incident mid-afternoon of the 23rd. It being Sunday there was little movement on the airfield as Harry and Tommy studied the scene through their binoculars.

"You could cut through that mesh fence with a pair of scissors," Harry whispered to his companion.

"You would think they would have something more substantial than that wouldn't you?" Tommy replied, scanning to the right with his glasses. He stopped, suddenly.

"Look."

Harry saw the direction in which Tommy's glasses were directed and followed suit. Lying on the ground near the fence was the new carcase of a forest deer. Three yards away the body of a wild boar. Both showed unmistakable signs of having parts of their limbs blown off.

"Mines," said Harry, "no wonder the bastards only had a mesh fence. I bet the deer wandered in and was blown up, the pig came along, saw a ready made meal and he then bit the dust."

"I can't see their logic though," Tommy mused, "with the numbers of wild animals about the things must be going off all the time."

"Well, we've got a problem my old son. We can't get down there to see what we can see in daylight, and I have no desire to go crashing around in a minefield in the dark. So what do we do?"

"This is one time when I am most grateful I am not the boss," came the reply.

They studied the spot where the two dead animals were spread-eagled, Harry, thinking aloud, said, "One, we don't know how far from the fence the mines are laid, or how close they are together. Two, they are anti-personnel mines. If they had been bigger than that the animals would have been blown to bits. Three, presumably they will replace the blown mines, first removing the corpses away from the minefield so that scavengers don't set more mines off. Lastly they may or may not use tripwires so that they can space out the mines. I reckon our best bet is to watch tomorrow, see what they get up to, and then plan how we get through to the aircraft."

Tommy's reply was droll in the extreme.

"How jolly."

It was getting dark so they made their way back to the bivvy area, getting their heads down soon after dark until the first light of day. As it got light Harry and Tommy, joined by Choon Guan made their way to the observation point. Both carcasses had been interfered with during the night, presumably by small rodents since they had not been moved. They waited and waited and at around 8.30 saw a small party of three Japanese soldiers, led by an NCO. They were following the line of the fence at a distance of only three paces from it.

"That's one problem sorted out," Harry pronounced, "it's not more than nine or ten feet wide," referring of course to the extent of the minefield.

When the troops reached the point where the animals lay, two of the men, who were carrying long bamboo poles with substantial hooks in the end, lifted the poles, plunged the hooks into each carcase in turn and pulled them clear of the minefield area. The NCO then took a cylindrical object from a satchel the third man was carrying and moved close to the wire.

"If he can walk like that they can't be very thick on the ground," Harry whispered to his colleagues.

The NCO then took a small trowel from his belt, tidied up the hole where the original mine had been and buried the replacement with its top at ground level. He then took a coil of wire from his pocket, measured off three arm's lengths, ("Ten feet of wire," Harry guessed to the other two), stretched it parallel to the fence away to his left and pegged it into the ground. Finally he went back to the mine and removed the safety pin. It was now primed.

Moving away from the fence about three or four feet from the first trip wire he repeated the operation, but placed the mine some four or five feet to the right of the first mine. Having planted the two mines and primed them the little group moved off back to the aerodrome.

"So now we know," Harry said, "two rows of mines at roughly ten feet centres, overlapping half way, with the rows three to four feet apart. All we have to do now is to unpeg the tripwires, and as long as we don't tread on the mines themselves, which are bound to have prongs on the surface, we can waltz through their impenetrable defences at will."

"Who's Will?" from Tommy.

"He's my uncle on my mother's side," from Harry.

A look of total incomprehension from Choon Guan.

Harry set about planning the attack. It was to be simple enough. He would unpeg two of the mines and cut the wire fence. The others would follow him in single file; they would place their explosive devices on the wing of each aircraft, set the timers and return in good order. Simple.

But as we have seen so many times before things don't always go the way you would like them to, no matter how foolproof or detailed your planning may be.

They returned to the bivvy area and slept for a couple of hours in the afternoon. As soon as it became dark they moved out following the game trail leading to the OP. At the observation point they moved down the escarpment towards the part of the fence nearest the aircraft, the same five as had been previously reported, an approach which gave them fortuitously the best cover from watching eyes on the small control tower which had been constructed on the galvanised shed noted in previous patrols. So far, so good.

Harry, using a thin wand of bamboo, and lying on his stomach with the rest of the force at a safe distance behind him, very carefully searched the ground until he lightly touched the tripwire. Now – which way was it pegged down, left or right? He moved to the right, lightly running the wire through his fingers until suddenly he found himself touching, not a peg, but the three upward prongs of the mine itself, not a pleasant encounter on a dark night. Slowly he moved back along the wire until he came to the peg. Here he came across another stumbling block. The peg was well driven in, with only a very small part of it above surface level. There was no way that, lying on the ground as he was; he was going to get sufficient vertical movement on it. He knelt up, and started carefully to pull upwards. It was very firmly embedded, and he was very much aware that any sudden movement in pulling the bloody thing out of the ground would almost certainly actuate the mine. Not something contained in the planning phase.

As he thought for a moment as to what he should do next, Tommy joined him.

"What's up?"

"Bloody peg's stuck in concrete I think."

"Why not cut the wire with the wire-cutters?"

"Would they do it cleanly enough without pulling on the wire?"

Harry had a point there. The wire-cutters had been used on thick barbed wire on numerous occasions, certainly not now possessing their pristine shearing ability they had when new.

"I've got an idea, hang on a minute." Tommy scrambled back to the waiting patrol.

"Anyone bring his parang with him?" One man had, the others knowing they would not need them had left them behind. They were encumbered enough with weapons, ammunition, food and explosive charges, parangs would only get in the way. Tommy crawled back to Harry.

"Dig around the peg with this," he suggested.

Harry knelt up again and slowly and carefully loosened the earth around the peg until he could get two hands on it and lift it straight upwards at first, then tilt it towards the mine. At last it came out.

"Not too many like that guv'nor," Harry whispered, looking up at the heavens. "Right, go back Tommy, and I'll remove the other one."

The second tripwire, nearest the wire fence was a piece of cake, to use Harry's description. Having pulled the peg out he cut a three feet hole in the base of the fence, marking the top of it with a piece of white cloth so that it could be readily found on the return journey.

By now it was past midnight, the guards would have been changed, the new ones settling in to the boredom of another four hours of doing nothing. It was time to move. It all went according to plan – up to a point! A point where having placed their charges and making their way back to the exit hole some stupid animal or other wandered into the minefield on the opposite side of the airstrip to the one for which they were heading.

"Run for it," urged Harry. They needed no second command. As they did so a searchlight was switched on mounted on the control tower, fortunately pointing away from them towards the place where the mine had exploded. There was no panic in the control tower, no alarm even. This sort of event occurred fairly regularly, they just had to check an animal had caused the alarm which they could readily achieve by lighting up the point of the incident and studying it through field glasses.

Harry's party made the fence and scrambled through one by one. Tommy and Harry waiting till last. It was at this juncture the operator on the searchlight, more through boredom than for any other reason, decided to make a sweep of his oversized flashlight around the remainder of the perimeter wire, which is when his observer spotted the backsides of the two officers crawling through his impenetrable minefield. He shouted. Mounted at the side of the searchlight was a type 96 light machine gun, attended by a gunner who, so far in this war, had not fired a shot in anger. He saw his chance to remedy this situation and excitedly pointed the weapon, as opposed to sighting it, at the illuminated backsides. He pulled the trigger. Nothing happened. In his rush to make a name for himself he had forgotten to remove the safety catch. During this delay Tommy had got through the wire to comparative safety leaving Harry to follow him. As Harry got half his body through the fence so the worst gunner in Hirohito's Imperial Japanese Army at last let off a long and totally useless burst in the general direction of one, Captain Harry Chandler. Despite his woeful incompetence however one bullet did make contact with Harry, furrowing the left cheek of his backside and ending up in his upper left arm. Harry roared with pain, which brought Tommy running back to him to help him to his feet and scramble into cover, accompanied by the cracking of innumerable bullets going everywhere except into their target.

"Where are you hit?" Tommy asked.

"Don't arse-k," Harry replied. Despite the pain, as he hung on to Tommy he was able to laugh at his reply, as did Tommy as he realised the situation. Harry continued.

"They will have a search party out soon, let's get out of here."

When they had put some distance between them and the wire they stopped and Tommy shone his flashlight on to Harry. He was bleeding quite badly from the flesh wound on his rear end, the bullet wound in the upper arm, although extremely painful, not bleeding too much.

Putting a field dressing on the cheek of a bum is not an easy thing to accomplish, particularly if you are possibly being hotly pursued. In this instance they need not have been too concerned about the latter in that the airfield guards were mustered from the ground staff. It was not considered necessary by the powers that be to have first line troops in such an out of the way place.

As they did their best to stop the bleeding, the local mosquitoes having a field day on the part of the exposed derriere not being treated, Harry held his hand up. They waited and listened. In a very short time, they heard the first explosion, followed by a second and then a third. And that was all for some very anxious minutes until two more went off almost simultaneously. What they had no means of knowing was that it was only a partial success. Two extremely brave young Japs had jumped on to a pair of planes as soon as the first explosion occurred, seized the bombs and threw them as far from the aircraft as they could, where they exploded harmlessly. Nevertheless, three out of five was not a bad result for a night's work.

At first light they moved off back to camp. Harry was in great pain now, and by midday was lagging badly. Tommy came back down the line to him.

"We are going to have to carry you."

"I thought you were going to say you were going to have to shoot me." Even in the straits in which he found himself Harry could still find a joke.

They quickly made a stretcher and put Harry on to it. Four men carried it unless the game trail was too narrow, in which case two men had the task.

"I'm very glad it is not Mr Ault we have to carry," said one of the stretcher-bearers. It's funny how you can find consolation somewhere, under all sorts of adverse conditions.

It was a cold, miserable, wet night. Although they tried to shelter Harry as best they could it is impossible to keep out tropical rain. As first light showed they moved on, not bothering to try and make a breakfast, they had time to make up if they had any hope of getting to camp before nightfall. The first aid man had done his best to make Harry comfortable, but was concerned about the bullet lodged against the bone in his arm. The arm had swollen badly and was giving a lot of pain. The earlier they could get Harry to Matthew Lee the better.

At long last they recognised the approaches to the camp. It was six o'clock in the afternoon and would soon be dark. As they got nearer, the picket sentry spotted them, pulled the warning cord, as a result a small party led by Reuben came out to meet them. Harry was quickly taken to the medical room while Tommy carried out the weapon and foot inspections. In the meantime Chantek was frantically pacing up and down her enclosure, emitting that sawing noise, banging on the communicating door to Harry's room without any answer forthcoming, totally unable to understand why she was not the centre of attraction to her newly returned master.

As a result of the air drops Matthew now had a supply of local anaesthetic equipment. He was therefore able to get the bullet out, although the entry point had started to become infected.

"You will have to have your tea from the mantelpiece for a few days I'm afraid," he told his patient, "otherwise you should be OK. You were very very lucky. If that bullet had been two inches to the right your spine would have been shattered."

Harry knew what that would have meant. You cannot carry a man with a shattered spine for two days; Tommy would really have had to carry out his gruesome task.

Chapter Twenty-Two

On the 18th June, as buzz bombs rained in on South East England David's company was dug in around some farm buildings facing a wooded ridge some four to five hundred yards away. It had so far been fairly quiet, except for sporadic shelling, along with the occasional incursion of night patrols. The company had a six pounder anti-tank gun in its position, with two more positioned out on their flanks. Their job was to prevent units of a panzer division known to be in front from reaching the Orne bridges thereby cutting the main road to Caen. The Second Army would soon be using that route to attack southwards to capture William of Conqueror's old capital city, an assault which would be as bloody as any during the war, taking weeks longer than at first planned.

It was just dark, the men not on stand-to, except for the sentries and forward pickets, gratefully tucking in to a hot meal, then to grab some sleep before themselves manning the guard posts. Paddy joined David in the small room in the farmhouse he had made his HQ.

"Mr Forster's sending me up another twenty-four blokes in the morning sir, before it gets light. I understand only ten of them are paras, from the depot, the others are general infantry reinforcements so I don't know what they will be like."

"Well, mix them in, as I have no doubt you were going to do anyway."

"I will that sir. Oh, by the way sir, the adjutant sent a runner. There's an 'O' group an hour after stand-down in the morning at battalion HQ."

"That probably means we are in for more fun and games."

"That's what I thought sir, so it was."

David got his head down. He was fairly happy with his newly reconstituted company. MacDuff had been allowed to stay with them as the Canadian battalion was well off for junior officers. Sandy Patterson still had 5 platoon, and a reinforcement officer, Lieutenant Roger Hammick, bringing his own personal batman to look after him, had taken over 6 platoon. The only problem was he still had no second in command. Paddy was carrying out those duties for the time being but obviously this could not last, Paddy had more than enough to do in his own job.

The night passed with only a couple of dozen shells in the company area and beyond. After stand-down the next morning, and a hurried breakfast of tea, bully and biscuits, David and Angus set off for battalion

HQ a mile or so back in some rather knocked about monastery buildings. When he arrived he was surprised to find he was the only company commander there. He was immediately grabbed by the adjutant and taken to the map room. The map room was an extremely scruffy monk's cell, a Tilley lamp hung from the ceiling over a camp trestle table and nothing else! except the maps of course. The colonel greeted him.

"David, how are your legs now, have they healed?"

"Yes sir, thank you, more or less."

"Which means they haven't bloody healed but you are not letting on – right?"

"Something like that sir."

Colonel Hislop turned to the adjutant. "Bloody heroes are all the same don't you agree Freddie?"

Freddie grinned.

"And how about those twins of yours, have they arrived yet?"

"Twins? You know more than I do sir, but no, they, I mean, the baby is not due for another month."

"Right then. Down to business. That big wood in front of your position. Divisional artillery are going to give it a good stonk at 1500 hours today for fifteen minutes. They are going to then put some smoke down in front of it and I want your company to do a reconnaissance in strength to see what's in it, and if possible what's behind it, and then retire to your company position. An FOO from the gunners will come with you and will be in radio contact so that when you leave the wood to retire over the open ground in front of your position they will put another stonk down to cover you. All clear?"

"All clear sir. Do you have any ideas as to what might be in it?"

"No. But aerial reconnaissance indicates numbers of vehicle tracks into it from the other side."

"Can I take a mortar man to bring down close support should I need it?"

"Good idea. Get that organised will you Freddie?"

David returned to his battered farm buildings and sent Angus off to get the platoon officers in for his company 'O' group. He explained the operation.

"Any questions?"

"What's in the wood sir?" from Sandy.

"Haven't a clue, that's one of the things we hope to find out."

As he spoke a battalion runner came in and gave Paddy a packet of half a dozen aerial photographs.

"The IO said they were taken yesterday sir, he has only just received them."

They studied them carefully, but apart from the fact they clearly indicated vehicle tracks from the road behind the wood across the open ground they told them little they did not know already.

"Right now. The most difficult part of the job is keeping together. Sandy, you go through on the left, Mac on the right, Roger you keep thirty to forty yards back in the centre. I shall be in front of you with my defence section pacing the reconnaissance. I will blow my whistle one blast every minute or so. That should enable you all to keep reasonably level with me. Two blasts means stop where you are. If you are fired upon go to ground and I will decide what the next step will be. Remember we are not looking for a fight; our orders are clearly to find out what is in there. The mortar platoon sergeant with radio operators will be with me to put down any close HE or smoke as required. An FOO from the gunners will also be with me to plaster it again as we leave so that no one can follow us up and catch us in the open. All clear so far?"

They each nodded.

"Right. When we leave the wood we will leave a platoon at a time. 4 platoon will go back half way at the double then go to ground to cover company HQ and 6 platoon. When they have carried this out 5 platoon will double back to their company positions to cover the return of the other two platoons. At this point I shall call down the artillery. Lastly, and this is most important, three long blasts on my whistle means the operation is completed. Either we shall have achieved our purpose or we have run into trouble or whatever. When you are in the wood, platoon commanders will move section by section covering one another, particularly on the return journey. If we do run into trouble you will find fighting in close country like that to be very very uncomfortable. Keep contact as much as you can."

They went their several ways, forming up as the barrage started. Apart from a sniper way over to the right who took one of MacDuff's men out, they reached the edge of the wood, the barrage having lifted. The wood itself was bisected laterally by, what David called, a ride, and in the direction in which they were travelling there were two such rides, each about ten feet wide. The wood itself was roughly four hundred yards deep according to the map. They had already found the maps, however, to be somewhat inaccurate.

Moving slowly through the thick undergrowth and waist high ferns in places, they met no opposition, until they came to the half way mark where the ground sloped down towards the rear edge, the open ground and the road. Paddy was up with David.

"This is too bloody quiet for my liking sir." David made no reply but had been increasingly concerned that things were going too well – the built-in pessimism of the professional infantryman coming to the fore! As Paddy's pronouncement and David's silence passed, so no fewer than four German MG42 machine guns opened up. Everyone hit the ground as a thousand rounds a minute from each gun cracked through the branches above them. The operators on the guns had no clear targets to aim at, relying on saturating the undergrowth with firepower. David turned to Angus.

"Follow me; keep five or six yards back."

He set off towards the guns, using trees for shelter as best he could. As he looked to his right he saw Paddy doing the same three trees away. What he didn't know was that Sandy and Mac had decided on the same plan of action, in fact Mac had found a gully running up beside the gun on his side, crawled along it with his batman in tow and lobbed a hand grenade. As soon as the grenade exploded his batman was over the top of the gulley and finished off two of the gun crew who remained, getting back into the gulley and back to their platoon position before another gun realised what had happened. There was no such approach for David or Sandy.

"Angus, get back to the mortar man. Get him to drop one on the back of the wood. Get the radio man up here and we will then talk him on to the targets."

Angus crawled back into cover then ran doubled up to the company HQ group, returning with an extremely windy radio operator, he who had volunteered for the radio operator's course since it seemed the occupation would be infinitely preferable to sticking a bayonet into a six foot Jerry.

As they settled behind the cover of the bole of a large chestnut tree, the first mortar bomb arrived. They were very well aware of its arrival in that it exploded only twenty yards in front of them. Luckily the chestnut tree had been there for a couple of hundred years and had no intention of being removed by a mere mortar bomb.

"Up one hundred right five degrees," David calculated.

In a few seconds the second mortar bomb arrived in the general area of one of the centre guns.

"Put ten down there," David ordered the radio man. Another slight delay and down they came, all the mortar platoon having a great time. Whether it was by luck, judgement, or discretion on the part of the gun team, nothing more was heard from gun number two.

"Left ten degrees. Put ten more down." The radio man passed the message, cringing a bit that the bloody major didn't even know how to order the shoot properly. Right or not, it had the right effect and both remaining guns gave up the ghost. David waited a while, gave one blast on his whistle and they all moved forward again until they came to the point at which they could see the edge of the wood. He gave two blasts. With everyone remaining where they were he, Paddy and Angus moved forward. The undergrowth here had all been cleared and there was evidence the cover from the trees had been used to conceal a very large petrol dump. A large number of jerrycans were lying around, presumably having developed leaks therefore not being removed when the dump had been either evacuated or put to use. This would explain the vehicle tracks on the aerial photos.

"Right, there's nothing more to do here. Let's get back," David said to Paddy.

They turned and went back to the company, David then blowing his three blasts to signify the planned withdrawal. As they commenced this phase of the operation they were given a parting present of a number of airbursts from the German positions. David blew two blasts and the men sheltered as best they could against the trees.

"Sir," the artillery FO called out to David, "I'm going back to the front edge to see if I can spot those guns and then organise a bit of counter-battery work."

"Righto lieutenant. By the way what's your name? – never thought to ask you."

"Middleton sir."

"No, your Christian name."

"Cuthbert."

Paddy, hearing the discourse said to David, "I'd better take a couple of blokes and go with him sir, don't you think? Can't trust these bloody gunners on their own, he'll only get lost."

"Good idea. Take three men from the defence section. But – don't get in harm's way."

"That sir, you can bet your life on."

'It's your bloody life I'm worried about', David thought.

David gave three blasts again and they all moved back, with the exception of the FOO party, which moved quickly to a convenient point behind some bushes. As they took up their position they spotted the gun flashes from a small copse over to their right. Cuthbert checked it out on his map, gave the grid reference number to the radio operator who in turn sent it back to the twenty-five pounders back behind 'R' Battalion HQ.

"They are sending a ranger sir."

As the operator spoke the shell whistled over them landing some three hundred yards in front, and a hundred yards to the left of the enemy guns. Cuthbert gave the corrections and a second ranger was sent over, which was very close. The message passed on, the operator said, "They are firing a mauve smoke shell on to the target sir, and leaving it to Typhoons."

The gunners had been told there was a flight of Typhoons patrolling Gold and Juno and would like to take a crack at the target. A minute later the coloured marker shell arrived very close indeed to the flashes, followed by the sound of aircraft.

"There they are sir," said Paddy.

The 'V' flight spotted the marker, peeled off, circled around over the wood, the leader then pointing its deadly weapons at the mauve indicator. As Paddy told David later, "The first one was about four hundred yards away when he let the first two rockets go. I don't know what it did to the Jerries, but it certainly put the shits up me just to watch it. He peeled off and the second one came in. The rockets from the first one must have hit an ammunition limber – there was a hell of a firework display. The second one let two more into the target and we saw vehicles trying to get away down the road behind them. The third one came in, did a turn so that he was flying in the same line as the vehicles, let a couple of rockets go, which hit a truck which blocked the road, then he carried on firing his cannons at the others. The first two planes, seeing what had happened circled round and plastered the whole bloody issue. I've never seen such a complete pandemonium in all my life, and it was all over in five minutes."

They had seen one of the first attacks by the 'cab-rank' Typhoons, a single-engined, single-crewed airplane which was to strike fear into the occupants any German vehicle or tank moving in daylight. On one day alone, as has previously been recounted, Typhoons destroyed 135 enemy tanks in France.

Having seen the carnage, the FOO with Paddy's party quickly made their way back to company HQ, David having already left to report to Colonel Hislop. Casualties had been reasonably light. One killed by the sniper early on, another killed by shrapnel, and four others being made walking wounded, again from the artillery fire.

They stayed in that sector for another comparatively quiet, four days, before being relieved to go back to a rest area. Not that the rest area was miles behind the lines. The bridgehead the division held was not only comparatively small, it was also overlooked in the main by a high ridge which ran in a sweeping curve from the sea, inland, then round towards Caen. Beyond that ridge, intelligence had told them a panzer division had moved in which had been sent down from the Pas de Calais – Hitler had at last realised Normandy was the main invasion point.

In the late afternoon of the 23rd June Colonel Hislop called his 'O' group.

"We are taking over the positions of 'L' Battalion tomorrow," he told them. "On Sunday night the battalion will attack the large village of Treville, just on top of and over the ridge. I shall be giving company tasks and so on once we have taken over from 'L' Battalion. This is an advance warning for you to get everything ready for our first major battalion attack." He paused for a moment. "Not that I thought for one moment you weren't always ready for anything of course."

Having passed the information on about moving out on the morrow, the platoon commanders following suit, he called them back in, along with Paddy, telling them of the proposed operation so that everyone and everything was in fighting order, but not to leak information about the target until he had more detail.

There was an awful lot to do before the attack was to take place. One ray of sunshine however illuminated their day – a big bundle of post. In addition to several letters from Maria saying how enormous she was and how unlovely she looked, there were messages from all sorts of people from whom he would not have expected to have heard. Karl, Doctor Carew, General Strich, whose life he had saved at Calais three years before and who was now back in England from North Africa. Even Ronnie Mascall from the riding stable had dropped him a line, but the biggest surprise was a most amusing and erudite letter from none other than Robin, as a result of which David at last learnt his real name, 'Robin' of course having been his code name. David was not unduly surprised to find that his mentor during the years he worked for Lord Ramsford doing foreign undercover assignments was none other than Sir William Blessinger. Bart – his address being the property at Wilmslow where David had spent so much time.

He saw Paddy passing by his doorway – I say doorway since the door had been blown off and subsequently chopped up long since for firewood to boil water for tea.

"Paddy!" CSM O'Riordan was surprised to be hailed like this; David was invariably meticulous regarding the military niceties of rank when others were around.

"Sir?"

"I've had a letter from Robin. Guess who he really is?" He handed the letter to Paddy.

"Well, sir, he must think we are near to winning the war to let on like this. Mind you, when I saw those Typhoons yesterday I had no doubts – I haven't stopped thinking about them since."

He had a long letter from Rose, passing on news she had received from Mark and Charlie. Emma was terribly upset their wedding had to be put back, but they were all much looking forward to Nanny and Harold's wedding on Saturday 24th June and the reception afterwards at The Angel which Uncle Jack was laying on. As he had said, "Well Nanny is more or less family is she not?"

"What's the date today?" he enquired of Paddy.

"Twenty-third sir."

"Nanny is getting married tomorrow. So come in at two o'clock and we will drink a toast to them."

"Do you mean like you did at my wedding sir?"

"Oh crikey, no. The memory of my pushing a dead drunk Father Kelly through Aylesbury in a wheelbarrow is constantly with me. I still pee myself with laughing at the thought of it."

"What time are we moving out tomorrow sir?"

"I haven't got the final movement orders yet. I'll give you a shout the minute I get them. Hallo, who have we here?"

A tall, rather scholarly looking officer, wearing the three pips of a captain on his shoulders and an ordinary infantry cap as opposed to a red beret had appeared in the doorway – I say doorway, but then I have already described the circumstances surrounding the doorway.

"Major Chandler sir?"

"None other. What can I do you for?"

The captain was a little taken aback by the somewhat unmilitary answer. He saluted.

"I've been sent to you as your replacement second in command sir. My name is Simon Finkelstein. I am in the Kings Royal Rifle Corps."

"The KRR's eh? We have vaguely heard of them sergeant major, have we not?"

"Very vaguely sir, though normally it's something we don't talk about in the City Rifles. It's a bit like saying you know somebody doing time, so it is sir, or your unmarried sister is in the club."

"Well Simon, KRR or not KRR you are now a member of the most illustrious regiment in the British Army, namely The Parachute Regiment." He stood up and shook hands with his new 2 i/c, Paddy too giving him a salute and shaking hands.

"Welcome to the best company in the best battalion in the best regiment sir, you've fallen on your feet here sir."

David intervened. "Mind you sergeant major; being a prospective parachutist he should always fall on his feet, should he not?"

"Oh, when he gets to Ringway sir he'll learn that quick enough."

Simon looked from one to the other thinking what the hell are they talking about?

"Well Simon, you are just in time to take part in a battle which I am assured from the highest authority will have a salutary effect on the ending of the war."

"I only came ashore yesterday sir."

"Look, my name's David, no sir's except on parade – OK? Anyway, tell us briefly what you have been doing so far in the war."

"Not a lot, I suppose is the answer to that. I was in the Queen Vics as a territorial." David swiftly interrupted.

"Were you at Calais?" and then added, "No, you couldn't have been. They were all killed or captured."

"No. As luck would have it I had been selected for Octu and left the battalion a week before they were rushed to Calais." At the mention of Calais where David's brother-in-law Jeremy, his greatest friend, had perished, David's face clouded over. Simon continued.

"I was commissioned at the end of the summer 1940, went to a battalion on coastal defence in the KRR's until the end of '42 when I was made up to captain, spent six months as an OCTU instructor, went back to the battalion and found I was supernumerary, so I missed the landings on D+3 when the battalion came ashore. When I came out on a draft we were warned we might be posted anywhere, not necessarily to our own regiments. I certainly didn't expect to end up as a paratrooper; I'm told they live frightfully dangerous lives."

"Well, I've had no second in command since we arrived. The Sergeant Major here has been doing both his job and the 2 i/c's for the past two weeks – God, have we been here only two weeks?"

"Two weeks and three days sir."

"To quote your proverbial comment Mr O'Riordan, bloody hell!"

"Is it in order to ask what happened to your previous 2 i/c?"

"The straight answer is, we don't know. His body has not been found, but by a series of reasonable assumptions and deductions we feel sure he was dropped in the River Dives and drowned. I am afraid a number of people from the battalion must have suffered that ghastly fate. We ourselves," nodding to Paddy, "were only inches away."

There was a silence for a few moments.

"Shall I take the captain and go through books and things sir? Then I will get down to Mr Forster to make sure my ammunition indent is made up."

"What you mean is RSM Forster will have a spare bottle of Scotch into which he may invite you to dip. Am I right, or am I right?"

"You may not be far wrong sir, let's put it that way."

Simon Finkelstein was beginning to feel he was in a very congenial company.

They had an 0430 reveille the next morning, moving up the five miles to take over from 'L' Battalion, well dug-in in hedgerows and light woodland some fifteen hundred yards from the enemy positions. Gradually 'L' Battalion filtered back out to prepared positions to act as reserve in the event 'R' Battalion failed in their attack, and the Germans counter-attacked.

At 2.30pm at David's company HQ he was joined by Paddy, who produced an army issue water bottle supernumerary to that which he wore on his waistbelt. "Mr Forster sent this up sir," he told David.

David grabbed his tin mug into which Paddy poured a generous measure of Vat 69. They both stood up.

"To Nanny and Harold," David pronounced.

Paddy repeated the toast, at which they both took a good swig of the usquebaugh, which undertaking was interrupted by the entry of the new 2 i/c.

"Are you toasting our success tomorrow night gentlemen?" he asked. David explained.

"Two friends of ours are at this moment getting married, hence the raising of glasses, well, not exactly glasses, but it sounds better than mugs don't you think Mr O'Riordan?"

"Oh much more better, sir, much more better."

Simon's first thought was 'how would a major and a sergeant major come to have mutual friends'? He asked.

"Army friends David?"

"Oh no, sort of family friends back home."

Simon was even more puzzled. The major was very young, the sergeant major was obviously a time-served Irish regular soldier, how could they be connected 'back home'. 'I'll find out one day I suppose', he told himself.

At 0900 hours on the 25th June David attended the battalion 'O' group. At 1000 hours he returned to his company HQ to hold his own 'O' group and instruct his platoon commanders as to the battalion/company/their specific platoon, task. Everybody was to know exactly what they had to do, furthermore to have a good knowledge of what the other companies and supporting arms were to do. It was not to be easy. They had been told that the ridge upon which Treville was lodged was held by a unit of SS Panzers. They were formidable opponents who would fight for every yard. It was to be a night attack. Control of night fighting was one of the most difficult tasks of any commander, from a lance corporal in charge of a section through to the colonel in charge of the battalion. David had this very unhappy feeling he was to lose good men tonight. In his gloomiest thoughts he would not have believed how many he was to lose.

Chapter Twenty-Three

It had been intended that Nanny's wedding to Harold James would be a quiet affair, with a small reception after the ceremony at The Angel. In the event Nanny, Harold and Jack entirely miscalculated, firstly how popular Nanny was with the wide and extended Chandler and Hooper families, secondly of how well regarded Harold was at Short's, and thirdly how much the people of Sandbury loved a good wedding. As a result the church was comfortably full.

On 26th June, two days after the wedding it would be Nanny's daughter Sophia's fourteenth birthday. Back in April, in the presence of Nanny's aunt Esther, who had brought Sophia up as her own, they had told the child the true story. Sophia of course, although a mature thirteen year old, was confused and bewildered by the revelation. For all her formative years she had called Esther 'Mummy', now she had a new mother and her 'mother' had become her great aunt. In addition she had to accept the fact that a man she hardly knew, although she thought him a very gentlemanly person, was in fact to be her step-father.

Fortunately Nanny, Harold and Esther had treated Sophia as a grown-up. Once she had accepted the situation they asked her whether she had views on the way they should live their lives in the future. Sophia suggested she lived on at Tankerton; after all, all her friends were there, she was very happy at the little private school she attended, and the social life she was beginning to enjoy at the local church. She could then visit Eleanor, it had been decided she should call Nanny by her Christian name rather than 'mother', on one weekend and perhaps Eleanor and Harold could come to Tankerton on alternate weekends, when he was not on duty with Sir Jack. Like all these sorts of situations the truth of the matter gradually leaked out, was perhaps a five minute wonder, then was promptly forgotten.

On the 24th of June therefore, Nanny Cavendish walked down the aisle of St John's on the proud arm of Sir Jack Hooper, attended by her daughter Sophia, marshalling young John Hooper, Elizabeth and Mark Chandler each now six years old, who Nanny had cared for from babyhood.

Whisper. "Who's the bridesmaid?"
Answer. "Some sort of relative I believe."

As the service progressed the sickening sound of a flying bomb, now known generally as the V-1, was heard approaching. The evil phut-phutting noise it made was listened to by people who fervently hoped that its engine would continue to function, therefore would not drop on them. Combined with that feeling would be the guilt that they were wishing the fiendish device to land somewhere else, which could well mean on someone else. As it was it phut-phutted on into the distance and disappeared. It was only one of a dozen they heard that day and during the following night.

The reception followed the pattern of most receptions. In addition to the short but very sincere speech by Harold, Eleanor expressed her deep gratitude to Sir Jack and Lady Moira for acting 'in loco parentis' as it were, in providing this beautiful reception. Not, she added, that either of them looked remotely old enough to be her parents. At seven o'clock the couple left to take the train to London, and then on Sunday to go on to The Crown at Lyndhurst in the New Forest for their honeymoon. At eleven o'clock the remainder of the guests who had not already drifted off, left for their houses, leaving Esther and Sophia to stay the night at The Angel and to have Sunday lunch with the Hoopers before leaving for Tankerton in the afternoon.

At eleven o'clock, as the last of the guests made their various ways homeward, Emma Langham, now a chief Wren, equivalent to a petty officer, made her way from the RM Barracks in Deal to her billet in a small hotel in a side street leading from the main street down to the front. It was a fairly light night. As she approached the turning into her side street she saw two American soldiers coming towards her. These she guessed were part of a large contingent of anti-aircraft troops drafted into Hell Fire Corner in an attempt to shoot down the ever increasing number of V-1's being directed at London and the South East, before they could reach their targets. The pavement was quite narrow. When she saw they were not going to make way for her she stepped into the deserted road. As she did so the one on the outer edge of the pavement also stepped into the road, rather unsteadily in fact – they had both been hitting the bottle was Emma's immediate appreciation of the situation.

"What have we here?" he asked of his companion.

"Looks like one of them sailor girls we heard about," was the slurred reply.

"Give me a kiss, sailor girl," said the one in the road. Emma tried to run between them but each grabbed her, one holding her tie and groping her breasts, the other attempting to get his hand up her skirt. She screamed,

"Let me go you beasts."

"Ho! We've got one of those hoity-toity ones Arni, not like them Lancashire girls."

By now her jacket buttons ripped off and her shirt being pulled open by one of her attackers, while despite her struggling, the other still endeavouring to get his hand up her knicker-leg, she sunk her teeth into the wrist of the one holding her tie, and kicked out at the second. It was a lucky kick for it caught him right in what Harry Chandler would have described as his wedding tackle. They each yelled furiously, she slipped away from them and ran around the corner of the street in which she had her billet, straight into the arms of two marine corporals just returning to barracks.

"What's up love?" but in asking the question they immediately knew the answer, since the Americans had decided to give chase to their victim. They slid to a halt as they saw the marines, but before they could turn and run they were grabbed. The shirt ripper got a thump in the solar plexus from marine number one which would have not done any good to anybody, let alone one whose gut at that moment was full of Kentish beer. He sank to the ground, his head on the edge of the gutter and vomited his heart up. Number two marine in the meantime had pushed the second American up against the wall.

"He was the one who indecently assaulted me," she said. She had a wry smile at herself later when she recalled the incident, thinking of how ridiculously legal she must have sounded, on the other hand she could hardly have said he had put his hand up her kilt.

"Oh, is he?" With that he used the American as a punch bag, an object to which the corporal normally had frequent access, since he was the light heavy-weight champion of the Corps. The American sank slowly to the ground.

"Where's your cap miss?"

"It must be in the main road."

They found it in the gutter. She shook hands with them both and thanked them for her deliverance, as they watched two would-be ravishers stagger away.

There was a predictable outcome to this incident. The Americans got back to their unit looking as though they had had a collision with a bus and had come off worst. They spun the yarn they had been set upon by half a dozen marines.

The corporals got back to their barrack-room and told the story of how they had given a couple of Americans a lesson who they found trying to rape one of the Wrens.

As a result the next night, small gangs of Americans, and small gangs of marines, roamed the fair town of Deal looking for a punch-up, and in the main succeeding, until the combined military, naval and US police – 'snowdrops', on account of the white helmets they wore – thumped a few belligerents with their staves, until the antipathy fizzled out.

The interesting factor about rape by American forces in Britain during the war was that some twenty-three black US servicemen were convicted and had their appeals refused. They were each hanged in Shepton Mallet jail in Somerset. Double that number of white US servicemen were convicted of the same offence, were not hanged, but were shipped back to the States to suffer imprisonment. They were all released early on in their sentences.

But, back to the wedding.

One of the guests was Major Margaret Coulter, who attended in company with Rose, Jeremy, Megan, oh, and Fred of course. She had not been to a wedding in an English church as yet.
"Well thank your lucky stars it's June," Fred had told her, "it's damned cold in that church in the winter I can tell you."
"How on earth would you know," queried Rose, "you never go to church anyway." She could immediately have bitten her tongue off on realising that her mother's funeral service had taken place on the coldest of January days. Fred passed it off in his own inimitable way.
"Well, you don't have to go to the Sahara to know it's hot."
Rose was so thankful he had let her off the hook of her indiscretion.

We have established on several occasions that things tend to happen at wedding receptions. There would appear to be a peculiar kind of miasma floating around on such occasions exuding influence on other people's 'affaires de coeur', besides that of the newlyweds. In other words people tend to get a bit soppy at weddings, as Harry undoubtedly would have put it. It was so with two couples with whom we are closely connected. Karl and Rosemary had been invited. After the speeches, the going around and saying goodbye, the waving away and the return to the tables to chat and drink a little – or a lot depending on who you were – Rosemary and Karl, who had previously been seated with Ernie and Anni and others of course, found themselves for a while by themselves.

"It was a nice wedding – ja? Oh Rosemary, I must get out of the habit of saying ja, Anni is often telling me of it."

"Yes, it really was a nice wedding, and don't worry about your habits, you have lovely habits."

"I may have some bad ones you don't know about."

"Then it would be up to me to gently wean you away from them. On the other hand of course I might not consider they are bad, in which case I could join you in them."

"Can you count what you are thinking, to being a habit?" he asked.

"I suppose you can if you keep on thinking it."

He paused.

"In that case I have a very bad habit. It is about you, and about making love with you."

She put her cheek against his.

"That is one habit I would encourage," a pause, "definitely."

They sat holding hands together.

"Would you marry me Rosemary? I know I am not a young man any more, but that I cannot alter, however..."

She put her forefinger on his lips.

"You are in the prime of life. Yes, I will marry you, but I must tell my family first – may I?"

"Yes of course." She kissed him lightly on the lips and was caught in the act by Anni and Ernie returning from having their conversation with Ray and June about their forthcoming wedding in September.

"Hallo hallo, snogging in public now are we?" asked Ernie and turning to Anni, "If this is what they get up to in public, what do they do in the back of that bus they travel on?"

Rosemary, normally most correct with her stepchildren-to-be, surprised them with, "Well, you will be interested to know that I made a curtain for the bus, so that when we get on we just pull it across. It is astonishing what you can do in a half hour journey there and a half hour journey back."

"I wonder you're fit for work," Ernie exclaimed, and turning to Anni, "No wonder your father gets out of the wiping-up at night nowadays. I had put it down to mental fatigue, now we know the real reason."

"Real reason for what?" said a voice at his elbow. It was Fred with a smiling Margaret at his side.

"Rosemary here has just admitted she's made a curtain they can pull when they get into their bus to and from work, so as to shut them off from the others."

Fred continued the leg-pull.

"To think such things go on in the God-fearing county of Kent. And right under our noses too. I shall have to have a word with Canon Rosser about this. And the ministry, they wouldn't like these goings-on on ministry property."

Rosemary turned to a chuckling Karl, taking his hand again.

"They are only jealous, dear," she said.

The Anni-Ernie-Margaret-Fred antennae noticed immediately a new level of intimacy in her method of address to Karl, which led to considerable, and as it proved, accurate speculation on the part of Anni and Ernie when they lay in bed that night.

In addition, it was a catalyst which directed Margaret and Fred's conversation later into realms which otherwise would not have been reached so soon, if at all. When Fred, Margaret and Rose reached Chandlers Lodge at around eleven o'clock, they sat for a few minutes in the kitchen.

"I wonder what the boys are doing tonight," Rose pondered. It was a question constantly surfacing in her mind, as it did in the minds of millions of others all over the world day in – day out, but as there was no positive answer forthcoming from her querying, it was left in mid-air. She followed a few seconds later with,

"I am rather tired. It's been a long day and I didn't get my usual afternoon rest, so I'll go on up." In another month both Rose and Maria would be producing additions to the Chandler family. Saying her goodnights she made her way somewhat heavily up the wide staircase. Margaret and Fred sat facing each other.

"I've got a tiny drop of Scotch left. Would you like a nightcap?" he asked.

"I don't think so Fred, thank you very much. But if you have two tiny drops why don't you put them together and give yourself a reasonable nightcap. After all, you don't have a wedding every day of the week."

"Would you like some of your coffee – I won't offer you ours." Margaret had raided the PX store at her HQ and brought coffee and other goodies with her for her short weekend stay.

"I'll make it; you get your nightcap."

They each attended to their task, then sat back at the huge deal table which had seen so many family gatherings over the years.

"I've heard that I might be posted again."

Fred's heart sank. "Oh no, don't say that, you're the nicest thing that has happened to us for years. Where will they send you?"

"I honestly don't know, what's more I can't even hazard a guess. I procure equipment. To procure equipment you have to have suppliers, where else are there suppliers but the UK? The war here will be over in the foreseeable future. I suppose suppliers would be available in India and to a lesser extent Australia for the war in the Far East, but they would take time to become operative. No, equipment will still come from Stateside and the UK." She thought deeply. "I wouldn't want to leave here. I've fallen in love with England, its greenness, its beautiful buildings, its general way of life."

"How about its people?" She looked at him, candidly.

"In particular its people."

Fred looked away.

"I've never wished to be younger than I happened to be, at any time in my life that I can remember. I do now."

"I don't see what age has to do with it. Correction. Age has to be taken into account, but it surely is only one of the many aspects that make up a relationship."

They sat silent for a while.

"When will you know if you are to be posted? After all, if the war ends as you predict, and I quite agree with you on that, you will probably be sent back home anyway."

"To answer your first question, I don't know – it could all be rumour, probably is. As regards my going home, because of my age and my terms of enlistment I can resign at any time, and if it comes to that, at any place. I shall not resign all the time I am needed and am doing a worthwhile job you may be sure, but I have been seriously thinking that when the war ends I shall stay in England." She hesitated again. "That's if they'll have me."

"Oh, we'll have you alright, you can count on it," Fred said enthusiastically, putting his hand over hers on the table top. She placed her other hand on his.

"You know, Fred, since my husband was killed I have been a sort of comfortable drifter. I have made a few friends, had a number of offers, as you can imagine, most of them of a fleeting nature, some extremely fleeting!" she laughed into his eyes, "but nowhere in all my travels have I felt at home, have felt settled. Even in London, which I love, it felt I was in just another city. A very knocked about city I agree, but beautiful all the same. Then I came down here to Kent and saw these rolling Downs, the oast houses, the orchards, the beautiful soft countryside, and I felt an immediate sense, at the age of forty-two, and of having travelled all over the world, of coming home. Does that seem ridiculous to you?"

"No, no definitely not. On behalf of the people of Kent I am flattered that you should feel that way."

"It wasn't only the countryside; it was the people as well. I haven't met people in other parts of the United Kingdom, and they might have welcomed me as warmly as the people of Sandbury have, but nowhere have I been taken in so kindly as I have been by everyone I have met here. We Americans are often treated with suspicion in different parts of the world on the basis of our only being there to make a fast buck. Here everyone, and you and Rose in particular, have made me feel welcome because I'm Margaret Coulter, not for any other reason."

Fred put his other hand on hers.

"Well, you see, the first time I saw you through the Venetian blinds in my window, getting out of your car with colonel Pompous I said out loud 'That lady is something special'. That opinion has grown stronger ever since."

She smiled at him, he smiled back. They stood up.

"I must go to bed." She kissed him lightly on the lips, squeezed his hands and made her way upstairs, leaving Fred to lock up and check the windows as he always did, and to wonder if there was any way he could overcome a twenty-two year age gap between himself and someone he was becoming very fond of indeed. He lay awake for a long time thinking the matter over from A to Z, but getting nowhere. One aspect he gave no thought to however, probably more important than any he was cogitating, was in which direction the lady in question was directing her thoughts, or having her thoughts directed. There is a difference.

On Sunday they all went to Matins, but not before Rose had remarked that with Fred Chandler going to church two days in a row the roof would fall in. There was in fact a precedent for this, well, not exactly a precedent but as near as makes no difference. Sir Oliver Routledge was the biggest landowner for many miles around. His family had lived in that part of Kent for four hundred odd years. One of his forebears, back in the early sixteen hundreds, had discovered to his horror that the crypt in which his family was interred was full up. In those days the nobility and gentry were buried inside the church in the nave, so that they did not have to lie with the hoi polloi in the churchyard.

Sir Oliver, therefore, he too having the name given to the eldest son, decided he would extend the crypt. After all, he paid the stipend of the priest, so he more or less could do as he pleased with the church property. He therefore got the builders and masons in to do the work. Under normal circumstances this would be fairly simple. A question of lifting some flagstones, digging out the extension to the existing crypt, walling-up the vault, putting in supporting beams on which the flagstones would be re-laid and bob's your uncle. The only problem was, that in digging out one corner of the extension it was found to foul the footings of a column which held up that section of the roof. The clerk of works, or whatever they called the boss man in those days, sent a message to sir Oliver to come and give advice and further instructions.

Now it must be said here that Sir Oliver knew a bit about farming, a bit more about hounds and a lot about horses. He knew bugger all, despite the fact he was a Freemason, about masonry. He therefore instructed the C of W to chop off the corner of the footings so as to accommodate his crypt, and stayed on to watch the men at work – a pastime he thoroughly enjoyed.

He should not have done this.

As a result of the ground support being weakened the column leaned, only slightly, at the base. Now, as you have already suspected I fancy, this small movement at the base was greatly magnified outwards forty feet above to the extent that a gap appeared in the heavily leaded roof which it supported, and which promptly fell in on top of Sir Oliver, the C of W and one unfortunate labourer. Needless to say, the new sir Oliver had the disaster put right, buried his father in the new crypt a good deal earlier than had been expected, having removed the somewhat battered carcass of the C of W and labourer to be laid to rest where they belonged – outside.

It is surprising what has happened under your very feet in years gone by. People walking down London's Cannon Street, in the heart of the City, walk over a plague pit every day and know not it is there. But that is another story.

The weekend over, Fred took Margaret to the station. As they waited for the London train Fred asked "Can you come down next weekend?"

"No, unfortunately. I have to travel on Sunday by train with a small party to a place called Barrow in Furness. Have you ever been there?"

"No, I can't say that I have. They make submarines there I believe, or used to. Probably now they make a bit of everything like a lot of the big firms."

"Well, I shall not know what it's all about until our conference on Saturday. But it must be a devil of a way away if it is going to take all day to get there."

"It's probably off the beaten track, so the train driver has to stop every now and then to milk the cows or something."

"The following weekend should be OK – if you'll have me."

"Definitely, and every weekend after, is my answer to that one."

"You really meant that didn't you, Fred?"

As the train pulled in, Fred held her elbows and kissed her, saying, "I've never meant anything more in all my life."

Driving back to the 'my little plant' as he jokingly referred to it on occasion, he pondered on the situation in which he found himself. Three months ago he would have considered, firstly that at sixty-four people don't go around being in love, that was for sixteen year olds. Secondly, the likelihood of his finding someone he could call a soul mate was remote in the extreme. Thirdly, if he did find such a being, the likelihood of her being attracted to him to the same extent would be even more remote. Now, it would appear that the world was standing on its head, and the impossible had happened. He then came down to earth with a bump. He could not get away from the fact he was sixty-four. If the three score years and ten lodestar was correct, he only had six years to go anyway! This thought came to him as quite a shock, despite the fact that like most people of sixty-four, three score years and ten applied to other people.

He arrived at the factory, and the immediate Monday morning problems hit him to the extent that even the thoughts of the beautiful Margaret went from his mind. But they returned during his coffee break. And his lunch break. And his tea break.

The following day came the great news that the Americans had captured Cherbourg. The Allies now had a major port in their hands. The bad news was that the Germans had demolished quays, cranes, warehouses, and anything else which would have helped their enemy. So efficiently had they carried out their task that it would take months to get the port open again. Ships had been sunk at the entrance, Cherbourg was one of many examples of the fact that the Germans may well be of the opinion they were losing the war, but they were not going to make it any easier for the Allies to get a quick victory.

Day after day V-1's attacked the south east. During the day fighter pilots found some of them and tipped them over. In the two weeks since the assault began Winston Churchill told the nation that 2750 of these hideous machines had been launched. They had killed 2752 people – an average of one per bomb, although to that had to be added some 8000 injured. They were absolutely indiscriminate. On the 30th June a nursery not far from Sandbury, near Chartwell, was hit. Twenty-two tiny children were killed, to be identified eventually in the main by the little labels they wore on their ankles. So far in this war 7736 babies and children had been killed, and as many again had been injured and hospitalised. One hundred launch sites had been found in France, Belgium and Holland and had been destroyed, to be quickly rebuilt.

It was not until the 11th and 12th of July that London had bomb free nights, but this was not the case in Kent which suffered badly during both those hours of darkness. The 12th of July also brought the news of another execution for spying. A Belgian, Joseph Vanhove, was hanged at Pentonville prison, raising the question from Sir Jack, "Why would a Belgian, whose country had been raped twice by Germany, spy for them?" As none in his small audience knew the answer to that, it remained unanswered.

Chapter Twenty-Four

Major David Chandler, 'B' Company Commander, took his three platoon commanders Sandy Patterson, Archie MacDuff and Roger Hammick, along with his new 2ic Simon Finklestein, Paddy his CSM, and of course Angus, his batman, to the observation point in the forward edge of a wood from which the western perimeter of Treville could be seen. On the way they met his friend Major Claude Warren, commander of 'A' Company, and his entourage. There was the usual good-natured banter, though they both knew it could well be the last time they would see each other. Attacking an SS unit well dug in, they too with the advantage of a commanding height, was obviously going to be a dicey business.

Reaching the cover of the observation point David said, "Right, you've seen the layout of the place on the aerial photographs. We are to attack to the right hand side of the church tower, 'A' Company are on the left hand side, and 'C' Company will be in reserve to be pushed forward if either of us get stuck. 4 platoon will be on our left, that is nearest to the line of the church tower, 6 platoon will be on the right, taking your line of advance Roger that white building in the trees there." They all trained their field glasses on to the objective. "I shall be with 5 platoon ready to reinforce where necessary. But remember this, I intend to reinforce success. If one of you gets stuck and the other is still bashing on, I will support him with the intention of getting in behind the resistance causing the hold up. Your final objective is the line A-A on the photograph, the track running across the back of the village, overlooking the valley on the other side of the ridge. Dig in fast, as soon as their artillery knows we have taken the place they will plaster us, you can be sure."

They all studied the objective intently. It was as plain as a pikestaff now, but in the dark, smoke from the inevitable burning buildings, and the general fog of war, it would be a very different place to the trim, neat vista before them.

Simon was standing next to David.
"What will happen to the residents do you think?"
"They either get moved out by Gerry, or they move out themselves when they see Gerry digging in, or they trust to luck in their cellars. Some of them unfortunately will die in the barrage."
They moved back to the company positions to wait for dusk and the move up to their start points. Colonel Hislop and Major Gillespie made

the rounds during this period, wishing the men well, telling them the village was to get a good stonking from the Highland Division artillery for half an hour as they moved off. "That will keep the buggers' heads down," he joked.

As 'H' hour approached David and Paddy too made their rounds. He was very happy with Sandy and Mac, Roger was still a bit of an unknown quantity, but looked good. On a night like this, on an attack like this, the main burden of leadership would fall on the section sergeants and corporals. This battle, a night fight in close or built-up country would break into dozens of smaller clashes where the individual's fighting spirit would win the day, or in this case, the night.

They moved up to the start line.
"Bit like going over the top sir, isn't it?" Angus said to David.
"I suppose you're right. Was your father in the last lot?"
"Yes sir. Seaforth Highlanders. Wounded twice. Second time a Blighty one. They saved his leg but he couldn't bend it again. Still he survived, most of the young men in the village didn't."

The officers looked at their watches. At ten o'clock the barrage started and they moved forward in the standard five yards apart formation. The barrage may have had its main purpose to keep the Jerry heads down; it also served of course to warn them that something was up. Immediately from the flanks of their positions came the menacing chatter of machine guns. Roger Hammick's 6 platoon was the first to take casualties. Three men were hit, others stopped to help their comrades until Roger roared, "Leave them, press on, press on." Medics following up would attend them. Nothing must jeopardise the compactness of the platoon advance.

They were half way to their objective, very much uphill now. The slope up to the village was much steeper than had been apparent from the observation point or the photographs, but the going was firm and the men very fit, as a result there was little straggling. There was however a tendency for some to bunch up until again Roger was heard to yell, "Open up, don't bunch."

Closing on the village, all platoons started to take casualties. Enemy fire was bad enough, but now the artillery supporting them started to drop shells short, in amongst them, one of them badly wounding Colonel Hislop and killing a navy FOO with battalion HQ, with them to call down ship's gun fire on any formations preparing to counter attack Treville once the paras had taken it. Hamish Gillespie took over command of the battalion.

The other problem was that the gunners had very neatly removed the church tower, and whilst this also meant they neatly removed several German observation posts established therein they also eliminated 4 platoon's guide to its line of advance. By now, with smoke from burning buildings drifting around on a windless night, both forward platoons lost direction and drifted in towards each other. It was then they hit the defences, resulting in going to ground, hand grenades away, sudden rushes as the grenades went off, bursts from Sten guns, followed by hand to hand fights with men running from slit trenches and into buildings. Sergeants trying to keep their sections together, men being killed and wounded, Germans being wounded and captured.

The first assault by the two forward platoons took them up to and beyond the first line of slit trenches. The SS then cascaded stick grenades on to the advancing paras, causing more casualties, making them shelter in the trenches they had just captured. A reserve force of the SS attempted to retake the trenches and drive 'B' Company back, but were beaten off with heavy losses. David and Paddy came forward to try and get some idea of what was happening to the forward platoons, saw they were entrenched in the main, and urged them on again.

"Where are Mr MacDuff and Mr Hammick?" David asked Mac's platoon sergeant.

"They are both wounded and having the wounds dressed sir." As he spoke they both appeared. Mac had been hit in the thigh and he was limping badly, Roger had his right arm in a sling but was waving his revolver in his left hand.

"Well done you two. Try and get to your platoons." The two lieutenants moved forward in the general direction of their leading men.

There followed, as is always the case in night fighting and house fighting, a series of mini-battles. In this case the fact that smoke was swirling around further making any semblance of overall control impossible, the small groups did what paratroopers are particularly good at. Commanded often by a lance corporal or even a senior private soldier as the NCOs became casualties, they moved forward, often using the bayonet to good effect, often drawing the fighting knife drawn from the special pocket built into the calf section of their battledress trousers for close quarter work. Just after midnight they had progressed past the church, which lay almost in the centre of the village. Dead Germans lay everywhere, others wounded or just plain defeated, sat against walls having thrown their weapons away, being treated where possible by paramedics, who seemed to be everywhere. All of 'B' Company medics were conscientious objectors, mostly Quakers. They had refused to fight, but would work, unarmed, to tend the wounds of their fellow men, risking their lives in the open even when the fighting men had gone to ground. Many of them died as a result, greatly esteemed by their fighting comrades despite their being 'conchies'.

David sensed the momentum of his company's attack was slowing. He had no idea yet of his losses, but appreciating the slowing up of his advance, he called up his reserve platoon, along with company HQ defence section. Three long blasts on his whistle indicated to Mac and Roger to hold firm while Sandy and Simon came up moving forward at speed through the remains of the two platoons which so far had borne the brunt of the fighting. The SS wilted at the sight, or rather the pressure of relatively fresh troops arriving and started to drop back down the reverse slope upon which the rear half of the village was situated. As they did this a sustained mortar barrage from the battalion three inch mortar platoon fell among them. This speeded their retreat. They must have been thin on the ground or had sustained a great number of casualties in the artillery bombardment since there appeared to be no attempt to counter attack.

"Dig in," yelled Sandy. This they started to do when a machine gun over on their right opened up on them. They raced back towards the German trenches they had overrun to get cover, but many were hit, many killed.

Simon and the defence section were on the extreme right, just beyond the fire from the MG42.
"Follow me," he yelled.

As a man they doubled off behind some bushes to get behind the machine gun position some one hundred yards away. In the noise of the battle the machine gunners did not hear them until Simon and his half dozen men were upon them. Even so they swung the gun round. To do this they had literally to lift it round and replace it on its bipod at the front. The number two on the gun, in his haste, picked it up by the barrel which was almost red hot from its previous heavy use, as a result he screamed with pain and had literally to pull his hand off, now almost welded on, with his free hand. Despite this, the number one got a burst off at the attackers, killing two of the men instantly and putting a bullet well and truly in the left shoulder of Simon Finklestein. As Simon said later in true film star fashion in westerns or war films, the hero always gets hit in the left shoulder! There was no film star fashion to the conclusion of this sideshow. The men went in with the bayonet; you take no surrender from machine gunners.

Over on the left hand side of the church Claude Warren's 'A' Company had been badly mauled. As a result Hamish threw 'C' Company in, who taking casualties again from machine guns, finally got through to line up with David's company. It was not however, over. A tremendous barrage hit them. With the three rifle companies now dug in, the worst of the casualties were taken by the signal platoon, mortar platoon and machine gunners who up until now had been in reserve. They dug like mad. It is staggering how fast a soldier can get under ground level when artillery is raining down on him. Nevertheless they took heavy casualties. David, sheltering in one of the trenches with Angus and Paddy, looked over the rear to see Hamish walking through the shell bursts, accompanied by his batman, as if he was taking a Sunday afternoon stroll.

"David, tell your blokes bloody well done when you get the chance. The colonel's been evacuated so I am taking over. If anything happens to me, you are to take over the battalion. Understood?"

"Yes sir, but isn't HQ company commander senior to me?"

"Don't bloody argue."

"Right sir."

Hamish turned away to resume his perambulations seemingly unconcerned that his arrangement with David might have to be put into effect at any moment. Paddy commented.

"They won't be queuing up to be his bloody batman after this lot."

By dawn the division had taken all the positions along the ridge, but had been badly mauled. The shelling gradually subsided when a replacement RN FOO arrived and started directing fire from six inch guns from a cruiser anchored out of Hermanville. 'R' battalion awaited the inevitable counter attack, which did not materialise. They ate the remains of their iron rations and awaited their relief. At 0900 hours the commandos started filtering in to take over their positions. Normally there would have been good-natured chaff between these two units who held each other in such high esteem, such as "Right-o cherryberries, you can sod off now and leave things to the men," but today there was a respectful silence as the green berets passed the stretcher bearers on the way up to what was a village no more, passed scores of dead paras laid out in rows and finally German prisoners being engaged in collecting their own dead and laying them side by side to be buried, before they themselves were shipped off to POW camps in England.

Jerry, observing some sort of activity was taking place on the ridge, and thinking presumably that the enemy was to reinforce success and proceed with their advance, began another stonk of 'R' battalion positions, which catching the men in the open during the takeover, produced casualties in both the paras and the commandos. The navy soon opened up, resulting in a desultory shelling from longer range German artillery, which was to last all the morning.

Gradually David's company filtered out, and marched some five miles to a tented area, where a roll call was carried out, they were fed, their weapons inspected, any minor personal damage attended to by the company medics, then sent to bed. David looked at the roll call. He had no officers left. Simon had been evacuated to UK, his shoulder blade much worse then he had let on. MacDuff's wound necessitated his return to Blighty, but he would be back in two to three weeks. Roger was a one-armed man for the time being, but was able to stay with the battalion. Sandy had been moved over to take over 'A' Company, where Claude Warren and all four of his officers had become casualties, Claude himself having several small chunks of shrapnel being carefully, but agonisingly, picked out of him.

From the one hundred and twenty odd in his company which had emplaned only three weeks ago, David was down to thirty-seven, seven of those being reinforcements he had received in the meantime. A number of the more lightly wounded would be coming back. As it was, including those, he would be fifty per cent under strength. He thought of all those telegrams the people back home would be receiving. The heartache, wives having to tell parents in law, explaining to children they would not see their daddy again, possibly facing severe financial strain in a society which as yet did not look after those in poverty to any great extent, even if the bread winner had given his life for his country.

David sat with his head slumped in his hands, with his arms resting on the camp table. Paddy joined him.

"Get to bed sir. Angus or I will wake you if we need to." Paddy knew how David must feel at the loss of those men. He knew his company commander as one of the few officers he had known in nearly twenty years of soldiering as one who really felt that he and his men were comrades in arms. They were not there just to be ordered about and win him medals; he felt their deaths almost as if they were family.

"Come on sir, get to bed, have a swig of this. A good sleep and you'll be back to yourself again, so you will." David took the water bottle from Paddy, and as invited, took a 'good swig'. It was army rum, and it nearly choked him. His eyes watered, he coughed, settled himself, and took another 'good swig'.

"Where the hell did you get that?"

"The QM has dished a large tot out to all the men sir. Being as how we are old mates he topped up my water bottle – after I emptied the water out of course."

"You realise that's against Kings Regulations?"

"So it is sir, so it is. But what the King doesn't know about won't hurt him, will it sir? Now, will you get to bed sir?"

He did, and slept for eight hours without moving, waking to face the prospect of having to completely re-organise 'B' Company.

They stayed in the rest area for a week, receiving reinforcements. Sandy came back to him and was promoted to captain, becoming his 2ic now that Simon was gone. One-armed Roger did the work of two men with two good arms, until replacement lieutenants arrived from the depot at Clay Cross. They presented themselves to David in his tent, saluting in a most regimental fashion, which David stood up, received and returned.

Paddy was standing beside him.

David's first question was, "How long were you at Clay Cross?"

"Nearly three months sir." One, presumably the senior, replied.

"And did you ever visit The Golden Fleece?"

"In Chesterfield? Yes sir."

"Did you meet the man on m'nishuns?"

They looked at each other, laughed uproarishly, the spokesman replying, "Yes sir, every Saturday night."

David looked round at Paddy. "Are you on m'nishuns?"

"No, I'm not on m'nishuns sir." They were all laughing. David explained. "The Sergeant Major and I used to go in there with the RSM, and this chap used to come in as pissed as a newt, take a drop of Scotch, put ten bob in the kitty and then move on to the next pub. If you were in civvies, as we were, he always asked 'Are you on m'nishuns, I'm in m'nishuns. M'nishuns all the week, pissed on Saturday, sleep it off Sunday'. And he's still making the rounds?"

"He is that sir."

"God, he must have the constitution of an ox. Right now, now we've got that sorted, who are you, where have you come from, and we don't go in for the 'sir' lark in this battalion except on parade. I am David, David Chandler."

The newcomers looked at each other knowingly. David's eyebrows raised in query.

"I'm Andy Gilchrist, this is the Honourable Reggie Pardew, he's a bit thick but otherwise alright. We're both from City Rifles originally. We have heard of you sir, I mean David, and the sergeant major."

"Have you now. Could we know, firstly the substance of your knowledge, and secondly the author of it."

"Well, taking those in reverse order sir, there were two sources. Firstly a chap of whom you may have heard named Charlie Crew, with whom we were at Eton, and who we met by chance at Arromanches when we landed two days ago. He was incidentally on his way back to Blighty with a bullet through his guts."

"Is he alright?" David asked anxiously. "I mean I know he can't be alright, but how was he, was he walking wounded, on a stretcher, or what?"

"He was on a stretcher sir, but was in good nick. We saw he had City Rifles pips up that's why we stopped to talk to him. Then we saw who it was! He told us that if we bumped into you to ask you how the hell he is going to manage without a best man."

David looked at Paddy. Paddy looked at David.

"If I accidentally shoot you in the foot sir, accidentally mind, perhaps you could still be best man."

"I shall seriously consider that sergeant major, though you shouldn't have mentioned it in front of these gentlemen."

"Don't worry sir, we'll turn our backs and pretend not to have noticed."

"Well, we'll discuss that later. Who was the second person?"

"Persons, actually. The RSM and CO at Clay Cross. They knew we were on a draught for 'R' Battalion, and they both told us to seek you both out and give you their best wishes."

Reggie Pardew chimed in for the first time.

"They knew sir, that neither of you had, as yet, bitten the dust as our quaint American allies express it. They would know since they are the first to get all the casualty sheets. As to the substance of the information we received, it was so damning we swore never to divulge it." He added after a short pause, "Particularly about the sergeant major."

Paddy looked at David.

"Do they breed them all like Mr Crew at Eton sir?"

"They do Paddy, they do, I'm sorry to say."

The new men registered the 'Paddy' and concluded they had struck oil in being posted to this company.

David saw Angus passing his tent.

"Oh Angus, see if you can find Captain Patterson and Mr Hammick will you?"

"They are in the company office tent sir."

"Ask them to come in please."

The two newcomers noted the method of address from the major to a private soldier. They did not appreciate at that time that Angus was the soldier's surname. They also found later that the major could be a right bastard if he had to be and the circumstances required him to be.

Sandy and Roger arrived and were introduced to the newcomers. Officer-wise they were now up to strength. The reinforcements they had received were either from infantry regiments, with a nucleus of paras from the depot. They were desperately short of NCOs. You cannot make an NCO merely by giving a private soldier a stripe or two. Similarly you cannot necessarily make a sergeant from a corporal. As in all walks of life army men have a level of ability. Because they are first class corporals it does not mean they will make good sergeants. The first thing the new platoon commanders had to do, under the continual guidance of Sandy Patterson, was to sort out their NCO structure. In the type of fighting paras are usually called upon to participate, as they had found at Treville, good section sergeants were absolutely essential. Fortunately several of the more lightly wounded were drifting back which helped matters, but it didn't cure the problem.

Three days later their new CO arrived. David had talked to Hamish, asking whether there would be any chance of his taking over the battalion.

"David my son," he had replied, "I am a major, I always will be a major until I retire. I have neither the brains, the ability, nor in fact the desire to be anything but a major. You know it. I know it. The whole bloody army knows it. There are plenty of colonels, brigadiers, and even people higher up the ladder than that, who have got there with the aid of large dollops of bullshit, or family connections. I don't believe in bullshit, I have no family connections, I am happy as a major. Now – does that answer your question?"

David grinned. "All I can say in answer to that is, you're not only the best major I have ever met, you are also one of the best blokes I ever met." He added, "And seeing you strolling through that barrage at Treville, Paddy O'Riordan and I thought you were the bravest of the brave, and that definitely is not bullshit."

The new colonel duly arrived. He instantly made his name by calling a battalion parade, finding fault wherever he could, and generally trying to impose his authority in the manner of a depot colonel. In the first instance, although they were some seven miles from the front line, it seemed to David, and others, to be utterly stupid to be drawn up as a battalion when one long range shell, or even the appearance of an enemy aircraft, an event which was not unknown, could cause serious casualties. They got away with it, but it left doubts in the minds of many.

However, travelling in a jeep up to the observation point of the position the battalion was next to occupy, the new C O along with the intelligence officer and the CO's bodyguard, met a military police roadblock.

"They've been mortaring the road ahead this morning sir," he told the colonel, saluting as if he were on Horse Guards Parade.

"I don't think we shall worry about a trifle like that," was the reply. After travelling a quarter of a mile a cluster of Moaning Minnies came down, blew the jeep off the road, killed the driver, severely wounded the colonel and his bodyguard, only Johnny Tate, the intelligence officer getting away with a few bruises.

"I did suggest to him it would be best to go up before dawn to that particular spot," Hamish told David, "that would at least have reduced the risk by half."

"So you are CO again?"

"Acting, unpaid, unwanted," replied Hamish.

But he wasn't unwanted. The brigadier came up that evening and told him was he promoted to lieutenant colonel and would take over the battalion straight away. There were sighs of relief all round from the janker-wallahs through to the company commanders. The brigade major was appointed to second in command and an obscure captain at divisional HQ who was related to someone very high up in the War Office was made brigade major. Actually, he made quite a good job of it! And good brigade majors are worth their weight in gold.

Chapter Twenty-Five

July 1944 was another disastrous month for the Wehrmacht in Russia. Minsk fell to the Soviet forces with the loss of one hundred thousand casualties by the Germans. Further south Lvov fell and the Red Army were within reach of Warsaw.

Dieter and his regiment, superior in armament though they were to the enemy, constantly had to retreat to prevent being encircled. Gradually his Tigers became immobilised for one reason or another, lack of available maintenance, lack of spares, even lack of ammunition and petrol. When you are retreating at the rate of fifteen miles a day, establishing fuel and ammunition dumps is a practicable impossibility.

The end came late one very dusty afternoon. Dieter had three tanks hulled down to cover the move back to another prepared line of the remaining six Tigers. Nine of his beautiful machines were all that remained of the thirty odd he had under command only a few months ago. They awaited the approach of the oncoming T34's with considerable trepidation. Tank for tank they were infinitely superior, but just as a pack of wild dogs can bring down a buffalo, so a herd of T34's will eventually overcome a Tiger.

Dieter had the sun more or less behind him. His three machines were well dug-in and camouflaged. His problem was that behind him he had several miles of plain open steppe, not an inch of cover of any sort, not even depressions or gullies in which he might be able to check his retreat and keep the bastards off. He therefore had to try and halt them until it got dark in about three hours, and then slip away. They would be unlikely to move in the dark.

Through his glasses he estimated around a dozen tanks approaching, most of them, except the forward three, having infantry shock troops riding on them. Because of the enormous amount of dust being thrown up it was impossible to be accurate in this respect, but it would not be wildly inaccurate. His three gunners carefully ranged at one thousand metres. As the T34's breasted a slight rise Dieter gave the order for all three to fire. Two out of the three point vehicles brewed up, the third turning back to get behind the rise, but before being able so to do getting a solid shot in its vulnerable side. When the projectile penetrated the tank it hit a solid piece of the steel framework in the centre, was deflected forward, promptly removed the raising and lowering mechanism under the driver's seat, lodged in the front armour, leaving the driver sitting on the floor of his otherwise fully mobile vehicle. The problem was he could not see out of his periscope, but knowing the position he was in when they were hit he made a blind left turn back over the ridge hoping he did not crash into another T34 in the process.

It was after making this instinctive move that he realised how close he had become to being emasculated, not by a surgeon's knife but by a solid piece of steel. He promptly fainted; the tank came to a halt. There was enough of the rear end of the tank showing to Dieter's right hand number to chance another shot, which he promptly carried out, effectively removing its turret, the shot this time striking way above the driver's head. How lucky can you get in one day?

Dieter watched his front. Nothing moved. For over half an hour nothing moved, then dragged on to an hour. Dieter was getting fidgety. On one hand the longer they left him the better his chances of getting away. On the other hand, when they so outnumbered him why didn't they attempt to surround him and finish him off? A few minutes later he had the answer. Out of the east came a flight of twin-engined fighter bombers. The Russian commander sent up a red Very light in the direction of the Tigers, the V formation flew into line and pointed their noses at Dieter and his comrades. In their first pass they fired cannon at the stationary tanks, several hits were made but the projectiles bounced off like tennis balls against a brick wall. On the second circuit they each in turn dropped a bomb, not very accurately; as a result no damage was done. Dieter realised that as things stood, he and his two commanders, along with their crews, had no chance. They could surrender, and trust to luck their captors would treat them reasonably, they could stay where they were and trust to luck the bombers would run out of bombs before they hit anything. Judging by their first run-in they were not the ultimate in marksmanship. Alternatively, they could make a run for it, but here they would be at a distinct disadvantage, or finally they could attack. Suicide probably, but at least they would go down fighting. Having considered the four options in less than half a minute Dieter made his decision.

Over the wireless he said to his two crews.

"We are sitting ducks here, or if we retreat. We are going to go at them and wipe a few out before we go down. Are you with me?"

There was an immediate and universal, "Yes."

"Right, reverse out of the position, move forward at top speed straight at them, keep apart, and good luck to you all."

The Tigers broke into life with a shattering roar and moved out swiftly straight at the spread out Soviet machines. In the meantime the aircraft had circled again and returned on another bombing run. Each plane took a separate tank but by the time they had reached them the panzers had covered half the distance to the enemy. Nevertheless they let their bombs go, one falling close to Dieter's left hand tank, slewing it round and in the process causing it to lose a track. It nevertheless trained its main armament on to the T34's moving about in front to give some covering fire to Dieter and the remaining mobile tank.

They were now in amongst them. At that close they did great damage but at the same time the T34's, at almost point-blank range, could penetrate even the thick frontal armour of the Tigers. There could be only one end. Dieter's companion went up in flames, and two minutes later there was a thunderous explosion at the rear of Dieter's panzer. It was the last thing he remembered until he awoke lying on the ground beside his stricken tank, with his head aching fit to burst, and his shoulder very sore indeed. As he gradually regained his senses he looked up to see a young officer holding his iron cross with oak leaves. Seeing Dieter was now conscious he said, "I've always wanted to get one of these," not, of course, since he was speaking in Russian, expecting a reply.

"To the victor belong the spoils, is I believe a well known saying," Dieter replied in excellent Russian. Just as his friend David had specialised in learning German resulting in its having saved his life when he was at Calais in 1940, so Dieter's command of Russian was now to save his life. The other tank commander and two crew from the one which had brewed up, the only two saved from it, listened intently, as the two officers had what seemed to be, an unexpectedly convivial conversation. They had expected to be shot, in fact had they been captured by infantry they might well have been. As it was there was the same sort of camaraderie between tank men as there was between fighter pilots and submariners, unless of course the Germans happened to be SS, in which case all rules went by the book, on both sides.

"So, you speak Russian. You are the first German prisoner I have met who has bothered to learn our language, except to say 'yes' or 'no' or demand vodka. Why learn your enemy's speech?"
"When I learnt your language we were not enemies."
"That is so? If we were not enemies why did you invade us?"
"You must ask the politicians that. I am just a soldier."
"What other languages did you learn?"

"I speak fluent French and English."

"So, you also invaded France?"

"Yes, we did."

"But you did not invade England?"

"No. They had a very strong navy which would have prevented it."

"And now they have invaded you and between us and them you will be squeezed into nothing."

Dieter remained silent.

"Well?"

"I fear you are right."

"And then we shall hang Hitler and Goering from Berlin lampposts."

"I think large numbers of Germans will applaud you for that." Stated sincerely, without his realising the disloyalty in the utterance, it caused the Russian to look at him keenly.

"Keep him here," he ordered an NCO, "send the remainder back to the prisoner compound."

Dieter's comrades clustered around him wishing him good luck, as he did to them. If they had known the sort of existence for which they were heading, they would have asked to have been shot instead. The evil stories of the Russian treatment of German prisoners of war would fill a book, or more than one. On the other hand, how many millions of Russian POWs were starved to death by the Germans in the first winter of the attack on the Soviet Union. Three million? – four million? – nobody knows with any degree of accuracy.

The officer turned back to Dieter, who by now was sitting up with his back against the bogies of his tank.

"Now major. I am Lieutenant Colonel Namoff."

Dieter was not entirely surprised that such a young man, no older than he himself was, was a lieutenant colonel. It was well known that thousands of Red Army officers from the rank of major upwards had been shot by the Russian security people before the war, as a result of Stalin's paranoia about plots against him. By the end of 1936 there was hardly a senior officer left of the people who had swept him in to power, along with those who had made their ways up the slippery slope of command. Combine this with the losses in the early years of The Great Patriotic War, as Stalin had named it, it followed that promotion to the brave and to the successful would be swift.

Dieter struggled to his feet and saluted.

"I am going to send you back to a special unit where I think your qualifications may well be of use to us."

Dieter's immediate reaction was to say,

"Sir, I have no love for the Nazis, but I will do nothing to betray my country."

The colonel looked at him.

"Major, you are now a prisoner of war. I suggest you think very well what you are going to say before you say it. We know how arrogant you German junkers are, a word out of place to some of my comrades would end in your being shot without their thinking twice."

Dieter decided not to argue the point. He was as far removed from being a junker, both geographically and politically, as it was possible to be, but in the present circumstances he had been taught a sharp lesson. Not all his conquerors were going to be as reasonable as Colonel Namoff.

It was probably a fact that in most armies, always excepting the barbarous Japanese of course, front-line soldiers were generally more civilised towards prisoners than those immediately behind the lines. This was particularly so in Russia. Of the 91,000 taken prisoner at Stalingrad, on reaching POW camps, fifty per cent were dead within three months, the few of those who survived remained prisoners until the German Chancellor Adenaur visited Moscow in 1955, when they were released, ten years after the war ended!!

An hour later a soldier came to where Dieter had been left seated.

"You are to come with me." He led him back over the ridge to a track some half a mile away where he saw the colonel seated in an American jeep, one of the tens of thousands of vehicles given to the Russians by their allies for which few thanks were ever received. A prime example of this ingratitude was 'The Sword of Stalingrad'. King George VI gave this beautiful bejewelled sword to the people of Stalingrad as a tribute to their bravery. No mention of the gift was ever made in Russia, in newspapers, on newsreels or over the wireless. Having been presented to Stalin by Winston Churchill at the Tehran conference, it was never seen again. Now that Stalingrad no longer exists, it is now called Volvograd, one wonders where it is today.

Dieter saluted. Was told to get in. He climbed into the back, lodging his field holdall on his lap. They travelled in silence for over two hours before reaching a fairly substantial tented encampment. He was directed to a bell tent, again American he noted, which was surrounded by barbed wire, and guarded at the entrance by a particularly stony-faced guard obviously from way beyond the Urals. The tent had no furniture and no other occupant. His first thoughts were 'how do I escape?' Getting out of the tent would be easy enough; the low sidewall was barely pegged down. Getting under the barbed wire presented few difficulties. The sentry stood at the front, ergo go out the back. The problem then arose he was at least thirty miles or more behind where the line was when he was captured. The Russians could well have advanced another ten or fifteen miles since then. The likelihood of being able to struggle through forty or fifty miles of very open countryside without being seen by one of the tens of thousands of Russian support troops between him and the German front line was remote beyond credence. He concluded he might just as well be locked in the Lubianka prison in Moscow, his chances of getting away would be roughly the same.

He sat on the dusty ground with his back to the tent pole, gradually becoming more and more despondent; particularly at the realisation that 'Monika' would no longer receive letters and would naturally fear the worst. He would almost certainly be posted 'missing', even 'missing, believed killed in action'. There was absolutely no way he could contact her or her family. Prisoners of war of the Russians were to all intents and purposes dead already, either on the way back to Siberian forest camps and coalmines, or in those and similar extermination centres elsewhere in the Soviet Union. It is calculated that of the German POWs and their allies, only five percent, possibly ten percent, survived to return to the Fatherland.

As his spirits sank to a new low he heard a fusillade of shots only a short distance from the tent. He pushed aside the entry flap and stepped outside. There was a different guard stationed there, in Dieter's assessment a Georgian or similar.

"What's going on?" he asked.

The guard shrugged. "Just the Hiwis getting their just deserts," he replied, "they deserve to be shot."

"I agree with you," Dieter replied, and returned to his tent pole. 'Hiwis' – Hilfswillege – willing helpers – was the name given by the German army to the tens of thousands of Russians, prisoners of war, civilians and deserters, who joined the Wehrmacht against the Red Army. They were employed as pioneer troops, camp guards, and eventually as front-line infantry. It was no wonder that when they were captured they could expect no mercy. In Dieter's code of honour and loyalty they deserved all they got. A curious ambivalence considering he himself had been required to swear an oath of loyalty and obedience to Adolf Hitler, yet would have readily assassinated him, given the opportunity.

During the evening some cabbage soup, black bread and weak tea was brought to him. He had a fitful night's sleep on the hard ground, waking soon after dawn, and at seven o'clock was given a repeat portion of the previous night's provender. An hour later an orderly came, spoke to the guard, then entered the tent.

"You are to come with me major, bring your things with you." Dieter picked up his holdall. He was still wearing his black tank overalls over his uniform, the holdall containing change of socks, underclothes, washing gear etc, sufficient for his needs for up to one week from his normal base. He followed the young soldier to the colonel's tent, was ushered in and saluted the colonel sitting at his camp table – a captured German camp table Dieter noted.

"I am to take you to my general," he was told. Dieter deduced from this that the colonel had discussed his capture with his commander, presumably over the field telephone land line. He wondered what on earth a general would want to discuss with him.

The journey back to divisional HQ was an eye-opener. As far as the eye could see on both sides of the rough track eastwards were countless thousands of troops, hundreds of horse drawn vehicles, horse drawn artillery units, ambulances, heavy motorised field guns, above all, masses of the fearsome Katyusha rockets mounted on lorry chassis. They were all moving slowly and inexorably eastwards towards the 'Thousand Year Reich'.

'How can we possibly counter all this. After all, these are just the reserves; they are not even the front line forces.'

'Where is the Luftwaffe – they would have a field day on a target like this.'

These thoughts, and others, running through his mind brought a feeling of despair upon him which he had never in all his life experienced before, one in fact he would never have believed existed. Although he had known for many moons now that Germany could no longer win, he had firmly believed that if they could conclude a peace with the British and the Americans, they could at least prevent themselves from being overrun by the Russkis. Now, when he saw at first hand the sheer volume of men and weaponry in this one small section of the front he realised the impossibility of the task.

After a little over an hour the jeep drove into another tented encampment. A large marquee with a divisional sign on a wooden board, guarded at the entrance by two very stern looking military policemen, indicated divisional HQ. As the colonel alighted the policemen sprang to attention and saluted. Noting this display of military correctness Dieter wondered whether they still addressed the officer as 'comrade colonel', as he believed was the case after the revolution. It is odd the trivial thoughts that occur to someone whose very life might be at stake in the next few minutes.

Dieter was told to follow, the colonel leading the way into a sort of anteroom partitioned off by a canvas screen from the main compartment. An attractive Red Army woman officer sat behind the desk which contained a battery of telephones, who asked the colonel to be seated, and whilst Dieter remained standing, waved him to a camp chair to be seated as well. Dieter again had the thought 'they'll be bringing the drinks out next'.

After some fifteen minutes a telephone rang on the desk, at which the receptionist, or whatever she was, asked the colonel if he would take the major in. They walked through the canvas entrance vestibule, emerged into the general's presence, halted, and both saluted. The general told them to be seated and regarded Dieter intently.

"I am General Vasili Gargarov. I am to be responsible for bringing to justice those people who tortured and killed our Russian citizens in their concentration and extermination camps. Did you know that your great, pure, Arian Reich had such things as concentration camps where they worked prisoners to death?"

"Yes, general, my wife is in one." It was a slight distortion of the truth.

"What! Your wife in a camp! You a decorated officer! Why?"

"She was found in possession of leaflets demanding the end of the war. She was given six years in Ravensbruk. She had not as yet distributed her leaflets as she had been away from her home in Munich, the six other doctors in her group had handed their bundles out. They were each hanged."

The general sat back in his camp chair.

"Yet you fought on?"

"I had my duty to do. We endeavoured to remove the Fuhrer as you will know. We were not successful."

"You were part of the plot?"

"On the periphery sir, only, but I had my function to perform had it been successful."

"And what was that?"

"I would have received further orders in that respect from my colonel. As far as I know plans were being prepared to sue for peace, but of course I was too far down the chain to know about that."

The general regarded him again closely.

"The colonel discussed you with me. He had the impression you were a highly intelligent young man whose word would be your bond. You speak almost faultless Russian; tell me, do you write our Cyrillic alphabet?"

"Yes sir, though I should need to practice somewhat to become fully efficient."

"The reason you have been brought here is for me to decide whether we can use you in our organisation. We are going to need many bi-lingual people in our interrogations and trials. You would still be a prisoner, but you will be better looked after than if we send you on to Siberia with the other prisoners. There is, as I see it, no conflict with patriotic duty, you will be acting purely under the law. Whether the accused are German, Polish, Czech, or Russian, your duty will be to the law. If you are prepared to accept this post and carry it out scrupulously, your prisoner of war status will be reduced so that you will get earlier release once the war is over. I shall require your sworn oath you will not attempt to escape in view of the extra freedom you will be allowed in order to carry out these duties. Is all that clear?"

"Sir, I am not legally trained."

"You have, I assume, been a member of courts martial?"

"Yes, sir, I have prosecuted, defended, and been a member of courts."

"These courts will not be nearly as technical as courts martial. We know most of the people we shall bring before the court will be guilty anyway. So, do you wish to join with the colonel?"

"Yes, sir, I would consider it a duty to see that these people, found guilty, are punished for the evil they have committed."

"I think that is the most intelligent decision you have ever made, major. But still remember this, you are a prisoner of war, you have no rank, if you step out of line in any way you will join the other hundreds of thousands out in Siberia. Always be aware of that. You are being saved from that because of our need, for no other reason. Take him away colonel."

They both stood up, saluted and walked out.

Dieter's immediate fate was therefore decided, but it would be a long time before he again became a free man, unless, that is, he could find a way. In the meantime he could play a part in punishing evil doers such as those that killed so many of his darling Rosa's fellow prisoners. His sworn oath not to escape was, as far he was concerned, and almost certainly as far as the Geneva Convention was concerned, invalid. It was a prisoner's duty to escape, using whatever means were available to him.

Chapter Twenty-Six

Charlie Crew had a bullet in his hip. The problem was it had arrived via his other hip, traversing his bowels on the way. When he saw his friends Gilchrist and Pardew at Arromanches he put a brave face on things, as one would anticipate from the indomitable Charlie, but despite the morphine jabs he still was suffering badly. The LST which took him to Portsmouth through a roughish sea didn't help. These are of necessity flat-bottomed craft, not exactly hyper-stabilised even when heavily laden with tanks. Being more or less unladen on the return journey to UK it bobbed about like the proverbial cork, severely increasing Charlie's discomfort.

At Portsmouth he was very swiftly transferred into an army ambulance and taken to Lord Mayor Treloar Hospital at Alton where he arrived just before midnight. After the preliminary examinations by the registrar and surgeon, it was decided he would be operated on that afternoon. He, with the help of another injection, spent the rest of the night and the following morning asleep.

The operation to retrieve the bullet was successfully accomplished, the surgeon, having had it cleaned up, presenting it to Charlie for a souvenir, adding, "But, young man, that projectile has done some damage on its way through, so as far as I can tell at the moment there will be further surgery and you can count on being here for quite a while yet!"

"But I am getting married."

"We have no facilities for weddings in this ward I am afraid. Added to which, the physical gyrations normally associated with weddings, or at least with the honeymoon after the wedding, would I am afraid, to put it plainly, be beyond you at present. I'm dreadfully sorry to put the kibosh on your plans for connubial bliss, but all the best things are worth waiting for, don't you agree?"

Still dopey from the anaesthetic and in some discomfort, Charlie lay in the half awake – half asleep condition most people experience after surgery. The next morning he was awakened by a gorgeous nurse who promptly undid his pyjama strings to examine and change his dressings.

Charlie, gathering his wits asked her, "Do you always monitor your patient's private parts without a by your leave?"

She giggled, and in a broad Hampshire accent replied, "Well, when you come in here nothing is private any more. But don't worry; I won't give your secret away."

"Secret – what secret?"

"Well, the first nurse that dressed you said you had 'Ludo' tattooed on it, but now I see it's 'Llandudno'."

"Nurse, you are a shocker. What's your name?"

"I am Nurse Stevens."

"Yes, but what's your Christian name?"

"We are not allowed to tell patients our Christian names, especially officers."

"How do you know I'm an officer?"

"'Cos you talk posh and it says so on your bed card – Captain Crew. Now, I must get on."

"Can you sit me up a bit?"

"After rounds if they say it's alright."

Charlie lay back on his pillows going over in his mind how he had landed here. He had taken part in attack after attack by his armoured division in the huge battle to capture Caen, the hinge of the whole Normandy campaign. With his company commander Mark Laurenson, their battalion of City Rifles had taken a hill overlooking the city, only to be driven off it again by a heavy German counter-attack backed by massive mortar and artillery bombardments. They reformed, although they had suffered heavy casualties, and with the cover of a heavy barrage from their own divisional artillery aided by accurate shelling by naval units off shore, attacked again, recapturing the hill. The Germans could not allow the British to stay there, from which they could observe the Wehrmacht movements, so again they deluged what already resembled the moon's landscape with seemingly endless quantities of high explosive. With men being blown to pieces as they frantically dug-in in an endeavour to escape the lethal storm, the order was given to withdraw. It was at this point an enemy attack was put in on the right flank, from which attack Charlie caught the bullet in his hip and fell to the ground.

He lay for a minute or so, thinking 'I'm a gonner', then raised himself in excruciating pain, to see his batman braving a veritable hail of small arms fire obviously looking for him.

"Over here Hankin." Hankin, bent double, ran over to where he lay.

"Bullet through the guts," he managed to gasp out. Hankin quickly undid his officer's belt and epaulettes and shed his equipment. Leaving his own rifle as well, he pulled Charlie up to his feet, slung him over his shoulder and began the long, hazardous walk back to the battalion lines, what there was left of the battalion that is. It was a miracle they got through safely. The regimental aid post bandaged him up, the field ambulance pumped him with all sorts of jollop and certified him for home via the casualty clearing centre.

And here he was.

A matronly looking lady in civilian clothes approached his bed. After the usual enquiries as to how he was feeling and so on, she announced, "I am the almoner; your next of kin will have been notified of your being wounded. Is there anyone else we can contact on your behalf?"

"I would be terribly grateful if you could let my fiancée and my grandfather know I'm here. You see, my father, my next of kin, is quite probably out of the country on active service somewhere, so that telegram will be nestling in a pigeonhole in his club."

"I will do that straight away. Will you give me their names and addresses?" She turned the flap back on her notebook. Was not unsurprised at the fiancée's name and address, but was most impressed with the name and address of the grandfather. She became, not exactly deferential, but certainly noticeably regardful of having an aristocratic patient with whom to deal, which showed just imperceptibly in her demeanour. We are a snobby lot, are we not?

Emma and the Earl each got their telegram from the almoner at almost the identical time. Each then found the telephone number and contacted the almoner, the Earl winning by a short head. They were told the visiting hours, that Captain Crew was not in danger and would be allowed visitors from tomorrow. The Earl at once made tracks for his club in London so as to be able to travel to Alton the next day, Emma got a forty-eight hour compassionate leave pass, and that was how the Earl and Emma bumped into each other on Waterloo station as they awaited the announcement as to on which platform the Winchester train would be standing. The Earl immediately realised that Emma would be travelling Third Class whilst he would, of course, be in a First Class compartment.

"You must join me on the train," he said, "we'll sort it out with the conductor chappie when he comes round." This was effected without difficulty, the two having a lively conversation for the hour and a bit to Alton. At the station they got a cab out to Treloar's, on alighting from which the Earl said to his companion and future granddaughter-in-law,
"Now you cut along to the ward, I have to see the almoner about his discharge."

Emma realised this was a fib, but kissed him lightly on the cheek. In Bentworth Ward she was directed by the sister to Charlie's bed, Charlie himself not expecting visitors having dozed off. He awoke to see his darling Emma looking down at him with tears running down her cheeks. He reached up to hold her suffering a spasm of pain from his wound as he moved which caused him to utter, "Ouch," and fall back again. Emma leaned over and kissed his lips, his forehead, his lips again, then took his hands and kissed those.

"Oh, darling Charlie, what have they done to you?"

"Nothing that cannot be mended my love, and certainly nothing to damage my important bits."

Emma laughed through her tears.

"How did you get away? You haven't hopped the wag have you?" he asked.

"I've been given a compassionate leave pass for forty-eight hours. I'll stay overnight in Alton and come and see you again tomorrow. By the way," (seeing the Earl approaching), "I am accompanied by a young gentleman friend."

"You had better not be."

"Better not be what?" enquired a deep voice from the other side of the bed.

"Grandfather, how great to see you. Oh Nurse Stevens, could you find a couple of chairs for my visitors," adding "this is my fiancée Miss Langham, and my grandfather The Earl of Otbourne."

Nurse Stevens did the next best thing to a bobbed curtsey seen on Bentworth Ward for many a year. They rarely saw an Earl or anything approaching a real live Earl, and with the countryperson's instinctive deference to the landed gentry she descended from her normal dictatorial position of Nurse Stevens of Bentworth Ward to Stella Stevens of Alton. But only for a moment.

"You must have your injection Captain Crew. Perhaps your visitors will wait while I close the screens round. I will then find some chairs."

"Does that mean they will hear me screaming like I did this morning?" He looked at his grandfather, "Nurse Stevens is very brutal when she gets behind that needle, that's why she puts the screens around so that the rest of the ward can't see what she's up to."

His grandfather laughed. "Well, the Hun may have put a bullet into you but it doesn't seem to have dampened your sense of fun."

"The only one having fun is Nurse Stevens with her confounded needle, I assure you."

The injection was given. To a certain extent Charlie's comments about the needle were well founded. It was as thick as a knitting needle and just as blunt, or so Charlie described it. Still it had to be done; they were very worried he could be seriously infected by the internal bowel damage.

They chatted away until four o'clock, arranging to come in that evening.

"Where are you staying?" the Earl asked Emma.

"I haven't booked anywhere yet. I'll find somewhere in the town."

"I'm at The Swan in the High Street. Let's go there and see if they have a room. I thought I would stay till the weekend and go back to London on Saturday, I've got to make sure he is behaving himself."

They were told they would have to wait a long time for a cab, but the bus went every half hour and one was due. Emma smiled.

"Do peers of the realm travel on buses?"

The reply came without hesitation.

"What about future peeresses?"

Emma clutched his arm. "If it means losing you, I would never want to be a peeress." Her eyes misted, "But I do love Charlie so very, very much. We should have been married on Saturday. It isn't fair is it?"

He put his hands on hers. "You have lots of time my dear. It won't always be like this."

The bus journey into town was eventful in that it was already full when it arrived. As a result the Earl and Emma had to stand with his lordship pressed hard up against an extremely stout lady possessed of whatever is the next size up from an ample bosom, the bosom itself showing abundant cleavage to the world in general and to the Earl in particular, who found it impossible to look anywhere else than into it, in view of the crush. To add to the entertainment, the road was somewhat bumpy, as were most roads at that stage of the war, and the bus seemed to either have solid tyres or no springs. As a result the aforementioned acreage, when not possessing a continuous surface ripple, every now and then threatened to jump out when a pothole was encountered. The Earl, seeing the lady was holding a small child in one hand and a shopping basket in the other, wondered to himself whether if one, or for that matter both, of these undoubtedly magnificent mammary glands escaped from their somewhat undersized repositories, should he offer to put them back? It was a warm day therefore his hands would not be cold. He then estimated one pair of hands would not be sufficient for the full load, it would be definitely a four-handed job. Was there anyone nearby who could help? Definitely not. A two-handed exercise would involve putting them in one at a time, which would be a little like getting into a hammock – when the weight is directed on one side, the other side tips up. This rehousing job was not going to be accomplished without a great deal of finesse combined with good fortune.

His mind then wandered to the old schoolboy joke about the topless lady with her arms folded across her chest, running into the sea to bathe, being followed by a little lad asking, 'If you are going to drown those puppies can I have the one with the pink nose?' This was followed by his remembering the story, told him by an ancient Scottish friend, of the well-developed young woman in a low cut dress seated at dinner next to an elderly gent. At length she said to him, 'Are you looking down my front?' to which he replied, 'Yes, I am, but I can't remember why'.

He smiled at the thoughts. The more than amply bosomed lady saw him smile and smiled back, saying, "The roads gets bumpier every day, don't 'um?"

"They certainly do, they certainly do."

"You been visitin' at Treloar's then, 'ave'ee?"

"Yes, my grandson was wounded in Normandy."

He endeavoured to turn to bring Emma into the conversation but due to the crush, was totally incapable of so doing.

"He was originally due to be married to the young lady behind me on Saturday."

"Oh, what a shame. Nell," she spoke to another well-endowed woman on a seat beside her, "this gentleman's been to see his wounded grandson in Treloar's. The young man was supposed to marry that young Wren lady on Saturday. Ain't it a shame?"

Nell and the lady next to her agreed it was wicked the things old 'itler was putting them all through. As a result the couple behind Nell, seated as they were next to the 'young Wren lady' started talking to Emma, commiserating with her on her misfortune and assuring her it 'would all come right in the end', so that by the time the bus arrived at The Swan, nearly everybody on the lower deck was on speaking terms with his or her neighbour. And all because of the lascivious thoughts of a peer of the realm who one would have thought would have been above that sort of thing at his station and at his time of life. But that, knowing the aristocracy, would have been wishful thinking.

The Swan found a room for Emma. They visited Charlie again on Friday afternoon, Emma then making her way back to Deal, while the Earl was to stay on in Alton for another day.

On the morning of Friday the 7th July she reported to Commodore Jenson's office sharp at 0800 hours. The rating in his office told her that the commodore had left a message he would not be back until lunchtime and that she should collect him at 1400 hours.

"So you've got a morning off, miss. How was your young man?"

Emma smiled. "How do you know about my young man?" she asked.

"Oh, just that the commodore mentioned you would be away to see your young man who had been wounded in Normandy, so I had to get him fixed up with a temporary driver. In fact yesterday he said he was praying – literally praying I mean – that you would soon be back, this driver he's got now is giving him kittens."

After a little more idle chat Emma asked, "Where are we off to this afternoon, do you know?"

"Only to Dover I believe, what for I can't tell you."

Emma wandered into the town. Since Deal Library had been hit by a shell earlier in the year, she had lost one of her favourite aiming points. However, the walk was not without incident. No fewer than four buzz bombs flew over, each time the pedestrians stopping to ensure they kept going, as in fact they did. Always there was the thought that someone, somewhere, would in a few minutes be receiving a two thousand pound bomb on them, unless it could be brought down in open country. Even then, cattle, sheep and rural dwellings could well be the unwitting targets of these indiscriminate, ghastly, weapons.

The eight mile trip to Dover passed without incident. The commodore was greatly pleased to have Emma in possession of his bodily safety again, to say nothing of his mental peace of mind. He was most solicitous of her fiancée's health and prospects, but exclaimed, "Look at my finger nails; I have bitten them down to my elbows over the past two days. They should put that Leading Wren Nicholls in a tank regiment. That's where she would be in the Red Army, without a doubt. I've never met anyone who could approach a roundabout at fifty miles an hour and still get round it. And as for passing other vehicles – it seemed a matter of principle she should not be following anyone, no matter what oncoming traffic there might be around. I tell you, Emma Langham, I have aged ten years in two days, I truly have."

The business completed in Dover, the return to Deal again passed without incident. It may be the subject of curiosity to wonder why the mention of a 'lack of incident' was in any way worth the mention. The reason of course is that this stretch of road was a frequent recipient of the shells being lobbed over on an almost daily basis at times. Whereas in Deal and the other towns there was a shelling warning, out here the first indication one had of an attack was a whoosh and a bang, always assuming of course it had not made a direct hit. One got little warning under those circumstances, and then it was too late.

At South Foreland the commodore suggested they turn off on a farm track he knew which would take them out on to the headland overlooking the Channel. It was a clear afternoon. About a mile out they saw a flight of Hurricanes, or Spitfires possibly, neither of them being particularly well up in the aircraft recognition stakes to be certain, patrolling parallel to the coast. Suddenly one of them peeled off heading back toward Ramsgate. Immediately they could see the reason why. Crossing behind their original path a buzz bomb had been spotted. From a safe distance the eight machine guns on the fighter opened up, blasting the V-1 and causing it to flip over into the sea, exploding as it hit the surface.

"That's one which will not get to London," said Commodore Jenson. In the next half hour before they resumed their return to Deal they witnessed two more flipped down into the sea. Over one thousand flying bombs were dealt with in this small stretch of water, and since it was calculated that, on average, one life was lost to each bomb, the saving of at least a thousand innocent lives took place in this small stretch of Kentish water alone.

Some did get through however. On Sunday 9th July, one landed on the Regent Palace Hotel. There were five hundred in the hotel at the time. Miraculously only one person was killed. At roughly the same time another struck the Guards Chapel at Wellington Barracks during a service. Casualties were heavy, but the numbers were not released.

On Friday evening Emma telephoned Chandlers Lodge to give them all the news. Having digested this Fred said, "I think I might pop down to Alton on Sunday and see him. It's only about seventy miles; I reckon I've enough petrol left to do that. I haven't used the Rover much at all during this ration period. Anyone like to come?"

Rose said she would love to come, but really wasn't up to it. Jack said he would come as Moira would be away over the weekend and would chip in some of the petrol. "But what about your Home Guard Fred?"

"Oh, they can do without me for one day."

"Suppose there was an invasion?"

"They would have to manage without me. How? – I don't know. But you know, I realise you have stated that in jest. But we don't know how many troops he may have in Holland, Denmark, Norway say, who could pose a threat to us while all our forces are committed in France."

Fred continued, "I think the answer is, all allied forces are not committed in France. There would not be room for them there at present.

However, I wouldn't mind betting Winnie hasn't thought the blighter might do an act of desperation if he though his secret weapon assault was doing what he hoped it would do. He will keep enough back here to cater for that sort of emergency you can be sure."

The three men took off on Sunday morning, Ernie having asked if he could join them. They took sandwiches; the likelihood of getting anything on the road on a Sunday would be pretty remote being the view of the level of catering held by the general public at that time. They stopped at a small pub at Holybourne, firstly to water the horses, as Jack always had described this necessary operation, and secondly to quaff a pint each of Courage's bitter, brewed in Alton, and according to Fred, 'almost as good as Whitbread's – not quite, mind, but almost!'

His grandfather, having gone back to Ramsford on Saturday, Charlie was not expecting visitors on Sunday. It was a most pleasant surprise therefore to have three of the nicest people he knew to arrive sharp at two o'clock visiting time to see him. How he got hit, where he got hit, etc etc – the full story was gleaned from him to pass on to everyone back at Sandbury and regions adjacent. Similarly the news from there, buzz bombs, Mrs Treharne's daily conflabs with the Earl, Typhoons on Sandbury aerodrome, the expectant mums – there was so much to talk about.
"Mr Chandler, I saw one of your Hamilcars come in a week or so ago. I've never seen anything like it. It did a big turn when it was released. Jerry was popping away at it like mad, and it landed in a field no bigger than an allotment. As soon as it stopped the nose whipped away and a jeep towing a seventeen pounder anti-aircraft gun roared out, followed by another jeep converted to carrying stretchers on the back. Then fellows started unpacking stuff, I couldn't see what, I was keeping my head down at the time. But I thought to myself, Jerry has got nothing like that, the very sight of it must put the wind up them."
"I shall pass all that round the works when I get back," Fred assured him, "now tell us, how was your grandfather?"
Charlie told them the story of the bus ride, his grandfather having had the time to invent a few embellishments as if the plain facts weren't hilarious enough, before relating it to Charlie on Saturday afternoon.
"Shall we tell Mrs Treharne?" Jack suggested. "She could really pull his leg over this."
"Good idea," agreed Charlie, "do you know, if those two were younger I bet they would be traipsing up the jolly old aisle."
"Perhaps I could suggest to your grandfather that he makes it a

double wedding when you and Emma name the day, or in your case rename the day."

"Yes, isn't it a dirty shame. At this very time I should be standing in front of some parson instead of being incarcerated here. I have little to forgive Mr Hitler for, least of all allowing one of his squareheaded lackeys to put a bullet in me. By the way they gave me the bullet as a souvenir." He rummaged in his locker, which caused him to wince at the sharp pain he suffered as he turned.

"There you are."

Ernie took it.

"To think something as small as that could cause all this suffering," he said.

"Could have been worse," Charlie joked, "six inches lower and there would have been no point in getting married."

The three visitors laughed with him, although when you come to think of it there could not be, in the whole wide world, less to laugh at than that incomparable catastrophe!

The four o'clock bell sounded, the visitors took their leave from a grateful Charlie, and made their way back to Sandbury. Since it was Sunday, and the pubs did not open until seven o'clock on Sundays, they made their first stop in the kitchen at Chandlers Lodge. There was general agreement that though the Courage's they had been only too grateful to sample at lunchtime had been very good, there really was nothing like the Whitbread's golden sublimity from under the stairs.

Chapter Twenty-Seven

Margaret Coulter's trip to Barrow-in-Furness turned out to be a lengthier project than had been expected. Instead of being back for the weekend of the 8th of July her small team ran into difficulties which necessitated their having to wait around while decisions were made in The Pentagon and cabled back. This would automatically be a slow process. As the colonel leading the team put it, "No one in the Pentagon will scratch his arse without getting authority from at least two ranks above him." With this inevitable delaying factor, combined with the necessity to code and decode all communications, they suffered a great deal of wasted time, since it would be illogical to go back to London and then have to return in a day or so.

On Saturday 8th July, Margaret put on her civilian clothes to do a little exploring. She took the train via Ulverston and Grange-over-Sands, to Carnforth. At Carnforth she found a cosy little tea shop on the main platform run by a charming lady who told her there was little to see in Carnforth itself but that she should get the bus to Lancaster. It was market day on Saturday, and whilst market days were not like they were before the war, it was still lively and interesting. She should also visit the magnificent Priory Church on Castle Hill. Although Lancaster was the county town, it did not boast a cathedral as such, but the Priory was as good as, she was told, "Of course, you know," the kind lady continued, "terrible things happened there a little while back. A doctor in the centre of the town killed his wife and chopped her up. Then he saw the maid had caught sight of what he was doing. She tried to get away but he caught her, and chopped her up too. Still, they hanged him – he got his just deserts."

"I'll make sure I don't need a doctor while I am there," Margaret said laughingly, and thanked the friendly lady for her help.

She visited the Priory Church as had been suggested. In studying one of the stained glass windows she stepped back to get a better view of some information contained in the glass in its base, accidentally knocking against a gentleman, almost putting him off-balance.

"Oh, I do beg your pardon, that was very clumsy of me."

"Not at all dear lady, not at all," came the reply. "I take it you are not from these parts."

Margaret explained briefly who she was, what she was, and why she was in Lancaster.

"Have you visited the castle?"

"No, I understand it is a prison?"

"Part of it is. I am in fact the governor. If you would like to see the remainder I would be delighted to escort you. It is not at the moment open to the general public."

By that fortuitous accident Margaret received a conducted tour of this ancient building, through the grim archway of John of Gaunt's Tower into another world. Throughout its nine centuries of existence, she was told it had held countless thousands of prisoners of all kinds. Catholics, Protestants, Quakers, debtors, witches and sorcerers, along with common criminals. They had all been housed here, many executed for their faith or their misdemeanours, executions up to as late as 1865 being a public event. As many as six thousand people had been known to crowd in to witness particularly notorious felons hanged, 'Hanging Day' being almost a public holiday.

From this grim account she was taken to see the magnificent Shire Hall with its unique collection of coats of arms of sovereigns, constables of the castle and high sheriffs dating from the twelfth century. Finally she saw the Crown Court, for hundreds of years the only Assize Court in Lancashire. It was in this court that a sentenced prisoner had his left hand put into a 'holdfast' and a branding iron with the letter 'M' for malefactor pressed into the ball of the thumb. Every prisoner coming before the court had to hold up his left hand to indicate whether he had been convicted before. It was not until 1811 that the practice was discontinued.

Margaret thanked her guide profusely for giving his time and imparting his unique knowledge. It was a memorable day for her which she would appreciate all her days.

At the end of the afternoon she got a train back to Carnforth where she changed for Barrow-in-Furness, to witness the sun lowering over Morecambe Bay as she passed south of Allthwaite. It had been a pleasant day. She would have dinner and then telephone Fred and at that thought gave an involuntary smile.

At 8.30 that evening the telephone rang at Chandlers Lodge. Rose answered it.

"Margaret, how lovely to hear from you. Where are you – back in London?"

"'Fraid not, Rose dear, they really are messing us about up here. Not your people I hasten to add, our people Stateside. I can't really see our being back in town – that is the way you describe London isn't it?"

"One of the ways. If you are going to London you are either going to Town, or The Smoke, or if to a specific part, to the City or West End."

"Well, I can't see our being back in The Smoke as you call it, for at least a week, maybe a bit more." She continued the conversation by telling Rose of her trip out today, casually adding, "Is your father OK?"

Rose did a little grin. "Fit as a fiddle – I'll go and get him." She put the receiver down and hurried to the kitchen where Fred was talking to Anni, Karl, Ernie and Rosemary.

"Margaret on the line for you dad."

Four sets of eyebrows raised in concert, as Fred made his way to the hall, studiously not hurrying.

"Margaret – having a good time?"

"Fred. In the comparatively short time I have been in the military I have learnt a deal of bad language. I have to confess to you that at Barrow-in-Furness I have used it all – frequently!"

"Don't tell me the place is as bad as that?"

"The place is fine, the people are fine, with a couple of exceptions, both in my party, and today I have had a lovely day touring into Carnforth and Lancaster."

"So when will you be back? We miss you."

"That's nice to know – who's the we?" she asked with a laugh in her voice.

"Oh, Rose, Jeremy, everybody."

"Including you?"

"Particularly me."

There was a distinct pause from Barrow-in-Furness.

"I'm pleased you miss me." Another short pause. "I have a ten day leave due after I return. Could you spare some time for us to make a trip somewhere?"

"Yes, of course. I've had no time off in years almost. Where would you suggest, South Africa? South America?"

"Now that is, as James Cagney would say, cooking with gas. But I fear we would need more than ten days."

"You could always desert."

Margaret laughed at the thought – not of her deserting but of Fred leaving his factory.

"Well, have some thoughts and we'll talk about it when I come back. I had better be off now. A gentleman has been waiting to use the telephone nearly all the time I have been here in the booth."

"How do you know he's a gentleman?"

303

"Well, firstly he is obviously an Englishman and secondly he has not tried to kick the door down yet."

"Alright, my love, see you soon."

"Goodnight Fred dear."

It can readily be established from those last two utterances that the air between Margaret and Fred would appear to be getting noticeably warmer.

Fred returned to the kitchen. The people sitting at the table looked at him enquiringly but said nothing. Silence reigned, until Rose questioned,

"Well?"

"Yes, she's very well. Sends her best wishes to all."

Addressing the company Rose announced, "My father has been on the telephone for eleven minutes and a half by the kitchen clock, and the only message he has is Margaret sends her best wishes. Now. I recall a couple of years ago at this very table, I returned from taking a telephone call from Mark, and said 'Mark sends his kind regards'. My father then recounted to all and sundry that Mark sent his kind regards and it had taken him twenty minutes to do so. The boot now is most definitely on the other foot. Assuming Margaret sends her best wishes takes five seconds; may we enquire what was discussed in the other eleven minutes and twenty-five seconds?"

Fred regarded the quintet of grinning faces.

"A gentleman would never disclose the contents of a discussion with a lady now, would he?"

Rose was ready for that.

"Yes he would, unless he had something to hide."

"Well, as it happens, Margaret will be getting a ten day leave when she returns, and it was suggested that I might take a little time off."

"She will be coming here?" Rose was well on the scent.

"No. We thought we might get away together for a few days."

The listeners made a real meal out of this announcement, with a chorus of 'Oooooh's' which could have been heard at The Angel, these causing Fred to respond quickly with, "All respectable of course, no hanky panky."

Leading Ernie to state "and if you believe that you will believe anything," followed up with the suggestion that perhaps they should take Miss Russell with them as a chaperone.

Fred knew there would be a good deal of leg-pulling when the announcement of his proposed trip away was announced, not only from those present but also from Jack in particular, the Rotary crowd, Ray Osbourne – they would all have a field day. 'Oh well! my backs' broad', he consoled himself.

Margaret, unaware of the ripples her stone in the water regarding the few days away had caused, went off to bed, read a book for a while then had a good night's sleep. Having enjoyed her rail expedition on Saturday, she decided to explore further on Sunday, on the local line along the coast to Whitehaven. Whilst the trip was not wildly exciting she thoroughly enjoyed seeing more of this country to which she was becoming increasingly attached. She was particularly intrigued by the different accents of the inhabitants of places only a few miles apart. In the States, the people in New England had a different accent to say those in Kentucky or Louisiana, but in those cases they were thousands of miles apart. Here she found the people in Carnforth spoke quite differently to those in Whitehaven, and they were only thirty odd miles apart.

She had discussed this with Fred and Rose. How, for example, the Londoners in the area in which she was billeted, spoke quite differently to the natives of Sandbury. They had told her that if she went to Newcastle or Belfast she would not understand a word said to her. She had taken this as a leg-pull, but with these new experiences she was beginning to think they might well be true. Which they are of course, or at least they were.

Margaret's sojourn at Barrow-in-Furness dragged on until Monday the 17th of July, when suddenly all was completed and arrangements made to leave the next day. She excitedly telephoned Fred on Monday evening, saying her leave would start on Friday 21st and that she would have fourteen days, not ten.

Fred, making plans as to where they should go had included Winchester as first on the list. In the meantime, Buffy having made his usual bi-weekly telephone call to Rose to see how his grandson was getting on, and with whom he would have little chats, was told that Fred was intending to take Margaret to see his home town of Winchester – or city as it should correctly be described. Buffy's immediate reaction was, 'they must stay here. I'll have a word with your father at the factory'. This he did.

"I understand you are going away with your lady friend and that you propose visiting Winchester," Buffy said.

In all innocence Fred replied, "Well yes. I'm very proud of my birth place, but I haven't settled it with Margaret yet."

"Then why don't you stay with us for a couple of days or as long as you like?"

"I'm sure Margaret would like that very much. Thank you, thank you indeed."

"No problem. Let me know when you are arriving and I will get you picked up at Winchester."

Fred sat back thinking, 'people are already taking us for a couple'.

Half an hour later his telephone rang again. "Mr Cartwright again Mr Chandler."

"Thank you Miss Russell."

"Mentioned my offer to the memsahib, Fred. She said ' will it be singles or a double room our guests will be requiring?' so I thought I'd better give you another ring. After all we wouldn't want to spoil your stay by getting it wrong would we?"

"We're not all like you, you know."

"I know, that's why I plumped for the double room, after all I know what a randy so and so you always were."

"Well, I'm afraid we're not at that stage. So perhaps you will kindly inform your boss that it is singles, and that I am very deeply grateful to her."

"I'll tell her that," then as an afterthought, "anyway, the rooms are next to each other, so your feet shouldn't get too cold padding back and forth." With that he put the receiver down leaving Fred with a bit of a daydream, into which we shall not intrude.

That evening, in the course of her daily chat with the Earl, Gloria Treharne just mentioned that Fred and Margaret were going to spend a few days together so that Margaret could see parts of England she had not so far been able to visit.

"Perhaps they would spend a few days with me?" he asked. "I'll give Fred a ring. Now, if they do, why don't you come down for a few days, make it a foursome?"

"If Cecely could look after Eric and Patricia. I would love to. They break up at the end of next week 28th July."

"Right then. When they break up you can all come down for the holidays. That would be very pleasant. Let's see what we can organise. In the meantime I will telephone Fred."

At nine o'clock the next morning Fred's telephone rang out. "The Earl of Otbourne Mr Chandler." Miss Russell always felt very important at taking calls from the Earl.

"Good morning my lord."

"Fred. I've heard on the grapevine that you propose cavorting around

England with a very attractive American lady. I wondered if you would like to spend a few days here – use it as your base you know, have a good shufti at Gloucester, Hereford and so on. Mrs Treharne will, I hope, be here. We could have a jolly time in the evenings when you come back from your travels."

As a result of this conversation Fred said he would be delighted to bring Major Coulter to Ramsford, and would confirm dates and times when he had discussed everything with her. It worked out therefore that Fred met Margaret at Waterloo Station on Friday 21st for the train to Romsey where they were to stay for four nights, moving on to Worcester on Tuesday 25th.

The time just flew past. Buffy met them at Winchester with the car. Rita took to Margaret immediately. On Saturday they all went to see Charlie, to find Emma already there. He was up and about now a good deal of the time, it being nearly two weeks since his operation to mend the internal damage. He was however strictly forbidden to bend, stretch or twist himself suddenly. On the odd occasion he unwittingly carried out one of these movements he was rudely reminded of the necessity for this regulation by the sharp stab in the guts which resulted. However, he was his usual ebullient self, looking forward to moving to a convalescent home in a week or so.

"Where would that be?" asked Buffy.

"I don't know. I plumped for somewhere in Kent for obvious reasons, but they told me it was infinitely too dangerous to send people to that neck of the woods. I said that my fiancée was there. The almoner replied, 'yes, but she's a Wren'. I haven't quite worked that one out yet."

After Fred's party left, Emma stayed on for a little while longer. She would be staying overnight in The Swan, where they had now got to know her.

"Do you think Fred and Margaret are a twosome?" she asked.

"Oh, I don't know. He's quite a bit older than her isn't he? Another thing, Ruth was such a perfect being, I loved her so much."

What he was trying to do was to express his loyalty to Ruth who was the nearest thing to a mother he had ever known. "I think Fred would find it very difficult to find someone to fill her shoes."

"What did you think of Margaret?"

"I thought she was utterly charming, articulate, and far from being at all pushy, as American women are reputed to be."

"So you think they could be, or become, a twosome?"

"I don't know. Let's be practical. There's always the sex side. It might be alright now, but what about in say ten years' time. She will be in the prime of her life and he will probably be past it."

"Would it be important at that stage?"

"Well, I suppose there is life without sex, as I can readily testify, though I give warning if it goes on much longer, I shall tear myself out of here, walk to Deal and carry you off on to the South Downs for an orgy of ravishment, until you scream for help – or for more!"

"It would kill you."

"Better than being shot."

She hugged him up and covered his face with kisses. "I must go. The bell went hours ago."

"Only five minutes ago."

"I'll see you tomorrow, bye bye darling Charlie."

On Sunday Buffy and Rita took their guests to matins at their local church, where a small plaque on the wall in the north chapel remembered one Corporal Jeremy Cartwright, City Rifles, Killed in Action. Calais. May 1940.

In the afternoon Fred and Margaret took a walk arm in arm along the river towards The Abbey. It was a calm, pleasantly warm day. As they strolled, Margaret said, "Emma is a lovely girl isn't she?"

Fred's instantaneous reply was, "So are you" followed after receiving a tug on his arm and a warm smile from his companion. "You know, it's all down to David. If he hadn't met his first wife Pat we would not be at Sandbury Engineering. Then I would not have met you. If he had not met and befriended Charlie, Maria would not have given Emma Charlie's address to write to in the Western Desert. David's great friend Jeremy would not have met our Rose, I would not have met Buffy again, therefore we would not be here. So it's all down to David."

"I wouldn't mind betting there's a flaw in that argument somewhere. I shall have to use my limited intelligence to try and find it."

"If your intelligence is limited, mine must be pretty well non-existent."

They walked on quietly for a while until Margaret broke the silence.

"I've found the flaw."

"Which is?"

"If it hadn't been for you and Ruth, David wouldn't have arrived. Therefore it's all down to you."

"Well, in view of the fact that I get blamed for most things I suppose I must agree. But then we could go on back to my father and his father and so on."

They laughed together.

"Have you been able to trace your antecedents?"

"Harry did, before the war. Luckily we are all country people, therefore births, deaths and marriages tend to get put into the parish registers. With a bit of diligent searching he got back to sixteen hundred and something, then Hitler came along and put the kybosh on everything. If I know Harry he will carry on again when he comes home, he never leaves things unfinished."

"Tell me about Harry."

Fred gave a word picture of his elder son, a committed family man, cheerful and generous, the sort of bloke you would want with you if you were in trouble. He had received awards for gallantry on the retreat to Dunkirk in 1940, and since then had won the Military Cross in his jungle hideout in Malaya.

"You haven't seen his photograph have you? Nor the drawings of his leopard?"

"His leopard?"

Yes. We'll get Megan to bring them round when we get back home. He's got a pet leopard," and he told her the story of Harry's acquisition of Chantek.

"I feel so desperately sorry for Megan."

"Fortunately she has a backbone of steel; she has needed it several times during this war. Her being a nursing sister and having the children to care for keeps her very busy which of course helps, but when she's alone it must be sickening. At least she knows he's alive now, but she still has the worry of knowing that he lives in one of the most unhealthy and inhospitable places on earth and is constantly involved in actions of one sort or another. There are few people I hold in higher regard than Megan."

After another silence, Margaret asked, "Could you tell me about Ruth?"

Whilst Fred had not expected Margaret to ask him the question direct, he had been preparing himself to tell her of how much he and Ruth had been to each other, how totally shattered he had been when she died. They had their little disagreements from time to time of course, as all people close to each other do, but their marriage was a true, open partnership. They enjoyed their intimacy with each other, and he relied totally on her intelligence and sound judgement in all things. When times were hard after the Great War she showed her mettle time and again, and of course when he went off to war in 1914 she was left as Megan is now with a child to look after. With the casualty lists coming in from the Mons retreat day after day, she lived a nightmare. So few of the Mons people survived the war.

"Let's go back," he suggested. "I loved Ruth very much. You must tell me all about you one day." He leaned over and kissed her on the cheek.

They enjoyed their stay at Romsey, being cosseted by Rita, exploring Winchester, visiting Bournemouth using almost the last of Buffy's petrol ration in the process, until on Tuesday they said their grateful goodbyes and boarded their train for Bristol, thence on to Worcester. After they had left Buffy turned to Rita and said, "You know, my friend Jerry Solomon at the Exchange once told me there is an old Jewish saying that guests are like fish, after four days they begin to smell a bit. I could have had those two here for four weeks if they could have spared the time."

Rita's reply did not entirely surprise him.

"Perhaps they would spend part of their honeymoon with us."

At Worcester they were met by the Earl and Gloria Treharne and warmly welcomed. Margaret was, like most people, a little reserved at meeting a member of the aristocracy, but when Gloria took her arm, the Earl took the other one. In this manner they walked ahead whilst Fred organised a porter to carry their luggage. Porters at that stage of the war were very thin on the ground. The days of a dozen waiting at the point at which the First Class carriages would stop were long gone.

Outside they met Captain Morgan, who had in the meantime visited the feed merchant for several paper sacks of provender stacked in the back of the large shooting brake. The cases were placed on top of this bird and animal feed, the weight of one case compressing a sack which emitted a quite unpleasant fishy pong. The Earl quite cheerfully announced, "Sorry about the aroma, we'll open the windows when we get going – soon get rid of it."

Margaret smiled. She was going to like it here. When they swung into the gates of Ramsford Grange she was even more certain. The long sweeping drive with the vista of the magnificent porticoed building she espied through the windscreen in front, was truly impressive. The Earl helped Gloria and Margaret to alight, whilst Fred, who was seated with them on the wide rear seat of the brake, used the off-side door. As the car pulled up, two servants appeared and carried the suitcases in, whilst the party, having thanked Captain Morgan, made their way up the wide frontal steps. At the top they turned to look south over the park, dotted with sheep grazing away, towards a long low wooded area. The sun shone in from the right, still fairly high although it was getting on for six o'clock, the whole panorama presenting a picture of peace, tranquillity and beauty.

Margaret was the first to speak.

"I think this is the most beautiful prospect I have ever experienced," she said, turning to the Earl.

"Yes my dear. Every day I regard it and think of all the evil being perpetrated across the water, and again in our own capital city and Home Counties. We have one major consolation. When those people who have brought all this wickedness upon us are dead and gone, this beauty will still be here. Now, that's the last dismal thing we shall say whilst you are here. Do you agree?"

There was a universal 'yes' from his three companions. But it wasn't the last dismal utterance of the day. That evening the cultured voice of the BBC announcer at nine o'clock told the nation that in a deluge of V-1's the south east of England had suffered in the past twenty-four hours, Saint Thomas Hospital, a famous London teaching hospital only a stone's throw from Buckingham Palace, had been hit, causing many casualties.

Before they retired the Earl asked them if they had made any plans for their stay.

"Well, I thought that on three of the days we could visit Worcester, Hereford and Gloucester, to see the cathedrals. I am ashamed to say I have never seen them myself, except from a distance," Fred replied.

"I particularly wanted to see those," Margaret added, "would it also be possible to walk around the estate?"

"Do you ride?" asked the Earl.

"Oh, yes, but I have no riding gear."

"Slacks?"

"Yes I have slacks with me."

"Right. We can find you some boots from somewhere, have no fear. Now Fred I know you can ride, your regiment were mounted infantry in South Africa. I was talking to Buffy about it when we were up at Sandbury on one occasion."

"Crikey. That was forty odd years ago!"

"Yes, but riding is like cycling, once you have learnt to ride a bike you never forget it. Mind you, if you haven't ridden either a bike or a horse for a while you can't afford to overdo it. Anyway, we'll get Tomkins to saddle up for us to suit your programme."

"I am a little confused my lord..."

"Oh for God's sake – we're all such jolly good friends, please drop the 'my lord' business and call me Christopher as Gloria does. I would much prefer that."

Margaret began again. "I am a little confused Christopher," with a smiling accent on the 'Christopher', "about this expression mounted infantry. If you are mounted do you not become cavalry?"

"Well you see my dear, it was like this," and the Earl explained to her that in the Boer war in South Africa, the enemy were all mounted. They would get up a defensive position on a 'kopje' or hill, leaving their horses in a safe place that they could retreat to and collect them when, and if, it looked as though they were going to be overrun. Having killed off a few of their attackers, the latter always being at a disadvantage since they would be assaulting a prepared position on an upward slope, they would beat a hasty retreat on their horses. They had the great advantages of knowledge of the territory, space to manoeuvre, and mobility, three things the British infantry did not possess. So someone had the bright idea of putting some of the infantry on horseback. They rode in fours, and when they met up with opposition they dismounted, one of the fours held the horses of the other three who then together put in the attack. Alternatively they were able if the ground permitted, to get round quickly behind the Boer, and unlike traditional cavalry could then dismount and climb where horses could no longer go. Now, having thoroughly bored you with all that, you are now informed as to how Fred knows all about riding horses."

Both the ladies laughed and clapped. It was decided therefore that Margaret and Fred would go to Worcester on the local in the morning and be back at Ramsford to ride around the estate at around four o'clock for a couple of hours. Margaret's immediate thought was that it must be a pretty big estate in that case, not appreciating it would probably take a full day to do the job properly, and then there was the land in Norfolk, to say nothing of the huge expanse of grouse shooting moorland Christopher and his cousin owned in Scotland. Successive Earls of Otbourne had been very careful in husbanding their properties over the past three hundred years, despite attempts by governments between the wars to tax them out of existence, as a result bringing about massive demolitions of mansions which were truly national treasures.

Margaret and Fred enjoyed their day out together to Worcester, returning, with a little trepidation on Fred's part, to mounting their steeds for a leisurely ride through the village and round part of the western borders of the estate, ending at the lake where four years earlier the Earl had taken David and Pat to wait to see the kingfishers coming back to their nest in the bank. They waited quietly for some while but were out of luck, until just as the Earl said that they had better make a move, a pair skimmed across the surface, their plumage brilliant in the sunlight, to provide Margaret, as it had Pat, with an indelible memory of their beauty and the beauty of the whole day.

As they turned, Gloria called to the Earl, "Race you back."

"You're on."

The two dug their heels into their respective mounts and set off across the front parkland towards the stables. Fred had been surprised to see Gloria mounted with them. Gloria always looked as though she had climbed out of a bandbox, she looked so immaculate – horsey she did not look! But Gloria had accompanied her late husband for years in colonial parts where the only means of moving from point A to point B was on horseback, the experience there gained, now being amply demonstrated. The Earl of course, being the gentleman he was, allowed her to win. Well, men are like that, are they not?

That evening as they were finishing their dinner, one of the servants hurried into the dining room.

"Telephone call for Mr Chandler my lord."

Fred got up and went to the main hallway.

"Dad, it's Rose. I'm afraid you've got another Christmas present to buy. It's for your grandson. Both he and Maria are well. She will telephone you as soon as she is able."

"What about you love?"

"I'm fine. I'll ring you again tomorrow."

"Alright, now take care mind."

"I will, have no fear."

Fred went back into the dining room, they each looked up expectantly.

"It appears I am a grandfather again," he announced. "Maria gave birth to a seven pound son this morning, they are both well."

There was a round of applause, which was added to by the two footmen waiting on them. The Earl stood up and announced, "To the latest addition to the Chandlers. May he live a long, prosperous and peaceful life."

"Hear Hear."

Chapter Twenty-Eight

There followed a quiet seven days for David and R Battalion when they moved up to their new positions on the 10th of July. They endured frequent shelling, but being well dug in suffered only a handful of casualties. David sent the new platoon officers Andy Gilchrist and Reggie Pardew out on night patrols, each on two occasions, Reggie on his second trip with half a dozen of his men returning with a prisoner they had snaffled from the enemy lines. From this captive the intelligence section was able to learn that the SS people had been withdrawn as a result of the casualties they had suffered, and had been replaced by an infantry division which was known to be second-rate.

In the meantime the bitter battle for Caen was gradually producing results. The evening before David and his men moved into their new positions, they saw, then heard, some five hundred Lancaster and Halifax bombers drop two and a half thousand tons of bombs on the northern outskirts of the city in front of the advancing British 3rd Division, 59th Division, the Canadian 3rd and flame throwers of the British 79th Armoured Div. As Paddy put the inevitable question, "How would you like to be under that lot sir?"

David replied, "I wonder how many innocent French people are having to be sacrificed, some of those bombs are bound to be dropped wide of the target area."

It was a fact of course. Many French civilians throughout Normandy, eagerly expecting liberation any day, became casualties of war themselves.

After a week holding this sector, during which two attacks were put in by the Germans using tanks and infantry, both comfortably beaten off, the battalion was taken back to reserve and their positions taken over by a Belgian battalion. General Gale's airborne division had now been reinforced with a Belgian brigade and a Dutch brigade, which along with the brigade of commandos already under his command made it a very potent fighting force indeed. However, for the moment the division's task was to keep the eastern flank secure to protect the divisions engaged in the mighty assault on Caen.

David was now anxiously awaiting the news from home regarding Maria and Rose, both due to give birth at the end of July. On the 24th July the battalion was withdrawn from reserve to a rest area. Here they were able to have hot showers, clean clothing and renew worn and torn battledresses and camouflaged smocks. On the day after their arrival the post Corporal arrived with a massive sack of mail for the battalion. It took him all the morning to sort it out into company lots, along with a further sad collection of those addressed to men who had been killed, or wounded severely enough to be sent back home.

After the distribution, Paddy went to David's tent, which he shared with his new second in command Sandy Patterson.
"Any news sir?"
"Not a sausage. Mind you, the last post mark from Maria is the seventeenth, so these have been a while getting here, which is a bit unusual."

Unusual it was. The Army Postal Service became renowned all through the war, in all theatres, for its superb efficiency. A letter taking a week to arrive in the BLA – British Liberation Army – from UK was by far the exception to the rule.
"What about Rose sir?"
"Her letter was sent on the 16th, saying she was well and as big as a house."
"Perhaps she's going to have twins, sir."
"I hope not for my father's sake. He would be saying 'don't I have enough Christmas presents to buy already?' He'll have a heart attack."

If David had known that at that very moment his father was on a train with a lady with whom he was spending 'a few days away', he would not probably have had a heart attack but the news might have induced a murmur.

The next day David's mind was put at rest. A telegram arrived from "Schultz," saying "Son born. Both well. Letter following." Coincidental with the telegram the officers' NAAFI ration arrived, comprising one bottle of Scotch and four bottles of beer to each officer and warrant officer, a monthly entitlement, but the first they had as yet received. That evening David, Paddy and Sandy pooled their resources and offered all the officers and warrant officers, to call and wet the baby's head, a call not one of them would have the discourtesy to refuse. RSM Forster was one of the first. He brought two bottles of Calvados which he had somehow acquired – one does not query sources of supply of an RSM. The RQMS, an old mate of Paddy's from days long ago in India, brought three bottles of champagne, and at nine o'clock Colonel Hamish Gillespie, never ever known to turn down an invitation of a drink, arrived. He already was three sheets in the wind from having more than sampled his own NAAFI ration before leaving his quarters. With contributions from other donors the party blossomed.

Just as it was getting dusk, David's bell tent, designed to cater at the most for eight men and their equipment, now contained two beds, a table, a forest of bottles, and around twenty well sloshed officers, each holding an enamel mug from which they each and all refused to be parted. Above the clamour Hamish was heard to bellow, "Drink up, and follow me."

The officers' tents were set a little way from the various company lines, but not so far that the men could not hear the hubbub. A small crowd therefore had gathered but could not see what was going on in Major Chandler's quarters. Imagine their surprise therefore, when Lieutenant colonel Hamish Gillespie, hatless and tie-less led a crocodile of their highly respected officers in a conga out of the major's tent.

'I came, I saw, I congaed' burst on the late evening air as Hamish led his snaking songsters' procession of commissioned rank in and out of the various bell tents – until, reaching the officers' dining tent he failed to see a particularly well pegged in guy rope which, in turn, failed to give way as his ankles connected with it, pitching him head first into the canvas side. The first half dozen behind him, unable to stop, went arse over tip on top of one another, the remainder slithered to a halt, splitting their sides, and the, by now, two hundred men of the battalion who had turned out to watch this carnival cheered lustily.

There were some terrible heads in the morning.

Henry Frederick Cedric Chandler's head had, however, been well and truly wetted.

There was however a downside to this memorable event. Two days later another telegram arrived for Major Chandler to the effect that he was an uncle again. Rose had been delivered of a girl, name as yet undecided. Another party was therefore called for. But as a certain William Shakespeare might have said, 'There's the rub!' To have a party you must have booze. As we know already the party of the night before last had left the would be celebrators booze-less, booze-less in fact for another month unless someone could find a source of supply of Calvados or some other inebriatory liquid. Step forward two men who would be able to find gin in the middle of the Sahara Desert, namely Regimental Sergeant Major Clifford Forster, and Company Sergeant Major Paddy O'Riordan.

Their first port of call was Madame Gondrand's cafe on what was to be called Pegasus Bridge. Her cafe was the first building in France to be liberated when Major Howard's men made their incredible landing in the early hours of June 6th. She found them two bottles of cognac and three of champagne, then gave them directions to a farm tucked well out of the way on the road to Ouistreham where they were reliably informed the farmer distilled a considerable volume of calvados. They were to mention her name because she and the farmer were at one time 'very good friends'. They found the farm with a little difficulty, expecting to find a thousand bods of some inferior regiment billeted on or around it. Their luck held. There was no military presence whatsoever. The farmer apologised for the fact that his stock from last year's distillation was not yet up to standard, but that it was drinkable – just.

Beggars can't be choosers.

With their prize hidden under a blanket in the back of the RSM's jeep they made their way back to camp and to Major Chandler's tent, where again they set his camp table groaning. The invitations sent out, Miss Unnamed Laurenson was welcomed into this world, not quite as liberally as had been her new cousin over the river in Essex, but sufficient to provide a renewal of the head problem experienced two days before, along with the inevitable 'mouth like the bottom of a parrot cage' syndrome.

Madame Darlet and her nineteen-year-old daughter Francoise lived in a somewhat run-down looking building overlooking the tented rest area. The property could be described as sizeable, that is, too large to be called a dwelling but not large enough to be called a chateau. Since 1940 she and her daughter had been obliged to live in apartments upstairs, whilst the remainder of the house was occupied by German officers, with whom they had little contact since they had their own stairway at the rear of the building, formerly the servants' access.

Madame Darlet's husband had been captured in 1940 in the Maginot Line. For four years she and her daughter had scraped a living growing vegetables and selling them in Caen market on Sundays, and rearing rabbits which they sold to the German officers' mess. They had had occasional brushes with would be lotharios from among their unwelcome lodgers over the years, but had escaped any serious harassment.

On Saturday morning, 29th July, Mademoiselle Francoise Darlet, looking out of her upstairs window towards the rest area, saw a party of men erecting what seemed to be canvas screens in a large square on the grass between the tented encampment and the stream which formed the boundary with Madame Darlet's property. Next she saw some German POW's digging three shallow parallel trenches across the green to the edge of the stream. Puzzled she called her mother and rummaged in the bottom of a large chiffonier to unearth two pairs of somewhat ancient, but still usable field glasses. Once the trenches had been dug, the POW's proceeded to lay a number of duckboards over and adjacent to them. British soldiers then erected a veritable maze of pipework, running back to a machine of some sort mounted on a lorry, which from where they were was partially obscured from them.

Nothing more seeming to happen, the two ladies enjoyed their coffee and croissants, talking of what to do with the excess of vegetables which had piled up since they could no longer go to Caen market, if the market area still existed after the bombing, which in fact it did not.

An hour later they went to the window again and received the shock of their lives. Some one hundred odd men, all stark naked, were lined up in rows of twenty ready to go under what were in fact hot showers – the first for a month. The screens, seven feet high, prevented any passing locals from viewing this ultimate in undress uniform, but could not conceal the spectacle from the elevated position possessed by Madame and Mademoiselle Darlet. They each reached for their field glasses. In the meantime a second company had lined up behind those now moving through the duckboard area. Behind them David's company lined up twenty abreast, ready for their dousing, with David and Paddy on the end of the line nearest to the two voyeurs, (or should it be voyeuses?). As the two ladies swung their binoculars on to the end of the line and rested on David and Paddy they simultaneously halted.

"Mummy."

"Yes dear."

"Do you think we could ask those two on the end to dinner?"

"I was just wondering about that myself dear. But how would we recognise them if we met them? I doubt if you have looked at their faces yet, I know I haven't."

"We couldn't invite them anyway, we haven't enough food."

"Oh, I don't think we would bother about food dear."

Few ladies can say they have seen four or five hundred naked men in the space of half an hour. The sight stayed with Madame and Mademoiselle Darlet all their days, and a good many of their nights!

Two days after the welcome shower the battalion moved back into the line. Apart from active patrolling and considerable shelling during which they suffered a few casualties, things were quiet. On 2nd August the brigade was ordered to move forward in a night attack on a slight ridge some one thousand yards ahead, 'R' Battalion and 'L' Battalion to lead the attack with the third battalion of the brigade in reserve. A preliminary barrage was put down for them as they advanced, after which they literally lay against it as it moved slowly, being uplifted a hundred yards at a time. It was a triumph of artillery shooting. As the shelling stopped the attackers were only a hundred yards from the enemy positions and went in with the bayonet through the defences to the stop line, where they dug in furiously. They were surprised at the number of prisoners they had taken, most of whom had just thrown down their weapons as soon as they saw their attackers upon them. They were even more surprised when they found that a large number of them were Russians!

Dawn was breaking as Paddy came up to where David was standing surveying the scene, watching in particular a very large feldwebel organising the dumping of some one hundred prisoners' weapons in an orderly manner, filling a large wooden wheelbarrow with ammunition and grenades, and then getting them into three files ready to march off, David called him over. He spoke to him in German.
"Where are you from?"
"I am from the small town of Oster on the River Desna about one hundred kilometres from Kiev. Probably half the men here are Ukrainians, some Georgians, Chechens and Uzbeks. We all hate the Russians. We were taken prisoner by the Wehrmacht in the early days and are fighting to regain our homelands."
"But you must know now that the Red Army is defeating Germany in the east, and soon they will be defeated in the west. Why do you hate the Russians? – we thought you were all Russians."
"The Ukraine is a separate nation to Russia. We have always wanted our independence but Stalin was determined we should be part of the Soviet Union. In the thirties he deliberately starved our country into submission. Two million people died of starvation in a land which was capable of feeding the whole Soviet Union. My uncle, aunt and three

cousins all died. That is why I fought with the Germans."

"What will you do now? You cannot go home."

"I shall try and get your country to take me in – we all will. We are very loyal people to those who will befriend us."

"Well, I wish you luck." David held out his hand which was taken firmly. The feldwebel stood back, saluted, turned about and marched his men off. One hundred and twenty odd of them, guarded by two walking wounded paratroopers.

"What was all that about sir?" Paddy asked.

David gave him the gist of the conversation.

"I never thought I would feel sorry for a bloody German," Paddy confessed. "Still, I suppose as he wasn't a German it's alright to feel sorry for the poor sod."

"There will be lots like him I am afraid Paddy. What the hell they will do with them all, God alone knows."

But of course, many did stay in Britain and were gradually assimilated into the population. This number did of course include some ex-camp guards who managed to talk their way through the initial vetting and were lucky not to have been caught and hanged.

Success had been general all along the divisional front, but there was no cause to become complacent. The division they had all but annihilated in one way or another would speedily be replaced by another, probably with panzers. They dug in rapidly expecting the inevitable counter attack. They had not long to wait.

Chapter Twenty-Nine

On Thursday 27th July Margaret and Fred were up early to catch the local to Worcester and then changed for Gloucester. Having walked around the city and enjoyed a light lunch they made for the cathedral. Again Margaret, and if he would be prepared to admit it, Fred himself, were overwhelmed by the majesty of this magnificent building.

"I always marvel how, all those hundreds of years ago, with the benefit of only the most elementary measuring tools, they managed to get the side walls up so that when they constructed the roof the sloping bits met at the apex. How they calculated the sizes of the buttresses required to prevent the weight of the roof pushing the sides out, I will never know, particularly when you realise the bulk of the roof is solid lead."

Margaret thought for a while.

"I can appreciate your looking at it from a sort of civil engineering point of view. There is also the source of wonder at the spiritual heights required to visualise such beauty, such immensity, purely in the praise of God." Fred nodded in agreement.

They continued their progress in companionable silence until just before three o'clock when Margaret suggested they sit in the nave for a while and just soak up the peace and serenity of this noble building. They had only been seated a few minutes when they were thrilled to hear the soft tones of the magnificent cathedral organ. There was to be a big society wedding on Saturday and the organist was now to practise the various hymns, anthems and of course wedding marches for the occasion. He ran through the hymns, with which he had no problem. The anthem he practised twice to the delight of his listeners, Margaret and Fred having been joined by some two dozen other visitors seated in the nave to enjoy some free entertainment.

Finally he came to the wedding marches. First the Mendelssohn, and lastly the Wagner, which played at full blast nearly lifted the roof off the cathedral, at the same time sending shivers down the spines of the listeners. Fred was not as appreciative of music as was his son David. Nevertheless the setting of this recital, the power of it, and the fact that it was obviously having a tremendous effect on Margaret, who had never been so close to its creation as she now was experiencing, had a profound effect on him. He took her hand and squeezed. She looked at him and kissed him lightly on the cheek. It was a very pleasant moment.

That evening during dinner they were telling the Earl and Gloria about the organ recital laid on for their benefit.

Margaret added excitedly, "And when he played the wedding march from Lohengrin the whole building, and I imagine the small number of us in there with us listening to it, vibrated with the depth and volume produced. I imagine he must have brought every pipe in that huge instrument to play."

"Now tell me," asked the Earl, "the Wagner one, is that the 'here comes the bride' one or is that the Mendelssohn?"

Fred hadn't a clue. Margaret was uncertain. Gloria had the answer.

"It's Wagner's Lohengrin. Act three. I know this because I was in a choir once, many years ago I hasten to add, and of course the libretto says nothing about 'here comes the bride', I don't know who put those words to it."

"Well come on then dear" (instant aural recognition of the 'dear' by Fred and Margaret, up until now it's not having been used in company), the Earl pleaded, "won't you please sing it to us?"

"I have a voice like a corncrake these days I'm afraid," she laughingly replied, "but I can remember the first few lines. They go...

Faithfully guided, come to this place
where the blessing of love shall enfold you.
Love, the reward of courage triumphant,
truly makes you a most happy pair.

...I can't remember any more. You have to admit it is a bit more romantic than 'here comes the bride', don't you agree? Mind you, it fits into the music more readily in the German."

"Well, I have to admit I have never been to a Wagner opera," the Earl confided, "I have always understood one needed a far stronger constitution than mine to sit through thirteen or fourteen hours of 'The Ring' for example. How about you Fred?"

"I have to admit complete ignorance of the subject," Fred replied. "Our David is the opera fan in the family, but whether he has a taste for Wagner I know not."

"But some Wagner is extremely listenable," Margaret suggested. "The Flying Dutchman, Tannhauser, Parsifal, for example. I must admit I have only heard them on records, maybe one day I shall be able to go to your wonderful Covent Garden and see them performed. Do they perform German opera in wartime I wonder?"

The Earl replied, "Do you know, I've never thought of that. They must do, after all they play Beethoven and Brahms on the wireless occasionally. Admittedly Wagner was anti-Semitic so that might put the kybosh on him – I shall not sleep until I have established the facts of the case," he ended with a smile.

On Friday they awoke to be greeted by a veritable downpour which continued all the morning preventing Fred and Margaret's journey to Hereford. They spent the morning in the house and when the rain eased up walked down to the village to have a drink at the pub. Christopher and Gloria stood at one of the big casement windows watching them as they made their way down the long driveway. They were walking arm in arm, the watchers noticing they were talking animatedly, with Margaret every now and then turning towards Fred and smiling.

"Do you think they make a good pair?" asked Gloria.

"Do you think we make a good pair?" replied Christopher. Gloria thought for a moment or two.

"We are never lost for conversation. We like or love similar things. We enjoy similar pursuits. Yes, I think we are a good pair."

"Then will you marry me Gloria? I knew we were soul mates the first time I met you. We can get Eric boarded at Cantelbury and Patricia can come here and live. There are one or two good girl's schools in easy travelling distance. Most of all I shall have you with me all the time, which I have been wanting for ages and ages ..." he ran out of pleading.

Gloria waited for a few seconds, then simply said, "Yes."

He held her close and kissed her gently.

"We'll tell them after dinner tonight, when the servants have gone, shall we?"

Margaret and Fred enjoyed their quiet drink, quiet mainly because the lunchtime trade was never exactly the mainstay of the business, except on Saturdays and Sundays. They had some soup and a roll, having told the Earl they would not be back for lunch. They had a most friendly chat with the landlord who remembered David and Pat very well. They were all so sad when that beautiful girl was killed. "Thank God this lot will soon be over," he had added; "although we've still got those..." he hesitated.

"Bastards?" suggested Margaret.

"That's right ma'am, those bastards out east to deal with, and that's not going to be easy, or quick for that matter."

"Mr Chandler's other son is out there now, fighting behind the lines in Malaya."

"Is that so sir? Your family has certainly done its share, that's for sure. When I think of one or two skivers we've got here in the village it makes me sick, especially thinking of your lads in the thick of it all."

"How do they avoid service?" Margaret asked.

"Mainly on medical grounds somehow, I don't know, neither does anyone else, how they get away with it. It doesn't stop them going to the dances in the city, and playing football at weekends, and I might add, knocking around with one or two of the women whose husbands are away. There will be some sorting out even in this small village after the war ends I can tell you."

He was most prophetic. In the two years after the war ended the divorce rate rocketed, due in part to hasty and ill-considered wartime marriages in the first place, but also largely due to returning soldiers discovering infidelities, even to the extent of finding increases in the family over which they could not have had any control whatsoever since they had been three or four years in India or somewhere!

At two o'clock closing time, they made their way back towards the 'big house'. The sun was shining through, hesitantly, the ground was wet underfoot, but since they both were wearing strong boots they decided to walk over to the lake. There was a fallen tree there upon which Fred laid his folded Macintosh on which they sat and watched a heron standing in the water only yards away. It was completely motionless until, like a rapier, it flashed its long beak into the water bringing out a small carp. Swiftly swallowing its catch it resumed its watchful stance, totally oblivious of its spectators. After a few minutes it decided to move on to a new killing ground, or I suppose it must be described as a killing water would you think?

The two had not spoken whilst they were observing the heron. When it slowly and deliberately had moved away, Fred turned to Margaret and asked, "Can I talk to you seriously for a few moments Margaret?"

"Yes of course, of course you can." She smiled at him.

"Well, we are very good friends and I don't want to spoil that. But I want to tell you that I have become very attached to you, very attached indeed. But there is a very difficult problem which faces me."

Margaret took his hand.

"Problems are best shared."

"Well this one had got to be – eventually."

He stared across the lake, not speaking for a few moments.

"You see, I would like to ask you if you would consider marrying me, but each time I bring myself to do so I think of the fact that I am over twenty years older than you are, and it would not be fair."

"Why would it not be fair?"

"Because I am sixty-four. The fact is that at sixty-four you can still feel the feelings of love, and desire, and fulfilment can be as strong as is required in a marriage. But it cannot be denied that the physical capability does not last as you get older. To put it bluntly when I am played out you will still be a seriously passionate woman."

Margaret did not answer straight away, but then replied, "You know, sex isn't everything. I am not underrating it. In many marriages that's all there is that keeps the couple together when otherwise they are poles apart. When people get older, as we are, they tend to consider other factors as being important. You can be passionately in love with someone, or unable to live without someone, even if there is no sex, although I am not denying it could be very difficult. It does so much depend on the two people concerned. There have been many instances where couples have lived platonic lives all through their marriage, it's not unknown."

There was again a short silence between them broken by Fred saying, "The first day I saw you getting out of that car on our forecourt I had the strongest feeling about you. I hadn't even spoken to you and yet I knew there was something about you that was different, more appealing if you like, than anyone else I had met, except for my dear Ruth of course who was the first and only love of my life, until now. I do love you sincerely and deeply, but I can't turn the clock back, much as I would like to." He turned and looked into her eyes. "There are also practical difficulties. You presumably have some commitments back home, you have your status in the army, you would be settling in a new country with new people, an impoverished country at that, all these things have to be taken into account." He wound up lamely, "And for all I know you might not think that much of me anyway."

She gave a little laugh, put her arms around him and pulled him to her, kissing him firmly on the lips. She just said, "Ask me."

He did.

She accepted.

They sat with their arms around each other for a while until Fred asked. "Can we tell Gloria and Christopher after dinner tonight when the servants have gone?"

"Yes, lets. They will be surprised!"

'They' would not be the only ones to be surprised that evening.

When the servants had cleared away and departed leaving coffee for the four friends in the sitting room, the Earl tapped on the low table with a spoon.

"May I call the meeting to order for a few moments please?" he joked. They each smiled, looking at him.

"I have known my dear friend Gloria for a long time now. During all that time I have been cognisant of the fact that we are true soul-mates. I have today asked her again if she will become my wife, and I have to tell you she has said 'yes!' You are the first to know."

There was handshaking and kisses all round. 'How marvellous'. 'We won't say a word', and so on, until the minor hubbub died down.

Fred came to his feet.

"My lord. I have a feeling there must have been some form of magic in the air of Ramsford today, since I too have asked my dear Margaret to marry me, and to my delight and astonishment she too has said yes."

There was a renewal of the congratulations, back slapping, and 'we won't say a word until you have told your families', assurances.

"Everyone at Sandbury will come in to see us on Sunday evening when we get home," Fred calculated, "we shall tell them then."

"Will your folks be able to come over Margaret?" Christopher asked.

"I am afraid I have none. On my late husband's side there are one or two, but because of our constant postings we rarely met them, and since he died they have dropped off completely. Actually, that's not quite fair; we were not close to start with so we just did not keep in touch. It was mutual."

As they spoke there came a knock at the door, followed by the entry of the resident cook.

"Mrs Harris, what can we do for you?" the Earl asked jovially.

"My lord, I am terribly sorry but young Maisie took a telegram in this morning for Mr Chandler and put it on the side. She must have forgotten to tell Joseph to bring it up to the dining room, because I've just found it there. I was frightened – I thought it might be bad news."

It was not an unnatural thing for people like Mrs Harris to be fearful of telegrams. In the days when few people had telephones the telegram was the only speedy way of getting news from person to person. Secondly, few people could afford the expense of a telegram over the cost of a stamp on a letter, which would have been delivered the next day anyway. Therefore telegrams indicated urgency, and urgent news was generally feared to be bad news. The Earl passed the small envelope to Fred. He read the contents.

"It appears I have yet another Christmas present to buy this year. Rose was delivered of a daughter this morning, six pounds and six ounces. Both well."

Before anyone else could say anything Mrs Harris burst out, "Oh, I am so pleased sir, I thought it might be bad news," and promptly burst into tears. The Earl turned to her.

"Now, now Mrs Harris – nothing to cry about."

Mrs Harris bobbed a little curtsey, turned and disappeared downstairs.

"Well now, a toast to the new arrival. May she be as beautiful and charming as her mother and her mother before her."

They raised their, almost empty, glasses.

On Saturday Fred and Margaret went into Worcester on the local and bought a ring. It was a solitaire, quite beautiful which was much admired by Christopher and Gloria when it was displayed to them later that day. On Sunday they made their way back to Sandbury. As they said goodbye to their hosts, Margaret told them, "Gloria and Christopher, these have been, I am sure, the happiest, most peaceful days of my life. Thank you, thank you both so much."

The Earl took her hands in his. "We trust you will be a regular visitor from now on, don't we dear? When we have both sorted out the details of the weddings, we must let each other know. Even more importantly you and Gloria must liaise to ensure they don't fall on the same day, for obvious reasons."

"Obvious reasons?"

"Yes I would like the honour, unless you have someone specifically in mind, to give you away. I've never done it before; I would try desperately not to muck it up. Don't answer now, have a word with Fred."

"I can't think of anything we would like more. Thank you, thank you dear Christopher."

They said their goodbyes on the little platform at Ramsford Halt, making an effortless journey home, where they were jolted back into the realities of life in London, Kent and the South East generally. Two nights before, Dulwich Picture Gallery had been hit by a buzz bomb, one of an absolute deluge which had hit Kent and the capital each day for the past week. Seven hospitals were hit on the Friday night and on Saturday night a block of flats was demolished causing dozens of casualties.

On the Sunday evening of their arrival home they were welcomed by all the Chandler family, actual and affiliated. Their first call was to see Rose and the new baby. Rose had had the baby at home and was sitting up in bed surrounded by flowers, congratulatory cards, even a large teddy bear. The baby of course was beautiful.

"What are you going to call her love?"

"I want to call her Ruth, but Anni called her little girl Ruth."

"Well that doesn't matter, we all agree it's a lovely name." He looked to Margaret for approval, she smiled in agreement.

"Well, as long as Mark agrees we will call her Ruth Naomi."

"Yes, of course, Mark's mother is Naomi isn't she? – another lovely name."

There was a hesitation in the conversation.

"Rose, love."

Up until now Rose had been so wrapped up in the thoughts of her new baby's names, the general euphoria of having another beautiful baby with no complications, and the pleasure of having her congratulatory relations and friends visit her, that her usual radar, as finely tuned as those enormous structures which surmounted the Dover cliffs, if not more so, had temporarily gone into limbo. However, the somewhat difficult tone of 'Rose, love', immediately switched her antennae on to receive news of obviously some importance.

"Dad?"

"Margaret and I are to marry. We haven't told anyone here yet until you were told."

Rose was taken aback for the moment, but having already suspected that the two were 'very good friends' was not entirely surprised.

"I really am very very happy for you, I really am."

Margaret gave her a hug, as well as you can hug anyone who is sitting up in bed, and as any newly engaged person would do showed Rose her ring.

"Have you decided when, and where?"

"No. Margaret has to sort out her situation with the American army people, so it won't be for a few weeks yet. But it will be here, in Sandbury."

Margaret added emphatically, "Most definitely, in that beautiful church, always assuming your vicar will have me – after all I am not a parishioner."

"Now, there is another announcement which I cannot tell the others yet. The Earl and Mrs Treharne are to marry, and the Earl wishes to give Margaret away. But we must not say anything until they have seen Charlie tomorrow and contacted Hugh. So keep it under your hat love, will you?"

"Oh how exciting it all is."

"Well, we will go down and tell the others now. We'll see you later love – you're a clever girl."

When the news was broken downstairs there was uproar. Jack thumped Fred on his back so hard he could have fractured his spine. Everyone clustered around Margaret to view what really was a very nice, but not extraordinary engagement ring. After all, unless you are an expert in such matters, a solitaire ring, whilst beautiful to look at, could be as beautiful at ten pounds or at five hundred. It was of course a means of congratulating the wearer to admire her ring and to acknowledge she was spoken for.

The party broke up. Margaret and Fred looked in on Rose before they too went off to bed. As they stood looking down at the tiny being in the cot beside the bed, Margaret said, "To think we were all like that once," but although she smiled gently, inside her she was sad that she herself would not experience the joys, and tribulations, of motherhood.

But you never know for sure, do you?

Inevitably, Rose asked the world,
"I wonder what Mark, and Harry and David are doing tonight?"

Mark and the few men left in his company were back in reserve. David we know about, and Harry? In a day or so news would come of Harry.

Harry's wounds were healing slowly. Nothing would heal quickly in that heat and humidity. Notification of his being wounded had been wirelessed off to Sunrise; he in turn had been obliged to notify HQ at Colombo. Colombo in turn passed the information to the War Office, as a result on Monday morning 31st July, just as Megan was leaving to go to Chandlers Lodge – it was her day off – the telegraph boy arrived with the hideously frightening buff envelope. Megan opened it with trembling hands.

'The War Department etc etc. Captain Chandler H etc etc wounded in action'.

And that was all. The telegraph boy had been waiting patiently while she read the contents of the envelope. Although he was only fifteen and a half he had already had considerable experience of the effect his messages, carried in that black letter box on his waist belt, sometimes had on the recipients.

"Any reply Mrs Chandler?"

"No, no thank you, no reply." She gave him the customary sixpence; the lad turned, remounted his bicycle and pedalled off.

Megan in her daily life as a sister knew only too well what 'wounded' meant. It stretched from a minor flesh wound through to having limbs blown off. Until she heard from Harry, she would not know how serious it was, and knowing Harry, when she did hear, he would make as little of it as he could. She called the twins, now nearly seven and on their summer holidays from school, put Ceri into the pushchair and made her way to see Rose and her baby and Margaret, who would be at the Lodge for a few days yet. When she showed Margaret the telegram it was the initiation of the real consequences of war to her immediate kith and kin confronting her. Up until now she could view casualty figures and individual obituaries with a distant sadness. Now, as she was to all intents and purposes a member of the family it became very real. Being a Chandler was not necessarily to be a life of permanent bliss, any more than it would be with any other family. But then, that is how life is constructed, she told herself.

Chapter Thirty

Margaret and Fred enjoyed the final few days of her leave. Margaret had suggested that Fred should go to the 'little plant', as they still jokingly called it, in the mornings, while Margaret spent some time with Rose and Megan. On one afternoon they took the bus to Maidstone, on another to Sevenoaks and Tonbridge. On Friday afternoon Fred suggested they walked along to Ronnie Mascall's stables and select a couple of hacks to ride on Saturday over to Beltring where Whitbread's grew the hops that flavoured his favourite tipple.

"Is there a Mrs Mascall?" Margaret asked in all innocence.

"Well, no. That is, not exactly."

"Fred Chandler, I sense a little story here. Now, come on, tell your Auntie Margaret."

"Well. As you are probably aware, one has to be incredibly careful in England, and the rest of Britain for that matter, about talking about certain friendships. Not only because they are illegal, but also because the people involved, if they are wealthy or in high social or professional positions, are wide open to blackmail."

"So you are saying that Ronnie Mascall has a boyfriend."

"Yes. What's more he is, as they say, of the cloth."

"A parson?"

"More than that, a canon working for the archbishop."

"Holy Moses!" Margaret digested this piece of information.

"And do they live together?"

"Oh no, the canon visits here occasionally, he's been to Chandlers Lodge a couple of times. I imagine Ronnie visits him at Lambeth or Canterbury from time to time."

"Well, bless my soul, things do go on in this quiet little old backwater of Kent don't they?"

"The strange thing is, no matter what we think in general of that sort of relationship we all like both of them enormously. They are both extraordinarily good-looking, well set up, blokes, both highly intelligent. Ronnie is very well off, was a major in the Lancers, John Husband has a great sense of humour." His mind wandered for a while. He continued, "You would have thought they both could have fathered families of distinction."

They had almost reached the stables by this time, to be overtaken by none other than Ronnie himself in his Armstrong-Siddeley, giving a toot-toot and cheery wave as he turned into the yard in front of them.

"Ronnie, you haven't met Margaret, have you?"

"No, but I have received innumerable accounts of her charm, her intelligence, and beauty from all quarters. So much so I wondered what on earth she could see in you?"

He took her hand and then lightly kissed her on both cheeks. "It is a very great pleasure to meet you Margaret."

Margaret stood smiling. She still could not get used to this British way of the best of friends insulting each other. Strangely enough, Fred answered in a serious tone, "To be honest Ronnie, neither can I."

Margaret immediately seized his arm, looked at him and said, "You're unique, that's why."

"And there I agree with you my dear Margaret," Ronnie concurred, "and so will everybody else in Sandbury who knows him" adding, "even those poor wretches in the factory he makes slave away day by day. Mind you, he would sack 'em on the spot if they didn't you may be sure. Now, how can I help you?"

"We are thinking of riding over to Beltring tomorrow to see the Whitbread shires. They finish work at midday so we shall be able to see them if we get there just after lunch."

"You'll see the hop pickers too. They change over on Saturdays at lunchtime, so if you go early you'll see them working. Take a packed lunch, the pubs will be full up, so you'd better put a couple of quarts of Whitbread's in your saddle bags. I'll put a couple of lengths of rope in them in case you need to tether the horses. I take it you'll be providing your own blankets and ground sheets!"

"Mr Mascall, what are you suggesting?"

"Oh, nothing, nothing, if you're going to sit on the grass in some hidden corner of the Kentish countryside you might just as well be comfortable don't you think? Anyway, come in and have a cup of tea."

This they did and spent a very pleasant half an hour with their entertaining host. After a walk around the stables, and the introduction to their prospective mounts for the day ahead it was time to retrace their steps to Chandlers Lodge. As they walked from the stables Fred asked, "How is John these days, give him my regards."

A disconsolate look shadowed Ronnie's face.

"I'm afraid they've made him a dean and posted him to York. He used to telephone regularly but I hear little from him lately. There it is, out of sight out of mind, as the saying goes." He smiled, but it did not reach his eyes.

They walked home slowly. Most people they met passed the time of day with Fred, at the same time taking careful note of the lady holding his arm without its appearing, in most cases, not too obvious. Nevertheless, the description of the tall, elegant, lady with Mr Chandler was a talking point in a number of Sandbury homes that evening.

On Saturday they cycled to the stables and by eight o'clock were on their way. With Fred's knowledge of the territory and the assistance of a one inch Ordnance Survey map of the district, property of Sandbury Home Guard, they made their way in a circuitous, but scenic route towards Paddock Wood, near which town lay the village of Beltring. A distance of some ten miles as the crow flies became nearer fifteen, when at last the line of five enormous oast houses came into view.

"There doesn't appear to be any pickers about," Fred observed, as they passed the rows of 'hoppers' huts', the raised wooden dwellings in which whole families from the east end of London spent what to them was their annual holiday.

"Do the pickers live in those?" asked Margaret.

"Yes, whole families. They come down from the slums in the East End in large Luton furniture vans. Shoreditch and Bethnal Green are centres for the manufacture of furniture and a whole street will hire a van or two to bring them and their cooking utensils, bedding and so on down every year. All the family mucks in to pick the hops during the day, for which of course they get paid, they have lovely days out in the open air, have a good booze-up in the evenings and in most cases go back home as broke as when they arrived. Not only that, the birth rate in the East End doubles around the end of May, so they tell me."

"Why aren't they here?"

"I believe the picking season varies with the type of summer we have. I rather suspected Ronnie might have been a bit out when he said they would be picking now, it's usually say another two or three weeks, through to the end of September."

They made their way to the first of the enormous acreage of hop fields surrounding the Whitbread farm, and sat looking up into the rows and rows of poles, each now encased with hops to a height of up to sixteen feet. As they sat there, the horses with their heads down idly snatching at the wayside grass, a tractor came towards them, driven as they eventually saw by a middle-aged man wearing a shirt and tie, the latter showing it was quite a few Christmases since he received it. The horses started to fidget as the unaccustomed noise approached them, the driver realising this, slowing down to a walking pace.

"Good morning. Can I help you?"

"No, thank you. I've just brought my American friend here over to see the hops and hopefully the shires. I've told her they are the finest in England."

"Only England?" he replied with a laugh. "Wait a minute. I know you don't I? Sandbury Engineering. That's it. You must be Harry's father, Chandler senior. Your photo was in the paper a while ago when you got the OBE. We knew Harry very well. In fact he sold us this tractor and several like it. How is he now? Look, don't lets sit here, come on over to the house and have a drink, and I'll get one of the lads to see to your horses."

"Thank you, that is most kind of you."

He puttered off, the horses taking little notice now since they had seen this noisy smelly object close up and found it was harmless. Margaret and Fred followed at a steady trot.

"The sun shines on the righteous," he suggested to her.

As they pulled in to the yard in front of a very substantial bungalow type building, their new friend appeared from stables at the side with a young Land Army girl.

"Sandy, unsaddle these will you, give 'em a quick rub down and a hay bag each and a drink."

"Yes, major."

"I failed to introduce myself," he told them, "I am Major Digby, the estate and farm controller. The farm is owned by the brewery of course. My friends call me Horace, or Horry for short." He shook hands with them both. "Now come on in, come on in." He led the way through the back door into an enormous low-beamed kitchen. Margaret looked around appreciatively.

"This, like Fred's, is what I call a kitchen," she said. At that a lady appeared from within the bungalow. She was very well dressed in sober country tweeds, achieving elegance without, it seemed, effort of any kind.

"Darling, this is Mr Chandler who owns Sandbury Engineering. Do you remember we used to see Harry, his son, until the war took him away. And this...," he was stuck. Margaret quickly stepped into the breach.

"I am Margaret Coulter of the United States Army. I am most pleased to meet you Mrs Digby."

"Well, sit down, sit down." Fred pulled a chair out from the big deal table for Margaret.

"Had we not better go into the sitting room?" asked Mrs Digby, who by now they had been told was called Lorna.

"We spend most of our time in the kitchen back home," Fred assured them, "what's more I should hate to leave a horsy smell on your pristine upholstery."

"I'm afraid our upholstery is far from pristine. Once this wretched war is over I shall throw the lot out on to a bonfire."

"Well, what would you like for lunch?" Lorna asked, then quickly wondering what the devil they had to offer anyway.

"All organised," Fred replied, holding aloft the food panniers he had removed from the horses before they were led away.

"You really are the sort of guests we love to have. Now, what would you like to drink?"

Fred dived into the heavier of the two panniers, pulled out a quart bottle of Whitbread's Light Ale and placed it on the table. "If you could provide some glasses I would be grateful. My organisational ability ran out when it came to glasses – we would have had to drink out of the bottle! Mind you, it's a good job it's Whitbread's. If we had brought Shepherd Neames, or Watneys, you would probably have thrown us out."

"Definitely," Horry affirmed.

They had a very pleasant hour or so over their simple lunch, which just goes to show you do not need expensive food to welcome and enjoy other people's company. Having said that, a chateaubriand followed by crepes suzettes, mocha coffee etc would always be acceptable.

Lorna and Horry took them to see the shires. In the first box – box? – it was as big as a football pitch according to Fred's description of it that evening back at Chandlers Lodge. Mind you, it needed to be. Victor, its occupier, was eighteen hands two and as broad as a London bus. But as gentle as a lamb, as Margaret described, in wonder still, that evening. She had almost cried at the pleasure of holding and stroking the soft silky muzzle of this glorious animal.

"Isn't he enormous?" she cried.

"There are two or three bigger than he is," Lorna told her. "Wait till you see Samson."

They moved through the central aisle of the stables to Samson's box. He was nineteen hands.

"These horses were used as chargers in the olden days," Harry told her. "They were not fast, but they were unstoppable. Can you imagine twenty of these in a line galloping into foot soldiers. They were I suppose the ancient equivalent of tanks."

"What a wicked thing to use them for."

"You are right of course. But then war is a wicked, wicked thing, always has been, always will be, and despite our incredible cleverness in that we can fly in the air, move under the ocean, send radio messages round the world, yet we still are unable to find a way to live in peace together."

"You are quite a philosopher Horry," Margaret jested.

"I imagine, like Fred here, I have seen what war does at first hand. Still, enough of that on such a lovely, pleasant day."

But they were to get closer to the war that day than they had expected.

At three o'clock or thereabouts they said goodbye to their new friends, Fred adding they would invite them over to Chandlers Lodge in the near future.

"Petrol permitting," joked Horry.

"You could always come on the tractor. Put a cushion on the bonnet for Lorna – should be alright."

As they rode away, turning to wave as they turned behind the high hedge on the border of the property, Lorna said to Horry, "What nice people, but he is a lot older than she is."

"I noticed that. It set me thinking. Perhaps I could trade you in for a younger model?"

"It's a thought. Perhaps she would have a twin brother for me."

They laughed, linked arms and returned to their very comfortable home. Well, if you had an executive job for a brewery you would expect it to be a bit above the average, would you not?

The horses trotted briskly up Seven Mile Lane, having the instinctive knowledge they were on their way home. There was no traffic about so they had the narrow road to themselves. As they rode, it crossed Fred's mind they had not heard a buzz bomb all day, which was decidedly unusual. Since the 13th of June, eight weeks ago, there had hardly been a day, or a night, when they had not experienced these awful weapons flying over them, along with the occasional one, destined for London, malfunctioning and falling near Sandbury. To add to this latter hazard, the RAF chasing those they could not ditch in the sea, were tipping them over into Kent in increasing numbers. There was a distinct disadvantage to living in Kent, East Sussex and parts of Surrey at this time.

As these thoughts passed through his mind he heard, as did Margaret, the distant hideous phut-phutting of one of these flying bombs coming towards them. Looking towards the east they saw it, flying quite high and being pursued by a Spitfire. The Spitfire slowed down, gradually positioned itself with its starboard wing a yard or so under the short stubby port wing of the buzz bomb, then flipped up, causing the gyroscope mechanism in the V-1 to go out of control sending the bomb down into the fair fields of Kent.

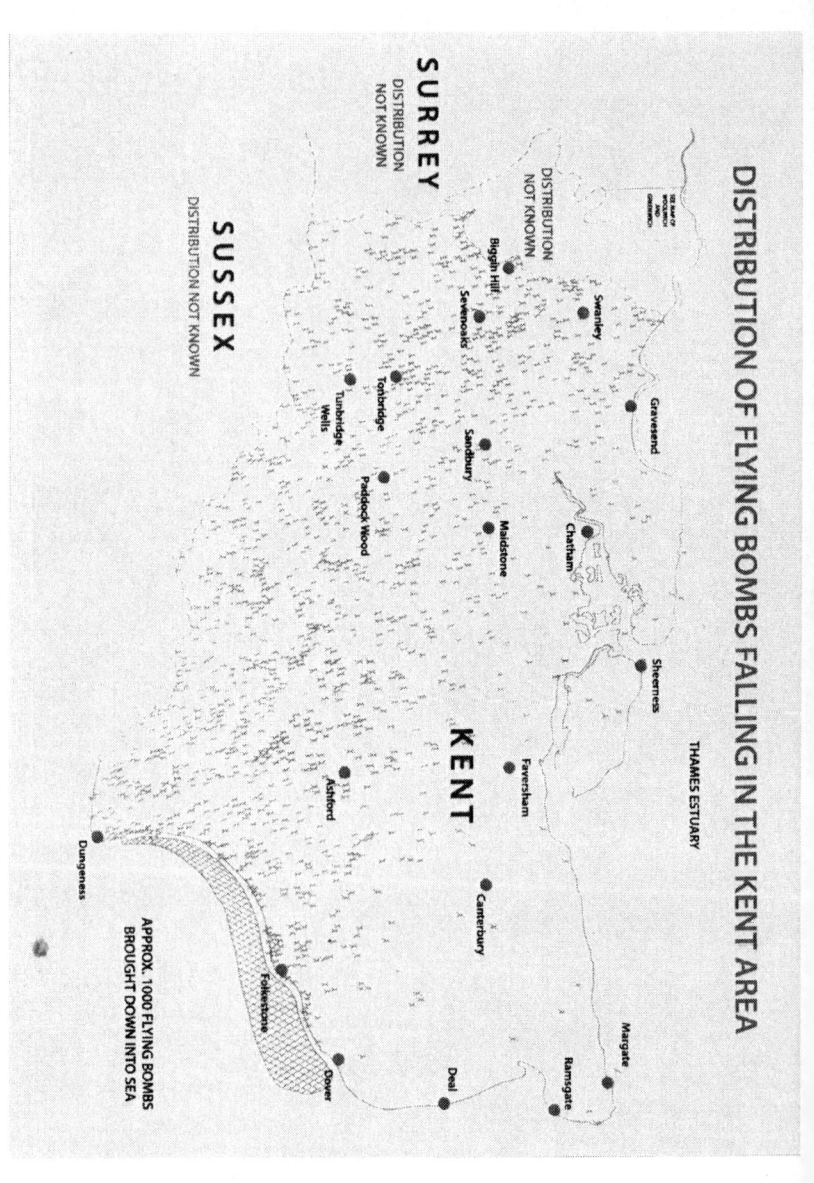

The map was drawn by the author's dear friend, Colin Scott, in 1947.

"Quick, off the horses, into the ditch," Fred shouted. Margaret needed no second advice. As they slid into the ditch at the side of the road – dry fortunately, it being August – the bomb landed two fields away with a thunderous roar. The horses were already panicking at the increasingly frightening engine noise; it being all their riders could do to hold on to them. Their ears were back, the whites of their eyes were showing, and they were snorting with fear. When the explosion came the riders were unable to hold them. They reared up, tearing the reins from the hands even of Fred, and took off down the road at a furious gallop, arched necks, high tails, both indicating how fearful they were.

It is instinctive for a horse, as for many other animals, to fly from danger. They are pack animals, and in the wild, centuries ago, they were much smaller than today. They had many natural predators, their main defence being in numbers. Hence if one animal sensed danger it immediately transmitted that knowledge to the remainder of the pack by pricking its ears, tensing its muscles so that it appeared more rounded than the normal, and adopting a high, jerky movement. These signals would immediately put the remainder on guard.

However, although Fred and Margaret may well have been cognisant of these undoubtedly interesting factors, their horses were a couple of hundred yards down Seven Mile Lane and legging it for Sandbury, transforming their riders, in the space of a couple of minutes, into pedestrians. Not a happy prospect.

As they stood for a few moments looking after the runaways they saw a man appear from a gap in the tall hedge a hundred yards or so in front of their mounts. He stood quite still in the centre of the narrow road. Instead of waving his arms about and shouting for them to stop, he appeared to have held his arms out towards them, his hands uppermost. He slowly moved his hands up and down, only a short distance but sufficient for them to notice. He called to them in a language, had Margaret and Fred been near enough to hear, was decidedly non-English. Gradually they lessened their pace; their ears came forward, their arched necks straightened and their tails lowered. By the time they reached their captor they had slowed up to the extent he was able to collect their reins and turn them about, talking to them all the time.

The two riders hurried towards their helpmate. As soon as Fred got a good look at him he said to Margaret, "He's a gypsy, a proper Romani, not one of your didikis." Their saviour was dressed in the typical Romani manner, broad brimmed, originally brown, now more or less black, trilby hat, corduroy trousers, supported by wide braces into which was tied the ends of a brightly coloured neckerchief around the collar of his flannelette shirt. A breathless Fred thanked him profusely, the thanks added to by Margaret, in response to which they gypsy said to her, "You ain't from these parts."

"No, I am from America."

He looked intensely at Fred. "You be from Mountfield."

A surprised Fred said, "God, that was a few years back, how the devil did you know that?"

"I never forgets a face. Your missus did us a great kindness once; we Romanis don't forget things. My missus and her sister and our little three-year-old Becky was pegging in Mountfield. It was early morning and Becky got bit bad by a dog. When they got to your farm she could 'ardly walk. Your missus took her in so the women could carry on pegging, see how bad she was and got the doctor. He got her to 'ospital. They reckoned it saved 'er leg. When I come to collect 'er that night you was there. That's when I see'd you. You sent me on to the 'ospital."

"I remember now, my goodness, there's been a lot of water under the bridge since then."

"You tell your missus we ain't never forgot 'er, 'specially about taking Becky in, not many people would take in a Romani and look after 'em."

"I'm afraid poor Ruth died three years ago," Fred replied.

"Then God rest her soul, sir, God rest her soul."

As they were talking Margaret spotted a couple of small children peeping round the hedge at them. She waved. They waved back.

"Your family Mr ?" she queried.

"Ephraim Lee, ma'am. Yes, them's mine."

Margaret, having moved forward to get a better view of the children saw the front edge of a caravan, hitherto hidden by the high thick hedge.

"This is your home?"

"Yes, ma'am." She walked to the gap in the hedge, Fred now having taken the horses in hand.

"It is beautiful, it is really beautiful. It is the first Romani home I have ever seen, except in pictures."

As she approached the home three whippets roused themselves from their slumbers under the caravan, closely followed by a large, vicious looking, black mongrel. Whereas the whippets were of the tail wagging friendly variety of canine company, the mongrel was already baring his fangs to the visitors until Ephraim spoke to him harshly in Romani at which he retreated to his previous resting place and turned his back on them.

The caravan was of the round top style, the main part painted a dark green. The front and the back were provided with a multitude of intricate designs, painted in yellow, black and white on a red background. A second caravan stood behind Ephraim's, congregated in front of which was his immediate family, his wife, his son and his wife, and an assortment of children ranging from a babe in arms to a strikingly handsome dark haired girl of around fourteen, as fully developed as any seventeen year old. Ephraim beckoned to her.

"Say hello to this gentleman and his lady. His missus saved your life." The girl, better described as a young woman, came forward, not knowing what to do next, furthermore not knowing from the introduction her father had made whether 'the lady' was 'the missus' referred to or not. She just smiled, bobbed a little curtsy to 'the lady', and said, "Thank'ee sir."

Having said farewell to their new, and somewhat unusual friends, they completed their journey back to the stables. Ronnie was most anxious to know whether they had been anywhere near 'the buzz bomb that came down'. By the time they had told him of their adventure, and meeting Ephraim Lee and his family, mounted their bikes and rode to Chandlers Lodge, it was getting on for seven o'clock.

"We were getting worried," exclaimed Rose, "what with the bombs."
"We only had one bomb, but that was close enough. Where were the others?"
"One up towards Wrotham, another towards Maidstone."
"Well, it's all very well the RAF tipping the blighters up so they don't reach London, but I wish they could find a way of just turning them round to go back where they came from instead of dropping them on us."

But despite the continual vigilance of the RAF and anti-aircraft crews, they heard on the nine o'clock news that evening that V-1 casualties in July had totalled 2441 killed and 7107 injured. Of the killed 1187 were women and 232 children, and worse was to follow.

During that evening Margaret excitedly told Rose, along with Anni and Ernie who had called in – Karl was babysitting, with Rosemary of course, his grandchildren David and Ruth – of her meeting with the Romanis. She said how they had invited her to peek into the interior of the caravan, a privilege Fred had told her very rarely accorded to non-Romanis.

"Ephraim Lee had a wife and five children. They all packed into the caravan in the winter, but the children would sleep outside in summer if the weather was reasonable, I believe. It looked very cosy, but would take a lot of getting used to if you were not born to it, I guess," Margaret decided. "Romantic it sounds, but give me a nice bed and a comfortable bathroom any time."

There was a chorus of 'hear-hears'.

Persecution of the Romani had been a fact of life since they arrived from India in the 13th century and spread across Europe, both by individuals and states. However, the folks discussing the Lee family would have no conception of the evil being perpetrated at that very moment against the Roma. The Nazis killed one and a half millions in what in, Romani was subsequently called 'The Porrajmos', meaning 'The Devouring'. The mentality of the people who planned, and those that carried out, such iniquity, is beyond comprehension.

Margaret returned to London on Monday morning with Fred extremely fearful of her being in the centre of the main target of Hitler's no longer secret weapon. To make them more evil, it had been given out on the wireless that some of the bombs were being fitted with twenty incendiaries which were blown off on landing, adding further horror to an already horrendous object.

That evening Rose quizzed her father as to what arrangements were being made.

"It all depends on how Margaret can arrange things. Whether they will release her or not, whether they will post her somewhere else, whether she will be allowed to be discharged in UK or have to go back to the US. It's all in the air at the moment. All I do know is that we have a batch of weddings coming up in the near future. Charlie and Emma, Karl and Rosemary, Roy and June, to say nothing of Gloria and the Earl at Ramsford. How the devil I am going to be able to afford all those wedding presents the Lord himself knows. Come the end of the year I shan't be able to afford any Christmas presents that's for sure."

Rose looked at Megan. Megan looked at Rose and said, "He always sounds so convincing doesn't he?"

Chapter Thirty-One

On the weekend after Harry's return from the raid on the airfield they received a coded message informing them of an air drop on the night of 1st/2nd August. Although Harry was up and about, Matthew had strictly forbidden him to lead the party to recover the 'goodies', as they were generally known. It always amused Harry to hear his Chinese chatting away, in the middle of their mainly Mandarin conversation hearing 'goodies' mentioned. Perhaps the Chinese had no word for 'goodies'. He resolved to ask Matthew.

The ringworm plague seemed to be dying down a little and there were no more cases of TB, although Matthew was keeping a close watch on any people with the slightest cough. Nevertheless, because of the current sick list they had difficulty in raising the required number for the 'goodies recovery squad'. Led by Reuben they moved out in heavy rain, which did not bode well for a successful operation. The rain eased somewhat as they reached the drop zone, but visibility was still very poor, low clouds with little wind not helping matters. Darkness fell, the party having taken up their positions to produce the flare path. There would now be a long wait, some five hours, before they would hear that beautiful sound of the four mighty engines of the Liberator. At midnight they lit their flares, they would last at least half an hour. Each man had a reserve, so that if the plane was delayed they could show for at least another half hour. This had happened only once; the air crew on that aircraft were more than well aware of the necessity of being on time.

At fifteen minutes after midnight they heard the throbbing approaching from the north, then to their horror heard the aircraft fly over them without any accompanying sight of white canopies drifting down. From their previous drop the navigator had been flying on dead reckoning, he could see very little on the ground other than white blankets of mist and cloud in the pale moonlight.

"We should see them in one minute exactly," he had told the pilot. The minute dragged on, they saw nothing. As they cleared the drop zone one of the gunners yelled into the intercom,

"Lights on starboard behind us."

The pilot put the huge plane into a sweeping turn to port to come back on to his original approach line.

"I'll come down a little," he told them.

"Not too bloody much," replied the navigator "we don't want to take any coconuts home with us."

"I don't think there are coconuts in the jungle, are there?"

"I would rather not find out."

These RAF types like a little chat whilst they are cavorting in their flying machines.

Having completed his circle, feathered back somewhat, and lowered his flight path a fraction, the pilot approached the point where the air gunner had said he had seen lights. A merciful break in the cloud showed he was almost on top of his customers; the loads were furiously pushed out, landing more to the end of the drop zone than usual, and a Liberator crew departed on its way to a well deserved breakfast.

The recovery of the loads was somewhat delayed. When Reuben tallied the number of parachutes found he discovered they were one short. He sent three-men patrols out in different directions in a search for the missing item – after all, it could have the rum in it – but in over an hour nothing was found. He decided to move back to camp and suggest a further patrol be sent out in daylight. Not only would they not want to lose a precious container, whatever was in it, but if it was hung up in the top of a tree in full view of a passing Jap aircraft flying overhead, it could well be suspected of being a pilot who had bailed out after engine trouble, and a ground patrol sent out to investigate. That was not to be desired from the point of view of not wanting nosy Nips on their territory, nor letting the thieving bastards pinch their goodies. Reuben made his way back to the camp and reported the problem to Harry.

"If all the others came down together at this end of the drop zone it can't be far away." Harry decided. "Tommy, get a dozen men together and go and have a shufti."

Tommy and his party were out for all the hours of daylight. They had three soakings during the day, but found nothing. A dispirited band returned to camp wet through and empty-handed only to be welcomed with the news that a message had been received from Camp Two, via HQ, that they had received a bonus, to whit ten pairs of boots and a jar of rum, for which many thanks. They would send the boots on to HQ in due course for forward delivery. It was regretted the rum jar was too badly damaged for onward despatch. The air at Camp Three was blue for some considerable while.

However, from Harry and Reuben's point of view, the end of the world had not completely arrived as a result of the loss of the rum, albeit they both added quite colourful opinions in the stupidity, carelessness, and typical balls-up capability of your average airman. The two officers had each received a sizeable packet of mail. Copies of 'The Times of India' for the past two weeks having been included, these were given to Matthew and his helpmates to read first, on the basis they received no mail. A sort of consolation prize I suppose.

As the last letter from Megan was dated 20th July it was obvious she would not have yet heard of Harry being wounded. It worried him he could not yet write and tell her he was recovering well from what was 'only a scratch'. He smiled to himself. Knowing Harry they would be as likely to believe that description as they would Joseph Goebbells.

He had sorted his mail into neat piles and date order when an urgent sounding knock came on his door. Chantek sat up, bristling.

"Come in." Choon Guan opened the door slowly, saw that Chantek was well clear and moved in quickly. Harry could see his normally unreadable face showed signs of agitation.

"What's up?"

"Two more men have gone sir."

"When?"

"They must have slipped out when Mr Isaacs's patrol went out. Their hut leader thought they were with him."

Harry looked longingly at his mail, but decided they had better have an 'O' group straight away.

"Ask Mr Isaacs and Mr Ault to come in will you please Choon Guan?" In a few minutes, Reuben was levered away from his highly scented mail, Tommy dragged from 'The Times of India', and they sat together in Harry's room with an extremely interested Chantek looking on.

"Who were they?" Harry asked.

"Ng Chong Lee and Cheong Kit Sing, they were not very good soldiers," Choon Guan replied.

"Do you mean they weren't good soldiers or they weren't good communists?" asked Reuben in his usual plain speaking manner. "I've said before, Choon Guan; if that commissar of yours was to speak to me the way he yells at your blokes I would bugger off too. Either that, or I would flatten him."

"We must have good party discipline; they must be instructed on the party line."

Harry broke in.

"Well, we won't go into all that again. We all have a job to do." He looked at Choon Guan, who was obviously very discomfited.

"They have taken their weapons and some ammunition."

"What?" Harry spoke so vehemently that Chantek sprang up in fright.

"How the hell did they do that?" Weapons were only issued by authorised section leaders from orders from an officer.

"They told their section leader they were detailed to go with Mr Isaacs. I have put the section leader under arrest," Choon Guan replied.

"They have had ten hours start and we don't know which way they went. All we can do is hope they took the weapons because they were afraid to be in the jungle without them and that they throw them in the river when they get to wherever they are heading. Which weapons were they anyway?"

"Rifles sir."

"Well, that's one consolation. You can't walk about a town with a rifle over your shoulder without a Nip being slightly suspicious. I would think they would head east for Raub, that's the nearest town, or west to Trolak, over the mountains. In case they get caught and tortured, and give our position away we had better have standing patrols out in daylight on both those approaches for the next two weeks." Harry thought for a moment.

"This has happened before Choon Guan. Your chief is not going to be very happy with you. I suggest you do something about that commissar of yours, particularly if you find out from questioning the men that what Mr Ault suspects was the cause of the desertion."

"The problem is he has equal rank with me."

Reuben chimed in.

"In that case the answer's simple. Take him behind the huts and knock seven shades of shit out of the sod, perhaps he will understand then."

Reuben always did have a subtle way with words.

Choon Guan departed to organise the standing patrols, Reuben and Tommy returned to their scented mail and newspapers respectively, leaving Harry to start opening his mail, now that it had been sorted into chronological order, as was his standard practice. A great part of the pleasure of receiving this pile of letters was in the preliminaries, a bit like making love I suppose.

The big news from Megan, after a very full description of the antics of the seven-year-old twins and little Ceri, now nineteen months, photographs of each included, was that Harry's father and the American lady, Margaret, seemed to be getting very close, to the extent they were going to holiday together at Romsey, then Ramsford Grange. She went on to say that everyone was very pleased. Margaret was such a delightful person. Harry's immediate thought was 'yes, but what happens when she is posted back to the States?' In order to get further intelligence on the matter he did something he had never done before, he dived into the letters he had received from his father, leaving Megan's pile for the time being. He gained little, his father was being very tight-lipped at the moment – or should it be tight-inked?

He went to bed with the usual mixture of emotions following the receipt of the mail, the euphoria of the initial reception, the pleasure of reading and re-reading messages from his loved ones, followed by the post perusal depression. As we have noted before, a bit like making love.

The next morning the standing patrols moved out at dawn, Harry had an early breakfast and picked up one of 'The Times of India'. He was shocked to read a special report of the V-1 attack on London and the South East, a report in which the sufferings of the people of Kent were emphasised. Yet there had not been one mention from any of his correspondents of the battering they were receiving. He knew very well why. They had all got together and agreed not to worry him, thinking he would not find out by any other means. He came to the conclusion he would have done the same, nevertheless he was, and remained, extremely worried for them all.

Making his usual mid-morning tour of inspection of the camp, the barrack-rooms, cookhouse, latrines and so forth, and noting the fatigue parties cutting back the inevitable onslaught of the jungles vines, he heard the knocking of the alarm stump on the front of the camp HQ hut. The stump was a piece of very heavy black wood to which was connected long lengths of joined-up parachute rigging lines leading out to the four sentry points. Immediately the solid clumping noise was heard the whole camp raced for their weapons and manned their stand-to positions. There was no shouting, little noise, the whole force in position in next to no time to defend the camp, the sentries would not have pulled their cord unless there was something unusual happening. Harry raced to the HQ hut and grabbed his tommy gun.

"Which cord was it?" he whispered to Tommy.

"The eastern one." They waited. It was a very long twenty minutes before the eastern sentries were seen emerging from the jungle driving in front of them one of the deserters. He was unarmed, his tunic was ripped, one of his sleeves was torn away exposing a badly lacerated arm, he was staggering, obviously on the edge of complete exhaustion. Matthew and two of his team ran forward, collected him as he fell, and carried him back to the medical room. Harry and Choon Guan called the patrol leader to them.

"What happened?" The patrol leader spoke little English. Choon Guan listened and translated to Harry. "Sir, apparently the two men were attacked by a tiger, they had no time to use their weapons. It killed Cheong Kit Sing straight away, attacked Ng Chong Lee then left him to feed on the dead man. Ng Chong Lee had passed out and when he came to the tiger had gone. He then made his way back to where the sentries heard him; they then pulled the stand-to cord."

"What about the weapons?" Choon Guan asked the question of the patrol leader.

"The man had no weapons sir; he must have left them with the body."

"Right, tell the patrol well done, stand down, and bring the other patrol in. I will go and see Matthew."

Harry made his way to the medical room.

"What's the score Matthew?"

"I don't think we shall save him sir, he's lost a lot of blood."

Harry thought deeply.

"I know what I am going to say to you is contrary to all your training and beliefs, but it will be better to let him die. If he lives he will face a charge of desertion, the only punishment for that is to be shot. We cannot shoot anybody here for obvious reasons which would mean we would have to hang him here, or send him to Cameron Highlands where they would be able to mount a firing party. How would you feel about being brought back to health, made to struggle all the way to Cameron Highlands knowing when you get there you will be put to death?"

"My professional duty and my duty to God, is to save his life. What other people have to do with respect to their duty is an entirely different matter."

"I appreciate that. I knew the answer you would give before I asked the question, but I had to put the other point of view to you. Surely sometimes you are faced with two evils, and you have to accept the lesser?"

"When it is a question of the Hippocratic oath and the gospel of our Lord there can be no contention. If this man lives and is then put to death my conscience will suffer all my days. However if he lives, and then those trying him find some extenuating circumstances in his case, or mercy is shown, or some sort of amnesty occurs, we shall have done the right thing."

"Well, all I can do is leave it in your hands."
"It is in God's hands, not mine."

Harry went back to his hut, angry at the blasted men for deserting, angry at the blasted commissar for allegedly causing it all, and angry at Matthew for being so bloody pig-headed. To save Harry further vexation the man died that night from his cruel lacerations and was buried without military ceremony by Matthew's little group who held a short prayer meeting over his grave.

On Sunday night 6th August, a message came through that Sunrise would be with them in a few days. He and his party, including of course Harry's friends Bam and Boo, of whom Harry made his usual fuss, arrived late on Friday afternoon.

"No planning tonight," he announced, "I've brought you a little peace offering from Camp Two, to whit a bottle of rum, which they swear is all they saved from your container dropped to them by mistake."

"Thieving sods," was Reuben's immediate and fully expected comment.

Nevertheless, the four officers had a jolly evening together, Sunrise providing the gossip from the other camps.

"And Mrs Rowlands?" queried Harry.

"She's running the TB section as well now," he was told "and running the risk all the time of picking it up herself, although she takes all the precautions she can of course."

The next morning they got down to business.

"We have reports from our northern patrols from Cameron Highlands that a great deal of rubber, tin and military supplies are being run on the metre gauge railway through the centre of the peninsula from Kota Bahru in the north down to Singapore. If we blow up the railway line in most places it can be repaired in days, but at one point, according to the map, it runs on a shoulder of a hill literally overlooking the river. The river is the same one in which you sank the patrol boat you may remember – the Pahang, although this point is a hundred miles or more from Kampong Bintang. To add to the picture a tributary of the Pahang runs into it at this point, over which is a bridge. A man with local knowledge tells me the bridge is made of wood. Now, if we derail a train on that bridge, and that train happens to be carrying rubber in the open trucks they use for the purpose, and we then plaster it with phosphorous grenades and Molotov cocktails it is highly probable the bridge will catch fire and we shall have killed three birds with one stone, that is, they will have lost a train, its contents, and a bridge. Furthermore they would not repair that lot in a hurry."

There was silence around the table, broken by Harry asking, "Do we know how often the rubber trains run?"

"I am told at least one every day. There is also night traffic, most of which is empty running north. It is as you know only a single track, just as the main broad gauge railway up to Siam on the west is single track."

Harry studied the map. "Between here and the target we have got Mount Benom, 7000 feet. We would be better off going around the north of it." And so he proceeded to formulate the method of getting to the objective. In their line of work it was frequently as big, if not a bigger problem, getting to and from the intended scene of an operation, as it was actually carrying out the task itself.

"May I suggest we do this in two phases?" he asked Sunrise.

"Harry, you now know the object, the method is down to you."

"Right sir, if I can look at it all the morning, perhaps we can have another meeting late afternoon, after we have all had a kip."

"An excellent idea. Now, where's this curry tiffin you promised me?"

When they resumed their talks, Harry put forward his plan.

"Sound reconnaissance will be needed if the job is to be done properly and without loss. I suggest I take Tommy and a patrol of six and find a place where I can study the target, then get out a final plan. Two days after I leave, Reuben follows with the main force, carrying the explosive and kerosene. When he arrives at the pre-arranged rendezvous point we will rest for a day. From then on the time factor will be determined by the train arrival."

"How long will it take to get there?"

"It's undulating jungle most of the way. Say three days, but allow four."

"So you will have to carry food and water for over a week?"

"Yes. We shall use a small number of the men as porters, as we have before."

"God, I wish I could come with you."

"Why not sir? Someone is in charge up in the Highlands while you are away?"

"That's true. I'll think about it overnight. Although let's be clear. It is your show, you will be in charge. I shall, if I do come, be just an observer – understood?"

"Just as you say sir."

It took Harry a week to get the plan thoroughly organised. On the 19th August he and his advance party, now increased by the presence of Sunrise, along with Bam and Boo who automatically followed, made their way east, skirting the northern slopes of Mount Benom then turning south east toward the target. At one point they had to cross the main Raub-Kuala Lipis road, which they did with no problems. At the end of day two they found the tributary of the Lampart River at which they camped. This tributary would take them direct to the target, all downhill, to an escarpment which overlooked the railway only two miles away. This was Reuben's rendezvous point. They made it without incident.

There was still an hour or more before darkness fell. Harry left the men to make a good camp, well hidden and secure enough to house Reuben and his twenty men when they arrived in two days time. He then led Tommy and Sunrise through the secondary jungle to a scrub covered hillock between them and the target which would, he hoped, prove to be a good observation point. Again luck was with him.

"Well, you have certainly been spot on so far Harry."

"Yes, sir, and I always get a bit windy when all goes well, wondering what's going to bugger it all up."

Sunrise laughed. "The funny thing is that thinking of your having to make a plan I've been singing a little ditty from Gilbert and Sullivan to myself for the last half hour."

"Which one is that sir?"

"Well, I can't remember which one it's from, but it goes,
'When I went to the Bar as a very young man,
(Said I to myself, said I)
I'll work on a new and original plan,
(Said I to myself, said I'.)"

His voice would not have been of a quality to pass a Covent Garden audition, even for the chorus, but it was sheer magic to Bam and Boo, who smiled widely and stamped their feet on the ground in appreciation.

They moved forward slowly and carefully to the edge of the scrub, making sure they kept any disturbance to the bushes to the absolute minimum, until they could see the railway line, the cutting and the Lampart River running under the wooden bridge into the Pahang River which seemed to be almost directly underneath the railway line from where they were.

"If we could tip a train off that stretch just north of the Lampart it could well go into the Pahang and cause problems for the Japs navigating that," Harry reflected. "Still, first things first, how to burn the bridge."

The ground, about three quarters of a mile, between their observation point and the target, was open country, very low scrub, but no cover. They were obviously not going to be able to risk crossing it in daylight. They had chosen these nights when there would be a full moon, it was lucky they had.

At nine o'clock that evening they made their first reconnaissance. The tributary which ran under the bridge at right angles, and into, the River Pahang was in a steep, jungle covered ravine – virtually impassable. The shelf on the side of the hill which carried the railway line was only fractionally wider than the train's wagons themselves. However, to their disappointment the railway was at least fifty yards from the big river, so there was no possibility of obstructing that passage in any way.

"Well, you can't win them all," Harry consoled his two colleagues. Bam and Boo nodded as if they knew what he was talking about.

The next day they spent watching, in turns, through their field glasses, the passage of the trains. Two factors soon became apparent. It was, of course, single track. To speed up the flow, trains were sent through each stage in pairs, two up, two down, with an occasional single, presumably if a second train was not available. The second factor, a very important one as far as they were concerned, was that there was no regularity in their movement. At four o'clock in the afternoon, Harry went back to the camp, ate a meal and slept till midnight. He and his Chinese bearer then relieved Tommy and the colonel to watch and take notes until dawn.

Significant factors registered in this night watch were that firstly the traffic was lighter and almost exclusively north to south, that is, laden, not the reverse as Sunrise had been informed. Secondly, the engines carried a large searchlight on the front which could be seen shining into the air when coming up an incline miles away, giving at least ten minutes warning of its approach before it hit the bridge.

Reuben arrived mid-afternoon having met no problems on the way. He went forward to the observation point to get a look at the target, leaving his men to organise their bivvies. They could not light fires, of course, so had to rely on water and their cold rations.

The next morning, Harry called an 'O' group to put forward his plan.

He commenced with, "We have a major problem. The bridge straddles the ravine. The ravine is virtually impassable; therefore if we put men on the south side of the bridge, or on the cutting overlooking it they would not be able to get back to the north side to rejoin us after the action. Unless we split our force in two we shall only be able to attack half the target. If we split the force in two, the party on the south side of the ravine will have to make its way back to camp around the south side of Mount Benom, while the north side party returns the way it came. As I see it, this is the only way we can do the job properly, and I propose to command the southern party."

"The plan therefore is that on the night of the attack North Force will lie in wait with their incendiary grenades while South Force crosses the bridge and prepares the rails so that they can be swiftly dislodged when a suitable train is on the bridge. We have done this before by unscrewing the bolts on the fish plates and leaving them in so that an empty train can pass over but can be swiftly removed, and the rails levered aside. Choon Guan and Choong Hong have the tools."

"Two men will be positioned a mile up the track. They will be provided with a hammer and when they can clearly see a rubber train on the track they will strike one of the rails hard three or four times with the hammer. We shall have seen a train approaching and will have our ears on the rail to get confirmation it is the target." As an aside to Sunrise he commented, "If only we could get some field wireless sets, we would be so much more efficient." Sunrise agreed and replied he would see if such animals were available.

"Finally, when the train is derailed we will plaster it from above with our incendiaries. If there are guards they will be eliminated. Do not wait around to see the results of your handiwork, get back to your bivvy area ready to move off at dawn. We shall see you back at camp in a couple of days, all being well. Right, any questions?"

After a number of questions of detail they split the force and went through the procedure with each man simulating what he would be required to do. Without actually visiting the target each had as clear a picture as possible of his proposed part in the operation.

At nine o'clock the next evening they moved out having had a good sleep that afternoon – they would get none for another twenty-four hours or more, that was certain. Harry's party got down into the cutting without difficulty and prepared the removal of the bolts and rail fixings, remaining concealed when an empty train ran northwards past them. A pair of trains, each with a dozen or so enclosed wagons came south and were allowed to pass. Finally, just before midnight they saw the headlight in the north, accompanied by four resounding reverberations in the ears of the bolt removing party. Swiftly this task was completed and the men scrambled back up the edge of the cutting to rejoin Harry and the remainder of his squad. They all primed their incendiary grenades to await their prey.

On this type of operation Harry was always utterly sick about the train driver, his mate and the guard. They would all be Malays of one race or another, often mixed, and it was highly possible they could come to harm. The trains themselves travelled slowly which lessened the possibility, but if an engine turned over when it was derailed they could well be in trouble. He kept his fingers crossed it would stay upright.

The two trains approached the bridge about two hundred yards apart, and it was at this point things did not go exactly according to plan. Somehow or other the first engine did not come off the rails, and travelled fifty yards or so before some of the wagons derailed, breaking their couplings and allowing the train and a couple of wagons to proceed unharmed. The second train however just had time to stop, screeching to a halt, the engine smashing into the guards' van of the front train but remaining upright.

The train crews jumped down. The trains were unguarded. As they jumped down with the intention of going to the scene of the derailment, the incendiaries started to rain down, they each decided this was quite an undesirable place to be and took to their heels.

The incendiaries took a little while to ignite the rubber packed in cubes. Just as a sheet of paper when lit will flare in an instant, so will a sheet of rubber. However if you have a bale of paper, or even a folded newspaper it does not light very easily. So with a cube of folded sheets of rubber, instead of an instantaneous blaze sufficient to light the whole countryside, all they could observe from the top of the cutting was a smouldering mass, rather like bonfire night on a wet evening, except of course few of them would have known anything about bonfire night.

As they waited for the wagons to start burning and drip their blazing latex on to the bridge, the driver and fireman of the front train had regained their engine. Choon Guan spotted one of them climbing in, the other waiting on the permanent way to follow him. He fired one shot which hit the side of the engine and ricocheted noisily into the night air. The two men stood still with their hands in the air. Harry called out – there was little need for silence at this stage – "Right, leave it, get back now."

Reuben waved an acknowledgement from the other side of the ravine, and they all got into their normal patrol order to get away as quickly as possible. It was disheartening not to see the results, if any, of their work, but the trains would be missed in the next hour or less, the quicker they put distance between themselves and the target, the better.

Four days later Harry and his party reached Camp Three. They were hungry and very tired having had to lie up on two occasions to avoid Japanese troops they encountered on their circuitous southern route around Mount Benom. He did, however, get some good news. When Reuben's party, which contained Sunrise, reached their original observation point near the bivvy area, they had a clear view of an enormous pillar of fire as one of the wagons, or perhaps more than one, suddenly flared up. Flames shot a hundred feet into the air and thick black smoke could be seen in the moonlight drifting away towards the east. They waited some fifteen minutes when a second and then a third conflagration erupted, lighting up the whole countryside. They decided then it was time to get a move on. Sunrise made the observation to Harry, "That bridge could not have survived through that lot."

The operation was not without its debit side. Three men went down with tick typhus, from which two of them died. Another scratched a leech off, leaving its teeth, or whatever they have, in his flesh which swiftly gave him blood poisoning. He too died before he could be got back to camp. Harry's men had no shovels or entrenching tools, they therefore had to hollow out a grave with their machetes and then cover the body with rocks. As they laid him in his last resting place, Harry said a prayer over him, working on the premise that he might have been a communist, but he still had a soul.

With a hug to Bam and Boo, Harry said goodbye to Sunrise a couple of days later, having received warmest congratulations on the planning and execution of a first class operation.

Chapter Thirty-Two

On the morning of the 5th August David was called to an 'O' group at Battalion HQ. Hamish told the company commanders that, with the capture of Caen and the complete rout of the German forces south of that city the Wehrmacht were retreating headlong to set up a defensive line behind the River Seine. The paras and their attachments were to make a dash for the mouth of the Seine via Troarn, Pont L'Eveque and Pont Audemer. And what a dash it turned out to be, punctuated at intervals by the difficulty of crossing rivers without bridging equipment, and the determined stand by the enemy at points, mainly at rivers, where they could hold up their pursuers.

Mile after mile the men marched and fought. By the 21st August David's men, dirty, tired, and with boots nearly dropping off them, were pulled back into reserve, but still having to march on behind the Belgian and Dutch brigades. On the 24th they were all halted. On the 27th they marched to Honfleur where, to their astonishment, they were told they were being sent back home to prepare for a jump over the River Seine. They were so dead tired that even the knowledge they were going back to Bulford raised only gradual euphoria.

After two days at Honfleur they boarded TCVs to Arromanches, crowded on to LSTs and the next morning arrived at Portsmouth. There, more TCVs awaited them and they found themselves back in Bulford by late afternoon. After seeing his men were properly fed and settled in, David went to his quarters and sank into a hot bath. It was the first proper bath he had had since the 4th of June – nearly three months. Although Angus was in a similar state, he had unpacked David's gear which had been left behind, and laid out a complete clean set of clothing, getting into which David later described as being one of the greatest luxuries in which he had ever indulged.

At 7.26 that evening the telephone rang at a house in Chingford. "I wonder who that can be," Maria asked herself as she hurried from the sitting room to the hall.
"Chingford 8134."
In a disguised voice David answered, "May I speak to Mrs Chandler please?" He singularly failed to fool his dearly beloved, disguised voice or no disguised voice.
"David, David darling, where are you?"

"We are back, and I understand we shall have two weeks' leave in a few days time."

Maria started to cry and cry.

"Oh, David, please forgive me. I feel such a fool behaving like this. We've been so worried not hearing from you for nearly three weeks."

"Well I will tell you all about it when I see you. Now, how is my baby?"

"He's wonderful – just like you."

"Poor little devil. Well perhaps he'll change."

Maria laughed through her tears.

"Can I tell everybody you are back and coming home?"

"By all means, although I shall be putting a call into Chandlers Lodge after I ring off from you. Now, what's all this about the American lady and my dad?"

Maria filled him in with the details of the romance, and the weddings soon to be taking place, then asked, "Have you contacted Charlie?"

"No, how do I get hold of him?"

"I'll give you his number. It's..."

"Hang on a minute; I've got no blasted pen."

He saw Sandy passing the booth.

"Sandy, can you take this number down for me?"

"What are you taking telephone numbers down for when you have only just arrived back into the bosom of your family?"

"Leave my family's bosom out of this and take down the number."

The number was duly given.

"Thank you darling. I'll phone Charlie after I've rung home. I'll ring you tomorrow, bye bye now."

He and Sandy went into dinner together. Sitting at the long mess table, covered in white linen, with civilised tableware, glasses and so on, being served by white coated mess waiters, it suddenly struck him how life can change in the space of a few hours. Filthy dirty, eating cold beans out of the tin, and a couple of days later enjoying a steak and kidney pie with a beautiful crust which could not have been bettered in Simpsons, or the Savoy.

The rest of the evening was spent in contacting Chandlers Lodge, where of course everyone wanted to speak to him, Megan, Anni and Ernie being there. He then telephoned Charlie, safely ensconced in a beautiful old manor house, turned convalescent home on the edge of the New Forest.

"So when are you being let loose again on an unsuspecting public?"

"In about two weeks, but I'm told I shall be sent to the depot as I shall be graded for the time being."

"How can they grade someone who is grade ten already?"

"You, my dear mucker, have lost none of your droll repartee, I am pleased to note. Now, down to serious business. My wedding to the delectable Emma has been re-scheduled for Saturday the 14th of October. Now, can you be my best man?"

"As I told Mark when he asked me the same question, yes, if the money's right."

"And as I believe Mark replied when he told me of that occasion, you don't have to pay. More to the point, do you know if you will be here then?"

"I shall know more in the next few days. There is talk of a drop over the Seine."

"I would think that's unlikely. They will keep running now until they reach the Rhine I reckon."

"Well let's hope you're right."

He was partially right. The battle for Caen had inflicted more casualties, more prisoners, and infinitely more loss of equipment than the battle for Stalingrad. With 240,000 Germans killed and wounded and 210,000 prisoners a total of 43 German Divisions had been destroyed. In the midst of this carnage, as a result of the Wehrmacht still employing large numbers of horse-drawn vehicles and guns, it was estimated that some 8000 horses were killed in the battle. It was apocalyptic.

The next few days at Bulford were spent in replacing lost, worn and unserviceable clothing and equipment. In a world where less than half of the population, including soldiers, owned a wristwatch, a most peculiar situation arose. All ranks of sergeant or above were issued with a particularly excellent piece of equipment known as an Army Time Piece. Why it was not just called a watch was anyone's guess. It was a Swiss made wristwatch, neat, shockproof, luminous, waterproof, but not loss-proof. Somehow or other ninety percent of them managed to get themselves mislaid and had to be replaced, much to the delight of the sergeant's/lieutenant's father, or father-in-law, or whatever, who became the final owner.

On the 3rd of September, a Sunday, there was a church parade at the magnificent Garrison Church at Bulford. It was the fifth anniversary of the start of the war. A number of the men in David's company were still at school when it all began, worrying that it would be all over before they had a chance to be in it. Now, they were blooded. They had, however, no false ideas of what war was like, although the Jerries were on the run at the moment, they were not beaten yet, and when they were beaten, there were the Japanese to deal with.

The next day they were given the news they were all waiting for. Leave on Friday. For David, as for all of them, the days dragged. It had been arranged that he would go to Chingford over the weekend then they, Maria, he, and of course little Henry, would go on to Sandbury for a week. Fred had arranged a party for the Saturday they all would be there, Charlie had organised a long weekend's leave prior to his being discharged, and Emma would have a forty-eight. With Mark being still in Normandy, Rose and Megan would be the only ones partnerless, except for Cecely of course, but then she would not be exactly partnerless as we shall establish in due course.

Leaving the hubbub of Waterloo station after saying goodbye to Sandy Patterson, who was en route to Blackheath to see Amanda One, David eventually arrived at the Schultz ménage at Chingford. After a long and impassioned welcome from his Maria, and a hug first from his mother-in-law and then from his father-in-law, he was led into the sitting room to where his son and heir was fast asleep in the big Pedigree pram. David looked down intently.

"Isn't he beautiful?" asked Mrs Schultz.

David was what you might describe as being caught on the hop, but quickly recovered from his moment of indecision – babies all looked the same to him.

"Yes, he's a little cracker, no doubt about it." Mrs Schultz persisted.

"Do you think he's like you or Maria?"

David thought again. Babies looked like babies. How could a six-week-old baby look like anyone else?

"I shall have to study him a bit to judge," he replied diplomatically. They left the little fellow to sleep and went into the dining room for the inevitable cup of tea, the first part of the arrival home ritual played out in virtually every household that day as paratroopers, and others, were welcomed home.

As soon as they were alone Maria asked him about his wounds.

"Well the one in the right leg gives me a little gip now and then but the chimney pot one is OK."

As he finished the sentence Henry Schultz came in. "The chimney pot one?" he exclaimed, "what is the chimney pot one?"

David then gave them a humorous and greatly exaggerated account of how the fallen chimney pot chased him around the room until it caught up with him and pinned him to the floor.

"Now, you have asked about me, what about you and these buzz bombs?"

"Well, all last month they arrived day and night. Towards the end of the month we had two days and nights when there was no attack. Then they started again. We were told they were now being launched from Belgium and Holland which meant they were coming from the east, so we thought we shall be even more in the line of fire. A few days ago one hit West Ham football ground, and then they stopped altogether. On the wireless today we were told that three hundred launch sites had been captured in our tremendous advance to Brussels."

Maria recounted these events in a calm reasoned manner, then added, "But the shelling has got even worse. I had a long talk with Emma. The view down at Deal is that Jerry is using up all his shells before he is overrun in a week or two. A week ago today Dover and Deal were shelled for six hours continuously and on the following day over one hundred shells fell on Dover alone, and it has been going on every day this week."

"Well, let's hope the Canadians soon clear up those coastal areas, although it won't be easy I'll wager."

David's real welcome home that night was as magical as he had dreamt it would be. Equally magical was the fact the baby slept soundly after his late feed until six o'clock the next morning, when evidence of an abnormally powerful pair of lungs shattered the peace of the Chingford air. Maria, still half asleep after her nocturnal delectation, correction, delectations, her husband had been away for several months, languidly wrapped her dressing gown around her, took her baby from his cot back to bed and fed him. David watched with keen interest.

"Could I have some when he's finished?"

"Go back to sleep."

David put his arm across her waist as she sat up against her pillows, and promptly did as he was told.

The news that evening was that although there had been no V-1s for the past two days shelling on Hell Fire Corner had increased. Civilian air raid casualties to date were 132,092 of which 56,195 had been killed.

"And when you think a good proportion of those were women and children it makes the figures even more horrendous," was David's comment on the announcement.

They went to Sandbury on Wednesday to a great reception from the family. The main, non-family topic of conversation was of course the shelling, which could be clearly heard on the previous Sunday when they were all at church. On the Monday and Tuesday the barrage lasted for over five hours each day, on the Wednesday when they arrived Dover was shelled from four o'clock in the afternoon until midnight, and on the day after they arrived the worst shelling of the war took place. For over thirteen hours it went on. Buses and trains were all stopped, cinemas closed, the towns of Folkestone, Dover and Deal were brought to a halt. The following day, the 15th, the assault continued, and then it ceased for good. The Germans had taken to their heels or been overrun. It is not generally appreciated that the first shell fell on Dover on August 12th 1940. For four years Hell Fire Corner had suffered bombardment by the heaviest of field and railway guns, a total of 2565 shells having landed in that time killing upwards of two hundred people, despite an extremely efficient shell-warning system being operated by the Observer Corps and Civil Defence people. With the banishment of the V-1 sites in the Pas de Calais, the folks of that corner of Kent could at last go about their lawful affairs in peace.

On Wednesday evening David at last got a chance to talk to his father alone.

"I hear there is a number of weddings scheduled very shortly," he remarked, with tongue firmly in cheek.

"You haven't met Margaret yet," Fred stated, "she will be coming down on Friday, she is looking forward to meeting you, I know you will like her, everybody does."

"Maria and I wish you all the very best, you know that. Have you named a date yet?"

"No, there are some extra formalities which have to be gone through, with Margaret being an American citizen, along with the fact she has to regularise her situation as a US Army officer marrying a foreigner."

"Well, there are plenty of Yanks marrying English girls, so I presume the reverse shouldn't present problems?"

"Well, that's one of the things we hope we shall know on Friday. I have had a chat with Canon Rosser and he said he would have to get in touch with the regional surrogate as we would need a bishop's common licence in order to be married. Now this surrogate chap, whoever he might be, has the responsibility of checking the American bride-to-be's eligibility for marriage, in other words to make sure she hasn't already got a husband tucked away anywhere. This would be done by checking with US Army records, and/or, a sworn affidavit on the part of the lady in question. In any case it will all take a little time."

"Well, as I say, I wish you both all the very best." They shook hands warmly.

"Now what about these other weddings. If they are at weekends I can probably get away by swapping duties if I'm down for field officer of anything."

"Right, let's look at my diary." Fred pulled a leather covered book out of his home desk drawer. "Well, first is Ray and June of course, but you've already had the invite to that. It's on the 30th of September."

"No. I've had no invitation, if it was sent it's still swanning around somewhere in Normandy."

"Well you and Maria are definitely on the list, and Nanny has volunteered to set up a crèche for all the infants that afternoon and evening."

"But doesn't that mean she will miss the wedding and the reception?"

"She says it's the least she can do after the marvellous reception Jack gave her and Harold back in June."

"Right, well that's only two weeks time. I'm going to have to play my cards very cleverly to get away for that one."

"The next one is of course Emma and Charlie at Buckhurst Hill. Emma's people are worth a bob or two so you can bet that will be a top hat affair. That's on the fourteenth of October."

"Well, I must get away to that one, I'm the best man. Incidentally who has Ray asked to stand for him?"

"Ernie."

"Right, who's next?"

"Next is Karl and Rosemary. Their wedding is on the twenty-eighth of October, two weeks after Emma and Charlie. That will be here in Sandbury of course. By the way has anyone told you they have found a nice house on the Mountfield Road? The ministry bus passes it I understand, so there is no problem with their getting to work.

"Last but not least then?"

"Last but not least the Earl and Mrs Treharne, or Gloria as she insists on being called now. That's at Ramsford on the eleventh of November. It is to be a quiet affair in their little local church. Quiet? I reckon the whole village and those from regions adjacent will turn out, to say nothing of the county press when the news leaks out, if it hasn't already. Anyway, we are all to go down and stay over the weekend."

"So how are you fixed for lending me a pound or two to buy all these wedding presents?"

"Don't ask. I reckon I shall have to take out a second mortgage."

"I thought the first one was paid up a long time ago? Anyway, that's not the last is it? What about you?"

"I'll let you know at the weekend."

The days at Chandlers Lodge passed quickly. On the Saturday Fred and Rose had planned a big party. Anni, Megan and Rosemary had all helped, along with Cecely and Gloria, to provide the food, Fred had made sure the liquid refreshment was adequate, correction, more than adequate for the occasion. There would be an excess of females due to the fact the general was away in France, but Lady Earnshaw was coming along with Doctor and Mrs Carew with whom she was staying. And of course Megan and Rose would be without their partners. The balance was, however, slightly redressed, with much excitement, late on Thursday evening by a telephone call for Rose. A very tired sounding voice told her he was on a ten day leave, starting tomorrow.

"Where are you?"

"I'm at Weymouth. There's a milk train leaving at four a.m. for a West London station somewhere. I will get into Victoria from there and be with you sometime during the morning. I will ring you from Victoria – I take it Victoria is still there after all the buzz bombs? How is my baby?"

"She's beautiful, everybody says so. Oh darling Mark, you are alright are you? I mean you're not wounded or anything like Charlie. That's not why you're home is it?"

"Apart from not having slept for thirty-six hours, not having had a bath for a month, I'm as fit as a fiddle. I'm on leave; it's six months since I had a leave. Now Jerry is on the run people who have been here since the landings are being given leave so don't worry your pretty head."

Rose returned to the family, complete with tear-stained face, to meet a barrage of 'what's the matter?' and similar queries, everyone being so happy for her and her unexpected news when all was explained.

On Friday Mark arrived closely followed by Charlie, followed later in the afternoon by Emma. Those who had not met Margaret until now were eagerly looking forward to so doing, particularly David of course. Margaret in the meantime, sitting back in a crowded compartment having traversed the long tunnel under the downs, was having a minor attack of the collywobbles at the thought of meeting David, despite the fact she had been welcomed so whole-heartedly by Rose, Megan, Maria and the rest of the extended family, particularly Jack and Moira.

Fred met her at Sandbury. She was dressed in a classical tweed suit and looked extremely elegant. Fred held her at arm's length.

"You look absolutely gorgeous," he told her.

"You, sir, are very kind. I hope your son thinks the same."

Fred immediately appreciated her qualms, and hugged her.

"He will be so appreciative of your style and grace he will be speechless."

"Fred Chandler, you are a flatterer."

"And you are beautiful. Come on," and with that he picked up her two holdalls, one of which was quite heavy, took her arm, piloted her to the Rover, and held the door open for her.

"I must say your attention is infinitely superior to my old colonel friend," Margaret remarked.

"You know," Fred replied, quite seriously, "my thoughts when he continuously left you to open your own door having clambered his own fat arse into the back seat left me absolutely furious." He then realised what he had said.

"Sorry about the basic language, but the thought still rankles."

Margaret laughed and swiftly pecked his cheek.

"Well, there's no gainsaying it, he did have a fat arse and no social graces. I suppose we should be sorry for him on both counts."

Arriving at Chandlers Lodge, Margaret's collywobbles were soon dispelled by the warm welcome she received from David and Mark. During the course of the evening she was able to tell Fred of the results of her initial enquiries at her headquarters.

"Apparently, at the discretion of the commander in chief, I can resign my commission at three month's notice. I do not have to return to the United States to do this; it can be handled in the UK. After the marriage I have to re-register at the embassy in London to retain my US citizenship, having dual citizenship as a UK resident. So that's all there is to it from an army point of view."

Fred thought for a while. "Now, what about this discretion business? Your commander in chief, General Eisenhower, is a bit busy at the moment isn't he? Might that not delay things?"

"Oh, he would delegate trivialities of that nature, I've no doubt."

"So, if you resign on Monday you could be out by the end of the year?"

"That depends on how long the discretion takes."

"If this blasted discretion takes any length of time, is there anything to stop your being married whilst you are still a major in the US Army? There's a thought!! Perhaps I could claim a marriage allowance and live in luxury for a while, free access to your PX store, the prospects are very enticing." They laughed together.

"To answer your question, I can, subject to your ecclesiastical clearances and formalities, marry at any time."

"In that case my love, can we pencil in a date, to be confirmed when I have had a further chat with Canon Rosser, as to when?"

"If we make it say at the end of January, how would that fit in with your programme at the factory – that after all comes first?"

"Nothing will come before you – that's a promise."

Margaret's suggestion had been conceived after serious thoughts as to what she would suggest given the circumstances which had in fact arisen with regard to the date. It was obvious that time was going to be required before they could be wed, probably three to four months. This then would bring that date perilously near to the anniversary of Ruth's death on New Year's Eve, with the attendant sadness felt by Fred and the whole family. If the wedding took place at the end of January this would, to a certain extent, if not forgotten, at least be allowed to slip from the memory for a short while. She so wanted Fred to be happy again.

On Saturday morning they all repaired to the factory to see a Hamilcar being taken away on its three separate sixty feet RAF trailers.

"I don't know how many more they will want," Fred remarked, "if things go on the way they are at the moment they won't be needed."

"I suppose it depends on how many years we take to see off the Japs," David remarked, quietly enough not to reach the ears of Maria and Rose. "I've got a feeling Jerry isn't finished yet either." How right he was, as would soon be evidenced.

The party that evening went off well, 'well' being the understatement of the age. The highlight of the evening as far as David was concerned was seeing his old headmaster, Doctor Carew, energetically taking part, later in the evening it must be said, in a convoluted conga wending its way in and out of the hallway, up and down the stairs until it came to a halt as a result of Ray Osborne slipping over, three stairs up, and almost bringing the rest of them down on top of him. It was one of the great Chandlers Lodge party evenings, at the end of which Jack called everyone to order.

"Ladies and gentlemen, we have all had a wonderful evening thanks largely to the great efforts of Rose, Maria, Megan, Anni and Gloria."

There was sustained applause, as the papers say.

"We always close our parties with a toast, so please charge your glasses, though knowing you so well I imagine that is something which you need no encouragement to carry out. Ladies and gentlemen, absent loved-ones and friends; Harry and his gallant company in the jungle, Nigel we know not where, Alex with his Canadians in France, the General, Lord Ramsford, and others you may know, of whom I have no knowledge. To absent friends."

They all drank the toast, each one thinking of those named, along with some thinking of others known only to them, the momentary solemnity swiftly being replaced by the conviviality of the saying of 'goodnights' and other leave takings.

Although there were one or two somewhat muzzy heads in the morning, those staying at Chandlers Lodge, The Hollies and at The Angel, made their respective ways to matins. Canon Rosser, having given the text to his sermon looking generally towards the Chandler party and pronounced, "I shall not talk too loudly this morning." They all, and some others of the congregation who guessed, smiled at the 'in-joke'.

The canon gave his usual excellent address. As he was drawing to a close, the congregation heard the distant noise of what sounded like literally hundreds of airplane engines. That level of sound far exceeded the noise they used to hear during the Battle of Britain when Kentish skies were filled with Dornier, Heinkels and Messerschmitts heading for London. As the noise increased the canon announced,

"I think we shall omit the last hymn and conclude the service now with The Blessing," which he duly did. Quickly the congregation filed out of the west door into the churchyard, and looking up saw the sky filled with row after row of Dakotas some towing Horsa gliders, along with a small number of Sandbury Engineering Hamilcars. It was an amazing, noisy, endless procession.

"God, I didn't know there was that number of planes in the world," Fred exclaimed.

"American paratroopers and support troops," David and Mark agreed. "I wonder where they are going?"

They would have been surprised to know that this was only one of three such columns heading east toward Holland. This, the American 101st Airborne was going to Eindhoven, the centre division, 82nd American going to Nigmegen, and north of them the British 1st Airborne Division heading for Arnhem.

It was Sunday 17th September 1944.

It was the beginning of a week of tragedy and heroism on the part of 8500 British paratroopers and glider men.

The name of Arnhem would go down in the history books for ever.

Chapter Thirty-Three

The leave, as always, flew past, and it was time for David to make his way back to Bulford. There was great sadness in the mess that evening. News had come through that, whereas the two southerly objectives, Eindhoven and Nigmegen, had been taken as planned, Arnhem was in flames and troops of the 1st Airborne were isolated in pockets of resistance. Many of the senior officers had friends in the 1st Div, friends they feared they would never see again.

After dinner, Sandy Patterson approached David.

"David."

"Yes, young man." Sandy was as old as he was.

"Amanda and I are going to marry."

"How marvellous. For you at least, I'm not quite sure of what sort of a bargain she's got."

"I'll ignore that. We would be most privileged if you would be my best man. I hasten to add that Paddy and Mary will also be invited."

"I shall be absolutely delighted, provided it does not clash with about a dozen other weddings in which I'm to be involved of course."

"It will be on the 2nd of December, which will be one of our non-working weekends, or so I calculate, so that various people from here can be present. You see, I have no family here to support me, so the battalion has to be in loco familias, or whatever the hell it's called."

"You're not inviting the whole battalion?"

"No, just one or two of its more select members."

"Are there such people?"

"Well, I suppose one has to be simply comparative on an occasion such as this."

"And where will this ceremony take place?"

"At St. John's, Blackheath, with the reception at The Shakespeare at Woolwich."

"That's settled then, and please tell Amanda One that Paddy and I are very happy for her."

Sandy wandered off back to his room leaving David in an armchair with The Times, reading about Arnhem. It would appear that the lightly armoured airborne troops had been dropped right on top of a panzer division being refitted behind the safety of the Rhine. 'Where the hell was the intelligence about the target?' he asked himself. It would be some years before the full story was told, when it would be known that intelligence regarding the presence of armour had been received, but had been ignored.

Over the next few days they were busy inducting replacements for the men they had lost in France. Not only did this involve putting the right people in the right place, but also required considerable retraining to weld the platoons into fighting units. The division continued with the practice of working through one weekend and having the next one free. David was going to have to play his cards carefully if he was to get away to his weddings, the first of which was to be Roy and June on 30th September. Now technically, as they had worked through the weekend of the 23/24 September, the 30th would be free. However, there had been no announcement to that affect, so David made a tentative enquiry of Tommy Atkins, the adjutant.

"I think you will be out of luck David," was Tommy's opinion. "I'm not being indiscreet or anything when I tell you that we are on a standby at the moment. I think the powers that be are considering whether we should back up the 1st Div."

As he spoke his telephone shrilled. He picked it up, listened carefully.

"Right sir, I'll put that in the diary. I can't say how relieved I am." He turned to David.

"That was Div HQ. 1st Airborne are coming back, what's left of them. We're to stand down. You can go to your wedding."

When Tommy said that 1st Airborne were coming back he had no idea that of the eight and a half thousand men who descended on Arnhem, only some two thousand were coming home.

So it was that David and Maria, along with young Henry, found themselves back in Sandbury, David all 'poshed up to the eyebrows' as he put it as befitted the attendance at a wedding of a captain with two MC's – there are not too many of those about. Roy, still a reserve officer, had been entreated by June and her mother Mrs Wilson, to marry in uniform. With Rose, Anni and others adding their pleas he was unable to resist. Ernie, in a very well fitting morning suit, performed his duties with supreme aplomb both at the wedding ceremony and at the subsequent reception at The Angel. On Sunday evening David made his way back to Waterloo, still suffering from a surfeit of the grape from the night before, followed by the post-coital exhaustion from later that night and again the following morning, a combination designed to dim the faculties of most men. He had forgotten one small factor. It was standard practice in 'B' Company that after each weekend break there was a five mile road run at 6.45am on the Monday morning. It nearly killed him, not being helped as he was by the bellowing of one CSM O'Riordan at his elbow, for the men to 'keep up at the back you nasty idle lot'. The rain didn't help either.

Well, 'B' Company had a reputation to keep up, did they not?

Two weeks later David again found himself at a wedding, as Charlie's best man. The press had got wind of an Earl's grandson being wed so turned out in force, as a result David's face appeared in all the Sunday papers, and, more importantly 'The Tatler', which cost him money when he got back to his mess at Bulford. If you got your picture in The Tatler it was drinks all round in the mess in due course, whatever the reason. At the reception, Charlie was called upon by David, as master of ceremonies, to speak. He commenced with the inevitable 'My wife and I', to loud cheers, thanked all present for their support on this great day in his life, continuing with, "There is one person who is not here who I would dearly have loved to have been here. A person who was good and kind to me and treated me almost as if I was another of her sons. A person who guided me and advised me and was always there when I needed someone to talk to. I refer to David's mother Ruth Chandler. I do trust that she is looking down on us now and witnessing how fortunate I have been in finding my Emma as a direct result of knowing the Chandler family."

After a second or two of contemplation he returned to his normal cheery self receiving sustained applause as he sat down. The new Mr and Mrs Charlie Crew went off to their London hotel for their wedding night, travelling down to Ramsford on Sunday afternoon to a welcome that the little station, Ramsford Halt, had not seen ever before. Virtually all the village turned out to welcome them off the local from Worcester, to ride up to the Grange in an open carriage which had been in the family for nearly a hundred years. Showered with confetti they were met at the steps by the Earl and Charlie's father, who had arrived earlier in the day, to spend their honeymoon in the seclusion of this beautiful house and park.

That evening David returned to Bulford in a similarly exhaustive state as he had enjoyed (?) two weeks earlier. We should here define the word enjoyed. It would be fair to say that getting into the state in which he found himself, was as a result of enjoyment of one sort or another, particularly another. However, after the feast comes the reckoning, the reckoning being, that five mile run again just as it was getting light, and again in the pouring rain, which literally put the damper on the previous enjoyment. Following on with another saying, this time evinced with malicious glee by an acutely observant CSM, 'You can't have your cake and eat it, sir', David responded with, "There have been many times sergeant major when I could have willingly strangled you; this morning is the closest I have ever been."

Paddy grinned, let out a roar to 'get fell in', which nearly shattered David's ear drums, followed by, 'by the left, double march', and they were off into three quarters of an hour of purgatory.

With the company now back up to strength it was time for a couple of jumps, both from Dakotas. The men liked Dakotas. They were easy to emplane into, easy to move around in, and when it came to the actual jumping you ambled down the fuselage and walked out of the doorway – simple. David had a little chat with his mascot, Cedric the golliwog, which Maria had given him to keep him company when he made his first jumps at Ringway.

"Now, my son, look after your uncle David again, there's a good chap."

The thought that his Maria had snuggled Cedric up in bed when she was a young girl and would never sleep without him gave him a lovely feeling of fondness. He gave the golli a little kiss and tucked him into his jumping smock as they climbed into the aircraft. It was to be the first jump with American crews for most of them, about which there was a certain amount of disquiet. In the event both drops took place without any serious injuries, one or two sprains, no casualties in David's company.

When the next free weekend came, David made his way back to Sandbury where Maria had arrived the day before. There had been some buzz bomb activity during the week. Although the sites in France and Belgium had been overrun, the Luftwaffe were now carrying the V-1s slung beneath bombers and releasing them off the Essex coast. Two such launching planes had been shot down on the previous Wednesday, which led to an all clear for a few days.

On Saturday 28th October it was Rosemary and Karl's big day. St. John's may not have been quite as crowded as for some previous Chandler weddings – Karl was fully considered to be a Chandler – nevertheless he had now many friends in Sandbury, in Rotary, at Fort Malstead, Rosemary of course also being well known in the small town.

When Karl had discussed with Fred a suitable town to go to for their honeymoon, Fred's first question was, "Where does Rosemary fancy?"

"That's the problem. She hasn't been around very much, apart from the seaside towns in Kent and Sussex; she said she would like to go somewhere else."

"Well, Ruth and I had a lovely holiday in Chester. Now it's not chock-a-block with Yanks it would be a nice quiet place to visit, away from the buzz bombs. We stayed at the Grosvenor, right in the middle of the city, beautiful place."

"I will write for a brochure."

In common with most 'brochures' at the time, a single sheet of paper, printed on both sides, arrived a couple of days later setting out the prices. Karl selected one of the two suites and sent a cheque off for the deposit, saving the knowledge of his extravagance as a surprise for his new bride on Sunday 29th October. Not everyone could say they had stayed in the suite used by the Earl of Derby when he came to Chester Races!

On Monday 30th October, the War Office stood down the Home Guard. The invasion of Britain was now deemed to be history. All ranks would receive Certificates of Service, all officers would bear the honorary rank to which they had risen, Fred therefore entitled to describe himself as Major Chandler. The vast majority of such officers did a little grin at the thought of giving effect to such a title, some pompous asses went around calling themselves Lieut Colonel Brown or whatever. They had been mainly managers of a utility or some similarly sized enterprise so had automatically assumed command of the newly raised LDV, afterwards to be put into uniform as the Home Guard.

Parades were to be held in all major towns on December 3rd and the King was to broadcast the thanks of the nation on that day.

"Well, we didn't fire a shot in anger," Fred expounded to the gathered Chandler clan on the Monday evening, "but at least we were here ready to do so."

"The problem with most of Home Guarders, or Home Guardsmen, whatever they are called, is that a lot of them are going to find it difficult to get out to the pub two or three nights in the week and on Sunday lunchtimes," Ernie suggested.

"How right you are," Jack replied, "we all know that was the only reason Fred joined."

With November coming, thought naturally turned toward Christmas. Charlie was to rejoin City Rifles at the depot, at Winchester after his wedding leave. However, before that happened his grandfather and Gloria were to have their quiet wedding at the little village church in Ramsford. With the invited guests almost filling the church seating, and then the villagers and estate staff packing the aisles, crushed round the font, and squeezed together at the back of the nave spilling out into the porch, it was, in the event, far from quiet. The reception, put out to a catering company, was held at The Grange, with the Sandbury people being accommodated in rooms in the main building, the remainder being squeezed into the village pub, and The Green Man in the next village.

David and Maria had the benefit of one of the four posters, which privilege did little to assist his readiness for the inevitable five mile Paddy-torture on the Monday morning.

Apart from the Ramsford wedding, November was a miserable month – well it usually is, is it not? They had two three-day exercises, which apart from getting somewhat footsore, they got soaking wet, and stayed wet for three days.

"What must it be like in the jungle with your brother sir?" Paddy asked.

"Yes, and not only the wet. All those nasties, and creepy crawlies, to say nothing of the bloody Japs. By God, I reckon they are absolute heroes just being there, without the fighting."

"Yes sir, you're right. The only thing is we're likely to end up there after Jerry's finished. We are in the BLA – British Liberation Army now, or we were, everybody is now saying BLA means Burma Looms Ahead."

Paddy could not know they would shortly be fighting in conditions so diametrically opposed to Harry's as he could ever have imagined.

During November, Margaret had at last established there would be no problem from the US Army point of view to her getting married to an Englishman and to resigning her commission. However, there seemed to be a hold-up between the US Army records people and the regional surrogate to give the go-ahead for the bishop's common licence. Eventually the regional surrogate informed Canon Rosser that if Major Coulter, presented her ID documents which indicated her to be a widow and a member of the Episcopalian Church, she could then be accorded a common licence.

"Who do I present them to?" she asked Canon Rosser after matins one Sunday morning.

"To me, I then confirm them to Rochester and the licence will be issued. We then go ahead with the banns as usual. You will both be described as from this parish."

During the second week in November, Winston Churchill announced a new and more frightful weapon which was being used by Hitler. Several explosions had occurred in London when no aircraft nor V-1s had been seen on radar or sighted. They were first reported as gas main explosions, but were speedily pronounced by the Prime Minister as rocket propelled bombs, known now as V-2s. They were being launched from Holland, Denmark and from Germany itself. Along with V-1s being launched from aircraft, Greater London and the south-east were deluged with these missiles all through November. The war-head on the V-2 was the same as the V-1 carrying two thousand pounds of explosive, but whereas the V-1 was both visible and audible, the V-2 was neither. Its arrival was not known until an almighty whoosh and immediate explosion took place, if you were near it that would be the last you would be likely to hear.

David had been warned he would have to forgo his weekend pass on 24th November as it would be his turn to be field officer, therefore being required to stay in charge of the camp whilst the CO and other senior officers were away.

"Would you like me to stay and keep you company sir?" Paddy asked.

"Your wife would kill me if you did."

"Sir..."

"Yes."

"Sir, I think we're a little bit pregnant again."

"What marvellous news. Good for you. When will you know for sure?"

"Well, sir, we know for sure now really."

"So when will be the great day?"

"Around the first week in June."

"But that's nine months to the day almost from when we went on leave from France."

"Yes, sir. You see sir, I'm a fast worker."

"I hope you let Mary get off the front mat."

"Not exactly, sir, but I did allow her to close the street door, so I did."

David grinned – "And I bet that's not far from the truth either."

On Saturday 2nd December David and Maria left baby Henry for the first time in the charge of his grandmother Schultz, while they made their way to Blackheath for the wedding of Amanda One to her Sandy. They were joined by Mary and Paddy, although as Mary said before the service "This will be the first time I have been in a Protestant church, so I hope I don't bring the roof in."

"Paddy will hold it up if it does," David assured her.

The wedding went off beautifully. Amanda and her parents, and half the police force of south-east London and their wives were present, Amanda making a tremendous fuss of her two old friends, telling everyone, "These are the two bravest men I have ever met," much to their mixed self-consciousness and pleasure.

On the 3rd of December Fred and twenty of his Home Guard company were taken by an army truck to Hyde Park where they joined hundreds from all over Britain in a final 'stand-down' parade. King George VI took the salute, it was a fitting tribute to colleagues who, despite not having been called into action, had spent many cold lonely hours watching the skies at a time when we were more likely to be invaded than at any time since Napoleon cast his covetous eyes across the Channel, a channel which would remain 'The English Channel' no matter how the French like to describe it.

Rockets rained in every day causing considerable damage. But then morale was boosted sky-high on Saturday 9th December when the blackout came to an end. To a population encompassed by darkness for over five years, a population that had to carry a torch when venturing out after dark, a population which had to ensure not a chink of light shone from its houses, factories, shops or vehicles beyond statutory limits, could now light a bonfire after dark if they were so inclined. Freedom takes many forms; the freedom to be lit up was one of the greatest blessings, and a sure indicator of the victory to come.

The second indicator was that the Kent coast was now a return home area. Children and expectant mothers, who had been evacuated, some for most of the war, to escape the bombing and particularly the shelling, could now go back to their own homes. Sadly, this was not the case with London, the V-2s and the occasional aircraft launched V-1s were preventing that.

At Chandlers Lodge they were making the inevitable plans for Christmas. David and Mark, with David's in-laws and Mark's parents were all staying over the holiday. Anni and Ernie would be spending Christmas Day at Karl and Rosemary's new house, then they would all come to Chandlers Lodge for Boxing Day. With the addition of Megan, Jack, Moira and all the children it was going to be a really festive time, even if the food was to be rather basic.

But things don't always go according to plan as we have seen in the past, and no doubt will see again.

Chapter Thirty-Four

At the end of July 'Monika' received a long loving letter from Dieter which had taken nearly three weeks to reach her. Three days later she received another one which had only taken ten days. Then nothing. All through August nothing came to the Strobel flat addressed to Monika, and then on Saturday 26th August the telephone rang as Fritz and Gita were eating a somewhat spartan breakfast – food rationing was biting hard now. It was Dieter's father calling from their home in Ulm.

"Fritz, I have some terrible news."

Fritz knew straight away what he was going to say and already was trying to decide how on earth he was going to tell Rosa.

"Is it Dieter?"

"Yes, we have a telegram saying he is 'Missing Believed Killed in Action'."

"So they don't know for sure?"

"Well, I suppose not, but as you know only too well when they phrase it like that they have a pretty good idea. Has Monika had any letters lately?"

"No, none at all this month, but that's not unusual. She sometimes gets two or three at the same time."

"Well they give the date of 27th July, so allowing a couple of days for the news to reach his HQ, the action must have taken place on 25th July. Wait a moment, the post has arrived. There's a letter with a field postmark. I'll read it and telephone you again."

"Very good Konrad, how we can break this to Rosa, God alone knows."

Gita looked up as he came back into the breakfast room. Instantly she recognised the pain on his face.

"Is it Dieter?"

"Yes. I'm afraid so. Konrad has had a telegram saying he is missing, believed killed in action."

"Then they don't know for sure?"

In circumstances such as this it is in the human nature to cling to every vestige of hope. 'They' do not say he is killed; therefore he may well be still alive. On the other hand the more realistic Fritz would read into that official communiqué 'they' have a damned good idea he has been killed but since they have not seen the body they will not commit themselves.

"Konrad has just this minute received a letter from the front. He is going to read it and telephone us again."

"How can we tell Rosa?"

"It might be a good idea to talk to Frau Doktor Schlenker and ask if we can bring her back here for a day or so."

"She would probably be reluctant to do that. They are so overwhelmed with wounded from both fronts, along with bombing victims, they don't know which way to turn."

"We can only ask. She can only say no. But let's wait until Konrad telephones again."

The call came within an hour.

"The letter was from Dieter's colonel. He described the action his major had been left to carry out, and they were obviously overwhelmed. Whilst they do not know for certain there were any survivors, from the last radio messages picked up as the three tanks went into the attack against very superior numbers, it would appear very unlikely."

Fritz repeated this to Gita, then expressed their sincere condolences to Konrad and Elizabeth, ending with, "But we shall continue to hope and pray for his continued survival."

"We shall too," Konrad agreed, "we shall too."

Fritz and Gita continued their discussion regarding approaching Frau Doktor Schlenker.

"If we telephone her first, dear, and ask if we can see her, or even ask her if she would care to come here, she would probably then guess what it is all about," Gita suggested.

"Yes, let's do that." Gita went to the telephone and was put through almost immediately.

"Klinik."

"Frau Doktor, it's Rosa's mother. We have had very bad news. Do you think we could see you?"

"Oh, my goodness, not her husband?"

"I'm afraid so."

There was a long pause. The Frau Doktor had lived with death for many years, an occurrence which had accelerated dramatically over the past two years, but she had grown fond of Rosa, without ever giving any sign of it, mainly through her acknowledgement of the professionalism her young colleague had shown day after day, night after night.

"Would you like me to send her to you?"

"That would be most kind of you Frau Doktor, but can you spare her?"

"Yes, I can manage for twenty-four hours or so. It is now Saturday midday. Ask her to be back at eight o'clock on Monday morning. I am terribly sorry, I really am. This terrible war. My aunt in Hamburg was killed last weekend in the bombing; they tell me there is little of the city left now. Paris has fallen I've heard today – when will it all end? When will it all end?"

"I wish I could answer that, and thank you again for being so compassionate." She rang off and moved back into the living room, taking station at the large window from which she had first observed her Rosa when Fritz had brought Gita from Munich. In less than five minutes she saw Rosa leaving the Klinik, looking up to the window, the fear on her face being visible even at that distance. She followed Fritz out to the landing to ensure the lift was at ground level, and finding it was so, waited for her to ascent. Arriving at their level, Rosa, with tears streaming down her face, had difficulty in opening the latticework door, Fritz moving quickly to help her.

"Mummy, it's Dieter isn't it?"

"Yes dear, did the Frau Doktor not tell you?"

"No, but I read it in her face when she just came and said 'you can go home for the weekend'. "

"Dieter's father telephoned this morning. He had received a telegram from the army stating that Dieter was missing, believed killed in action. Shortly afterwards he received a letter from Dieter's colonel saying that they were in action against very superior numbers and it was unlikely there would be survivors."

Rosa sobbed and sobbed, then composing herself a little she said, "But they don't know he is dead," accenting the 'know'.

"No dear, they don't."

"Then I shall not believe he is until someone can give me proof. I shall believe he is still alive."

Neither Gita nor Fritz argued with her to the contrary, each thinking if she can keep hope in her breast, that will at least help her a little in the immediate future. Then with time, a great healer, the final acknowledgement of his passing will be easier to bear.

"I think I would like to go back to the Klinik. I shall be busy there. I have two births scheduled for the weekend, and one soldier from Normandy has dreadful burns, it is unlikely he will survive. If I stay here, even though I love being with you very much, I shall just think and think. It will be better if I have things to do."

Gita folded her into her arms.

"You are a brave, brave girl, which you have inherited from your father. He bore the pain of his war wounds with courage for many years, never complaining. We will walk back with you."

They parted at the Klinik doorway. Rosa walked to the Frau Doktor's room, tapped at the door and walked in.

"Frau Doktor, I think I shall be better here." She then saw her colleague had been weeping, but pretended not to notice.

"Thank you Rosa, thank you. You are a brave girl."

It was the first time she had ever addressed her assistant by her Christian name.

Dieter was introduced to the Russian army legal system by the end of September. It involved the trial of six 'Hiwis' – Russians who had gone over to the Germans after having been captured, subsequently falling back into the clutches of the Red Army. A fearsome looking major was president of the court martial, assisted by two lieutenants, one a woman. The major read out the charge to the six men.

"You are charged with giving aid to the enemy. Do you plead guilty or not guilty?"

The young officer defending answered, "Not guilty sir."

The major said, "How can they plead not guilty when they are wearing German uniforms?"

"The men all swear they were forced to work for the Germans."

The president looked at the other two officers. They each shook their heads.

"The plea is not accepted. Have you anything to say in mitigation of the sentence?"

"Nothing sir."

"They are found guilty and are sentenced to be shot. The sentence to be carried out immediately."

The trial had taken a little over three minutes. They were led out and were dead within half an hour.

Dieter's first case as defending officer involved the prosecution of a Russian civilian accused of stealing food from a Red Army store where he had been engaged to work when his district had been retaken.

"You are accused of stealing three kilos of potatoes. How do you plead, guilty or not guilty?"

The poor devil, having been found with the potatoes stuffed into his somewhat capacious trouser pockets had no option but to plead guilty.

"Have you anything to say in mitigation?" the president asked Dieter.

"Yes sir. The man's family, a sick wife and three small children had, because of the battle which took place around his village, no food. He realises it was wrong to take the potatoes but his family were starving, and he asks for the mercy of the court."

The three members consulted briefly.

"It is a serious matter to steal from the Red Army. He will serve twenty years in the Gulag organisation."

After this, and several similar offences producing similar sentences, Dieter realised that a not guilty verdict was going to be a virtual impossibility, and that long sentences for trivial offences were the norm. What he could not know of course was that this was Soviet Government policy. As many people as possible, for little or in many cases, no reason, were needed to feed the system of camps spread all over Russia, particularly in Siberia and elsewhere in the Arctic circle. The camps provided the country's main income for export goods, timber, silver, gold, coal and other minerals, and contrary to popular belief, did not house purely political prisoners, in fact these were in the minority, but in the main comprised hardened criminals, recidivists, and petty thieves. A ten year sentence for being drunk was a common occurrence. The chance of surviving for ten years was remote.

The numbers over the next six months would be swollen by the hundreds of thousands of Red Army POWs rescued from their German captives as the Soviets advanced. These, having been suspected of being tainted by western influences – many had been set to work on German farms and in factories – were, instead of being returned to their families, or reinstated in the Red Army, sent direct in to the gulag system. The gulag system was, if that is possible, even more evil than the Nazi concentration and extermination camp systems. Stalin killed vastly more of his own people than did the evil Hitler.

In later years, when Soviet Russia came to an end and the archives of the NKVD, later known as the KGB, were thrown open, it was estimated from the records kept there that between twelve to twenty million men, women and even some children died in the gulags. These records did not cover the numbers who died on the month long journeys in box cars to the gulags in sub-zero temperatures, many of whom were stripped of their clothes and thrown out for the wolves. Nor did it include the two million odd Ukrainians starved to death in the late thirties by Stalin's orders, nor the officer class who were decimated in 'The Terror' of 1938. When you consider that an ordinary worker, late for work for three days in a week, would end up with ten years in a Siberian gulag, leaving his family without a provider, one gets a true picture of communism in action.

Dieter was being extremely circumspect in his attitude to his captors. He was punctilious in his saluting of senior officers, at no time did he rock the boat in any way, or give any impression to his immediate contacts he was being nothing other than a compliant captive, anxious to carry out the tasks he was allotted in the hope of receiving reductions in the time he would be kept a captive. Not that he had many illusions about this latter factor, he had a pretty good idea that when this present job was completed he would be packed off to a gulag the same as everyone else. In the meantime he was being adequately fed and housed, and all the time taking notes as to how he would escape. First things first, get 'them' to depend on him thereby obtaining a relaxation of supervision over him. Don't try and rush things; wait for a good opportunity; don't take some half-baked chance.

By the end of October they had moved into the centre of Poland to encounter their first concentration camp. It was not a main extermination camp, it was what was known as a satellite unit, one in which the inmates, male and female, were worked to death instead of being gassed and cremated. Due to the speed of the advances of the Soviet troops, over half of the Totenkopf SS guards failed to make their escape, along with a variety of Hiwi's, a mixture of Ukrainians, Lithuanians and other Balts. The inmates were mainly Jews from Russia and Poland, along with a hundred or so out of the two thousand odd prisoners, who were Hungarian and Serbian.

Dieter was called into the colonel's HQ, a solidly built single storey dwelling previously the camp commander's home, which he had shared, as indicated by the cosmetics in the bathroom, with his wife, or girlfriend.
"There are some fifteen SS officers of various ranks. You are to interview them, prepare charges and prosecute them to a court martial panel in four days' time. A political commissar who knows a little German will sit in with you for two reasons. Firstly to ensure you show no leniency during your interrogation, secondly so that my superiors know that the NKVD have been properly represented."
"There will be no leniency sir. I have no love for these people."
"I know. That's the only reason you are here and not in Siberia. Now, evidence against each one is being gathered and will be presented to you.

It will be your responsibility to translate it into German for the benefit of the accused, and likewise translate any material facts from the German into Russian."

"Sir, why have they not been shot already?"

The colonel looked at him closely. A German asking why other Germans should be shot without trial?

"Our allies want trials, so we must give them trials."

"The English and Americans always were chicken-hearted sir." The colonel made no reply but mentally noted this young man was somewhat after his own heart.

The next three days produced evidence that sickened Dieter to his very stomach. The deputy governor of the camp, a captain, was in the habit of walking around carrying an old cavalry sabre. If he came across an inmate, man or woman, not working as he or she should, he would not hesitate to bring the weapon down and cleave their skulls. There were children in the camp. Another officer, a lieutenant, although around forty years of age, was in the habit of almost daily, seizing any child, boy or girl, between the ages roughly of eight to twelve years old, sexually abusing them, then taking them at night to a small copse at one corner of the camp and strangling them. Another had trained an eight-year-old boy to use a Schmeisser sub-machine gun. The officer used to carry the gun around with him, the boy trailing behind. If he came across someone obviously too ill to work he would get the boy to empty a magazine into the prisoner, he and the boy then laughing uproariously as the unfortunate man or woman expired before them. Virtually all the remaining officers had killings on their hands, with vicious ill-treatment of prisoners a daily pastime.

Dieter had seen and heard of many, many evil things in the five years he had been at war, but nothing was to prepare him for the depravity and wickedness which had occurred in this small tract of land in the middle of Poland. How could people who had bred Beethoven, Goethe and Schiller have spawned scum like these, scum whose activities were known all the way up the military ladder to the very top. It was a grim faced Dieter who finally presented himself to the colonel with his findings, on the evening before the day of the trial.

"Everything is ready sir."

"You look rather disquieted major."

"I am nauseated beyond belief sir. With all my experience of war, and what happens on both sides, I have never ever considered that people could be as evil as most of those men."

The colonel had at one time as a young officer commanded a company of men, most of whom had been released from the gulag system. They had told him from time to time of what happened in those places, a world as vile, depraved and corrupt as any known to man. For the first time he felt sorry for Dieter. Dieter would, he knew, end up there one day, one day when his use to the Soviet Union had run its course in his present task. If he survived for more than two years in a gulag it would be a miracle, strong and resilient even as he was.

On Monday 30th October Dieter presented himself to the court martial building when it was barely daylight. A heavy mist hung over the camp and the surrounding forest. It was very cold even though it was nearly November. Dieter introduced himself to the members of the court, who he had not met before, a lieutenant-colonel, a major, a captain, and an NKVD officer, the latter tall at least two metres, very thin, and with the coldest, light blue, almost colourless eyes Dieter had ever seen. He gave Dieter an exceedingly penetrating gaze which he interpreted as being his normal interrogative opening gambit. 'I would suspect there is little of the milk of human kindness in that bastard', was Dieter's judgement.

The trial opened with the captain in the dock, well it wasn't a dock as such, it was a square on the wooden floor where he had been indicated to stand. He faced the table behind which the four members of the court were seated, Dieter's table on his right. There was a further mark on the floor where the witnesses would stand – only as Dieter had been informed there would be no witnesses and no defence counsel. Evidence from the inmates would be read by Dieter in Russian, then interpreted into German for the benefit of the accused. Since the evidence would be so damning perhaps for the benefit of the accused should be stated differently. In any event it had already been determined what the verdict of the court would be.

"You are charged with the murder of prisoners. How do you plead?"

"Not guilty." The members looked at each other almost laughing.

"Read the evidence major."

David read the evidence in Russian, from five inmates, each totally dooming the vicious beast. He then read his translations to the accused. The court president said, in Russian, which again Dieter translated,

"What have you to say?"

"It's all lies. You know that all Jews are liars, that's why you tried to wipe them out with your pogroms in days gone by. You have killed as many Jews as..."

"Quiet!!" The bellow was from Dieter, which not only silenced the captain, but made the members of the court sit up sharply. He continued.

"Two of these affidavits are from German Quakers. They would not lie even to save their own lives. So what have you to say?"

Again Dieter translated the proceedings; the captain remained silent. Dieter turned to the court. "The accused has no answer to the charges, gentlemen."

At this stage the court would normally retire to consider their verdict, but since they had known what the verdict would be before they came into the room they felt no need to exercise themselves for that purpose. They just looked at each other and nodded.

"You have been found guilty. The sentence of the court is that you shall be taken from here and shot immediately."

Dieter having translated, the captain sprang to attention, threw his right arm up and yelled "Heil Hitler." He was bundled outside where a firing squad awaited, and within ten minutes was dead.

TO DIGRESS.

Having used the word 'bundled' I am reminded of my German master, a Scot named Willie Wilson, who had a leg blown off in Italy during the war. Marvellous chap. We were discussing the word 'bund', which can mean many things in German, particularly bunch, or bundle.

He then went on to say there was a similar word in Scotland – 'bundling ' which was the practice of courting couples in the Highland crofts being allowed to lie on the double bed built into the side of the single roomed dwellings, when it was too damned cold to go outside. There was a drawback. A bolster was put down the middle between the couple. I am given to understand by an ancient Scottish friend of mine that the contraceptive effect of the bolster was not always one hundred per cent, with the obvious consequences. As he told me, the general opinion of others in the more southerly parts of the country excused this minor mishap with the feeling 'well there isn't much else to do up there anyway is there?'

DIGRESSION COMPLETED.

The trials of six more of the camp officers followed, all with the same result. The next day the remainder were tried, again all but one receiving the death sentence. The one who escaped did so because he proved he had only been posted to the camp two weeks before it was overrun. He was a baby-faced eighteen year old, had been employed purely as assistant to the administrative officer, who had managed to escape, and had therefore no evidence of cruelty or murder made against him. He was given twenty years for offences against the Soviet Union, and despatched to Lubianka prison in Moscow. From there, after three years, he was sent to the Vorkutlag gulag in the Arctic Circle to dig coal. He served only a further three years of his sentence before he was murdered by a Russian criminal prisoner who hated Germans, particularly SS Germans, and whose crime was ignored by the camp authorities.

The trials completed, the papers were sent to Moscow, with continual and prominent reference to the 'Prosecuting Officer' Major D. von Hasselbek. Summaries of the proceedings were then despatched to the British and American Embassies where the immediate perception, having checked out Major von Hasselbek in the German Army Officer's list to come of a solid old South German family, that fair trials had taken place. Not that they were not a bit puzzled as to what a German officer was doing working for the Russians but then as one of the British diplomats said, "If Field Marshall Von Paulus can work for them there is no reason why a major shouldn't." Von Paulus, captured at Stalingrad, was a frequent broadcaster over Soviet radio of anti-Hitler, anti-Nazi propaganda, who returned to Germany after the war where he gave evidence against a number of defendants at the Nuremberg Trials.

At the end of November the war crimes unit was moved further west. By now Dieter had 'found' a German Army map of Western Poland, from which he could readily establish the impossibility of immediate escape westwards. He would have to continue to keep his head down.

It was Christmas Day. Two weeks before the festive season, not that there would be a festive season, the Klinik had been instructed to clear all patients – ALL patients. Frau Doktor Schlenker telephoned the chief of staff of the large municipal hospital in Hannover, an old flame of hers years ago, to try and find out what was happening. He told her he knew as much as she did, but as she had probably guessed, when this sort of instruction was issued, it invariably meant there was to be a big push somewhere and as we are only some two hundred odd kilometres from the western front, it was probably going to be there. And so it was. The Fuhrer had effected one of the greatest achievements of WW2, in assembling a complete army group to strike through the Ardennes against the Americans without a glimmer of his intentions being discovered by allied intelligence. On the 17th December Von Runstedt, brought back from retirement to mastermind the battle, launched his panzers and paratroops against an unsuspecting enemy, about which a great deal more will be dealt with in later pages. On Christmas Day the Klinik received the overspill from the Hannover main hospital of the first wounded from the battle, including for the first time three badly hurt American soldiers, one of whom died on the following day, holding her hand and asking that one day would she write to his mother, and tell her he did not suffer, this despite the fact he was in dreadful pain. He was just twenty years of age. He gave her an envelope with his address on in Ohio, she could not tell him that she was a concentration camp prisoner and as such could not be sure she would survive the war herself, nevertheless she promised to do as he asked.

The new year came with no rejoicing, but only for fear of what 1945 would bring to the German nation.

Chapter Thirty-Five

Harry's company, reduced as it was by the loss of the deserters and the fatalities of the three men on the August railway job, was further decreased by two men sustaining fractures, another dying from snake-bite and yet another being attacked by a swarm of wild bees which had suddenly appeared on the edge of the camp where the unfortunate man had been returning from the latrines. These two latter occurrences were most unusual, snakes generally speaking are themselves very vulnerable therefore only attack when cornered or trodden on. Wasps and bees however are very aggressive and will attack anything that moves. It had been drilled into the men that if a swarm should suddenly appear they must stand perfectly still, in which case they would be ignored. The unfortunate Chinese in this case was only ten yards from the hut and decided to make a run for it. He was half way there when they descended upon him until the upper half of his body was totally covered in a crawling mass of vicious stinging insects, each twice the size of the European bee, with a sting to match. It was a quick death, the combination of the poison, the intense pain, and the traumatic effect of being deluged by a seething, deafening, blinding swarm from which there was no escape brought a speedy end. Men in the hut who had witnessed the tragedy watched in silence. There was nothing they could do. The bees swarmed on the dead body for several hours before they all up and left as if from a central command leaving Matthew to arrange for the burial. The jungle is not a very nice place.

At the beginning of October they received another drop. A patrol was sent out to establish whether the railway they had attacked the month before was still out of action. It was. Reuben, who led the patrol, established that the bridge was being rebuilt by POW and white civilian prisoner labour.

"God, you should see the state they are in," he reported to Harry. "It takes twenty of them to lift a length of timber that you and I could shift on our own. I saw one poor sod drop his end of a length of wood. The bloke at the other end – it was like four by two timber about eight feet long – he couldn't hold it and let it go, as a result it fell into the river below. Two guards immediately rushed up and beat the daylights out of the pair of them. I can tell you this Harry, it took all my will power not to take one of the men's rifles and plug the pair of them. They were only two to three hundred yards away; I could have done it easily."

Whether Choon Guan had taken Reuben's advice and knocked seven shades of you know what out of the commissar was unknown. It was noticeable however that the high-pitched evening harangue from the dining hall had substantially reduced in both volume and quantity. The subject was not raised with Choon Guan. On the one hand he would gain face having achieved his object, on the other hand the movement would lose face if it was acknowledged to have been achieved by others, and the movement was vastly more important than the individual.

The news was getting a little brighter week by week. They heard on their radio that the port and large town of Padang on the west coast of Sumatra had been bombed by carrier borne aircraft. The Japs now were going to receive some of their own medicine. This news was particularly cheering to Harry and his men since Padang was only three hundred and fifty miles from their camp – a little over an hours flying time.

"Malacca next," said Harry.

"But who protects the innocent civilians?" asked a sad faced Matthew, "The innocents are the ones who always suffer most. The next target will be Singapore I have no doubt.

Matthew was correct in his assumption. Three weeks later Superfortresses of the US Army Air Force bombed Singapore Naval Dockyard and oil refinery – The dockyard we had left absolutely intact in 1942 for Japan to use all through the war until now.

On November 15th Choon Guan and his commissar left for Kuala Lumpur to collect six new recruits who had been vetted and trained by the MPAJA, the Malayan Peoples Anti-Japanese Army, the new name for the Malayan Communist Party. Prior to collecting them they were to attend a conference in a hotel situated in the middle of a busy street market in Jalan Benteng in the town centre. With the throng filling the market place, a dozen or so insignificant Chinese making their individual ways to Happy House Hotel would excite no curiosity whatsoever. There would be two representatives from each of the four camps, two from the central HQ, that place known only to them, the commander of the MPAJA and his two lieutenants. There would therefore be a total of thirteen of the top communists of the Malay Peninsula in one place at one time. The Chinese, being an extremely superstitious race, should have taken note of that.

Their arrival having been spread over some twenty minutes, they got down to the order of business. Ever since they had arrived Choon Guan's stomach had been playing up, rumblings reminiscent of the hot springs his parents took him to when he was a child, at Pedas, near Seremban. His gurgling became so pronounced he had to ask the commander to be excused. Having left the room he realised he had no idea where the lavatory was. He scooted along the corridor on this floor, there was nothing. He raced up the stairs to the next floor, fully aware that he had left things a bit late and if he did not find sanctuary immediately he would disgrace himself. As he reached the next landing he spied his objective at the far end of the corridor, prayed it would not be occupied, (to whom he prayed, being a communist, we shall never know), burst in, slammed the bolt and he was saved.

He was, in fact, saved in more ways than one. As he breathlessly surmounted his panic, he heard a fusillade of automatic fire from downstairs. That could only be one thing he told himself. Somehow they had been betrayed and the Kempetai had raided the conference.

This had happened before at a meeting at the Batu Caves when the then Chinese commander and others had been killed.

Quickly he dressed deciding the only escape was upwards. He ran up to the top floor, climbed through a window on to a tiled roof which looked and felt decidedly unsafe. About thirty yards away there was an open skylight. He made for it, lifted it up and laid it against the roof and lowered himself into the room, only to realise immediately he was in a brothel. A portly middle-aged Chinese was sitting up on a bed alongside a girl young enough to be his granddaughter. There was no top sheet on the bed with which either could cover themselves, there was therefore the ludicrous situation of the man, having disentangled himself, covering his vitals with his hands, whilst the girl just sat quite unabashed, not attempting to cover anything up. I suppose in her line of business she was used to men seeing her in the altogether.

Choon Guan opened the bedroom door slowly, then walked downstairs, past a Madame in her little box. He put his finger to her lips, she having heard the gunfire just nodded, realising since he had not come in the front door into the building, he could only have come in via the roof. Choon Guan melted into the crowd in the street to try and find out what had happened. There was a Japanese truck parked outside the Happy House Hotel, in a few minutes Japanese military police started to come out carrying bodies, throwing them one by one on to the truck. He counted eleven. There then emerged a Jap leading Choon Guan's commissar, his arms bound, his head streaming with blood. He was pushed into the cab to be seated between the policeman and the driver and driven off.

Choon Guan's first thought was ' I must get back to the camp'. He had a fair idea of what the commissar's captors were going to inflict upon their prisoner; the question now was would he tell them about the camp, or would he hold out? Choon Guan had his doubts about the resilience of his comrade. He had the feeling that the man was a bully, able to rant at his captive audience, because of his position on the political ladder, but like most bullies, yellow when faced up by superiors, whether within the party or of the enemy.

He then had a second thought. It would be highly probable that the main line station would be under surveillance after a major security operation of this nature, particularly if the Kempetai had not been informed of the exact numbers attending the conference. His mind in a whirl, he puzzled who the betrayer could have been. It was the second time this had happened. Two years ago a similar conference had been betrayed at Ipoh, and most of the delegates killed. It must be someone at headquarters, or someone in the British command structure with knowledge of MPAJA operations. One day he, she, or they would be discovered and would regret the day they were ever born.

He brought his thoughts back to the present. He was supposed to collect six men. He had no idea where, that was to be told to him at the conference, that part of the plan therefore had to go by the board. He had to get out of KL. The railway station would probably be unsafe therefore he must get a bus to a station further up the line. He saw a bus, a rickety, no glass window affair, with rolled up blinds to pull down when it rained. It had 'Kuang' on its front board, which he knew was on the line on his way north to Trolak, where he would alight. He whistled shrilly, the driver pulled up. They did that in Malaya. After some ten minutes they were reaching the outskirts of the town, when, turning a sharp left hand bend they found themselves at a road block, manned by civil police, backed up by a contingent of Japanese military police and an escort of Korean soldiers lining either side of the road. A Malay policeman boarded the bus followed by a nasty looking little Japanese whose collar badges denoted he was military police.

They ignored women, old men and children, concentrating on the dozen or so young men and others up to the mid forties or thereabout. They examined identifications, searched bags, baskets, and the men themselves, two men who had no papers whatsoever but rather large quantities of Japanese occupation banknotes were taken off, later to be let go with a caution – less their money of course. It was well known that the Kempetai ran, not only a very lucrative personal benevolent system, but to augment it operated an extremely efficient scam in the production and distribution of counterfeit notes.

"Papers." Choon Guan produced his immaculately produced identification documents, a product of one of the most prolific forgers in pre-war Malaya, now a comrade at Camp Three.

"Where are you going?"

"Kuang, to see my uncle who lives in Jalan Bahra." He had no idea if there was such a road as Jalan Bahru, but then he was confident neither the thick headed policeman and certainly not the shit-pig of a Jap would know either. The policeman looked at the Jap, the Jap nodded; they passed on to the next seats. Having removed two more young men stupid enough to have travelled without papers, they allowed the bus to proceed, with loud sighs of relief from all the remaining passengers, whether they had anything to hide or not. Just being near a Kempetai man was enough to require one to speedily make an extremely necessary call, which most did when they reached the bus station at Kuang, conveniently situated as far as Choon Guan was concerned on the railway station forecourt.

Despite the persistent rumblings in his stomach he made his way safely back to Trolak, a three hour journey, during which there were no further alarms. Arriving there he made his way to the safe house on the outskirts of the town to stay overnight. The elderly Chinese couple who owned the house fed him and bedded him down for the night. They had expected eight men in dribs and drabs, Choon Guan told them he would now be the only one. They did not query this change of programme, it was not their business, what you don't know cannot be got out of you.

As dawn broke he left the house to get into the nearby beluka as quickly as possible, to find his heavy jungle boots and clothing left in a waterproof bag, along with his tommy gun. It was a two day journey up to the camp, his hosts at Trolak having provided him with sufficient water for the first day – there would be plenty of fresh water from the mountain streams on the second day – along with a plentiful supply of rice and fruit. On the second day, as the last of the sunshine gave notice it was leaving, he was challenged by the western outlying picquet.

"Where are the others? I was told you were bringing six comrades with you."

"When you need to know you will be told." He was tired, dispirited, disappointed at the failure of his task, sad at the loss of his comrades in KL and looking forward to a hot meal. The last thing he wanted was to be cross-examined by a bloody sentry. The sentry pulled the nylon communication cord to warn the camp guard Choon Guan was approaching and said no more, he himself would be leaving in another twenty minutes or so.

The three officers came out to meet the party, only to find the solitary figure of Choon Guan approaching. They led him into the company office, sat him down, gave him a mug of tea well laced with rum, and waited for his story. Harry commenced the questioning to an obviously shaken and dispirited Choon Guan.

"What happened old son?"

"We all assembled at the Happy House Hotel. I had an attack of diarrhoea and had to race upstairs to find a lavatory. While I was there I heard a number of sub-machine guns being fired in the room below. I climbed out on to the roof and got down to the street through a brothel. I saw the Kempetai carry out eleven bodies and throw them in a truck and then bring out our commissar with his arms bound."

"Was the commissar wounded?"

"He had a head wound but was walking without any difficulty."

There was silence for a moment or two, broken by Harry.

"So, we were betrayed. The question is by who. It could be one of three sets of people, someone in MPAJA headquarters, someone in our command HQ at Cameron Highlands, or someone at the meeting who was the only one allowed to live. We can do nothing, others will investigate options one and two, but if it was three we could be up the creek. Even if the commissar was not the betrayer, if he gives way under Kempetai persuasion, and there are few who don't we could find the nasty little men knocking on our door in a day or two, or dropping their calling cards as they did at Camp Six."

"There is another possibility sir," Choon Guan suggested.

"What's that?"

"We delegates were in KL overnight before the meeting. One of them might have had too much to drink, or gone with a whore, or even let it slip out to a relative or friend he was here for a big meeting. The Kempetai pay big money for that sort of information, that's how they get most of their intelligence."

"Right. Well, let's give our commissar the benefit of the doubt. He's as clean as clean. It still doesn't alter the fact that when they have finished with him they will know a great deal more than when they started. So from tomorrow morning we will be on full alert, outlying picquets doubled, defence camouflage in position, parade ground covered with vines. After a week we will phase back into alert and then standard defence." Harry sat back and mopped his brow. "To cap it all we are now seven more men short. Oh, by the way, radio silence until next weekend, those bastards will be doing all they can to pinpoint us, let's not give them any help."

Some very harsh things had been said about the commissar during the previous months, he was heartily disliked even by the comrades. He did however; prove his devotion to the cause. As a direct contrast to his usual verbosity he remained totally silent with his torturers, until in the middle of the night, three days after his capture, the warrant officer endeavouring to get the information from him, lost patience. Unsheathing his sword he decapitated the almost lifeless body as it sat bound in a rickety chair.

As was so often the case in war, the commissar's heroism went unrecorded, unknown, and unhonoured.

From then on for the next three weeks there was tension in the camp, but as the time went on it gradually lessened until on Sunday 10th December they received the coded message over the airwaves there would be a 'drop' on the night of 16/17 December. Following this message they were told Sunrise would be with them at the end of the month.

"I wonder if he has any info on what happened?" Reuben asked of no one in particular.

"You mean on what caused it to happen I suppose," Harry answered, stating it as a fact. "The more I think of it the more furious I get that somewhere in our organisation there is someone who can live on blood money."

There was general agreement on that point, which is curious when you consider that in a few short years blood money was being paid by the Malayan government authorities to people to inform on those in that organisation, and that those killed in KL could equally well have been eliminated by British or Ghurkha troops. It is a funny old world.

They were lucky on the night of the drop in two respects. Firstly and most importantly the weather was good, secondly the precious rum container was dropped in the right place. As a result, in addition to the welcome mail, Harry received not only another brandy soaked cake, but also a carton of three little Christmas puddings, sealed again in stainless steel and containing a note from the craftsman in Sandbury Engineering wishing him 'Good luck, looking forward to seeing you next Christmas!'

On the 'down' side was the news in the copies of the 'Times of India' of the deluge of V-2s hitting London and the Home Counties, over 700 killed in November including 450 women and children.

"I suppose our David has wangled Christmas leave," Harry said to Matthew as they sorted out the goodies.

But as Harry sweltered in the tropical heat waiting for the monsoon to arrive there could not be a greater contrast to what David, Paddy and the others of 'R' Battalion were about to endure, with little or no warning, seven thousand miles away as the crow flies. Having made that statement I must agree it would have to be a fairly robust crow to prove my point.

Chapter Thirty-Six

'R' Battalion had rejoiced to hear that they would be sent on Christmas leave for 10 days from 23rd December to return on 2nd January. The weather was appalling in the two weeks before Christmas, a jump had to be cancelled and little outside meaningful work could be done. It was on Friday morning 15th December after company orders, when David usually had a little chat with Paddy and his platoon officers that Paddy said, in reply to David's melancholy comments on the weather situation,

"Never mind sir, in another week you will be all snuggled up and won't give a damn what the weather's like."

"You're right of course, and I wager I shall not be the only one," looking at Sandy and then the sergeant major himself. But they were to be oh! so disappointed.

On the morning of the 17th, being a Sunday and especially as it was the last Sunday before they all left for Christmas leave, there was to be a church parade. It was greatcoat weather as the company, less the Catholics, Jews, and other infidels, paraded for inspection by a Catholic CSM, and were to march to the garrison church, the company clerk, he a Methodist, ran out of the office on to the parade ground.

"Sir." Paddy just about to give the command to march off turned toward him.

"What's up?"

"Parade's cancelled sir, all ranks to return to their barrack rooms."

"Why, what's happening?"

"Don't know sir. All I know is there is a stand-to situation."

"Righto, my son, get back on that switchboard and find out what the bloody panic is." Paddy turned to the assembled one hundred or so paratroopers.

"There's a stand-to. When I dismiss you, get back to your billets. Platoon sergeants see me in the company office." With that he called them to attention and dismissed them, hearing as he had expected the usual "Get us all bloody bullshitted up for church parade, then cancel it – typical army."

Shortly after getting to the company HQ Paddy heard David in the outer office.

"What's on sir?" Paddy asked.

"We've to stand-to to get ready for an operation. I've got to go to Battalion HQ 'O' Group at 1100 hours. It was then 1030. As he spoke his

2ic and platoon commanders arrived at the double.

"Right. Platoon commanders. Do a check on clothing, equipment and arms. Any deficiencies let Sandy know straight away. Sergeant major, see what you can find out from the RSM, only be quick because he will be in on the 'O' Group in a few minutes."

"Right sir, straight away sir." Paddy left very speedily, returned ten minutes later.

"He knows nothing either sir."

"Oh well, you had all better get on with getting prepared to move at a moment's notice, and I'll send a runner for each of you when I get back."

David went off to the CO's office with very mixed thoughts. What on earth, with the state of the war at present, could there be such a panic about? How disappointed everyone at Sandbury and elsewhere would be if the Christmas leave were cancelled – particularly if it was a false alarm. What the hell would he do with all the presents he had bought and Angus had packed away in his valise ready to take home?

They were ushered in to the CO's office by the adjutant.

"Gentlemen, I have to tell you the Germans have launched a major offensive in the Ardennes. I understand that at 0530 yesterday, 16th, over 2000 guns opened up on the Americans in that sector, they then attacked with what is estimated some seventeen to twenty divisions with SS armoured divisions leading the assault. They have walked through the Americans and are heading for Antwerp. It will be our division's task to make a parachute landing on the northern sector to assist in preventing their so doing, and to turn them back from whence they came. That's all I can tell you at present. There will be another 'O' Group at 1500 hours, unless I call one before that time. Any questions?"

"Sir, where the devil did he get all those troops from, and why the devil didn't we know they were there? You can't hide one division of tanks from the air let alone twenty."

"I can't answer that. I'm afraid, though no doubt the question is going to be put to the Americans in due course. Anyway, up to war footing immediately, deficiency lists immediately to the QM, ammunition requirements to Mr Forster, you all know the drill. That's all gentlemen."

David made his way back to his spider through flurries of snow blowing across the parade ground, thinking to himself, 'you've got to admire the buggers, they may be down but they're certainly not out. Attack through the Ardennes always recognised as a job and a half. In winter, impossible. Now they were on their way to Antwerp. Holy mackerel, they will take some stopping cutting through reserves and support troops as they will be, and how can we drop in this weather?'

Paddy was waiting for him in the company office when he returned.

"'O' Group straight away sergeant major please."

Paddy went out in to the company clerk's office where platoon runners were waiting.

"Officers to 'O' Group straight away," he told them. They scampered off at the double. Five minutes later they were all assembled in David's office, Sandy Patterson, now 2ic, Andy Gilchrist 4 platoon, Reggie Pardew 5 platoon, and Roger Hammick 6 platoon. David repeated to them the substance of the CO's briefing, ending with,

"The time between now and when we actually move from here will be the most testing for the men. Try and keep them occupied. Talk straight to your NCO's to jump on any soldier moaning too volubly about missing Christmas. They are here to fight and to live up to the reputation of those we left in Normandy. I have another 'O' Group at 1500 hours; we'll meet here again after that. Any questions?"

"Can the men telephone or write that they will not be home for Christmas?"

"Yes, there has been no instruction otherwise. It is not like Normandy where the day date and place to remain a secret until we landed. The enemy knows where this battle will be, and when, since they are the ones who have started it. Anything else?"

Roger asked, "How can we jump in this weather David, and I bet my last fiver it's ten times as bad over there?" He did not realise how prophetic he was being.

"I raised the same point in my own mind and came to the conclusion it would not be on. We shall see pretty soon now. So, back to your platoons and break the good news!"

Contrary to all their expectations the officers found little bellyaching among their rank and file. Those who had been in Normandy were somewhat more sombre than the replacements. These latter were split between the excited ones, looking forward to finding out what real soldiering was all about, and those who chattered away to conceal their tension, their worry whether they would measure up to being shot at or in the final analysis having the courage to put the bayonet in.

There was no further news at the 'O' Group at 1500 hours, other than the reports that all ammunition, mortar bombs, and Piat anti-tank projectiles were issued.

The next day, 18th December – one week to Christmas! – they were told they would not be jumping. Weather conditions were so bad over there, visibility almost nil in places, with snow and fog, that aircraft would not be able to find their drop zones. As a result they were told to be ready to move by road to Tilbury the following day to embark on landing ships for Ostend where they would be collected by TCV's – troop carrying vehicles – to take them to wherever they would be sent into action.

Every telephone in Bulford was in full use right up until lights out on the night before they moved, those who could not contact loved ones in that manner scribbling messages of undying affection to their wives or girlfriends, or in a few cases, both. David was no exception. He had a long talk to Maria, a very subdued Maria, trying to brush away from the back of her mind that her David had survived Calais where her brother had been killed, he had been with the Resistance for three months in France, he had spent six months in desperate fighting as part of Tito's Partisans, and then the hell of Normandy. She had this stomach churning thought that a soldier's luck can run out, then brushed it aside. Thoughts, however, have the habit of returning, especially at night when you are finding it impossible to get to sleep.

'B' Company embussed at 0800 hours, the long procession of TCV's leaving shortly afterwards on its journey to Tilbury. They hit the bridge at Kew soon after midday, crossing over on to the North Circular Road. At the Woodford Green roundabout David recognised he was only a couple of miles away from where his darling Maria was sitting, probably in front of a blazing fire, in her family home at Chigwell, in total ignorance of the fact he was so near. As he thought these thoughts the driver said,

"One day they will think of putting a blooming heater in these things sir, I don't know about you but my feet are frozen stiff."

"I was just thinking of my wife, just a couple of miles up that road, sitting in front of a lovely warm fire."

"Are officers allowed to desert sir?"

"I'm very tempted to find out, I can tell you."

They came alongside the landing ship at Tilbury, the advance party, which had travelled up the day before, having been marshalled by the quartermaster, swiftly leading the various platoons to their berths. It was now dark and very cold.

They remained on the LST all the next day whilst other units of the division arrived and were embarked. At dawn they moved out. On

Christmas Eve they arrived at Ostend after an horrendous crossing. The ship was lightly laden since it had only a few soft skinned vehicles on board instead of the thousand odd tons of tanks it normally carried. It was, of course, a flat-bottomed craft. There was a force seven gale blowing, as a result, big though it was, it went up and down like a demented lift, those who weren't sick, even among the crew, being in the minority. When they pulled in at Ostend, Reggie Pardew was heard to say, "If we were asked to go into action now I wouldn't be able to fight my way out of a paper bag," a statement agreed, nem. con. among his subaltern companions.

It might well have been cold in England. In Belgium it was bloody cold. They were met again by TCV's, with military police outriders, to proceed, as they had been told at an 'O' Group on the ship, to receive further orders at Dinant, some one hundred and twenty miles from Ostend. They had been given two days' rations on the ship. As they passed through Brussels they were given a hot drink, and by jove they needed it. The pavé roads were poor to start with. They were badly iced up; as a result progress was slow. There was however, one very strange and totally unexpected situation. The men on the trucks were actually sorry for the redcaps on their motorcycles, sliding arse over tip at frequent intervals. As David said to Paddy at one of the stops,

"I never thought I would see the day when your average squaddy would express anything but unadulterated hatred for the military police."

Paddy thought for a moment then voiced the view, "Serve the bastards right." Paddy always had his priorities right.

At Dinant the men were kept on the trucks while the company commanders went to a hotel on the river to receive their orders. Haimish Gillespie, their colonel eventually arrived from his briefing with the brigadier saying,

"They are being held on either side of us here by the Americans in the south and to the north. We are to push forward between them and drive the Boche back on the axis of this main road." He indicated the proposed line of advance. 'C' Battalion will be on our left and 'L' Battalion in reserve following us up. I want 'B' Company to take the lead, followed by 'C', followed by 'A'. It will be a narrow front since the deep snow on either side prevents our spreading out." He went on to say they had little intelligence of enemy strength or composition, nor whether they had armour. He finally added, "Because of the fog and snow storms we cannot expect any air support. The mortar platoon will be deployed behind the assaulting company on immediate call, and a troop of airborne artillery will be supporting us with their FOO Mr Ranson up with the forward company. The rest of the battle gentlemen we play by ear, a situation which is not unknown to you all. Any questions? Right, 'B' Coy move out 1800 hours."

David went back to his company and passed on the good news. Boiled down to basics, what it meant was that a platoon had to lead the company down a snow covered road, in the dark, although to be sure the snow helped to lighten up the proceedings a little. This they would continue to do until they bumped into Jerry, whose greeting would comprise either a shower of potato mashers, or a few hundred rounds from their MG42 machine guns, or both. Depending on how long Jerry might have been in that defensive position there might also be a nice carpet of anti-personnel mines in the line of the paras advance. All in all, Reggie Pardew and his No 5 platoon, who had been given the privilege of leading the way, were a trifle apprehensive.

David had his little coterie of Paddy, Angus, two signallers, a mortar platoon sergeant, and two medics tuck themselves in behind Reggie's platoon as they moved off along the road, shielded on either side in the main by high, snow covered banks. There was desultory shelling, long distance stuff, being sent over by German artillery, obviously more in hope than anger. 'B' Company moved on steadily until a cluster of buildings appeared. Reggie halted and studied them with his field glasses – he had learnt in the short time he was in Normandy how useful field glasses can be even in the dark. Seeing nothing untoward he moved on. The buildings were not defended. At 2000 hours David sent Angus forward to Reggie saying Roger Hammick would now pass through with 6 platoon to take the lead, Reggie would then follow on at the rear of the company.

At around nine o'clock, or 2100 hours since we are talking army language, Paddy said to David, "You know sir; we'll walk all the bloody way to Berlin at this rate so we will."

He no longer had voiced this prophecy when all hell was let loose. From a small wood on either side of the road machine guns opened up. Everyone hit the ground. David said to the mortar sergeant, "Smoke down on that wood," the sergeant immediately wirelessed instructions to the mortar section behind who in less than a minute began putting smoke down. As soon as it was thick enough David yelled, "Right 'B' Company, at 'em."

As one man his company charged down the road, the forward ones firing from the hip as they went. Into the chaos of the smoke they stormed, then having go through the smoke, there began hand-to-hand fighting through the trees, until Roger blew his whistle recalling them back to him on the road. In the short engagement Roger had lost three men killed and three more wounded, whilst company HQ right at the back had suffered two wounded from stray machine gun fire.

Colonel Gillespie, who had been following 'B' Company hurried forward. David told him of his losses, which by now were being evacuated on jeeps by the medical section.

"Right, stay put, I'll move 'C' Company through to take the lead. That was obviously an outpost; the main force cannot be far away. Get yourselves sorted out; we may all be up to our necks in it soon."

Half an hour later Haimish's hunch proved correct. Rounding a bend in the road 'C' Company could clearly see a village in a slight valley ahead, some two to three hundred yards away. At once they came under fire and went to ground in the snow filled ditches at the side of the road. Haimish came forward to get a clear view of the lie of the land, standing in the middle of the road, oblivious to the streams of tracer flashing above and beside him.

"Mortar sergeant," he bellowed. The mortar sergeant reluctantly left the relative shelter of his ditch.

"You can see where that tracer is coming from, put HE down on them."

"Right sir." He dived back into his ditch and gave the necessary orders over his wireless, in less than a minute the first two bombs were loosed off, each falling short and to the left of its respective target. A quick correction from the sergeant and two more were fired falling close to the targets. As they landed the mortar platoon officer, Nick Dale, braving the tracer, slid in beside his sergeant.

"They close?"

"Yes sir, very."

"Right, tell them to stonk until further orders."

The sergeant did just that. Under cover of the barrage 'C' Company rushed forward to reach the houses, closely followed by 'A' Company with David's 'B' Company following up in the rear. The village nestled, around a crossroads, the houses stretching some one hundred and fifty to two hundred yards in each direction from the crossing point. Just a short distance from the crossroads was the massive church, a building it would seem incongruous, in that it would be more suitable to be sited in a city than in a small hamlet such as this.

There followed a soldier's nightmare. House-to-house fighting in the dark. The ground floor cleared, were there enemy upstairs waiting for you, or down in the basement? Were there civilians still there? Were SS hiding among the civilians if there were, to use them as shields? That's the sort of thing they did. Were the houses booby-trapped? Steadily 'C' Company moved forward on the left hand side of the road, with 'A' on the right. Haimish sent his runner to the two company commanders to order them to stop at the crossroads, a task which was easier said than done. Finding a company commander, or in this case two company commanders, in the dark, in a row of houses you have never been in before, with bullets flying around all over the place, to say nothing of the frequent plethora of German potato mashers being flung more in hope than anger, all in all was a somewhat difficult task. He carried it out with the same degree of equanimity possessed by his colonel, as a result the two companies halted in considerable disorder, leaving David's 'B' Company to pass through them and carry on the good work past the church.

The battle raged until dawn when the last of the defenders had been killed or captured, a few having made their escape. It was not without serious loss to 'R' Battalion. 'A' and 'C' Companies had nearly fifty percent casualties, including, in each, some twenty killed. David's company did not suffer to the same extent, but even he had two of his platoon commanders, Andy Gilchrist and Roger Hammick wounded, not badly, but bad enough to be sent back to the field ambulance. The battalion was halted and a battalion of the Cheshires passed through them.

The various platoons got themselves sorted out, by 0800 hours on the 28th having got their heads down for a few hours' sleep until midday in the houses they had fought through. David, Paddy and Angus, having made the rounds of their three platoons to check they were all settled, and having warned them to mount guards in case of a counter attack, moved into a small detached property surrounded by its own garden. It had not been too badly knocked about, although the front door hung on one hinge and all the windows on the front of the building had been shattered. They made their way through a reasonably spacious hallway into the kitchen at the rear. As they passed the stairway, David heard a noise from what was presumably a cellar beneath. In the dim light of early morning he put his finger to his lips. Paddy unslung his Sten gun as David slowly lifted the catch to open the cellar door, while Angus stood ready to shine his army torch on to whoever would appear. It was unlikely they judged to themselves it would be a Jerry, but you never know.

As the faint noises approached the door David whipped it open, Angus shone his flashlight and Paddy pointed his Sten. To their astonishment it shone on to an SS colonel. He was hatless – or helmetless, they had no means of determining which – his tunic was unbuttoned to the waist, he was unsteady, looking at them myopically without it appeared being able to fathom what was going on. David spoke to him rapidly in German.

"Put your hands up and come out here."

He looked as though he was going to turn and run. He had nowhere to run to; therefore he instinctively would be planning to reach his weapon. Paddy dissuaded him from doing just that by putting a burst of the Sten into the ceiling above him, bringing down a shower of plaster. The colonel turned back and staggered out into the passage. He was obviously still quite drunk and had slept through the battle that had raged over and around him.

"Get his gear up from the cellar will you Angus?" David asked. Angus disappeared down the stairs, the next minute calling up.

"I think you had better come down sir."

By now several of company HQ personnel had found their company commander and were filing into the house. Paddy detailed two of them to guard the prisoner.

"And shoot the bastard if he tries anything," he ordered. They both joined Angus below. A dull paraffin lamp hung from the ceiling. On a bunk on one side there was a shapeless form covered by a heavy striped blanket. With Paddy covering him with his Sten, David pulled the blanket back to reveal a middle-aged, fully clothed couple, embraced in each other's arms, both shot neatly through the head in the 'goodnight kiss' method of dispatch which was the trade mark of the SS executioners. On a shelf above the bunk was a row of bottles of Cognac. There were two empty bottles on the floor and a third one, which had been sampled, sitting on a small table fastened to another of the walls. The SS officer's tunic, greatcoat, helmet, belt and revolver were slung over a chair in the corner. Paddy looked at David.

"What do we do sir, hand him over or sentence him ourselves?"

David's face was livid with rage. His overwhelming instinct was to storm upstairs and put a bullet through the head of that drunken, murdering swine. No one but his immediate comrades would know, and they would stick by him through thick and thin. On the other hand, that too would be murder and he would be no better than the thug himself.

"We'll get the adjutant here, Angus, see if you can find him and tell him we have a war crime here, could he please come immediately."

They went upstairs to where the colonel had slumped off into a sound sleep again.

In less than ten minutes Angus was back with the adjutant, who having visited the cellar, said they would contact Div HQ and get the Military Police Provost Marshall to take over. In the meantime the prisoner was to be securely held – "And I mean, securely." David took this to mean bound hand and foot which Paddy very speedily put into effect.

That was not the only murder perpetrated by the SS in the Ardennes. A few days before, after the first push by the Wehrmacht, the SS massacred one hundred and fifty US prisoners at Malmedy. Flushed with the success of their initial attack they again began to consider themselves above the laws and usages of war, committing a crime which set America seething with rage, and which later, as we shall see, brought terrible retribution upon others of their breed.

They remained in the village for two more days, then on New Year's Eve were withdrawn to Namur. The new year was seen in with a copious supply of beer and Cognac obtained from avaricious French cafe proprietors and grocers shops, all charging at least double the standard price made to their fellow frogs, without the slightest feeling of gratitude to those very men who had just saved them from being under the jackboot of the Nazis once again.

"Business is business I suppose," as David said as he raised his glass to Paddy and his two remaining officers. "I give you a toast – Absent friends and loved ones, and may we all be home by this time next year."

They drank to the toast, but the hope expressed in the second part was, sadly, not to be fulfilled for any of them. It had been a very long war already, but with the evil in the east to be contended with, it was not over yet.

Chapter Thirty-Seven

On the 17th December the devout of Sandbury heard Canon Rosser's stentorian voice proclaim;

"I publish the Banns of Marriage between Hector William Loveridge, bachelor of this parish and Ethel May Rose Trevelyan, spinster of the parish of All Saints, Truro. And between" – there were two other couples before he came to – "and between Frederick Chandler, widower of this parish and Major Margaret Jean Rosemary Coulter of the United States Army, widow, also of this parish. If any of you know of any just cause or impediment why these persons shall not be joined together, ye are to declare it."

There were no dissenters.

The word of the proposed marriage soon got around Sandbury, most of whose population, if they did not know Fred Chandler personally, knew of him. There were many who said 'isn't he a bit old to be marrying again? and to an American too?' Some who had known Ruth well were a little miffed at what they thought was disloyalty almost. Most of the men, particularly those who had seen the very attractive Major Coulter, said 'jammy sod', or something similar, agreeing of course with their wives opinions when under domestic restraints. Nevertheless, the couple walked home with the rest of the family to Chandlers Lodge happy in the knowledge that the first step in their matrimonial venture had been successfully achieved.

A problem however had arisen. The banns are called three times, which in Fred and Margaret's case fell on the 17th, 24th and 31st of December. But, the 31st December was the anniversary of Ruth's death two years before in 1942. Margaret had pointed this out to Fred when the first date had been decided upon. As Megan and Rose were with them at the time, Fred turned to them for an opinion. The unanimous feeling was that, firstly, Ruth would have wished Fred to find happiness after she had gone, and secondly it was not as though the day would be a celebration, it was purely a date upon which certain ecclesiastical requirements were being met. If the wedding had been arranged on that day it would well have been considered to be in bad taste. There were still some people in Sandbury however who were unhappy about it, despite the fact it was none of their business.

That evening there was a gathering at Chandlers Lodge, as was often the case on Sunday evenings, when the telephone rang for 'Dad'.

"Dad, we are off on a job. The Germans have broken through the Americans in the Ardennes and we are being sent to help contain it. I can't get hold of Maria – they must all be at neighbours or something, I will try again in the morning, but perhaps you will give her a ring sometime tomorrow to make sure she has heard from me."

"I'll do that. Now you just take care, do you hear me? No heroics at this stage of the game."

"You know me; 'takecare' is my middle name. Now, how did the banns go today?"

"Oh, very well. I mean nobody stood up if that's what you are insinuating."

"As if I would, bloody good luck to you is what I say."

With those few words they rang off, Fred having the dismal task of telling the others of what David was up to again.

Fred telephoned Maria soon after nine o'clock the next morning. It was a very downcast Maria who answered him.

"Has David telephoned dear?"

"Yes, at eight o'clock. How could Germans who have been on the run for four months suddenly find enough strength to turn to the attack?"

"I think everybody is asking that my love. Hopefully it is one last desperate gamble. There is a news blackout at the moment but it seems obvious to me Jerry is heading for Antwerp to kill two birds with one stone. Firstly Antwerp is the only usable port in the northern sector to supply the BLA, they demolished all the others, and secondly, if they are strong enough, they can cut off the Second Army in Belgium and Holland hopefully preventing a British invasion of Germany."

"Well, all I know is our David is back in the thick of it. I really do think he has done his share."

"I agree with you, but the army wouldn't. The more experienced their company commanders are the more they need them. But David is like Harry, he can look after himself you can be sure."

With final enquiries about the baby and the Schultz's, Fred rang off and got back to work, although, unusually, his heart and soul were not in it. He knew that however much David and Harry could 'look after themselves' it only needed one lucky sniper to get them in his sights for their luck to run out, or in David's case to tread on one of the millions of mines the German army had planted to cover their retreat.

On the 20th of December Margaret arrived for her final fourteen days' leave.

On the 3rd of January 1945 she would be returning to her HQ for two weeks or so to obtain her discharge. They would then decide on the date of the wedding.

Christmas this year would be unlike any previous one. David, Mark, Charlie and Alec were all in the BLA. Gloria and her grandchildren were at Ramsford, as also would have been Cecely and Greta. Cecely had been invited to Ramsford but begged to be excused as Greta's boyfriend, John, would only be given four days over Christmas, that is, the normal weekend of Saturday and Sunday plus Christmas Day on the Monday and Boxing Day on the Tuesday. He was on the afternoon shift at the mine, so could at least stay over on Boxing night and travel to Betteshanger on the Wednesday morning.

"Will there be many turn in on the morning shift on the Wednesday?" Fred had asked him during his previous visit.
"Those that do will be pretty useless if last year is anything to go by," laughed John.

Greta was now nearly seventeen, an attractive vivacious girl, now in the lower sixth at Benenden. She missed her father still, much more than she would admit. The family still had not received news from him since that one letter two years ago. The hatred of both Cecely and Greta, and Gordon as well, now in BLA, of the Japanese, was intense, as indeed it was for many thousands of civilian and service families of those unfortunate enough to be in the hands of those beasts.

Fred met Margaret off the train on the afternoon of the 20th and it was a jolly good job he did! She was laden with boxes and parcels of all sizes, plus a sizeable plain cardboard box she could hardly drag from the guard's van until Fred ran to help.
"What the devil have you got in there?"
Giving the guard a half crown for being so kind as to keep an eye on her parcels and packages – a sum duplicating the half crown she had donated to a porter at Victoria for transporting them from her taxi to the guard's van – a similar sum having been given to the taxi driver for his extra kindness in allowing her to pile all the bundles in the cab (kindness? – taxi drivers? – rubbish!). As we were saying, giving the guard a half crown, and a smile which brightened the dull but frosty Platform Two of

Sandbury station, Fred piled the goodies on to a trolley clearly marked 'To be used by staff only', then turned to his Margaret and said,

"Right, where's my half crown?"

He was rewarded with a pair of welcoming arms thrown around his neck, and a firm, and somewhat lingering kiss fully on the lips, the smiling guard in the meantime waving his green flag to signify departure to a somewhat impatient driver wondering what the hell was going on. The guard was not the only witness to this oscillatory performance on Platform Two. To be fair, it was not an extraordinary occurrence on this or any other platform. In fact far more erotic events had taken place in the blackout, usually at the far end of the platform, when wives and girlfriends were saying goodbye to service men going back off leave, not necessarily their own men in many cases, if you follow me. However, in this case it was the eagle eye of Canon Rosser, whose wife was the first to behold the 'more than friendship' between these two, and had left the station on that occasion bursting to impart her chronicle of events to her dearly beloved. Now the boot was on the other foot and the canon could hardly wait to get back to the rectory to wildly embellish Fred's lascivious performance on Platform Two, lucky devil, to his better half.

The couple arrived at Chandlers Lodge. Margaret went on in carrying an armful of parcels, while Fred made three trips from car to hall carrying the others, to the wide eyes of six children, all of whom would be at Chandlers Lodge on Christmas Day, Megan's three, young John Hooper, young Jeremy and Anni's David. The children, under the tutelage of Rose, had spent all the afternoon making yards and yards of paper chains which the grown-ups would hang that evening.

When Megan arrived at six o'clock she was bursting with excitement. On her way from the hospital she had called in at her home backing on to the small river which ran through Sandbury, and among other little chores had collected the post, delivered that morning after she had left to bring the children to Chandlers Lodge.

"Look at this," she cried out to the general assembly, and took a folded piece of foolscap paper from an envelope, which judging by its somewhat tattered edges had seen better days. Carefully she unfolded it to show a drawing of Harry, sitting on a camp chair with Chantek squatting beside him, her large eyes staring up at him from what appeared to be a massive head resting on his thigh. There was no doubt it was a beautifully crafted study which brought forth very varied comments from the viewers, the first of which was Margaret.

"What a superb drawing. Harry is so handsome." She took another long look. "Do you know dear," she added to Fred, "that could almost be a picture of you, you are so much alike."

"To which if Harry were here he would add, 'only I'm that much better looking', meaning himself of course."

There was general laughter at this, but it did not escape either Rose or Megan it was the first time a term of endearment had been uttered between the two in public.

The children were studying the leopard as closely as they were their Uncle Harry. Elizabeth turned to her mother and said, "Do you think daddy will be bringing Chantek home with him? I do hope so, she is so beautiful. What do you think grandad?"

"I don't know love. She is a wild animal and could be dangerous to people she doesn't know, so I don't expect he will be able to. We shall have to see."

As we have observed before 'we shall have to see', falls in the category of 'I don't really know' or 'I don't want to be unpleasant by saying that it would be impossible'. Grown-ups are good at that sort of subterfuge.

There were things in the picture that Rose and Megan had however perceived. Whilst it was a pencil drawing delicately shaded, it was apparent that Harry's hair was no longer the lustrous brown it had been when he went away. Secondly, there were lines about the eyes and vertically on each cheek which he had acquired during his sojourn in the jungle, and which Rose suspected had probably been understated by a sympathetic draughtsman. Nevertheless, they all were thrilled by the beautifully drawn picture with 'Happy Christmas' as a heading and 'Next Year is Our Year' in stunning calligraphy across the base.

Despite the absentees it was a jolly Christmas at Chandlers Lodge with the children all staying there and their presents piled up under a large tree Fred had established in a half-barrel in one corner of the large sitting room.

The party was increased on both Christmas Day and Boxing Day by the presence of Lorna and Horry Digby from the Hop Farm. Since their first meeting back in August they had been regular visitors to Chandlers Lodge, resulting in Horry becoming a member of the Sandbury Rotary Club – much superior to that lot at Paddock Wood, Fred had assured him.

But it was soon over and on the day after Boxing Day, on which day they had all turned out to see the hunt off from The Angel forecourt, they all struggled back to work. And struggle it was, not only because they had to surface after four days of unaccustomed leisure and in some cases the overindulgence in liquid refreshment of the alcoholic type, but also because from four o'clock on Boxing Day it snowed like the clappers. The children, of course, woke up to the gleeful sight of a foot of beautiful crisp snow, whilst their unfortunate parents and grandparents wondered how the devil they could get to work, those who had to that is. John Power was included in the latter category. He made an early start to Sandbury Station for the train to Dover and then out to Betteshanger, a journey which would normally take around an hour and a half, having left a tearful Greta the previous evening sad at not being able to see him again for four whole days. The journey took four hours, after which there was a struggle to get to the snow-bound pit on foot – no buses were running, or able to run for that matter. As he got into his pit-black, he commented to Mike, one of his workmates,

"I don't know about you but I'm knackered before I start."

"Why? What have you been up to over the holiday then? Don't tell me, I'm too young to know about these things."

It was the usual banter between mates who in many cases, because of the way pitmen work, only saw some of their fellow workers in the showers or in the locker rooms.

When John reached pit bottom, having left his token on the board before taking the chair, the deputy called him over.

"Your collier had a motorbike accident over the holiday. You wait here on the market and I'll see you in a few minutes. You will be on dataller today." This meant he would be on a fixed wage instead of piecework.

The few minutes stretched to half an hour until he returned.

"You have worked with the electricians haven't you?"

"Yes, earlier on."

"Right, you five," he pointed to four others, "go to the electricians' room and wake the buggers up – they've probably all gone back to sleep again as soon as they arrived. We've to take a motor out of a worked out seam. You can help there."

John and his companions made their way to the electricians' room. It was commonly believed by colliers that electricians, and certain other maintenance staff only worked for half a shift and spent the other half locked in their cubby holes having a kip. When John had worked with them in his early days down the pit he had found this to be, if not entirely true, at least not far from the mark. The electrician was waiting for them, with a deputy, who would supervise the job in hand and look to their safety.

"Right. We've got to go in-bye about a thousand yards. I will come and disconnect the pump motor, then leave you to get it out on to the main road," the electrician told them.

"Then I suppose you'll go back to kip again," was the inevitable wisecrack from one of the gang.

"You're only jealous," being the equally inevitable reply.

They made their way long the main road until they came to the branch where, some three hundred yards distant the seam had petered out. This road undulated badly, the original seam obviously having been far from horizontal. The problem was that in the dips the water had accumulated which meant they had to wade through knee-deep slurry in places, and since the roof was only about five feet high the going was, to say the least, uncomfortable. At last they reached the end of the road to find, not only a large pump, complete with motor, but also an equally big conveyor motor. On the roof of the walkway in this section there was an I-beam. They had chains and manual hoisting gear with them, once the electrician had disconnected the motors they were to un-bed them, hoist them up on to carriers on the I-beam and push them to the main road, where they would be put onto a tub and taken to the pit bottom. Easier said than done, they were huge flameproof motors weighing over half a ton each, plus the weight of the pump.

The method of disconnecting the wiring was an eye-opener to John. The electrician took an extremely well honed axe out of a scabbard on his belt, and with a few deft strokes sliced through the inch thick cables in less than two minutes. They were not, of course, live.

"That's his day's pay earnt," was the comment from the wise-cracker. The electrician grinned.

"It's all yours lads, don't be late for the chair," and with that he left them to it. By now it was well past four o'clock, they only had six hours to free the machines, get them to the main gate, and then get themselves to the chair.

The deputy allocated the men to their tasks, working from the light from the overhead fittings. With the general wet conditions in the mine, not only were some of the holding down bolts difficult to find, having been well silted up, but all were rusted in to a lesser or greater extent. After a couple of hours they broke off for snap, the conveyor motor having been freed, the pump and its motor still providing a headache.

Snap over, the deputy said, "Right, let's get the conveyor motor up on the I-beam and get that out of the way." This they accomplished without difficulty other than the expenditure of a certain amount of sweat accumulated during the previous two days of overindulgence.

"Right, you two, pull that down to the main gate," he instructed two of the men, they being pleased to have this job to do rather than trying to free rusted in, underwater nuts as big as door knobs. They moved off, pulling the heavy load suspended from the beam, having been given a shove by John and another to get it going. They moved away, around a curve in the roadway, and were lost to sight.

"How many left here?" the deputy asked, referring to the number of securing bolts still to tackle.

"Only one on the pump but three on the motor," the senior hand replied.

"Well, let's get the pump free and get that away, we may have to leave the motor."

As he spoke he glanced at the Davy lamp deputies carry when traversing the pit. It was showing a flickering blue flame inside the mesh.

"Hey up – firedamp," he exclaimed.

Kent collieries were generally free of the explosive gas methane, commonly known by miners as firedamp. Nevertheless there had been a bad explosion at Chislett Colliery nearby some while before which had cost lives, and it was not unknown in Betteshanger. Their eyes were all glued on to that fluctuating blue cap until gradually it flickered and disappeared.

"I've never seen that before," John told the deputy.

"Well lad, it's not common here, not like it is in some places up north. It's not dangerous until it reaches a certain proportion with air, around about twenty per cent I'm told, then a spark will set it off. Our Mr Davy," he tapped the lamp affectionately, "our Mr Davy has saved more lives than anybody else in the world I reckon."

The little discourse was interrupted by a rumbling, roaring noise from the section of the road around the bend, along which their two workmates would be pulling their heavy load. This was followed immediately by a huge cloud of dust completely filling the tunnel, racing towards the four men in the dead end, billowing upwards and back over again, terrifying to observe. Not that they observed very much. As the deputy yelled, "Cover your faces," the lights went out, they were left in absolute pitch darkness being bombarded with tiny pieces of stone, breathing as best they could through the sweat rags or neckerchiefs being held over their faces. As the noise ceased and the dust began to settle John took his neckerchief from his mouth and eyes, experiencing for the first time in his life absolute darkness. There is nothing, but nothing, to compare with the density of blackness which exists three thousand feet down in a tunnel in the ground, a black place to start with in view of its purpose. He was very frightened, totally disorientated, suffering an acute feeling of vertigo as a result of the total inability to register with some other object.

In a few moments the deputy's lamp snapped on, the others following suit. They found themselves facing a completely blocked tunnel, the rockfall ending about a hundred yards from them. One of the men said, in a low, strangulated voice,
"Jesus Christ, Matt and Gareth must be under that lot." The conjecture was received in silence from the others. The deputy took charge.
"Right now. We must work in pairs to take the top off the fall from this side; others will be doing the same from the other side."

By this he meant it was no use trying to shift the fall as a whole, all they could hope to do was to excavate a cavity on top of the fall to crawl through, and hope like hell it was not too long a cave in. He continued, "Now, we each have a lamp. The battery lasts six hours. We don't know how long we shall be here before we get through or they get through to us, so we will only keep one lamp on at a time. That way we shall have twenty-four hours of light, piss-poor though it may be. Water. I assume you each brought your usual five pints and if you are anyways like me, you've drunk a pint or so. I want all your water bottles and I will ration it out. Matt and Gareth left their bottles with their snap tins over there; I'll take them as well. We can last for days if necessary without food or light, but we can't last without water. The chances are we won't have to do either, but you never know."
They handed their bottles over to the deputy who stacked them on a ledge at the blank end.
"Right, John, keep your light on and you and Fergus make a start. Don't rush it, and keep listening while you work."
"Mr Evans."
"Yes John?"
"How will they know we are here?"
"Well, if no one has heard the fall, and if Matt and Gareth are under that lot, they won't know until they check our tokens at the end of the shift. Then they will alert the rescue people."

"Yes, but they still won't know we are here and alive. Can I make a suggestion?"

"Fire away lad."

"If we hit the overhead I-beam with a hammer every so often, even if the sound is deadened by the rock fall, the reverberation may be felt by people on the other side of the fall. I know Morse code, if someone out there recognises it they could get a Boy Scout or a soldier or ex-soldier or somebody to communicate with us."

"That's assuming the I-beam isn't broken of course. Worth a try, worth a try. But first let's get moving, you and Fergus start throwing rock back, everybody else, lights off."

It was in the dim light of that one lamp John and Fergus gradually made an entry into the fall. In places it had not reached the roof, and after their half hour stint they had made an appreciable inroad, albeit working on their bellies to the detriment not only of their shirts and trousers, but also of their knees, elbows and worst of all their bellies and thighs. They were given a welcome swig from a water bottle.

Although the deputy was around the fifty mark, he was a lean, wiry, typical pitman, brought up on coal dust since he was fourteen. Nevertheless, several years of supervising others doing the hard work very soon proved to him by the pain they were producing, that he had muscles about which he had long forgotten. Nevertheless he carried out his half hour before reversing out to his well-earned water ration. By now it was nearly eight o'clock in the evening.

"Try your signalling John," the deputy suggested. John took up the heavy club hammer and struck the overhead gantry, three heavy, three light, three heavy. He waited for ten seconds then repeated the SOS and then again, and again once more. There was no reply.

"That means either the gantry's down or they haven't missed us yet," decided the deputy. "Right, back on the rock." John and Fergus resumed their labours, hoping all the time they would reach the cavern above from which the rock had fallen in the first place, but knowing that could be hours away, in fact may not even exist!

At ten o'clock the deputy decided they would have a break.

"They will know we're missing now," he told them. "Let's wait and see if we can make contact."

At ten o'clock the chair hurtled its load of weary, black-bodied humanity up into the showers and then into the cold night air. As all cleared the discharging area the deputy in charge made an automatic, and usually unnecessary, inspection of the token board. He stopped short at the sight of six tokens not taken up, noted the numbers and hurriedly made his way to the office to check to whom they belonged, and what work those men had been detailed to carry out. It took only seconds for him to establish they had an emergency on their hands. He went through the procedures required on such an occasion, mercifully a rare occurrence, sounded the alarm siren so that men in the nearby housing who would be part of the emergency rescue team would race to the pit, even if they were just getting into bed, even – but we won't go into that.

Next, he made a warning order to the Area Rescue Section at Snowdown Colliery to assemble and stand by. They had specialised equipment to meet all emergencies there, and could be called in by any one of the collieries in the Kent Coalfield should the necessity arise. He then took three maintenance men and went down, and in-bye, to the road in which the men had been working. The lighting on the main roadside of the fall was still functioning. Two hundred yards from it they rounded a bend and immediately were confronted by a solid mass of rock, chalk, lumps of coal from a seam above not worked, dust turned into mud by the seeping water. It was nearly half past eleven.

The deputy ran back to the nearest telephone, these being positioned at intervals in the main road. His ringing was answered immediately from the control room now set up in the main office.

"Major emergency. Get pit rescue team straight away. Rock fall. Get area rescue people here as quickly as possible."

In their small cavern the beleaguered men, encompassed by the pitch blackness of their surroundings, waited with all lamps off, listening and listening, trying to get some indication their plight had been discovered. The deputy put his light on; he had been putting it on for five minutes every quarter of an hour so that the alarm and distress they all felt should not deteriorate into hysteria – unlikely, but it had been known.

"John, have another go with your hammer."

John carried out the instruction, repeating the distress signal a dozen times. It did not give out a ringing sound as it would certainly have done had the rail not been buried, but this was to be expected. As John was about to cease his efforts for the time being, the deputy on the main road side returned from his telephone conversation.

"What was that?" he asked. His small party immediately went quiet, listening intently.

"It's the monorail," one said, and put his hand on it, to feel the last of the reverberations from John's dozen or so hammer applications.

"Hit it back," ordered the deputy, another of the men taking a crowbar and giving the rail a succession of blows which clearly carried to the entombed men.

"They've heard us," the deputy said, his fist clenched on to the gantry. John found himself crying with relief. He need not have worried at the thought of shedding a few tears, the others were not far behind him, although of course none of them would admit to it later.

"Right now. We don't know how long they will take. Could be a couple of days, so we will carry on with rationing the lamps and the water. That way we could last two or three days. We will get some sleep in turns. Get close up together to get a bit of warmth. John, take my watch – it's got an illuminated dial. You take first watch after we have contacted them again, then wake Taffy."

"Would it be a good idea if I started tapping out more messages? They might then cotton on and get someone on the other end who can decipher them."

"Good idea. Keep it simple. Tell them about Matt and Gareth."

John started sending his message. Lighter taps at quicker intervals for the dots, heavier blows at slower intervals for the dashes. They were received but not understood at the rescue end, but at least the deputy realised what was going on and hurried back to the phone, the control centre quickly organising an RAF signals man from a nearby airfield to come and see what it was like three thousand feet down as opposed to three thousand feet up.

In the meantime the mine hooter had executed another chain of events. A stringer from the Daily Express living nearby heard it, pedalled furiously to the mine, got to the control room by some devious means to discover there was disaster down below.

"Can I borrow your phone?" he asked the deputy in charge, and in typical newspaper reporters' fashion, not waiting for an answer, grabbed it, giving the operator the Daily Express number in Fleet Street. He then proceeded to give a highly spiced account of men trapped thousands of feet below etc etc, most of it the produce of his somewhat fertile imagination, which was immediately headlined in the first editions, a copy of which landed on several doormats in Sandbury including that of Cecely and her daughter Greta. But more of that later.

It was now after midnight on the 28th of December. The rescue teams, working a well-organised drill, gradually tunnelled across the top of the fall, twice meeting large solid pieces of rock upon which they had to use their pneumatic drills. All day on Thursday 28th they inched their way forward while the entombed men sat in the impenetrable blackness surrounding them. At midnight they calculated they were well over half way, knowing of course that what lay ahead was as much a lottery as had been the stretch they had already covered.

In the cavern the men dozed fitfully. John had sent his messages regarding their situation, and the loss of Matt and Gareth. Messages in return had been sent by the RAF signaller, telling them of progress, which kept their spirits high. How terrible it must be for men trapped in this manner, with no communication whatsoever with their colleagues, no knowledge whether help was at hand, and all in that horrifying pitch blackness.

All through Friday 29th they tunnelled. They had to cease work on several occasions to shore up suspect parts of the roof, all of which not only took time but considerable expertise, and not a little risk. As it was, two of the rescue team had had to be withdrawn when minor pit rock falls had caused them injury.

Back at Sandbury the news soon flashed around the extended Chandler family of a 'pit disaster' on the Kent coalfield. Because of wartime restrictions on the issue of information, the pit containing the 'disaster' was not specified. This did not lessen the anxiety, particularly of Greta, but also of the Chandlers as a whole, that John might be involved.
"Very unlikely of course," Fred surmised, "although it was during his shift, so Greta tells us. On the other hand it could be in one of half a dozen mines." However, early in the morning of the 29th, a telephone call was made to John's uncle, with whom he stayed when away from his mine digs, to say his nephew John Power was one of the men trapped, but was alive and well, and it was hoped would be reached soon. John senior immediately telephoned a retired colleague of his who carried out locum duties for him during holidays or time off, getting him to come over to take his surgeries for the day. Immediately after that he telephoned Cecely with the news, leaving it to her as to whether she should tell Greta, or wait for a few hours for more definite news. He then got in his car and drove to Betteshanger; doctors had fairly generous petrol allocations, particularly in country areas.

It was Saturday morning just after ten o'clock when the breakthrough came, and the long crawl back over the fall took place. They were still not out of the woods. The roof was decidedly insecure in places, small pieces of debris falling on all of them at one time or another. Stretchers were waiting for the four men as they finally tumbled out, but as a matter of pride they each determined to walk to the chair, first thanking their rescuers and the RAF man who had been their lifeline, staying at his post continuously for two and a half days, living on a diet of tea and bacon butties brought to him from the staff canteen.

When the chair reached the top of the shaft and was unbarred, the men and their rescuers emerged to a barrage of flashes from an assembled press from all the nationals along with, of course, the Kent locals. The four were put into an ambulance and taken to Dover Hospital for a thorough examination, put to bed, their abrasions and injuries attended to, and mildly sedated so that they slept for the next twenty-four hours. When John awoke on Sunday he had difficulty in remembering where he was, until it all flooded back to him. It brought about a mixture of feelings, relief, fear, sorrow as he remembered Matt and Gareth, exhilaration he was alive, apprehension that in a few days he would be hurtling down again in that chair to do his loading job. 'I suppose', he said to himself, 'it's a bit like an infantry man having to go into another attack', but with second thoughts agreed that it wasn't really – no one was trying to kill him, it was just the mine showing who was boss.

He dozed off again to be awakened at two o'clock by a kiss on the cheek from Greta, she trying hard not to cry. John the elder had brought her with him for visiting hours, along with copies of the Mail and the Mirror, both of which had pictures of him with his workmates on the front page. Smiling as he looked at them he remarked, "Fame at last," at which Greta did dissolve into tears.

On Monday night, New Year's Eve, there was the usual gathering at Chandlers Lodge. Although, being the anniversary of the death of Ruth, it had not been a boisterous affair, this year, as a result of John's deliverance, the forthcoming nuptials of Margaret and Fred, and the favourable war situation; it was a great deal less subdued than that a year earlier. After they had all sung 'Auld lang syne', or at least the few words of Robbie Burns's poem with which Sassenachs are acquainted, Jack was given the floor.

"Ladies and gentlemen. Despite the absence of many of our dear ones facing what sorts of tribulation we cannot even dream about, I am confident that this year of 1945 is to be a momentous year. Let us drink to absent friends, and victory ahead."

They drank the toast.

An hour ahead of them David and Paddy had already raised their glasses in a shabby cafe in Namur.

Ten hours ahead Harry and Matthew had performed a similar procedure in the noisy, steamy jungle in Malaya.

Mark and Charlie had acquired a case of vintage champagne in their comfortable lodgings in a small chateau at Reims where they were in reserve, jammy sods. By the time they came to toasting the new year in, they were not too sure of the time anyway, but who cares?

Nigel Coates died on New Year's morning at around two o'clock from beri-beri and a number of other diseases. You rarely died from one complaint in a Japanese camp.